I0762269

Double Crossed

Play the Hand You Are Dealt

Anthony Anthamatten

Published by Sincerity Press, a division of Sincerity Media Group, LLC
https://sinceritypress.com

For more information about the book, author, ordering signed copies or contact information please visit: https://double-crossed.com

First edition
First Paperback Edition: August 1, 2020
First Hardcover Edition: September 1, 2020

Cover Design: Anthony Anthamatten (https://anthamatten.com)
Editor: John David Kudrick (http://johndavidkudrick.com)
Illustrator: Jeff Brown (https://jeffbrowngraphics.com)
Images: Adobe Stock

ISBN: 978-1-7352720-1-6

“Your life is not falling apart. It is falling into place.”

Dedicated to the underdogs.

Justin's Story

CHAPTER ONE

DEVEREAUX PARISH, LOUISIANA

To say Justin "JC" Carter entered the world with any chance of happiness is beyond an understatement. The heartache began when a tiny blue plus sign appeared on a home pregnancy test. Sixteen-year-old Mattie Carter trembled as she stared at the bad news she held in her hand.

How could she have become pregnant the first and only time she'd ever had sex? The father, twenty-two-year-old Demarcus Jackson, didn't seem to care. It would be his third child by an unwed mother, and he had no intention of sticking around for this one either. Demarcus considered it Mattie's fault, since she wasn't on birth control. Mattie's own mother, Ula Mae Carter, had her at age sixteen, and Mattie never knew her own father. Ula Mae had even warned her daughter something like this could happen. But, like every teenage know-it-all, Mattie didn't believe her.

Now Mattie sat in the bathroom, all alone and angry for allowing Demarcus to pressure her. He'd said he loved her, and in a moment of weakness, she believed him.

Mattie understood how difficult it could be for a single mother. She continued to watch her mom struggle to raise her. Mattie, though, had always envisioned a different life and wanted to be the first in her family to go to college. She hoped for a rewarding career and to one day meet the man of her dreams; to raise a family they planned together. But, as the little blue plus sign faded into existence, all her hopes and dreams faded away.

She also knew, of course, that people would ridicule her for being so young and pregnant. And even Mattie had to ask herself: *How can I raise a child with a ninth-grade education and no way to support myself or the baby?* Maybe this was all a nightmare she'd wake up from. But, unlike the common cold, this "contagion" only grew with every passing day, bringing with it greater concerns for the teenage girl.

For instance, she barely weighed a hundred pounds at five-foot-two. So it wasn't long before the pregnancy showed. She tried to conceal the swell of her belly by wearing her mother's larger clothes.

One morning after a shower, Mattie stood in front of the mirror and admired her naked body. The protrusion of her tummy reminded her of the life she held inside. She smiled at the sight, but then a frown fell upon her face, like some thief on a mission to steal all her happiness. Mattie wished it was a different time in her life; a time when she could care for her child; a time filled with joy.

Meanwhile, Ula Mae noticed the change in her daughter. She initially assumed Mattie was just going through a growth spurt. But it didn't take long before she realized her little girl was pregnant.

For a third morning in a row, Ula Mae heard Mattie throwing up in the bathroom. When Mattie came out, she almost ran into her mom in the hallway.

Ula Mae glared at her with her hands on her hips and shouted, "You're pregnant!"

The outburst caught Mattie off guard. Her mother had never yelled at her like this. She exclaimed, "No I'm not,

Mama! I'm just sick to my stomach."

"Don't lie to me!" her mother shouted.

Mattie cried because the truth was out. The one person she never wanted to disappoint was her mother. Through honest tears and a quivering voice, she whispered, "I'm sorry, Mama. Demarcus said he loved me."

"Demarcus is a bastard just like your father! You are not having that baby! No child of mine will mess her life up like I did!" Ula Mae bellowed.

Mattie's tears burst into a waterfall.

Ula Mae realized what she'd said and tried to retract it: "Mattie, I didn't mean that like it sounded. You are the best thing that ever happened to me. I only want you to have a better life than I did."

"I am not having an abortion!" Mattie yelled.

"We're going to the clinic in a few days, young lady, and you'll thank me for it later," her mother sternly said.

Mattie ran to her room and threw herself onto the bed. She sobbed and felt like she'd never stop crying—not that she hadn't considered an abortion, of course. It would definitely be the easier thing to do. But she'd be damned if her mother would force her to make such a horrible decision. It was her body and her mistake. She would decide what to do. Lying there, Mattie prayed like she'd never prayed before, begging for an answer to this life-changing question. Feeling almost crushed by an overwhelming sense of despair, Mattie cried herself to sleep.

During her slumber, she heard a voice: *"Don't cry, Mommy. It will be okay."*

"What did you say?" Mattie replied to the voice within her dream.

"Everything will be okay, Mommy," the child-like voice repeated.

"Where are you?" she asked.

A little boy emerged from the center of a misty cloud. The gentle face seemed so familiar to Mattie as he walked toward her, extending his hand and saying, *"Everything will be okay."*

Mattie reached out to touch the child. But a wisp of air puffed the mist away and the little boy disappeared into darkness.

Drawing in a sharp breath, Mattie sat up in bed and realized it was a dream. But what a vivid dream! And what did it mean? She placed a hand on her stomach and felt the life within her move. Was this the answer she searched for ... or was she losing her mind?

She did not go to school that day. Instead, she stayed in her room, recalling the dream and contemplating her decision. If she had the abortion, her life would return to normal. It's what her mother wanted, and Demarcus would prefer it—if he even cared at all. But something tore at Mattie's soul and said it wasn't right. And why was the little boy in the dream telling Mattie that everything would be okay?

Later on, her mother knocked on the bedroom door, then opened it and asked Mattie if she wanted dinner. Mattie said "No!" so absolutely that her mother knew not to ask again. Ula Mae understood how upset her daughter was and gently closed the door. She hoped once this was over, Mattie would return to her sweet and cheerful self.

That night, Mattie waited until she was certain her mother had fallen asleep. Then she wrote a note and left it on top of her dresser. Next, she packed her school bag with clothes and emptied her piggy bank into a small purse. Across the room sat her favorite teddy bear. The gaze of the stuffed animal looked sad, as if to say he didn't want her to go. She slung her bag over a shoulder, picked up her fluffy companion, and tiptoed past her mother's room. Mattie eased open the front door and stepped into the night. Her head didn't know where this journey would lead her. But her heart told her, *This is the way to go.*

The air felt cold and damp as Mattie walked through the empty streets. A streetlamp glowed yellow-green in the distance, like a lighthouse guiding her to nowhere in particular. She remained lost in her thoughts as she took each step to some unknown destination. Where would she go? How would she raise her child all alone? Why did her life feel so miserable?

Hours later and miles from home in an area she'd never been before, Mattie neared exhaustion. She needed rest and a place to stay, but who would rent a room to a sixteen-year-old pregnant black girl? It didn't matter anyway, because she only had the $24.89 from her piggy bank. And that money wouldn't last very long.

Glancing around, Mattie noticed an abandoned railroad car ahead. The graffiti-covered box on wheels looked like it hadn't moved in years. The place felt as creepy as a haunted house but seemed safe enough to shelter. She climbed inside the rusty container, which smelled like a zoo for dead animals. With a brush or two of her foot, she cleared away debris and then sat near the open door. She stared at the dank, dark night and knew there was no point in complaining. Mattie drew the hood of her coat tightly around her head and positioned her backpack for use as a pillow. She lay down with her teddy bear and sighed.

"Teddy," she whispered, "you remind me of happier times when life was carefree and fun."

Mattie awoke at sunrise with a rumble in her tummy. She wished she hadn't been so stubborn the night before and had instead eaten the dinner her mother offered. Mattie gathered her belongings and climbed out of the train car. She walked along the railroad tracks until she noticed a diner in the distance. Being just a teenager, Mattie felt out of place as soon as she opened the door of the busy restaurant and looked inside. Enormous men filled most of the seats, and their appearance said they worked for the railroad ... or maybe as professional wrestlers. Loud conversations and clinking tableware went silent as everyone stared at the out-of-place teenage girl. Mattie skulked to the counter with her head bowed low and sat on a stool at the end. She placed the backpack and teddy bear on the floor beneath her feet.

A heavyset waitress with a nametag that read *"Annie"* set a napkin and glass of water in front of her. She handed Mattie a menu and said, "Hello, sweetie. Shouldn't you be in school?"

Without looking up, Mattie replied, "We don't have school today."

The waitress sensed it wasn't true, but just smiled and said, "Let me know when you're ready to order."

Mattie stared at the menu, looking at prices. This was the first time she had ever been to a restaurant alone. She finally landed on the cheapest thing she could find on the menu.

When Annie the waitress returned, she asked, "Are you ready to order?"

"Yes ma'am, I'll have the toast."

Annie paused before saying, "Is that all you want to eat?"

It wasn't, but Mattie said, "Yes ma'am, that's all."

Annie smiled and called out to the scruffy man working the grill, "One toast!"

Mattie felt hungrier than toast, but she had to save her money. The toast cost 75 cents, and she calculated she would still have a little more than $24.00 after tax. Then she imagined her mama's breakfasts. Ula Mae fed Mattie so much food that she could never finish it all.

Annie returned with a plate of buttered toast and asked, "Would you like jelly with that?"

Mattie looked up. "Yes ma'am, please."

The waitress placed two packets of grape jelly in front of her. "Enjoy!"

Mattie spread jelly over the two pieces of toast and took the first bite. She'd of course eaten plenty of toast before, but never realized it could taste this good. Knowing it might be her only meal today, she savored every bite. When she finished, Mattie wiped the crumbs from her fingertips, then took a sip of water. She grabbed her belongings and walked to the register, where Annie was waiting.

"That's 82 cents, sweetie," Annie said. "And was everything okay?"

Mattie nodded. "Yes ma'am, it was very nice." She reached into her purse and counted out 82 cents in coins.

Still sensing the child was hiding something, Annie said, "Don't worry, honey, it's on me."

Mattie felt her cheeks flush. "Are you sure?"

The waitress gave her a warm smile. "It's my treat."

After she left the diner, Mattie thought of how nice the waitress had been. While the gesture of paying for breakfast only cost 82 cents, it might as well have been $82.00. Annie's simple act of kindness gave Mattie a reason to smile on an otherwise dreary day.

That same morning, Ula Mae peeked into Mattie's bedroom and discovered she wasn't there. Ula Mae checked the bathroom and then the kitchen, both of which appeared undisturbed. Checking Mattie's bedroom again, Ula Mae noticed that her book bag was missing, so she assumed Mattie went to school early, although it wasn't like her daughter to leave without eating breakfast. But then Ula Mae remembered how upset

Mattie had been the night before. She looked around Mattie's bedroom again and found a note lying atop the dresser. Unfolding it, Ula Mae read it silently:

"Dear Mama, I am sorry you're angry with me for being pregnant. I didn't mean to let you down and I'm disappointed in myself. It was the only time I ever had sex. The reason I did is Demarcus said he loved me and now I know he lied. But, Mama, I had a vivid dream and believe God wants me to have this baby. It is my body and my child. I cannot allow you, or anyone, to force me to have an abortion. That is why I left. Please don't worry or look for me. I hope you will forgive me someday. Love, Mattie."

A lump formed in Ula Mae's throat, so large that she could not swallow. She braced herself against the dresser to prevent dropping to her knees. How could she have been so stupid? She remembered what it had been like when she was Mattie's age—an unwed teenager and pregnant. History was repeating itself. At least Ula Mae's own mother had been supportive. But instead of being like her mom, Ula Mae had given her own child a reason to run away.

She felt like the worst mother in the world. All Ula Mae ever wanted was the best for her daughter, such a sweet and intelligent kid. While it was a strain raising her daughter alone and working two jobs and barely getting by, she wouldn't change a thing. Mattie was a blessing and always came first.

Ula Mae had to find her daughter—now. Mattie couldn't survive on the streets alone. Ula Mae grabbed her car keys and rushed out the door. *Maybe Mattie's still nearby*, she thought as she drove through the neighborhood, peering between houses. She expanded her search to outlying neighborhoods. Finally, Ula Mae drove through parts of town she was certain Mattie would never go. But, as each hour passed, feelings of desperation turned into raw fear.

Grief-stricken and panicked, Ula Mae returned home and

called the police. When two officers arrived a short time later, they could see the anguish in Ula Mae's eyes. Before they could even ask anything, Ula Mae blurted, "My daughter has run away! It was a big misunderstanding. I spent all day looking for her!"

She handed Mattie's note to one of the officers. He read it and said, "I see from the note she's pregnant. How old is she?"

"Sixteen," Ula Mae replied in a shaky voice.

"Have you tried to call her?"

"She doesn't have a cell phone. I wouldn't let her have one. Now I wish I did." Ula Mae looked at the floor, embarrassed at her admission.

The officer asked, "Can you provide us with a picture and description of your daughter? I'll write a missing person report and notify the other officers to keep an eye out for her."

"What? That's all you're gonna do?" Ula Mae asked.

"I'm sorry, ma'am, but kids run away all the time. Most children return home in a day or two, and we only have so many resources."

Ula Mae frowned, but then she described Mattie and handed the officer a recent school photograph. It was impossible to hide the hopelessness Ula Mae felt as the police left her home. All she wanted right now was to have her child home safely. Ula Mae sat on the sofa and cried.

Mattie entered a nearby library when it opened and looked over at the tables lined with computers. She walked to the information desk and asked the librarian if she could use one of the devices. Mattie produced her library card, which thankfully provided her access to all the libraries in the county. The attendant gave Mattie the log-in information.

After sitting down at a computer, Mattie opened a web browser and typed "homeless shelters" into the search box. The closest center was over ten miles away. *That's a long walk*, she thought. Maybe she could ask Annie the waitress for a ride tomorrow when she went back to the diner for breakfast.

The thought of breakfast made Mattie's stomach grumble again. She still felt hungry, as the toast had done nothing to fill her up. She looked at the computer clock and realized it was lunchtime. She sighed, wishing she was in school and eating with her friends. But then she thought, *Oh well ... I better get used to this. It's going to be my life for a while.*

She decided to stay at the library and study the same subjects she had in school. She found online classes for English, social studies, math, and science. Mattie laughed when she thought of her PE class. *I can skip physical education considering all the walking I'm doing.*

Science and math were her favorite subjects. For many years, she'd dreamed of pursuing a career in medical research. There was something intriguing about discovering new cures and helping others. Then she again realized that such a career would never happen. How could she possibly finish high school or go to college as a single mother?

Mattie hung her head and slumped in her seat, feeling tears welling in her eyes—until she recalled the vivid dream she'd had two nights ago. She wondered how she knew it would be a boy.

She studied for several hours until the library announced it would close soon. She wanted to check out a book to read when she returned to the rusty railroad car. Reading would give her something to do other than think about her dire situation. So Mattie searched for books about pregnancy. She selected *What to Expect When You Are Expecting*. She jotted down the number and located it on a shelf. Then she gathered her belongings and headed for the counter. The librarian smiled when she saw the book.

After she left the library, Mattie realized she needed a flashlight. It would be hard to read in the dark—and being alone in that railroad car was scary enough even in daylight. Mattie walked to a general store a block from the library. She looked at several flashlights and chose the cheapest one they had. She clicked the button, and it seemed bright enough. Mattie looked at the candy bars at the checkout counter but knew she should save her money, so she paid the cashier and headed back toward the railroad tracks. Her stomach rumbled louder as she passed several fast-food restaurants along the way. She didn't stop but promised herself to eat a bigger breakfast in the morning.

It was dusk when she reached the railroad car and climbed inside. There was still enough light from the open door to read. She pulled out the library book and stared at the cover. It had a picture of a happy pregnant woman with her hands on her belly. Mattie sighed at the sight and wished she felt as happy as the lady looked on the cover. The first line in the book said, "Pregnancy is one of the most joyous times in a woman's life." Mattie laughed at that. She closed the book and curled up with her teddy bear. It had been an exhausting day.

CHAPTER TWO

DEVEREAUX PARISH, LOUISIANA

The sound of gravelly footsteps startled Mattie awake, and then she heard a light rain tapping on the railcar's roof. She fumbled for the flashlight as the crunching steps grew closer. Through the inky blackness, she made out the shape of a shadow crawling inside. Her shaking hands finally found the flashlight button, and she clicked it on. It illuminated a man—a scary-looking man—only inches from her face. But it seemed like the sight of her frightened him as much as he terrified Mattie.

He whispered, "Hey, I'm sorry. I didn't mean to scare you. I was looking for a place to sleep. I didn't know anybody was in here. You mind if I share this car with you? My name's Johnny. I promise I won't hurt you."

He had a sunken face with inset eyes and a mouth void of anything but a few broken teeth. The appearance was like a zombie from the scariest horror film. His skeletal frame looked to be nothing more than skin stretched taut over bones that were ready to break. He wore a dirty T-shirt and equally dirty jeans. His unkempt blond hair and scruffy beard looked at home on his pale, transparent face. Overall, the man appeared sickly ... and smelled of rotting flesh.

"I ... I'd prefer you sleep somewhere else ... if you don't

mind," Mattie said.

"It is raining, you know ... and this is the closest thing I could find. You want me to sleep outside?"

Mattie preferred he would sleep anywhere but here. But she finally relented: "Well, if you have to stay here, can you please go to the other side? I don't feel very comfortable."

"I understand," Johnny said. He moved to the far end of the container. He sat down and asked, "How 'bout this? Is it okay?"

"I guess," Mattie said, despite thinking that Mars or some other planet wouldn't be far enough away for this crazy clown to move to.

"What's your name?"

"Mattie."

"That's a pretty name. Matches your beautiful looks," Johnny said.

Mattie swallowed, feeling even more uneasy. She kept the flashlight pointed in Johnny's general direction, not planning to try to rest until he was asleep.

The horror show of a man reached into his pocket and pulled out a syringe. "I hope you don't mind if I take my medicine."

"What's the matter with you?"

"Oh ... I'm diabetic and this is my insulin."

Mattie thought it might explain this freak's sickly appearance. She watched him take out a spoon and crush something into it. Then he lit a flame with a lighter and held it under the spoon. After the stuff on the spoon melted, he set the lighter down beside him. Next, the creep picked up the syringe and used it to slurp up what looked like a sticky brown liquid.

Though Mattie had never seen illegal drugs before, she felt pretty sure this wasn't insulin. Now Johnny took a length of thin rubber tubing and wrapped it around his right arm. He pulled the tube tight with his few remaining teeth, tapped a vein, and then slowly inserted the needle. Mattie put a hand to her mouth, ready to throw up, but thankfully she didn't.

Johnny pushed the syringe plunger, draining the brown liquid into his body. Then his eyes rolled back in his head. An eerie smile crept over his face, and his hands dropped to his side, leaving the needle hanging from where it was stuck in his arm. As he sat there, Mattie noticed he had a skull-and-crossbones tattoo on his left hand.

A few moments later, Johnny's glazed eyes focused on Mattie. He pulled the needle from his arm and then untied the rubber tube. "Ah, that feels better," he said.

Mattie shouted, "That wasn't insulin!"

Johnny's mouth formed a wicked grin that nobody would mistake for a smile. "Would you have let me stay here if I told you I was a homeless heroin addict?"

"Hell no!" Mattie yelled.

"Well, I didn't lie when I told you it was my medicine. I'd die without it."

"Yeah, and you look like you're almost dead because of it!" Mattie said as she pushed her back against the wall, trying to keep as much space between them as possible.

"Maybe so, but at least this makes me feel better. ... So what's your story? Why is a young girl like you sleeping in a railroad car?"

"It's a long story you'd never understand. Can you just leave now? I don't feel comfortable with you being here."

"But I'm tired. Please let me sleep here, okay? I'll leave in the morning."

Before Mattie could respond, Johnny closed his eyes and drifted into a coma-like delirium. The guy looked like he was dead, and if that was the case, she couldn't care less. All she knew was she didn't have to talk to the creep any longer.

Mattie adjusted her backpack and picked up her teddy bear. She turned off the flashlight and lay down, eager for this night to be over.

Mattie had no idea how long she'd been asleep, but she startled awake when she felt something touch her hair. At first, she thought it was a bug and tried to swat it away. Then she realized it was a hand. "Oh my God!" She jumped back, remembering that a man was with her in the railcar.

"What are you doing?" she yelled, pawing around for the flashlight.

A moment later, she found it and turned on the light—only to see Johnny's leering face inches from hers. It looked even scarier and more demonic than before.

"You have such pretty hair. I just wanted to touch it," Johnny said, giving an evil grin.

Mattie cringed at seeing his few teeth again, all broken and brown.

"You mind if I kiss you?" Johnny asked, leaning in closer.

Mattie could smell his sickly garbage breath. "Hell yes I mind!" she shouted.

Without warning, Johnny smacked her so hard her head spun. "I *will* kiss you!" he growled.

"No you won't! Get your hands off me!" Mattie yelled as she tried to push Johnny away.

Johnny's rage took over as he began punching Mattie's face. The blows were crushing, and she felt blood dripping from her nose and lips. He continued to beat her until she finally fell unconscious.

It was daylight when Mattie awoke. Her head pounded and her body ached. She didn't know where she was—or even who she was, at first. The fogginess began lifting, and she remembered that someone had beaten her. As her senses came into focus, she realized she was naked, except for her socks.

"My God!" she cried.

Feeling something wet on the floorboards, Mattie looked down between her legs and saw a puddle of blood. "Oh my God oh my God oh my God!" she cried, knowing she had been raped.

Mattie sobbed. How could this happen? What did she do to deserve this? Now she felt a surge of anger. She would never be in this position if she had not slept with Demarcus. Her life would be happy, and she would be in school with her friends right now. But here she was: another stupid, pregnant runaway teenager who had put herself in a position to be raped!

She slowly stood up and saw her clothes scattered around the railroad car. Her shirt was ripped, and her jeans were turned inside out. She also saw her bra and panties, along with her shoes. The violence of the attack seemed apparent. Then she realized her backpack was missing.

"Oh noooo! He stole it—and the only money I had!" Mattie slumped back down, naked, and cried to the point she could not breathe. "What am I going to do?" as she burbled through her hyperventilation.

After a while, Mattie picked up her clothes and put them on. She also found her teddy bear. Mattie climbed down from the railroad car, and the sunlight almost blinded her. Should she go to the police? No, because they would return her to her mother, who would no doubt still insist on her having the abortion. Then, after finding out that her runaway daughter had been raped, her mother would disown her. No, going to the police was not an option.

The only person she knew nearby was the diner waitress, Annie. She'd be ashamed to see her, but Mattie needed help. She adjusted her torn shirt and walked to the diner. The place again fell silent when Mattie walked through the door. This time, though, everyone stared at her battered face. She wanted to turn and run.

Annie saw her and rushed over. "What happened to you?" she exclaimed at the sight of the child.

Mattie cried again, and she didn't care who saw it.

Annie put her arm around Mattie and said, "Come with me, sweetheart."

They walked to the bathroom, and Annie locked the door behind them. "What happened, honey?"

Mattie dropped to her knees and sobbed some more. Annie's heart melted at seeing the girl in this condition. She kneeled beside her and wrapped her arms around Mattie, who continued to cry on Annie's shoulder.

Through stuttered breaths, Mattie said, "A man ... A man raped me."

"Oh my, honey! How did it happen?"

Mattie told Annie everything about the attack as best as she could remember. Then she revealed how she was only sixteen and pregnant, and how she'd run away from home, which was why she had been staying in the abandoned railroad car.

Annie's mouth was agape. She could not believe what this poor child had been through. She said, "Baby, we have got to get you to the hospital and call the police. Then we need to call your mother."

"No! I can't call my mother! She'll make me abort my child."

"We can talk about that later, but we have to get you to the hospital. And we have to call the police so they can find the person who did this to you. ... And before we do anything, what's your name, sweetheart?"

"Mattie," she whispered.

Annie wiped the tears from Mattie's eyes with her apron. "Come on then, Mattie, let's go."

Annie helped Mattie stand up. She straightened the child's

torn shirt, and they exited the bathroom.

Out front, Annie yelled to the owner/cook, "Max, I have to leave. It's an emergency."

Max shouted, "You can't leave! It's breakfast rush hour!"

"You deal with it, Max!" Annie hollered back.

Annie placed her arm around Mattie's shoulder and hustled her out of the diner. She opened her car door and helped Mattie inside, saying, "Everything will be okay."

Those words haunted Mattie as Annie drove to the hospital. They were the same words the little boy had said in Mattie's dream. But how was all of this okay? ... And why did she have that dream?

Annie pulled in front of the emergency entrance with Mattie. She told her to stay in the car. Annie returned with a nurse, who assisted Mattie into a wheelchair. Once inside, the nurse pulled Annie aside and asked what happened.

"She was attacked and raped last night," Annie said. "She's only sixteen years old ... and pregnant."

"Are you her mother?"

"No, I'm a friend," Annie replied.

"We're required by law to contact police," the nurse said.

Annie nodded.

The nurse returned to Mattie. "Hi there. My name is Angelina. I'll be your nurse. What's your name?"

"Mattie," she said in a voice almost too quiet to hear. "Mattie Carter."

"It's nice to meet you, Mattie. You can call me Angel, okay?"

Mattie tried to smile. Even in her darkest moment, God had sent her an Angel.

When they reached the examination room, Annie waited outside. Inside the room, Angel said Mattie would need to remove her clothing. She laid a hospital gown on the bed and then handed Mattie a clear plastic bag. The nurse explained they needed to save her clothes for evidence. Then Angel left the room while Mattie changed, but she soon returned with an ice pack for Mattie's swollen eyes and lips. Angel helped her position it, then said she would get Annie to come in while she went to find a doctor.

A few minutes after Annie came in to be with Mattie, a doctor entered. He took a deep breath when he saw Mattie so battered and bruised. The doctor knew he'd never get used to seeing children in this condition. It troubled him even more that the patient was the same age as his daughter.

"Hello, Mattie, I'm Dr. Powell. Can you tell me briefly what happened and where you're experiencing pain?"

"A homeless man beat me unconscious," Mattie said, her words flying out of her mouth. "When I woke up, I was naked and my private parts hurt. ... Oh, he said his name is Johnny, and I think he's a drug addict. I saw him inject something into his arm he said was medicine."

Dr. Powell's expression changed to concern. "Mattie, I'm very sorry to hear this. We will do everything possible to comfort you. Unfortunately, we need to conduct a personal examination. Has anyone explained what that involves?"

"No sir," Mattie replied softly.

"I'll ask Nurse Angelina to speak with you about that. Sit tight and I'll be back soon," Dr. Powell said, with a gentle touch to her hand.

Dr. Powell approached Angelina at the nurse's station. "Please explain the rape exam to the patient. We also need a full STD workup, including hepatitis and HIV. She mentioned the man who raped her was an intravenous drug user."

Angel nodded, then finished her notes and walked to Mattie's room. "Hi again, Mattie. Dr. Powell asked me to explain your examination and other tests we need to conduct. Is that okay with you?"

"Yes ma'am."

"Mattie, this examination may seem uncomfortable, but we have to do it to collect evidence. It's also to protect your health. There is nothing to be embarrassed about. The exam is like a gynecological exam, but a little more thorough. Have you had one of those before?"

"My mama took me to the gynecologist when I started my period two years ago," Mattie replied.

"Okay, sweetie. We'll be as gentle as possible and try to get this over with as quick as we can. I'll be back in a few minutes. While you wait, there's a police officer in the hallway that would like to speak with you, all right?"

The officer stepped into the room. "Hello, Ms. Carter, I'm Officer Davis. Would you mind if I take just a few minutes to speak with you? We were notified that you were assaulted. Is that correct?"

Mattie looked at Annie, then back at the officer. "Yes sir."

"Could you start at the beginning and tell me what happened?" he asked.

Mattie stared at the floor. She swallowed and took a deep breath, then she again described the violent encounter in a voice that was barely a whisper. When Officer Davis asked for a description of her attacker, a chill ran down Mattie's spine. She recalled the terrifying moment when the flashlight shined on the sickly man's face. Her recollection was so vivid it caused uneasiness in the seasoned officer. That face would be forever burned in her mind.

The officer looked toward Annie and asked, "Are you her mother?"

"No, I'm a friend ... Annie Barnes. I brought her to the hospital."

"Has anyone contacted her mom?"

Annie motioned for the officer to step outside. She

explained Mattie was pregnant and had run away from home. Annie told the officer that Mattie's mother insisted she have an abortion, but Mattie was adamant she would never do so. So the scared kid had no intention of contacting her mother.

"I can't force her to speak with her mother," Officer Davis said. "She can emancipate from her parents at sixteen years old. But she'll have to go through the legal process. And we did receive a missing person report from her mom. She's very worried."

"I'll speak with Mattie and encourage her to contact her mother," Annie said. "In the meantime, I'll take care of her if she agrees."

"Will you bring her to the police station later? Our detectives will have an artist create a composite sketch of her attacker."

"I will when we finish here," Annie said, wishing Mattie didn't have to go through that.

Annie returned to the exam room. Mattie appeared helpless, sitting alone on the medical table in the sterile hospital room. *What pain the child must be feeling ...*

A technician walked in. "Mattie, we're ready to begin your exam." Then she turned to Annie and asked, "Ma'am, would you mind sitting in the waiting room?"

Mattie looked up with fear and insisted that Annie remain. Thankfully, the technician agreed.

For what seemed like hours, the technician poked, prodded, swabbed, combed, and stuck Mattie. She felt so violated all over again. Even though the technician was gentle, Mattie couldn't wait for this nightmare to end.

After the medical technician had finished, Nurse Angel returned to the room. "Mattie, we're all done. The doctor will be in to see you in a few minutes. Do you have any other clothes to wear?"

"No, the man stole my backpack. I have nothing else."

Mattie's innocent response almost made Angel and Annie cry.

Annie told the nurse, "I'll get her clothes as soon as we leave."

Angel nodded and said she always kept a couple sets of extra clothes on hand in case a patient needed them, although they might be a little big for Mattie.

Then Angel left the room, and a few moments later, Dr. Powell entered, with a change of clothes in hand. He smiled at Mattie and said, "I know this was difficult, Mattie. I have a few prescriptions for you. And I need to see you again next week to review your test results and perform a follow-up exam."

Mattie cringed at the thought of coming back to this place. But she nodded to the doctor.

Dr. Powell gave Mattie a fatherly hug and said, "Get some rest. I know your friend will take good care of you."

Annie helped Mattie step down from the table and then turned around while Mattie changed into the baggy clothes. Afterward, Annie helped her sit in a wheelchair.

Angel waited with Mattie inside the door as Annie went for the car. "Mattie," Angel said, "I know how traumatic this has been for you. I promise everything will be okay."

Mattie reached for the nurse's hand and wondered why she'd once again heard the same words as in her dream: "Everything will be okay."

Annie pulled up with the car, and Angel helped Mattie inside. As they drove away, Angel said a silent prayer.

CHAPTER THREE

DEVEREAUX PARISH, LOUISIANA

Mattie stared out the car window, lost in thought. Her spirit felt as dull as the cold, gray day. Annie wished she could take Mattie home now, but they still had two stops to make.

"Mattie, I need to get you some clothes ... and the police need to speak with you again."

The crushed teenager glared at Annie with a scorn that could have melted the upholstery. Mattie's expression said a thousand words that Annie understood.

"Don't you want them to catch the man who attacked you?" Annie asked.

"I want them to kill him! He ruined my already messed-up life!" Mattie shouted.

Annie said nothing and soon pulled into the police station parking lot. When they approached the counter, a female officer recognized the youngster from a missing person photo. It was a small police department, and everyone knew of the teenager's brutal assault.

"You must be Mattie Carter," the female officer said kindly. "We've been expecting you. Please have a seat and a detective will be with you soon."

A few minutes later, a tall gentleman wearing a dark suit approached. "Hello, Miss Carter. I'm Detective Hodges. Would you mind if I speak with you?"

Mattie looked toward Annie for reassurance.

Annie told her, "Go ahead with the detective and I'll go get clothes for you while you talk with him. That way, we can go right home after this, okay?"

Annie didn't feel comfortable leaving Mattie alone, even with the police. Her motherly instincts told her she would look after this sweet girl for as long as she needed to, but she knew the detective had to speak to Mattie, so she reluctantly left to buy clothes.

Detective Hodges led Mattie to a small conference room and asked her to take a seat. He offered her a bottle of water and sat in the chair across from her. "Mattie, my name is Detective Robert Hodges, but you can call me Rob. I'm a criminal investigator with the Devereaux Parish Police Department. How are you feeling?"

Mattie thought that was a dumb question. She replied sarcastically, "Like I've been beaten and raped by a drug addict. How are you feeling?"

Detective Hodges realized that it wasn't the best way to break the ice. "Sorry. I know this has been a horrible experience. The reason we asked you to come in is to record as much information about the incident as you can recall. We would also like you to sit with a forensic artist to help create a sketch of the person who did this to you. Even though we're a small police department, you're very lucky. There's a retired FBI criminologist who lives in town. He's an expert in making composite sketches and forensic identification. I told him about your case. He'll be here to visit with you later ... if that's okay with you."

Mattie knew she didn't have much choice and dreaded the thought of revisiting the awful attack again and again. But she understood it was necessary, so she shrugged and mumbled,

"I guess."

Rob pressed Record on the device in front of them, introduced himself and Mattie, then asked Mattie if he had permission to record her testimony. After a moment of silence, Mattie agreed, then Rob nodded at her and she began to relate her encounter with Johnny the heroin addict, starting from the moment he entered the abandoned railroad car. She described the events in such detail that the detected felt uneasy. When she finished, they were both quiet. Rob stared at Mattie, not with the look of a police officer, but more like a concerned father.

Shaking off his emotions, the detective said, "Mattie, I'm sorry this happened to you. I promise we will do everything in our power to capture this person. You have my word."

The conference room door opened after a slight knock. "I'm sorry to interrupt," said an older gentleman who appeared to be in his mid-seventies.

Rob rose and shook hands with the man, then turned and said, "Mattie, this is Clive Fennimore. He's the gentleman I mentioned to you earlier."

Clive stepped forward and shook Mattie's hand. "Hi, Mattie, it's nice to meet you."

Mattie noticed his hand felt soft. He wasn't what she expected an FBI agent to look like. He was tall and fit, with silver hair—more grandfatherly in appearance than she'd seen FBI agents look like on television.

"I'll leave you two alone," Rob said before he left the room.

Clive pulled up a chair next to Mattie and placed a large pad and several pencils on the table in front of him. "Mattie, I hope you don't mind that I'm sitting so close to you. Did Rob tell you I'm a retired FBI criminologist and draw sketches of people?"

"Yeah ... I mean, yes, he did," Mattie replied, staring at his pad and pencils.

Clive saw where her eyes had gone, and he smiled. "I wanted to be an artist growing up—a painter, actually. But the FBI recruited me when I was in college and that's how I became a forensic artist. Now that I'm retired, I spend most of my time painting watercolors." He paused, then continued, "When Rob told me what happened, I insisted on helping them catch the person who hurt you."

Mattie could tell Mr. Fennimore cared. She felt at ease with him and suddenly wished he was her grandfather. For the next hour or so, Clive sketched as Mattie described Johnny's features. They began with his skin tone, then the shape of his head, and the color and style of his hair. She related every horrible detail of the evil man.

When it was time to describe the eyes, Mattie paused.

After several moments, Clive asked, "Do you remember his eyes, Mattie?"

She remained silent as she recalled those scary, deep-set eyes. It was the feature she remembered the most. Then she said, "His eyes were evil. They were dark and sunken into his face, almost like he was dead, but alive. ... I don't know if that even makes sense."

Clive nodded. He understood, having seen that look on many drug-addicted faces that he'd sketched over the years.

As he drew the eyes, Mattie looked away.

Clive sensed her uneasiness. "Is everything okay, Mattie? Is this what his eyes looked like?"

Mattie glanced at the drawing and whispered, "Exactly."

Clive finished the sketch and showed Mattie. Seeing it made her stomach churn. He had captured the attacker's appearance so accurately that Mattie wanted to stab the drawing. It felt as if she was staring at the demon again.

"Is there anything else you can recall about him? His height, weight, clothing, or any unusual scars or tattoos?" Clive asked.

Mattie said he was skinny and wore a dirty T-shirt and jeans. She didn't know his height, so Clive asked several officers to step inside the conference room.

After looking at them, Mattie pointed to an officer and said, "He was around that height, I think."

The officer told Clive he was five-foot-ten.

After the officers left, Mattie related two other features she remembered vividly: Johnny had several missing and broken teeth, and he had a skull-and-crossbones tattoo on his left hand.

In her angered mind, she thought, *Raped by some kind of pirate wannabe!*

When they finished, Clive said, "Mattie, you have been one of the most helpful witnesses I have ever worked with. I believe this drawing will assist our officers in capturing the man. This community and others will be much safer when he's off the streets."

Clive shook Mattie's hand before leaving the room. In the hallway, he met Detective Hodges and handed him the sketch. Clive told Rob, "Please keep me informed about this investigation. She's a sweet young lady."

Detective Hodges returned to the conference room. "Thank you, Mattie, for helping Mr. Fennimore create this sketch. It will be helpful to our officers. Your friend Annie is waiting for you in the lobby, but I have a few more questions ... if you don't mind?"

Mattie felt a little more relaxed after her time with Mr. Fennimore and said, "I don't mind."

"Mattie, there's a missing person report for you, filed by your mother. I understand that you're pregnant and there's some tension with your mom, which caused you to run away, right?"

She nodded. "She's making me have an abortion. It's why I ran away."

"Well, since you are sixteen, you can legally leave home in this state and we can't force you to return. But your mother is very worried. I hope you'll consider calling her and telling her you're okay?"

Mattie frowned. "I don't want to talk to her after what she said ... and after what happened to me! ... But, well, could you maybe tell her I'm okay?" she asked. "Oh, but please don't tell her about the attack! She'll only worry more."

Rob was disappointed but understood how Mattie felt. "Sure, I'll call your mother if that's what you want me to do. How can we contact you?"

"Oh ... uh, just call Annie. I'm staying with her for now."

The detective patted Mattie's shoulder. "Get some rest. I'll check on you in a few days."

Mattie nodded and mumbled, "Thanks."

They returned to the lobby, where Annie was waiting.

The detective said, "Hi again, Annie. Mattie was very helpful. Please take good care of her. I have your number, so we'll be in touch."

Annie and Mattie returned to the car. Even though Mattie's face was still swollen and battered, Annie sensed a relief in the teenager. She said, "Honey, I picked up clothes for you. I'm sure you're ready to get out of those baggy clothes, even though it sure was nice of Nurse Angel to give them to you."

Mattie gave a weak smile. "Yeah. ... She really was nice." Hanging her head, she whispered, "I know all people aren't bad in the world."

Twenty minutes later, Annie turned down a small country road and then up a gravel driveway. She pulled alongside an old gray trailer and turned off the ignition.

Mattie was quiet and didn't seem to notice the car had

stopped.

Annie broke the silence: "Here's where I live. Not much, but it's home."

Mattie felt surprised when they entered the trailer. The interior looked neat and cozy, in contrast to its worn exterior.

"I'm sure you want to take a shower," Annie said, directing Mattie to the bathroom.

As the water poured over her battered body, Mattie wished it could wash everything away: Wash away the mistake of sleeping with Demarcus. Wash away the pregnancy. Wash away the violent attack and rape. Wash away the anger between her and her mom. Wash away all the pain.

She felt like such a fool. All she ever wanted was to be a good person and make her mother proud. This was not the life she dreamed of. Mattie began to cry.

After her shower, Mattie stood in front of the mirror, staring at her disfigured face. She wiped away her tears and then opened the bag of clothing Annie had given her. She found a pair of pink pajamas with little yellow flowers and matching fluffy slippers.

When Mattie walked into the kitchen, Annie was cooking.

Annie turned and smiled when she saw her wearing the pajamas. "I hope you like them. You look cute."

Mattie gave a little smile, "They're perfect, Annie. Thank you."

"Are you hungry?"

Mattie realized she was starving, since the only thing she had eaten in the past thirty-six hours or so was two pieces of toast. Annie put two plates of food on the table, and they sat down. Mattie crossed her hands and bowed her head to whisper a prayer, as she always did before meals. Annie listened to the sweet child pray.

At the end, they both said, "Amen."

Annie never saw anybody eat food as fast as Mattie. She acted like a fat guy at a buffet. It tickled Annie watching her gobble everything up, and she soon pushed her own plate toward the hungry girl. Mattie didn't even notice it was Annie's portion as she dove into the second plate.

Annie thought to herself, *What a wonderful kid.* Even though she'd never had children of her own, Annie always wished she had one just like Mattie.

When she finished eating, Mattie took a long drink of orange juice and burped. It made them both laugh, and Mattie said, "Excuse me."

Annie saw a little flash of peace and contentment in Mattie's eyes. She reached over and held Mattie's hand. "You need some sleep. I only have one bed, but I want you to take it."

"No ... I can't. It's your bed."

"I insist, Mattie. I'll sleep on the couch. I don't mind."

Annie walked with Mattie to the bedroom. Mattie smiled and almost started crying when she saw her teddy bear resting on a pillow. Annie pulled back the covers as Mattie took off her slippers before climbing into bed.

Annie kissed her on the cheek. "Sleep well, Mattie. Tomorrow will be a better day."

Mattie slept for the next twelve hours and woke up sore. She climbed out of bed and walked to the kitchen, where she found a note on the table: *"Mattie, I hope you slept well. I went to work, but I left breakfast for you in the refrigerator. There are more clothes for you by the bed, and my laptop is on the coffee table (no password needed). Love, Annie."*

She put the note on the counter, then found a plate of fruit and a bowl of oatmeal in the refrigerator. As she ate breakfast, Mattie thought how lucky she was to find such a caring friend as Annie. She washed the dishes, then took another shower. When she returned to the bedroom, Mattie found two more bags of clothes sitting beside the bed. She put on a T-shirt, shorts, and sandals. The T-shirt was a little large, causing Mattie to smile. Annie no doubt knew she would grow into it.

Mattie walked to the living room and sat on the sofa, wanting something to do—anything to keep from thinking about all that had happened the past few days. She noticed Annie's laptop and picked it up. She logged on to her school's website and found her class assignments. What she really needed was her schoolbooks. She sent a private message to her friend, Mollie: *"Lots going on. Won't be back for a while. Can you get the books from my locker? Here's the combination ..."*

Mollie messaged back: *"What's going on? Your mom called and said you ran away?"*

Mattie replied: *"Yeah. Tell you more later when we meet. Don't have a phone so this is the best way to reach me. Love you."*

Mattie searched for online classes in her subjects. Maybe she could keep up with her studies and get her GED—and she'd of course have to declare herself as an emancipated minor, so she sent another message, this time to the school guidance counselor, telling her about her plans. When the counselor messaged back and asked to talk to Mattie over the phone, Mattie replied that she had made up her mind.

A few hours had passed when the door opened. It was Annie.

"Hi, Mattie. I'm home for lunch before my second job. Did you sleep well?"

"Yeah. I don't think I dreamed at all."

"That's good. It's what you needed. Can I make you lunch?" Annie asked.

After Mattie nodded, Annie prepared sandwiches for them.

When they sat at the table, Mattie said, "Annie, I appreciate all you're doing for me. I ... I hope I'm not a burden."

"Honey, you are not a burden at all. We'll get through this

together. Besides, I like the company. It has been so lonely around here since my husband passed away."

"Oh. ... Your husband died?"

Annie looked down at her plate. "Winston was the love of my life, Mattie. We met when I was fourteen years old. He passed away last year after a long battle with cancer."

Mattie didn't know what to say, and Annie could sense it, so she said, "Mattie, I hope one day you will find love like what Winston and I had. I miss him every day."

After they finished lunch, Annie put the plates in the sink and said, "I'm off to my next job. Is there anything you need?"

"No thanks, Annie."

"All right. There's food in the fridge if you get hungry. I'll see you this evening."

Mattie returned to the sofa and began to study again. At 2:30 p.m., she realized school was over for the day. An instant message popped up from Mollie: *"Got your books. Where are you? Brian can drive me over."*

Mattie gave Mollie the address. She didn't mind Mollie seeing her in this condition, but she'd feel embarrassed for Mollie's boyfriend to see her. *Oh well* ... There was nothing she could do about it. Half an hour later, a knock came at the door. When Mattie opened it, Mollie and Brian stood there, clearly in shock at seeing Mattie's battered face.

"Oh my God! What happened to you?" Mollie exclaimed.

After Mollie and Brian came in and sat down, Mattie told her friends why she ran away. Then she shared the terrifying ordeal of the attack and rape, the hospital, and her visit to the police.

When Mattie finished, Mollie was in tears, and Brian sat in disbelief.

"Please don't tell anyone about this, especially my mom," Mattie said.

"We won't say a word," Mollie promised, and Brian nodded in agreement.

Mollie gave Mattie a hug and said, "We have to go. My mom is expecting me home now. But if there's anything you need, please let me know. You know how much we love you!"

"I do, Mollie. Thanks." Mattie walked them to the door.

Brian hugged Mattie, then stepped back and said, "If they find out who did this to you, I'll kill him!"

CHAPTER FOUR

DEVEREAUX PARISH, LOUISIANA

The most unusual circumstances of life became a new normal for Mattie as she settled into a daily routine with Annie. While Annie worked her two jobs six days a week, Mattie focused on her studies. They enjoyed each other's company, especially when Annie had a day off.

One afternoon when they were both at home, a knock sounded at the door.

A moment later, Detective Hodges and a female police officer greeted Annie. "Good afternoon, Annie," the detective said. "Is Mattie home?"

Annie invited them inside and called for Mattie.

When the teen walked into the living room, Detective Hodges smiled and said, "Hi, Mattie. You look better ... and maybe a little bigger than the last time I saw you. Please, have a seat."

After all of them had sat down, the detective began, "Mattie, we received information last night that I wanted to share with you in person. We sent copies of the sketch of your attacker to every police department in the state. New Orleans PD contacted us about a man they believe may be your attacker. Please prepare yourself for what I'm about to show you."

Detective Hodges handed Mattie a photograph. Shock ran

through her as if she'd stuck her tongue in a light socket. She stared at the photo. Her hands shook and her lips quivered.

She looked up, fighting back tears, and said, "That's him."

None of the adults in the room wanted to see the teenager cry. The female officer's first instinct was to move closer on the sofa to the girl, but she was afraid to touch her in such a vulnerable moment. This was a time that only Mattie could indicate if, or when, anyone could invade her personal space.

Detective Hodges said, "Mattie, they found him dead in an alley in New Orleans. The coroner believes the cause of death was a drug overdose. We hoped to capture him so he would face justice for the crime against you. But please take comfort knowing he will never harm another person again."

Mattie wiped her tears with the collar of her shirt and handed the photograph to Annie. Then, looking at the officers, Mattie whispered, "Thank you. I'm glad he won't hurt anyone else. I have forgiven him. Now I hope God forgives him too."

They all stood up. Detective Hodges gave Mattie a hug like he would with his own daughter. "Mattie, you are a sweet person and I wish you all the best in life. I hope this gives you closure."

"It does," Mattie said, still teary-eyed as she clutched the detective's arm.

Annie thanked the officers and escorted them to the door.

After they left, Annie sat back down with Mattie and asked, "Are you okay?"

Mattie shrugged. "Yeah ... I am. Just need a little time to process this."

Annie changed the subject: "Let me take you shopping. That always cheers a girl up. Besides, you've outgrown all your clothes."

Mattie managed a small smile because Annie was right: Mattie's stomach was getting bigger. She'd complained more than once to Annie that she was huge and waddled like a duck. Annie reminded her there was nothing more beautiful than an expectant mother. Mattie said to tell that to her fat feet. "They'd look more at home on a baby elephant!"

Ultrasound revealed Mattie was having a son. It made sense to her, because each time the child kicked, it felt like her intestines would explode. Mattie was convinced the boy would be an athlete one day, maybe even a boxer.

One evening, a few months later, Mattie mentioned she had a stomachache. Annie asked if she wanted medication. Mattie said it was probably something she ate and would lie down. She woke a few hours later in excruciating pain. It felt like somebody was stabbing her in the gut. Mattie sat up and held her stomach, then noticed the bed was wet. She scooched to the living room and woke Annie.

"Annie, something's wrong with me. I'm in so much pain and I think I wet the bed."

Annie was awake in an instant and exclaimed, "Mattie, you're going into labor! Your water broke!"

Mattie didn't believe it. "The doctor said I wasn't due until next month."

"Girl, you are having that baby now! Forget what the doctor said!"

Annie rushed to get dressed. She grabbed Mattie like an expectant father would and hurried her out the door. Mattie huffed for every breath as Annie ignored speed limits, stop signs, and red lights along the way. She screeched to a halt in front of the emergency room and ran inside for assistance.

A nurse wheeled Mattie into the delivery room. The hospital called her physician, but it was too late for him to arrive in time. The doctor on call examined Mattie and determined she was dilated seven centimeters.

He told her, "Your baby is ready to see the world, Mattie.

Let's help him out."

Mattie was in such pain that she felt like she would rather get beat up again than go through this!

Annie dabbed Mattie's forehead with a cool towel as the nurse coaxed her to take deep breaths.

"It hurts!" Mattie screamed.

"I need you to push, Mattie," the doctor encouraged as the child's head began to crest.

Mattie roared like she was possessed and spewed a slew of profanity. Nobody in the delivery room acknowledged her remarks. They had heard it all before. But, coming out of Mattie's otherwise quiet and polite mouth, it sounded kind of funny.

"That's it, Mattie," the doctor said while pressing on her belly.

Mattie gasped and pushed again, and her son's head finally came all the way out. With another painful thrust, the shoulders were free. Summoning all the energy she had left, Mattie made one more agonizing push. With that, the son she had dreamed of entered the world.

Annie cried tears of joy when the doctor held the baby up with the umbilical cord still attached. He patted the child's back, and after a small cough, the infant took his first breath.

The doctor smiled and said, "Mattie, you have a beautiful baby boy!"

Then the doctor severed the umbilical cord and handed the baby to a nurse. She removed the fluid from his lungs, then cleaned the child. She wrapped the baby in a light blue blanket and placed him on Mattie's chest.

Tears flowed as Mattie looked at the tiny face of her son. "Hello, Justin Carter," she said through her tears.

Annie had never seen anything so beautiful. The sight of Mattie holding the child she fought so hard to bring into this world was the very picture of an unbelievable act of courage and love.

A few minutes later, the nurse walked over and said, "I need to take him to the neonatal unit. He's premature and requires special care. But don't worry, he'll be back in your arms before you know it."

Mattie hesitated to let Justin go. He had been a part of her body and through every ordeal with her recently. She relented in her exhaustion and had no choice but to trust the nurse. For the next twenty-four hours, Mattie rested and recovered. Her friends Mollie and Brian stopped by to visit. Annie asked Mattie if she wanted to call her mother now that the baby had arrived. Mattie declined by saying that now was not the time.

Annie wheeled Mattie to the neonatal unit before her discharge the next day. She watched her son lying in an incubator next to the other premature babies. He seemed so tiny and fragile. But Mattie knew her son was a fighter like her.

For the next month, Annie took Mattie to visit Justin every day. She enjoyed watching Mattie rock the baby. He had grown stronger, and Mattie could now nurse her son. Annie sensed something special in the bond between this mom and son. Like any mother and child, there was of course a nurturing instinct. But this was something different. It was as if some glow or magical aura surrounded them.

Mattie loved this child more than her own life. But the unknown destination of their future tormented her. Was she selfish for bringing a baby into this world without every advantage he would need to survive? She prayed for wisdom or some divine message to tell her what to do.

Little Justin Carter—JC, for short—had gained four pounds and was healthy enough to go home soon. The news excited Annie like a doting grandmother, but she sensed Mattie's concern. Mattie showed symptoms of postpartum depression, as new mothers often experience. Annie thought shopping for baby clothes would cheer Mattie up. But whenever Annie held up a baby-blue outfit, the only blue Mattie saw was the color of her own heart. It was a deep blue, like that of the ocean just before the last glimmers of light fade into the night.

The day before Justin's discharge from the hospital, Annie took Mattie to visit her son. As she rocked her baby and stroked his face, he gave her an innocent smile. Mattie leaned down and kissed his cheek, then whispered in his tiny ear, "God blessed me to be your mother. One day, you will grow up to be a great man. I don't know what life holds for either of us, my sweet child. But I will always love you. Please forgive me for what I must do."

The nurse returned to take Justin to his crib. His little hand wrapped tightly around Mattie's forefinger as if to say he did not want her to go. It would be the last time Mattie would hold her baby boy.

That evening, after Annie went to sleep, Mattie packed a plastic grocery bag and left a note on the kitchen table. She did not know where life would take her and prayed one day that God and her son would forgive her for this heart-ripping decision she had made. But it wouldn't be fair for Justin to go through life raised by an unwed black teenager with no job or education. She wanted the best for him no matter how much it hurt. Sacrificing her life for his happiness was the price she would pay.

Mattie opened the door and stepped into the darkness.

The next morning, Annie discovered Mattie's note. "No!" she shouted as she read it. Annie understood Mattie's reasoning, but her heart sank at the teenager's decision. She spent the rest of the day searching for Mattie to no avail. Out of desperation, Annie even went to the abandoned railroad car where Mattie had been attacked.

Then Annie drove to the hospital, hoping Mattie would be there. She went to the neonatal unit and saw little JC lying safely in his crib, along with the empty rocking chair. Annie bowed her head and knew it was true: Mattie had left. How could she tell the hospital staff that JC's mother had abandoned her child?

Annie went to the nursing station and requested to speak to a supervisor. A few minutes later, an attractive Hispanic woman dressed in business attire arrived. She introduced herself as Maria Jiménez, the senior administrator of the children's unit.

"May we speak in private?" Annie asked.

Maria escorted Annie to a small office and closed the door. She offered Annie a seat and asked how she could help her. Annie handed Mattie's note to Maria, whose brow furrowed as she read it.

"The mother has run away?" Maria confirmed.

"Yes, for what she believes is best for her child."

Annie described the extraordinary ordeal Mattie had endured. She told Maria that Mattie ran away from home because of her mother's insistence she abort the child. She then spoke of her attack and rape.

After a long pause, Maria asked, "Do you believe she'll return?"

"No, I don't. Mattie is a determined young lady and believes she has done what she feels is best for the child."

"What about the father? Can he care for the child?" Maria asked.

"No!" Annie said. "He cares less for that child than he did for Mattie. He already has two other children by different mothers and he doesn't support either of them."

A nurse knocked on the door and apologized for the interruption. She asked to speak to Maria in the hallway.

Maria excused herself and left the room. The nurse handed her a note she had found tucked inside Justin Carter's jumper. Maria read it and thanked the nurse for bringing it to her attention.

Maria returned to the office and handed the note to Annie. Maria said, "It appears Mattie did her homework. She has requested to apply for Louisiana's Safe Haven Law."

Maria explained that the law allowed a parent to relinquish custody of an infant without question when they felt they had no alternative. Since Mattie had handed the baby to a healthcare provider, she could exercise this right.

Annie asked, "What will happen to Justin?"

"We'll continue to care for him here. However, we are required by law to notify the Department of Children and Family Services. They will begin a process to gain custody of him."

"May ... May I adopt him?"

"I'm uncertain how that will work in this case, since I've not dealt with the Safe Haven Law before," Maria said as she handed Annie a card. "You'll need to contact them."

Maria paused. "Annie, I have some unfortunate news. Normally, this information would only be shared with the parents. But given this situation and your relationship with the mother, I feel you should know. A test revealed the infant has human immunodeficiency virus."

"What? He has AIDS?" Annie shouted.

"No no, Annie." Maria explained that HIV was a virus that could lead to acquired immunodeficiency syndrome—or AIDS. She assured Annie that there had been advancements in the treatment of HIV and that Justin could live a long and healthy life.

"How can this be possible?" Annie asked.

"We suspect the man who raped Mattie was HIV positive,

or maybe the baby's father. Has Mattie been tested?"

"She was tested the day after the rape, and it came back negative," Annie replied.

"Unfortunately, it may have been too soon for the virus to be detected. It's important Mattie get tested again."

Annie's blood boiled. Mattie had already endured so many terrible things. Now she and her son might have to live with this disease for the rest of their lives. Annie could only wonder, *How can this happen to such innocent kids?*

CHAPTER FIVE

DEVEREAUX PARISH, LOUISIANA

Gina Harper, a child welfare supervisor from the Department of Children and Family Services, arrived at the hospital to meet with Maria Jiménez. Gina said, "Ms. Jiménez, I have read the case file. It is very unfortunate what happened to this child and his mother."

Maria handed Gina the note Mattie had placed with her son. Gina read the note and asked if there had been any progress locating the mother.

"Neither the police nor her friend, Annie Barnes, has been able to find her," Maria replied.

Gina hated to be the bearer of bad news but the thirty-day waiting period had ended, and so the department would take custody of Justin Carter that same day. Gina reminded Maria the mother had sixty days to appeal the decision and reunite with the baby.

Maria mentioned Annie Barnes' desire to adopt the child if his mother did not appeal. Gina assured her that Annie would be the department's first consideration and said she understood the special relationship Annie had with the mother.

With regret, Maria signed the paperwork and accompanied Gina to the nursery. Justin Carter was dressed in pale blue pajamas and wrapped in a white blanket. Maria handed the infant to Gina, who placed him in a baby carrier. Maria then gathered a small bag and walked with Gina to her car.

Two days later, Annie arrived at the Department of Family and Children Services. She met with Gina Harper in a conference room.

"Hello, Ms. Barnes. Please have a seat," Gina said.

"How is JC—Justin?"

"He's a happy baby. We've taken him to Mission of Hope." Gina handed a card to Annie. "You can visit him anytime. Just show them that card."

Annie spoke of her desire to adopt the baby or become his foster parent.

Gina explained the process and then handed Annie a stack of forms to complete. "Our goal is to find the best home for the children in our care. I understand your relationship with his mother, and I believe you would be a great fit for him, based on what I've heard and researched about you. I will do everything within my power to support you during this process."

After the meeting, Annie drove to Mission of Hope. She expected it to look like a daycare center but found that it appeared more like an ancient fortress, with its high stone walls and turrets. The only things missing were armed guards and cannons on the roof.

An assistant escorted Annie to the nursery. Four rows of cribs filled the dorm-like room, all with crying babies. The assistant directed Annie to Justin's crib. Annie found him napping, oblivious to the racket going on around him. When she picked him up, Justin opened his eyes and smiled at her. Annie spent the next hour rocking JC in the nursery. She considered putting him in her big purse and taking him home with her. But she decided the legal process would be a better option than a kidnapping charge.

That evening, Annie completed the paperwork Gina Harper had given her. She dropped it off at DCFS on her way to work the next morning, so she arrived late for her shift at the diner.

Max barked at her, "Ever since that kid walked into this place, you've been distracted. Keep it up and you're fired!"

Max saw the scornful look on Annie's face as she put on her apron. He could tell this was not the day to cross her. If he said one more word, she'd probably kill him with a spatula.

Annie enjoyed her job at the diner and the regular customers. But underneath the cheerfulness was concern for the baby and the safety of his mother. Mattie had been gone for weeks now, and her whereabouts remained unknown. Annie's only relief to the constant worry came in the form of her daily visits to Mission of Hope to spend time with Justin.

Soon, Annie received a letter from the Department of Children and Family Services. It requested her appearance at a determination hearing for custody of Justin Carter. She could not contain her excitement. Annie had always wanted children and wished that she and Winston could have had kids of their own. Maybe adopting Justin would be God's way of saying there was a different plan.

Annie went dress shopping the day before her meeting at DCFS. She couldn't remember the last time she'd worn a dress, but this was as good a reason as any. Annie wanted to look her best when they delivered the wonderful news that she could adopt Justin.

She arrived early for her appointment the following day. Two administrators, Shirley Jones and Richard Barker, met her in the lobby. They escorted her to a formal conference room, unlike the casual one she'd been in before. Annie looked across the dark maple table, where she expected to see Gina

Harper. Without explanation, Shirley Jones informed her that Gina would not be attending the session. That was when Annie sensed something wrong.

Annie sat at the large conference table, facing a quartet of officials. Shirley Jones started by saying formally into a microphone, "Good morning, Ms. Barnes, thank you for coming today." Then she opened a folder and reviewed her notes. She looked at Annie and said with feigned compassion, "I am sorry to inform you that after our review, we find you unqualified to adopt the child, Justin Carter."

Annie's heart dropped. An uncomfortable quiet followed before Annie finally spoke: "What do you mean? There's no better person to care for him than me."

"We understand, and we considered your close relationship with the child and his mother," Jones said. "But, unfortunately, you do not meet the minimum financial requirements. Also, since you are single, there was concern about the child's care while you are working."

"I'll get a better job! I'll hire a babysitter when I'm not home. Please let me adopt him!" Annie said, near tears.

"I am sorry, Ms. Barnes, but we have made our final decision."

"What will happen to Justin?" Annie said, just above a whisper.

"We will take good care of him and find an appropriate foster home, since the father has no interest in him, and his grandmother just recently passed away suddenly or we would have tried to place him with her. You are welcome to visit him until we find him a home."

That was no consolation to Annie. She rose from the table and said, "What that child needs is love, and I am the closest thing to his mother! You won't let me adopt him because I don't make enough money? Seriously?" Annie shouted.

Shirley Jones, Richard Barker, and the other two officials did not say a word as Annie stormed out of the room, slamming the door behind her.

Annie drove home, knuckles turning white from gripping the wheel so hard. Never had she felt so angry at bureaucracy. How could they not let her adopt that wonderful child? She loved him and his mother like they were her own. Annie just knew deep down that Mattie would come back and rejoin them later.

As these thoughts spun through her mind, Annie didn't notice the traffic signal ahead turning red. She barreled through the intersection, where a truck T-boned her driver's door. Annie was killed instantly.

As with most funerals, Annie's was a somber affair. So many people loved her and the kindness of her heart. Max, the diner owner, paid for her expenses. He loved Annie like a sister and would miss arguing with her every day. As he stared at the casket, he regretted not having been kinder to her. Many of the diner customers were there. Maria Jiménez, Gina Harper, and personnel from the DCFS and hospital also paid their respects.

Happy moments of Annie's life played on a screen behind her casket. There were photos of her as a child and some pictures of her in college; loving photos of her wedding to Winston and the wonderful life they shared. There were photos at the beach and others she'd posed for with her favorite customers. But the last two photographs were the most special. They showed Annie at her happiest. One photo was a selfie she and Mattie had taken while Mattie was pregnant. The other was a photo of Annie holding baby Justin Carter. She beamed with joy in that photograph, and little JC was grinning too.

Pallbearers carried Annie's casket to the white hearse on the gray and rainy day. Motorcycle escorts guided the car carrying

Annie's mortal remains on the slow drive to the cemetery. Everyone gathered around the grave site, and then the pastor said a final prayer. Gradually, attendees walked away, leaving Annie's casket alone in the rain.

After everyone had left and before cemetery workers showed up to lower Annie into the earth, a hooded figure approached from behind a tree and laid a rose on the casket with a note. It read, *"Thank you for loving me and my son. May you always smile in heaven. Rest in peace, my dear friend. With all our love, Mattie and Justin."*

As silently as she had arrived, Mattie turned and disappeared into the distance.

Stenson's Story

CHAPTER SIX

POLKSVILLE, ALABAMA

"Stop, Daddy! You're hurting me!" six-year-old Stenson cried as his father struck him with a thick leather strap.

"Quit your whining, boy, or I'll give you something to cry about!" shouted Tug Beckett, a big, burly man who looked much older than his twenty-four years.

"What did I do?" the little boy whimpered.

"You left your goddamned bike in the yard and I tripped over it!" Tug growled.

"I'm sorry, Daddy. I promise I won't do it again!" Stenson said.

But his father didn't care and hit him again. Then the man stormed off with the belt in one hand and a bottle of whiskey in the other. Stenson wondered what was wrong with leaving his bicycle in the front yard. His father could be so mean sometimes.

Tug was even more violent with his wife, Betty. He blamed her for his misery and stolen youth. Tug believed she tricked him into marrying her when she got pregnant with Stenson, and he'd resented her for it ever since.

Betty Adair was fifteen when she met Tug Beckett in high school. She was a freshman, and he was three years older and the quarterback of the football team. Betty could not believe such a popular guy had even noticed her.

They went on a few dates that Betty never told her strict parents about. She knew her dad would never approve. She'd say she was going to a friend's house to watch a movie or study.

Those "dates" with Tug were always the same. He would drive to a deserted road in the woods where they would park and kiss. At first, Betty found it electric. But it was not long before Tug wanted more. Betty felt uncomfortable on one date when Tug attempted to go further. She panicked and pushed him away.

"Stop!" Betty exclaimed.

"Don't you love me?" Tug said, pouting.

"I love you, Tug, but I'm a virgin. That's something I am saving for my husband. I hope you understand."

"Whatever! I'm taking you home! Better yet, get out and walk!" Tug yelled.

His reaction shocked Betty, and she started to cry. "I thought you loved me and would understand."

"What I understand is you better get out of my car before I drag you out!" the jock snarled, which made her tears flow even more.

Betty opened the door and stepped out. She hoped Tug was teasing. Instead, he reached over and slammed the door shut. He put the car into gear and stomped on the gas, kicking up gravel and dust over her as he sped away. Betty stood alone in the dark woods, wiping the sticky dirt from her face and wondering how this date had gone so wrong.

Tug ignored Betty for more than a week despite her repeated phone calls and messages. She begged for his forgiveness and told him how much she loved him. Betty asked Tug for another chance.

This played right into Tug's hand. He knew that ignoring Betty would get him what he wanted. That Friday night, he met her at the mall for a date, and then, like always, they drove to the secluded woods. Betty decided this time she would do anything for Tug.

It didn't take long before he removed her pants. Despite her uneasiness, she allowed him to do it. It hurt when he entered her body, but she tried to feign enjoyment. A minute later, it was over and Betty thought, *That's it?*

Tug pulled up his pants and didn't bother helping Betty with hers. He turned on the ignition and drove back to the mall without saying a word.

When they arrived, Tug said, "I have to meet some friends. Talk to you later."

As he drove away, Betty tried to wrap her head around what had just happened. After all her begging and pouring out her heart, she'd lost her virginity in one minute of sex and was dropped off at a mall? *What a jerk!* she thought. Betty decided that would be the last time she'd ever see Tug Beckett.

A month passed and Betty didn't hear from Tug. She reminded herself that she could do better. But then she missed her menstrual cycle and began to worry. Betty asked a girlfriend to take her to the store, where she bought a home pregnancy test. Her heart sank when it revealed she was pregnant.

Betty waited several weeks before she spoke to Tug. They were sitting in his car when she told him she was pregnant.

His first response was, "It isn't mine!"

"Tug, it is definitely your baby. I only made love to you that one time. And I was a virgin when we did it."

"So get an abortion!" Tug shouted.

"No. I am having this baby ... with or without you."

"Well, then you'll have it without me!"

"Fine!" Betty said as she got out of the car.

Betty had expected that to be Tug's response and she didn't

care. Her parents would be supportive and help her raise the child. She was certain her mom would be excited. But her dad would be another story.

One Sunday after church, Betty asked her parents to sit down. Not knowing a gentler way to say it, Betty blurted out, "I'm pregnant."

Her mother took it well, but her father made a groaning sound she had never heard him make before. After she explained it had happened the only time she'd ever had sex, her dad asked who the father was.

When she told him it was Tug Beckett, her father seethed. "I'll kill him!"

The next day, Tug noticed a truck parked in front of his car after football practice. Sitting in the driver's seat was Betty's father, James Adair.

"Hi, Mr. Adair. What are you—"

"Get in!" James demanded.

Tug did as he was told because James sounded serious—and was much bigger than Tug himself. At six-foot-seven, James towered over Tug by seven inches. Betty's father was a farmer, and Tug was sure the man could crush his head with his bare hands if he wanted.

"You got something to tell me, boy?" James asked, as if commanding a police interrogation.

"I don't know what you mean?" Tug said, trying to play dumb.

"You know exactly what I mean!" James snarled, daring the boy to lie again.

"I ... I was meaning to talk to you about that, sir," Tug said. "I, uh, was planning to ask Betty to marry me."

"You're damn right you are! And it better be the nicest, most heartfelt proposal I have ever heard of in my life. My daughter better be over the moon with joy when she tells me you asked her. You got it?"

"Yes sir, I got it," Tug whimpered.

"Now get out of my truck!"

Tug couldn't get out of the truck fast enough, and then he watched Mr. Adair roar away. He was glad he made it out in one piece because he knew Mr. Adair might kill him and feed him to his pigs. He imagined that all they'd find of the school's star quarterback would be tiny pieces of him in a pile of dung.

Two months later, Betty and Tug were married in a small ceremony at the church she attended. After the wedding, Betty's father pulled Tug aside with a grip like the Jaws of Life that rescue workers use to extract people from a crumpled car.

"You better make my daughter happy, boy."

"I will, Mr. Adair. I promise!"

Their son, Stenson, was born a few months later. Tug didn't want to be a father at eighteen, but he tried to make the best of it. He settled on a job at the plumbing manufacturer like his father and grandfather before him.

Betty enjoyed married life and being a mom. But Tug struggled as a husband and father with all the responsibilities he had to bear. The only home he could afford was a beat-up trailer on the outskirts of town. Gone were his dreams of being a college quarterback, getting out of this hellhole town, and basking in the adoration of girls he used to enjoy. It was not the life Tug expected. That was when his drinking and abuse began.

The first time James Adair discovered that Tug had hit his daughter was when Betty came over for dinner with a black eye. He knew Betty was lying when she told him she had fallen. James drove to the trailer and found Tug passed out drunk on the sofa. James ripped him off the couch and flung him across the room, smashing the delirious guy's head into a picture frame on the wall. He beat the drunken man to within an inch of his life. James told Tug, as he lay bleeding on the floor, that if he every laid a hand on his daughter again, he'd be back to finish what he started. James returned to his house and demanded that Betty and the baby move back home.

Tug felt miserable without his Betty and Stenson. Once he sobered up, he gathered the courage to go to the Adair home to speak with Betty and her father. Tug promised he would never be abusive again. He convinced Mr. Adair to allow them to return home. But James warned him, as only a father can do, that there would be consequences if he ever laid another hand on his daughter or grandchild again.

Things were fine for the next few years. Betty and Tug had two more children: James and Mary. Tug worked his mundane job building propane gas meters and stayed away from alcohol. But things changed for the worse when the plant manager called a meeting one day. He informed employees that the plant was closing and moving to Mexico. Like that, 1,200 employees were without a job in a small town with few opportunities. That was when Tug's tailspin into madness began.

Stenson avoided his father as much as possible. School was a refuge where he could avoid the chaos and anger at home. His father's abuse made him quiet and shy. He wasn't like other boys his age. When they went to the playground, Stenson was content sitting at a table drawing cartoons. He dreamed of one day becoming a video game designer.

He had met his closest friend, Luna, back in kindergarten. They were both nerdy and had a similar sense of humor.

"Hi, I'm Luna Jean LeRoux. But call me Luna, because I hate when my mom calls me Luna Jean. She only says that when I'm in trouble."

Stenson smiled and replied, "My name's Stenson Beckett,

but you can call me Stenson because Beckett is my last name and I don't have a middle name."

Luna laughed, and the two became inseparable friends.

Every day, they walked home together after school. Stenson noticed how Luna's life differed from his own. She lived in a nice house with a trimmed yard and a dog named Fluff. Her father worked at a job where he wore a tie, and her mother stayed home with the kids. They didn't drink, smoke, or curse. And the whole family went to church every Sunday.

Stenson's home was the opposite. He lived in a beat-up trailer, and his father was an unemployed, violent alcoholic. Once, he asked his dad if he could have a dog. His father yelled, "We have enough mouths to feed in this house, much less a scroungy animal!"

None of it mattered to Luna. She understood that you cannot choose your home or your parents. But they shared one thing in common: they both had great moms. Stenson's mother did the best she could with what they had and always took the kids to church. But it was pointless asking his father to go with them. Stenson thought the church might burn down if his dad ever stepped inside.

After school, they would stop by Luna's house, where she would tell her mom she was going to play with Stenson. Luna's mother liked Stenson and told Luna to be home by dinnertime. When they arrived at Stenson's trailer, he would run inside and tell his mom he was going to play, then dash out the door. He never let Luna go inside, because he wasn't sure what state of mind his father would be in.

Stenson and Luna built a tree house in the woods behind his parents' trailer. The kids called it their "fort," and they worked on it every day. They scavenged dumpsters for anything to make the tree house nicer: an old rug, a table, or a broken chair. They hung drawings on the walls for decoration. One day, Stenson taped an illustration of his family to the wall.

When Luna asked where his father was in the drawing, he replied, "Dead."

The remark puzzled Luna, and she asked Stenson, "Why?"

"My father drinks a lot and beats my mom and me." Stenson was quiet for a moment, wondering why he had told Luna a secret he hadn't shared with anyone. "It makes me sad when he hits my mother. She cries and I try to stop my dad, but I'm too little."

"Stenson! Tell somebody!"

"I can't, Luna, 'cause I'm afraid they'll take us from Mama. I'm the only one who can protect her." Tears welled up in the little boy's eyes. Stenson tried to hide them and quickly wiped his face with the sleeve of his shirt, hoping Luna didn't see him cry. "Please don't tell anybody, Luna. I don't want to lose my mama, and I've never told this secret to anyone but you."

Luna crossed her heart. "I promise."

The rest of the afternoon was quiet as they worked on the fort. It was the last time they would talk about it. Luna knew how much Stenson's father bothered him. She wished, even at her young age, that there was something she could do to help him.

When Stenson returned home that day, his father was passed out drunk on the sofa. Stenson went to the kitchen to discover food all over the walls and floor, along with a broken plate. It looked like a tornado had blown through the kitchen.

Stenson went to check on his brother and sister, who were lying on their beds, silent. They looked at Stenson with blank expressions of fear.

He went to his mom and dad's bedroom and found the door locked. Stenson gently knocked. "Mama, are you there?"

After a moment, he heard a click. Stenson opened the door and found his mother sitting on the bed, holding a washcloth against her face. Her hair was strewn, with her shirt stretched so wide that it hung off her shoulder.

Stenson sat on the bed next to her. “What happened, Mom?”

She looked at him with a strained smile. In a shaken voice, she said, “I'm fine, sweetheart. How was your day?”

Stenson reached over and pulled the washcloth away from his mother's face. Her left eye was swollen shut, and her lip was puffy and had a small cut. He saw blood on the rag as well.

“Mom!” Stenson exclaimed in a voice not loud enough to wake his father. “Let me call the police!”

“I'm okay, honey. It's my fault. We didn't have much food, so I tried to prepare something with what we had and your daddy got upset.”

“Mom, it's not okay!” the boy yelled, now not caring about the volume.

Even though he was a little boy, Stenson had the fury of a grown man. He was ready to grab a knife from the kitchen and stab his father as he slept. Nobody would blame him if he did.

His mother tried to assure him, “Stenson, I'll be okay. I just need some rest. There's a plate of food in the refrigerator. Please eat dinner and make sure you do your homework too. And will you help your brother and sister put on their pajamas and get ready for bed after you eat?”

“Yes ma'am,” Stenson said as he leaned forward and kissed his mother on the cheek. He locked the bedroom door as he left, in case his father woke up later.

Stenson walked past his drunkard dad lying on the couch and scowled. He cleaned up the mess in the kitchen, then took out the food his mom had left for him in the fridge. She'd made spaghetti, which was his favorite. He didn't understand what his father had complained about, nor did he care. He would have heated the food in the microwave, but his father had destroyed it in one of his rages. As he ate the cold spaghetti, Stenson thought of how much he loved his mother and hated his dad.

After dinner, Stenson went to see his brother and sister. "Hey, Mom said it's time to put on your pajamas and get to bed."

"Where's Mama?" James asked.

"She's sleeping, like you need to," Stenson said to his little brother.

Stenson helped his baby sister put on her pajamas.

She climbed into the bottom bunk with James and said, "Read us a book!"

Stenson smiled, knowing his mom always read to James and Mary each night before they went to sleep. He chose one of their favorites: *Where the Wild Things Are.*

He read, "'The night Max wore his wolf suit and made mischief of one kind and another his mother called him "Wild Thing!" And Max said, "I'll eat you up!"'"

Mary giggled, and soon the children's mood changed to a cheerfulness that every child should have.

After the kids fell asleep, Stenson slipped away from the bed and sat at his desk, staring at his homework. The only thing he had to do was practice cursive writing.

"Who writes like this?" he whispered. "This is like from the 1950s ... when dinosaurs roamed the earth!"

Stenson finished the assignment and put on his pajamas. He climbed onto the top bunk bed and said his prayers: "Dear Lord, I pray for Mama, James, and Mary ... Granddaddy and Grandma. Please make them happy. I pray for Luna, because she is my best friend. And, Lord, I pray that Daddy will never hurt Mama again. Amen."

CHAPTER SEVEN

POLKSVILLE, ALABAMA

The next morning, Stenson found his mother in the kitchen preparing breakfast. He was glad his father wasn't around. The wounds on his mother's face looked different than the night before. Her eye was no longer as swollen, but it now showed a deep purple crescent beneath. Betty's lip, though, remained bulbous, with a scab over the cut.

"Good morning, sweetheart," she said through a beaten smile.

"Mornin', Mom. How are you feeling?"

"I'm better. Nothing like a good night's sleep."

Somehow, Stenson didn't believe it as he sat down at the kitchen table. His brother and sister soon ran in, still wearing pajamas, and joined them. Betty placed plates of scrambled eggs and toast, along with orange juice, on the table for James and Stenson. Two-year-old Mary wanted cereal. Betty did not make a plate for herself. Instead, she took a seat to enjoy the company of her kids. The reality was that she only had enough food for her children. Betty would forgo breakfast until their welfare card renewed in a week.

Betty slid a pamphlet across the table to Stenson. It showed a group of cheerful boys on the cover. Stenson flipped through the pages and saw that the boys were camping and having fun.

It was a brochure for the Cub Scouts.

"They're starting a new Cub Scout pack at the church. I thought you'd like to join, Stenson. They teach camping, wilderness survival, and other fun things," his mother said.

"Don't you need a father to go with you?" Stenson asked, frowning.

"No, honey, they have Scout leaders. You can join without your father," Betty said, offering a knowing smile.

Stenson felt relieved. The last thing he wanted was people seeing what a piece of work his father was. Then he asked his mother if it cost money. She told him it didn't. What she purposely failed to mention was that their pastor and his wife offered to pay for Stenson's dues and uniform, which, she said, he would get after school that very day.

Stenson's eyes grew bright, and he grinned. "Okay, I'd love to join, Mom!" He jumped up from his chair and gave his mother a big hug and a kiss. Then he grabbed his book bag and told his siblings to be good as he dashed out the door for school.

When Stenson caught up with Luna, he told her he was joining the Cub Scouts, and he beamed at her. She laughed and said she signed up for the Brownies. They each said they were getting their uniforms later today. That was when they knew their mothers had planned this together. The kids could not wait for school to be over that day.

Luna's mom picked up Betty and they met the kids in front of the school, then they drove to the store that sold uniforms. Stenson walked out of the dressing room wearing his Cub Scout clothes, while Luna waited in hers.

Luna said to Stenson, "You look like you're in the military in that blue uniform."

Stenson grinned and said, "Well, you look like a chocolate cupcake. I guess that's why they call you a Brownie."

The kids giggled while their mothers enjoyed seeing the children so happy. The moms asked if the kids wanted to change clothes before returning home. They pleaded to keep their uniforms on. They were so proud to be a Cub Scout and Brownie. It was a cheerful drive home as the mothers listened to Stenson and Luna talk about their next great adventures.

Luna's mother dropped Stenson and Betty off at their trailer. A lump formed in Stenson's throat when he saw his father's truck parked in the front yard. Maybe his dad would be in a good mood and feel proud of his son, the little boy hoped. When they walked in the door, Tug was sitting on the couch, watching TV and drunk as usual.

He took one look at Stenson in his Cub Scout uniform and yelled, "What the hell is this?"

"Stenson joined the Cub Scouts! Yay!" Betty cheered as she looked down at Stenson.

"We don't have the money for no damned Cub Scouts. Besides, he looks ridiculous!" Tug bellowed.

Stenson's heart sank. He ran to his bedroom and slammed the door.

Betty looked at Tug and said, "I think he looks cute, and Stenson wants to be a Cub Scout. You were mean to say that, Tug!"

"I don't give a damn. That boy needs to grow up and not play some stupid games!" he growled. "While you were out spending money we don't have, where is my dinner? You want me to starve to death?"

"It didn't cost any money, Tug. The pastor and his wife paid for it. Besides, he's a little boy. Let him be a child while he can."

Betty went to the kitchen to prepare dinner. She knew it was useless to argue with Tug in his current state of mind. All she hoped was that he would eat what she prepared. She didn't want him throwing food at her again or ruining what had been a wonderful day.

Stenson loved Cub Scouts. With Scouts, his mom, and his friendship with Luna, he almost felt like he had a normal life. The only problem was his alcoholic father, and he couldn't change that. For the next two years, he spent his time going to school, camping with the Scouts, and hanging out with Luna, building their tree house.

One day after Cub Scouts, Stenson brought over his black friend Bryan after inviting him to play at his fort. Stenson's father was standing in the front yard when they arrived.

Tug took one look at Bryan and said, "What are you doing hanging out with that nigger, Stenson?"

The question shocked Stenson. "Dad! Bryan is my friend!"

"You ain't bringing no nigger around my house!" Tug yelled.

Stenson looked at Bryan. "I'm sorry, Bryan. My dad is mean. I guess you have to go."

Bryan understood and said goodbye. Stenson walked past his father, head hung low with tears in his eyes. His mother saw him when he went inside.

"Hi, honey, how was your day?" Betty asked.

"It was fine ... until Dad called my friend Bryan the N-word."

Stenson sat at the table with his head in his hands. Betty placed a plate in front of him and caressed his head.

The boy looked up at his mother and said, "Thanks, Mom, but I'm not hungry. May I go to my room?"

"Of course, Stenson. I'll put your food in the refrigerator in case you want to eat it later."

Stenson went to his room and climbed into bed. He overheard his mother arguing with his father. She said something about leaving and moving back home with her parents. Loud banging sounds came from the kitchen, then

Stenson heard his mother yell for Tug to get out. The front door slammed, and Stenson jumped out of bed and ran to the kitchen. He had never seen his mother look so mad. She hugged her son and told him things would change. Betty gave him a kiss and asked him to go back to his room, saying she needed time to think.

Tug Beckett drove to the bar in a fury. "That bitch thinks she'll throw me out of my own house and take away my kids? She's got another thing coming!"

He got so drunk that his otherwise tolerant bartender insisted he leave at 11:00 p.m. Tug sat in his pickup truck outside the bar, slugging a bottle of whiskey he kept under the seat. He stewed at the thought of Betty and the kids moving in with her parents. There would be no way her father would let her return to him this time. Tug knew that James Adair hated him.

With his headlights off, Tug pulled down the long gravel driveway that led to the Adair home. The house was quiet at 12:30 a.m. Tug stopped and took out a bag of tools from his truck bed, then crept along the side of the house. He lit a small flashlight and held it in his mouth. He inspected the gas meter and laughed to himself. It was the type he used to build when he had a job. After putting on a pair of gloves, he manipulated the contraption until he heard the hiss of gas, sounding like an angry snake. He gathered his tools and returned to the truck, then drove home and rushed inside.

Soon, a loud crash and screaming awoke the kids.

Stenson whispered to James and Mary, "Stay here and lock the door!"

Then he jumped out of bed and ran out into the living room and over broken frames of family photographs that had shattered on the floor. Stenson found his father on top of his mother, beating her face with his bare fists atop the cheap blue sofa they'd purchased from Goodwill. It was the most violent abuse Stenson had ever witnessed from his father.

"Stop it, Daddy!" Stenson screamed as he tried to pull his dad off his mother.

Tug looked at Stenson with evil in his eyes and then struck the boy with a right fist to the temple. The blow knocked the little boy to the floor. Stenson struggled up and jumped on his father's back, trying to pull the large man off his mother. That angered Tug even more. He grabbed Stenson and slammed the child into the glass coffee table, shattering it with the boy's back.

"This is all your fault, you little brat! Your mother tried to tell me that little nigger boy you brought over is welcome here! Then she said she's leaving!" Tug punched Betty's face again. "I say who is welcome here!" He struck Betty again. "I say who stays and who comes and goes!" He bashed her head with a fist yet again.

Stenson ran to the kitchen and grabbed the largest knife he could find. He rushed back to the living room and, with all his might, plunged it deep into his father's back. It penetrated below the shoulder blade but seemed to have no effect on the giant man.

Tug leaped up from the sofa and grabbed Stenson by his hair. He hit the child so hard in the head that the boy's body fell limp to the floor. Through blurry eyes, Stenson saw Tug back on top of his mother again. This time, he was holding the bloody knife against her throat.

Tug roared, "You ruined my life, bitch! These children ruined my life! This is the last time you ruin my life because now I'll ruin yours!"

Stenson could only watch as Tug ripped the blade across Betty's throat.

Then Stenson screamed "No!" so loud that God and all

eternity could hear it. He struggled up and stumbled out of the house before the maniac noticed. He ran to the next-door neighbor's trailer and banged in a panic on the front door.

"Mr. Massey! Please open up! Please!" Stenson yelled as he beat the door with his little fists in a drumroll of terror and fear.

The porch light came on, and then the door opened. Standing in his bathrobe, Mr. Massey said, "Stenson? What's going on? Don't you know it's 2:00 a.m.?"

"Mr. Massey, call the police and an ambulance—please! My father hurt my mama really bad!" Stenson pleaded through tears. "James and Mary are still in there!"

Richard Massey knew all about Tug's temper and saw the wounds on Stenson's face. "Come in, Stenson—hurry now!" Mr. Massey said and then grabbed the phone to dial 911.

The commotion had woken Mrs. Massey, and she'd overheard her husband's conversation with Stenson. She rushed out to the sobbing boy and pulled him to her side. Minutes later, the police arrived. Mr. Massey met them in the yard. He relayed what Stenson had told him and said he believed Tug had a knife. He also told the officers there were two other children inside.

Officers approached the door with weapons drawn. They rapped hard on the door, and one of them yelled, "Police! Open the door!"

"Screw you!" Tug shouted.

"Sir, open the door! Don't make this worse!" an officer yelled.

"Go away!" Tug shouted.

The officers knew it was a dangerous situation with children held as hostages. And the police had encountered Tug Beckett several times before and knew his volatility. They wouldn't have time to wait for a prolonged hostage negotiation. Two more units of officers arrived, along with an ambulance.

Officers gathered and decided they had to get inside immediately. They would enter the trailer simultaneously from the front and rear. Two officers in tactical gear went to the back of the trailer while two prepared at the front. Others trained their weapons on each window.

The lead officer whispered into his shoulder microphone, "Ready."

In turn, the three other officers replied, "Ready."

"Three, two, one!" the leader whispered.

An officer fired a flash-bang grenade through a front window while the front and back doors were kicked open simultaneously. Tug was stunned but still standing in the living room, holding two-year-old Mary with the knife at her throat and a crazed look on his face.

"Put the child down!" the lead officer commanded.

"I dare you to make me! I'll kill her!" Tug yelled.

Before Tug could say another word, officers in the rear fired Tasers into his back. Two 50,000-volt probes stuck in his body from the left and right. He started shaking, letting go of the child as he dropped to the floor. The lead officer sprang forward and caught the girl before she fell, while the other three leaped on top of Tug Beckett and secured him.

A female officer quickly entered and escorted James and Mary out of the trailer, making sure she shielded their eyes from the sight of their dead mother. Paramedics attempted rescue efforts until the coroner arrived and pronounced Betty Beckett deceased.

Detective David Patterson arrived and was briefed on the horrendous situation. He investigated the bloody scene while technicians photographed the evidence. Knowing that James and Mary were safe in a patrol car with the female officer, Stenson stood with the Masseys as paramedics removed his mother's body around 5:00 a.m. The little boy wailed as he realized this nightmare was true.

A news crew arrived and began filming the scene. Detective Patterson declined to give a statement until they gathered more information. Knowing this would lead the morning news, the detective needed to notify the next of kin. He spoke with Richard Massey and learned that Betty Beckett's parents lived in town. He dispatched officers to their home to relay the news.

Then Detective Patterson kneeled in front of Stenson and introduced himself. This felt different for Patterson. He was used to seeing violence, but not when it involved kids. He hated his job right now.

Patterson asked the little boy if he could talk with him down at the police station. Stenson grabbed onto Mrs. Massey's leg, too fearful to answer. Stenson didn't trust anybody other than his brother and sister.

The detective offered to let Stenson ride in a real police car. He would even let him turn on the lights. Any child Stenson's age would have jumped at the opportunity. But at this moment, Stenson was too traumatized to consider it. Everything was a daze. Mr. Massey suggested to the detective that he and his wife could take Stenson to the police station instead, and Patterson agreed.

Meanwhile, officers arrived at the Adair home just before dawn. The house was quiet as they knocked on the door. James Adair awoke and heard the knocking. He couldn't imagine who it could be at such an early hour. He reached for his glasses and looked at the clock. It was 5:47 a.m. His wife stirred in bed and asked what was happening, but he told her to go back to sleep.

After sitting up, James noticed a faint smell of rotten eggs as he turned on his bedside light.

Suddenly, the home erupted into a gigantic explosion, hurling officers from the porch like Hollywood stuntmen. By the time the fire department arrived, the house was completely engulfed in flames. It took several hours and three fire companies to bring it under control. Later, two victims were discovered in the rubble. They were eventually identified as James Adair and his wife.

Mr. Massey followed the detective on the short drive to the police station. Detective Patterson took Stenson to a brightly lit interview room and offered to get him a soda. Stenson took a seat while the detective left the room to get the drink.

An officer stopped Detective Patterson in the hallway. "You won't believe this. Officers went to notify the parents of the deceased and the house exploded."

"What?" David Patterson looked at the officer, not believing what he'd just heard.

"The house exploded. Must have been some kind of gas leak. The fire department is still on the scene. It is a real mess over there, Dave."

"This has to be more than a coincidence. Get some people over there to figure out what happened."

Detective Patterson indeed couldn't believe it: A murder and a house explosion on the same day in this quiet town? And he would bet his pension that Tug Beckett was responsible for both. The detective could not wait to get his hands on the man, but right now he had a traumatized little boy to deal with.

The detective returned to the conference room with a soda

for the boy and a cup of coffee for himself. *This is going to be a long, hard morning*, he thought.

Before David sat down, he looked at the boy and said, "Stenson, as I said earlier, I'm Detective David Patterson, but you can call me Dave."

The youngster cocked his head like a puppy trying to understand a command. He looked confused, like he didn't know where he was or what the man just said. It seemed as if was he was in a big, empty white room and everything was so far away. He felt tiny and insignificant. Numbness filled him with a sensation like he had never known before.

The detective had met with traumatized victims before, but no one he'd encountered ever had the look he saw on little Stenson's face. The boy's distant eyes spoke a thousand words of loss and incomprehension.

David pulled out a chair and sat down in front of Stenson. He stared at the little boy and wondered if he should proceed. The look on Stenson's face had the seasoned detective confused. He regained his composure and pressed a red button on the recorder between them to begin the interview. He waited a few moments before asking: "Can you tell me your full name and age?"

The little boy stared at him, still lost in his dream—or nightmare. David reached over and gently touched the boy's hand, which seemed to bring the child back to reality.

He asked again, "Can you tell me your full name and age?"

"My name is Stenson Beckett, and I'm eight years old," he said, his words slow, almost robotic. "My birthday was last week."

"Happy belated birthday, Stenson. My son is eight years old also." The detective smiled. "Can you tell me what happened at your home this morning?"

Stenson stirred in his chair, visibly uncomfortable.

"Take your time, Stenson," David reassured.

Stenson stared at the table and then related how he came home with his friend, who was black. He mumbled through how his daddy had cursed him, using the N-word. Then he told the officer it upset him so much that he couldn't eat dinner and went to bed. Then he heard his mom and dad arguing before his daddy slammed the door when he left the house. Stenson told the detective his father drank every day, and it caused a lot of fights between his parents. He said his father often hit his mother and him. Stenson paused.

It always pained Detective Patterson whenever he heard details about violence against a child or spouse, but he pressed on. "Can you tell me what happened to your mother this morning?"

Stenson remained silent for several moments. Finally, he said he woke up to a loud crash and screaming. He told the detective he saw his father on top of his mother, punching her in the face. He said he tried to stop his father, but his daddy hit him and threw him into the coffee table. Then he ran into the kitchen and found a knife and stabbed him in the back.

"You stabbed your daddy in the back?"

"Yes," Stenson cried. "He was killing my mother. I had to do something!"

David remained quiet for a moment. Then he said, "Stenson, your father said it was your mom who stabbed him."

"He's lying!" Stenson yelled. "After I stabbed him is when he knocked me down! When I was lying there on the floor, he screamed that he would kill my mom and then he did it! I saw him cut her throat and all the blood and ..." Stenson hyperventilated and tried to catch his breath.

The detective stopped the interview. Stenson had experienced enough trauma for one day. He shut off the digital recorder and handed Stenson a box of tissues. He then moved closer and placed his arm around the sobbing boy.

After getting Stenson comfortable in the hallway, Detective Patterson took statements from Mr. and Mrs. Massey, both of whom confirmed what Stenson had told him. After they finished, all three of them walked into the hallway and found Stenson asleep in a chair.

Mrs. Massey woke him and said, "Come on, honey, let's go home."

They said goodbye to Detective Patterson and went outside. It was a bright morning when they left the police station. Stenson remained quiet in the back seat of the car. As they pulled up to the Masseys' home, Stenson saw that crime tape surrounded his trailer next door. Mrs. Massey hurried Stenson inside.

She asked if he wanted breakfast. He declined and said all he wanted to do was sleep. Mrs. Massey prepared the couch and helped him lie down. She covered him with a blanket as inconsolable tears poured from his eyes.

Stenson looked up at Mrs. Massey and asked a question nobody could answer: "Why did my daddy kill my mom?"

CHAPTER EIGHT

POLKSVILLE, ALABAMA

Detective David Patterson could hardly contain his anger after interviewing eight-year-old Stenson Beckett. A boy his own son's age had witnessed the violent murder of his mother at the hands of his father. It truly infuriated David. Then there were the victim's parents. David felt certain it was more than a coincidence their home had exploded the same night as the murder.

The seasoned veteran knew he'd better calm down before he entered the interview room again. Otherwise, there would be another murder today when he killed Tug Beckett. David resisted the urge to kick down the door. He calmly entered the room and pulled up a chair.

"Good morning, Mr. Beckett. I'm Detective David Patterson. I would like to speak with you about the events at your home last night into early this morning."

Tug wore a white tank top covered with brown stains of dried blood. His hands were cuffed to the table.

In a boozy breath that could peel paint, he said, "I told you guys it was self-defense. She stabbed me!"

"If that's the case, then why did my officers have to storm your trailer? And why were you threatening your daughter with a knife to her throat?"

"I don't know. I was scared," Tug suggested, giving a shrug.

"I have testimony from your son, who says he was the one who stabbed you before he saw you cut your wife's throat."

"That little brat doesn't know what he's talking about. He would say anything to protect his mama." Tug shifted in his seat. "I'm not saying another word until I speak to my attorney."

"Who is your attorney?" the detective asked.

"I don't have one." Tug smirked with a wild grin. "Y'all have all the money. Get me one."

"That's fine if you don't want to talk to me now. But you are being charged with first-degree murder, aggravated assault on a minor, and a long list of other offenses." The detective tossed the charge sheet in front of Tug. "And I thought you should know your wife's parents are dead. It seems there was a fire at their house this morning. You wouldn't know anything about that, would you?"

Tug Beckett leaned back and howled with laughter at the ceiling. The reaction confirmed David's suspicion that Tug was behind it. Unfortunately, laughter from a psychopath would not be evidence he could use in court. David picked up his notepad and left the room quickly—before he choked the man to death.

David phoned the public defender's office to request counsel for the suspect. A few hours later, attorney Martavius Green arrived from the DA's office. Detective Patterson handed him the case file. Martavius shook his head as he read it. He had recently joined the district attorney's office after graduating from law school. He could not believe the first case they gave him was capital murder. *Nothing like trial by fire*, he thought.

Martavius entered the room where Tug sat, still shackled. "Hi, Mr. Beckett. I'm Martavius Green, and I'll be your attorney."

Tug looked at the attorney. "Oh hell no! Ain't no nigger representing me!"

Martavius wasn't fazed. "Mr. Beckett, I am your attorney, so you better get used to the color of my skin. And given the details of this case, I can understand why nobody else would take your case."

"I'm not saying a word to you. I don't talk to niggers."

"Mr. Beckett, you are facing a capital murder charge, among others. You can work with me or plead guilty and take the death sentence. It's up to you."

"What do you want to know?" Tug asked.

"I would like to hear your version of events."

"It's simple: My son brought a nigger boy home with him. He knows I don't like niggers, and I told him so. He ran inside and told his mother. Later, she confronted me about it. She got crazy and pulled out a knife and stabbed me in the back. That's when I grabbed the knife and cut her throat. I was defending myself."

"Mr. Beckett, according to your son, he stabbed you," Mr. Green replied.

"That boy was asleep. He must have been dreaming. She stabbed me!" Tug shouted.

"Okay, Mr. Beckett. I assume you wish to plead not guilty?"

"Of course!" Tug snapped.

"Your arraignment is tomorrow morning. I'll see you in court."

"You better be a good nigger lawyer and get me out of this!"

"I'll do my best," Martavius replied as he ignored the racist comment, picked up his notes, and left the room.

Martavius wasn't sure how to approach this case. He listened to the recorded testimony from Tug Beckett's son. Besides being heartbreaking, it sounded very convincing. Should he claim the child was under duress during the interview? Should he contend the child hated his father because the man killed his mother? He knew juries did not like when attorneys bullied children on the stand. If the boy cried during his testimony, it would not bode well for his defense. He also had to contend with the fact that his client was an unapologetic racist.

At the arraignment, Judge Matt Stephens denied bail to Tug Beckett. He cited the brutal nature of the crime and the threat he posed to his children, one of whom would be a witness. It didn't matter anyway because Tug Beckett was broke and couldn't post even the most minimal bail if he wanted to.

Detective David Patterson received the fire investigation report for the Adair home. It concluded a gas leak had caused the explosion and arson was suspected. The report stated that the home's gas meter had been modified to bypass the safety mechanism. This alteration allowed unregulated gas to enter the home. The ignition source appeared to be a lamp in the master bedroom of the home.

David looked at photographs of the gas meter. A pipe led from the main gas line into the house, bypassing the meter altogether. An amateur could not have done this. Somebody knew what they were doing. He pulled the file on Tug Beckett. The man had been unemployed for two years. Tug's last employer had been a plumbing manufacturer that produced those very same gas meters.

David laid down the file. He knew Tug Beckett would be convicted for the murder of his wife based on his son's testimony. But the man should be charged with triple murder for the death of his wife's parents. David had to find more evidence aside from Tug's previous employment with a plumbing manufacturer.

This case was crazy, and Martavius Green did not look forward to the deposition of Stenson Beckett. The police interview with the eight-year-old was just so convincing. He knew the prosecution would introduce it as their first piece of evidence. He needed to get the child to contradict his recollection of the events.

A paralegal escorted Stenson Beckett into the conference room and had him take a seat. The little boy seemed frightened at the sight of six adults surrounding the table with microphones and a video camera.

“Hello, Stenson, I’m attorney Martavius Green. I’m representing your father in court. This is a deposition. Do you know what that is?”

Stenson shook his head and looked at the tabletop as he mumbled, “No sir.”

“It’s a chance for us to understand what happened the night your mother died,” the attorney explained.

Now Stenson looked up and stared hard at Martavius. “You mean the night my father killed my mother?”

“Well, yes, Stenson. The night your father attacked your mother in self-defense,” Martavius said.

“He did not! He slashed my mother’s throat!” Stenson yelled.

Martavius realized this would be more difficult than he imagined. He chose a softer approach with the traumatized child: “Stenson, on the night in question, you said you were asleep when you heard the commotion?”

“Yes, I was asleep when I heard a crash and my father screaming at my mother,” Stenson replied.

“What did you do then?”

“I locked the bedroom door and pulled it shut behind me to protect my brother and sister, and I ran into the living room.”

“And then what?” the attorney asked.

“I saw my dad on top of my mother on the sofa beating the shit out of her in the face with his fists!”

“You mean you saw your father strike your mother?”

Martavius asked, trying to get the boy to rephrase his response.

"No, I mean my father was on top of my mother, screaming and beating her to death!"

Martavius took a deep breath. "Stenson, I know you're upset. We are not here to upset you. We are trying to understand the facts."

Stenson's face grew redder as the attorney continued, "You said in your testimony that you stabbed your father, is that correct?"

"Yes," the boy replied.

"Your father said your mother stabbed him. We are trying to understand how a child your size could stab a man as big as your father."

"He's lying! I stabbed him! And just because I'm small doesn't mean I wasn't angry!" Stenson shouted so loud that the recording device peaked. "I wish I killed him before he killed my mother!"

Stenson had apparently had enough. He stood up and shoved the chair away, then stormed out of the conference room. Martavius Green and the others sat speechless. This was not the deposition Martavius had been hoping for.

Over time, everyone noticed the change in Stenson's personality. He became more withdrawn and not as cheerful as before. His grades dropped, and he quit the Cub Scouts. He even stopped spending much time with Luna working on their tree house. Luna understood how much losing his mother had hurt him. He never wanted to talk about it, and she didn't press him for the sake of their friendship. But she missed the old Stenson.

He went to specialized counseling for children of violent crimes. Stenson was reluctant to go at first until he met his counselor, Dr. Angela Stewart. She had a pleasant personality and reminded him of his mother. He talked of the abuse he and his mother had experienced from his father. But one topic he never wanted to discuss was the murder. Dr. Stewart instead focused on the grieving process. She helped Stenson understand he was not responsible for his mother's death. Angela admired the little boy's chivalry.

It took months, but the counseling sessions seemed to help. Stenson became more interactive with the Masseys. His grades picked up, and he rejoined the Cub Scouts. Luna was happy when Stenson wanted to play with her in their tree house again. But she could sense that the tragedy still affected him. Luna knew it was a burden he would carry for the rest of his life.

The trial date approached for Tug Beckett. Richard and Marie Massey met with the district attorney. She explained to the Masseys that Stenson's recorded police interview would be introduced as evidence. But the most important witness would be the boy himself. Richard Massey voiced concern about Stenson appearing in court. The little boy was returning to normal, and Richard worried this might set him back. The attorney wished there was another way, but the case depended on the child's testimony.

Richard and Marie held off discussing the trial with Stenson until the day before it was set to begin. They reasoned there was no point in making the Stenson worry unnecessarily. When he arrived home from school, they asked him to sit down.

"Am I in trouble?" Stenson asked.

Richard laughed. "No, Stenson. We need to talk to you about your father's trial. It starts tomorrow."

Stenson's face turned from cheerful to troubled. Richard explained how Stenson would need to testify in court. He assured Stenson that it only involved answering a few questions from the attorneys and then it would be over.

"They'll ask me about the murder?" Stenson said.

"Well, yes," Richard replied.

"I can't do it."

Mrs. Massey said, "I know how difficult this is, Stenson, but you must. You want to see your father convicted for what he did to your mom, don't you?"

"I do, Mrs. Massey," he replied. "But I can't relive that nightmare again. I can't even be in the same room as my father. I never want to see his face again. Please don't make me do it!" Stenson's lip quivered like he was about to cry.

Mrs. Massey leaned over and hugged the boy.

Stenson asked, "May I go to my room?"

"Of course, Stenson," she said.

Richard and Marie looked at each other as Stenson walked away. It broke their heart to ask him to do this thing he did not want to do. They hoped a night of rest would help him understand the importance of testifying.

Stenson lay in bed, recalling the night his father had killed his mother. He remembered each vivid, tiny detail of the violence, the screams, and the blood. It felt like watching a horror movie play all over again in his head. The thought of sitting in a courtroom with the man who killed his precious mom angered Stenson. And the way his father had lied and called it self-defense made Stenson sick. They had the recording of Stenson's testimony and they could use that. But there was no way he could face his father.

Stenson made up his mind and climbed out of bed. He took his Cub Scout backpack from the top shelf of his closet. He gathered a few clothes and books, then stuffed them in his pack. After jotting a note to Mr. and Mrs. Massey, Stenson crept down the hallway past the sleeping couple's room. He opened a cabinet in the kitchen and chose several cans of food, along with a can opener he got from the drawer. Stenson placed the note on the counter and slipped out the door.

He made his way to the tree house, where he gathered his sleeping bag, knife, and fishing pole. He wrote a note for Luna and pinned it to the wall. Stenson climbed down from the tree and tucked the rest of the items in his backpack. He lifted it over his shoulders and set off into the darkness.

The next morning, Mrs. Massey discovered the note. It read: *"Mr. and Mrs. Massey, thank you for taking care of me. I can't testify at my father's trial. It will be too hard for me to do. I love you both. Please don't worry. Love, Stenson (P.S. I hope you don't mind if I took a few things to eat and the can opener.)"*

Mrs. Massey's heart sank. She went to Stenson's room and confirmed he wasn't there. She rushed to wake her husband and told him the boy was gone. Richard jumped out of bed and read the note. He threw on some clothes and dashed out the door. Richard combed the streets looking for Stenson. Marie Massey called the prosecutor's office to let them know Stenson had run away.

It was 9:15 a.m. the morning of the trial when the lead prosecutor, Paul Stanley, received the news. "What do you mean the kid ran away? I have no case without him!"

Tug Beckett was in the courtroom, with the jury already seated. Paul requested a meeting with Judge Stephens in his chambers. Defense counsel Martavius Green joined them.

"Your Honor," Paul said, "I must inform the court that our key witness, Stenson Beckett, has disappeared. However, we request his recorded testimony be allowed into evidence."

Martavius seemed relieved, but knew he had to object.

Judge Stephens made his decision: "I am sorry, Mr. Stanley. The recording is not admissible since the defense cannot cross-examine the witness. I will not allow it."

Paul looked at Martavius and said, "Listen, Martavius, we all know this guy is guilty as hell. You've heard the recording.

I'll request a continuation, but if we can't find our witness, this is what I am prepared to offer: your client can plead down to manslaughter with ten to twelve years."

David thought about it. "I'll present it to my client."

"And I'll give you two weeks to find your witness, Mr. Stanley," Judge Stephens said.

The attorneys exited the judge's chambers. Martavius Green returned to the defense table and informed his client there would be a delay. He did not mention the reason was that his son had run away.

Detective David Patterson received the news Stenson Beckett was missing. He'd been told about the plea agreement if the child could not be found. David knew Tug Beckett was responsible for two more deaths by blowing up the Adair home. But the only evidence he had was still circumstantial: Tug worked at a manufacturing plant that made the very gas meter at the Adair home. They'd also recovered plumbing tools from Tug's truck. And he had the motivation to kill his wife's parents. But what David Patterson lacked was physical evidence. They had no fingerprints, and no one could place him at the scene.

David presented what he had to prosecutor Paul Stanley. Paul agreed with David that everything pointed to Tug Beckett. But Paul also did not believe there was enough evidence to convict. So the prosecutor's office declined to add the additional charges. It forced them to go with the capital murder charge and hope their witness would be found. David understood the situation, but he hated the way the system worked sometimes.

Two weeks passed and Stenson Beckett had not been located. Martavius Green met with Tug Beckett and presented the prosecution's plea agreement. He handed the document to Tug and said, "If you plead guilty to manslaughter, you will serve ten to twelve years. It's the best deal you will get."

Tug Beckett said loud enough for all to hear, "Ten to twelve years?"

"Yes, Mr. Beckett. Otherwise, you are facing life in prison without parole. Or, even worse, the death penalty," Mr. Green replied.

Tug considered it and said, "Fine, nigger. You suck as an attorney." Then he signed the document.

Martavius Green made an announcement at the start of the trial: "Your Honor, my client has agreed to plead guilty to manslaughter. All other charges will be dismissed per our agreement with the prosecution." He handed the document to the bailiff.

Judge Stephens reviewed the terms and asked, "Counsel, are you both in agreement?"

"Yes, Your Honor," attorneys from each side replied.

The judge asked the defendant and his attorney to rise. Judge Stephens read the terms of the agreement to Tug Beckett. He asked him to confirm his understanding and agreement through a series of questions.

At the conclusion of the proceedings, the judge slammed the gavel. "Mr. Beckett, the court finds you guilty of manslaughter. You are hereby sentenced to the Alabama State Penitentiary to serve no less than ten years."

Martavius Green felt glad it was over. He hoped he would never have another case or client like this. Paul Stanley, the prosecutor, and Detective David Patterson felt dejected. The Masseys looked on with disappointment. So much for justice.

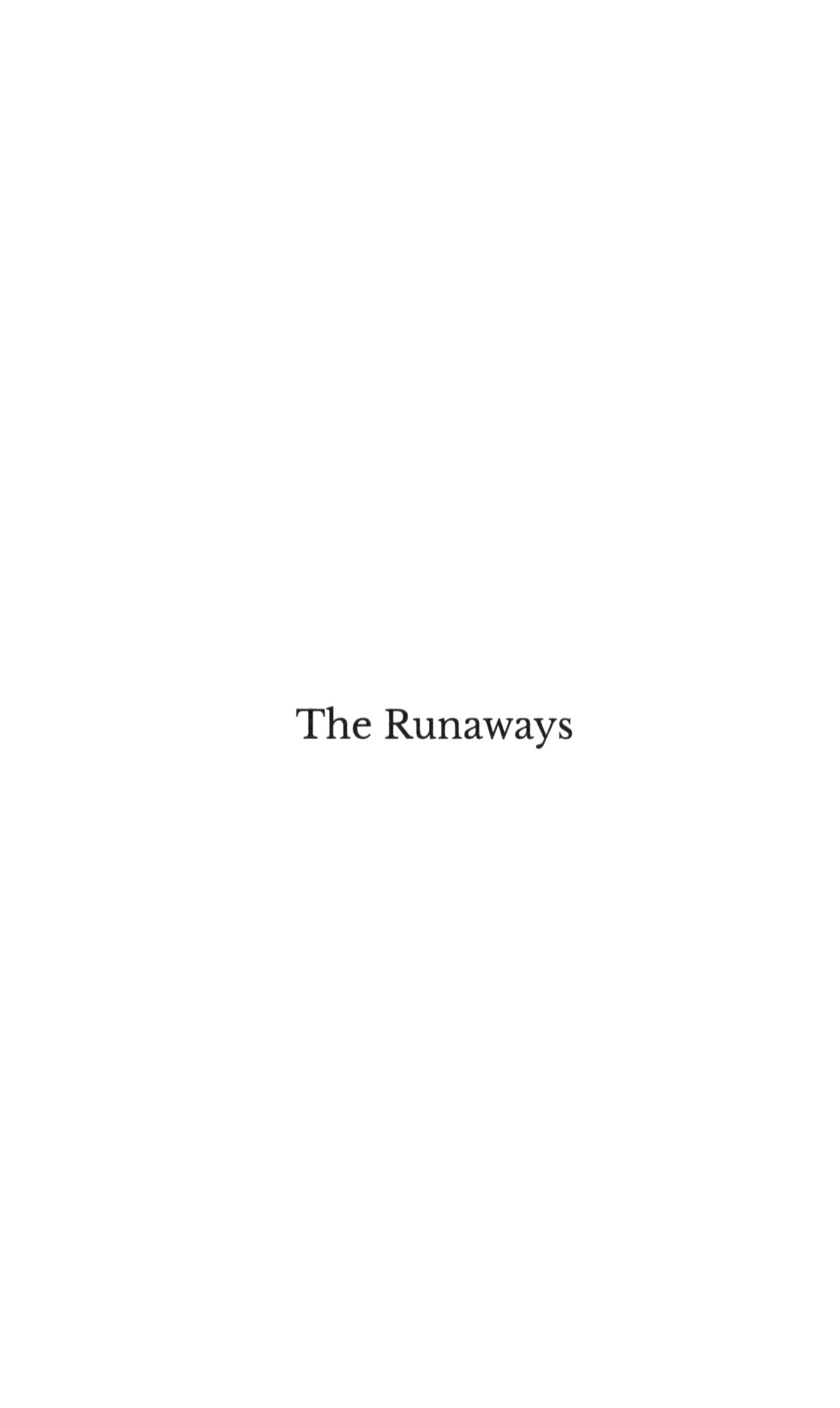

The Runaways

CHAPTER NINE

DEVEREAUX PARISH, LOUISIANA

Ten years had passed since Justin "JC" Carter arrived at Mission of Hope. In that time, the Department of Children and Family Services could not find a suitable home for him. Nobody wanted a black child with HIV, and it frustrated his case workers. One compared it to a puppy up for adoption: "It always gets passed by because it's not pretty enough or the right breed."

JC himself felt like a broken toy. He watched kids come and go over the years. Yet he remained in a sort of purgatory without hope. He found that ironic, considering the name of the place where he lived was Mission of *Hope*. His mother hadn't wanted him either. And he was born with a disease that scared off other people. And his skin was brown. It was like having three strikes before you even swung the bat in a baseball game called *life*.

Religious groups often visited Mission of Hope. JC remembered the first time he asked a minister, "Why did God do this to me? What did I do wrong?"

The answer was always the same: "God loves you and has a special purpose for your life."

What purpose? JC thought. *To be born into a life of misery?* JC believed it was all nonsense.

He questioned another pastor, "Would you trade places with me? Swap bodies and let me drive to your house and you stay here unadopted, unloved, and live with my disease?"

Rather than answer the question, the pastor said, "I will pray for you." Afterward, he got into his nice car and drove to his nice home, feeling better about himself for visiting orphans.

JC hated his life. But most of all, he hated his mother. He often wondered why she'd discarded him like trash. Was his life even worth the sack it took to carry this emotional baggage? Sometimes JC thought it would be easier to end his own life. He could jump off the roof or run out into traffic. But every time those thoughts came to mind, he heard a mysterious voice inside. JC wondered if God was talking to him. If so, God was a woman. The voice always said, *"I love you. One day, you will be a great man."* As if he didn't have enough problems, now he was going crazy.

There were other misfits at Mission of Hope. The only difference was that they were white. Being bullied was a daily occurrence for JC. It could be as simple as jokes about his race. But other times, kids attacked him like they were a pack of dogs. Then they'd laugh at him as he lay on the ground, beaten and humiliated.

Administrators always blamed JC for starting the fights. The kids who beat him would snicker as the mission workers led JC away. None of this improved his already bad attitude toward white people or authority.

There was one kid at Mission of Hope that JC liked, though: Jesús Fernando Alvarez. His parents were illegal immigrants from Mexico. Jesús had been born in the US, which made him a citizen. One day, Immigration and Customs Enforcement detained his parents during a raid. Because of some mismanaged US policy, Jesús remained in the country when ICE deported his parents to Mexico.

JC and Jesús liked each other because they were both bullied for their skin tone. But that wasn't the only reason they liked each other. They also shared a sense of humor. Jesús spoke with a heavy Spanish accent. JC remembered the day Jesús told a teacher how to pronounce his name. When the teacher called roll, she said, "Jesus, raise your hand."

Jesús said, "My name is 'hay-SOOS.' No 'jee-ZUS.'"

That made JC laugh, and the two became best friends. JC helped Jesús speak better English, and Jesús taught JC Spanish. They also had each other's back when it came to fighting the bullies. JC was in the hallway one day when a group of kids surrounded him. "What's up, monkey boy?" a kid said as he pushed JC to the floor. His books scattered across the tile. Other kids laughed and taunted him more. Jesús saw the commotion and ran to JC's defense. He shoved the biggest kid out of the way and stood inside the circle next to his friend. Jesús pointed at the bully and yelled something in Spanish that JC felt certain wasn't polite. Whatever Jesús had said scared the gang enough to run away.

Constructed in the mid-1800s, Mission of Hope looked and felt like a prison. With towers like European castles and high stone walls, it seemed out of place in the middle of Louisiana. An eccentric millionaire had originally spent years building it as his home. Soon after he'd completed it, he died. Since then, it had been a Civil War hospital and then served as training facilities during World Wars I and II. Later, it became an insane asylum and finally an orphanage. Many people had died within its walls, and everyone believed it to be haunted.

The headmistress, Ms. Illowich, was a mean and gnarled woman who looked as ancient as the building. She was so evil that the boys called her "Ms. Evil-Bitch" behind her back. One evening, JC and Jesús watched the movie *The Wizard of Oz* and compared the headmistress to the witch in the film. JC said,

"The only thing she's missing are the flying monkeys and a broom!"

Ms. Illowich didn't care for JC and Jesús either. She considered them troublemakers. The boys loved to play tricks on her. One day, they snuck into the teacher's lounge and waited for Ms. Illowich to go to the restroom. When they saw her approaching, they covered the toilet seat with superglue. Everyone at Mission of Hope heard her yell when she tried to stand up. She screamed, "JC and Jesús!" She knew it was them but could never prove it.

Mission of Hope was indeed an unhappy place for JC and Jesús. They were browbeaten, bullyragged, and couldn't get adopted. All they could do was survive. One day, a group of kids ganged up and beat both boys.

That night, as he lay on his bed, swollen and battered, JC told Jesús, "I am out of here!"

"Where will you go, homie?" Jesús asked.

"As far as I can get from this place."

JC had been planning his escape for a while. He told Jesús he had already cut a hole in the perimeter fence with wire cutters he'd found in a shed. He would set off the fire alarm later and take off during the evacuation. With all the chaos, it would be hours before anyone would discover him missing.

Jesús replied, "Yeah, but like I said, where will you go?"

"I haven't figured that part out yet," JC answered. "Come with me."

"I have nowhere to go, JC," Jesús replied. "But I'm glad you are leaving. I will sure miss you, my friend. We're a good team. But we will see each other again one day."

Carrying out his plan, JC escaped Mission of Hope that night. He ran through the woods for several miles until he made his way into town. It began to rain, and JC took shelter inside a large cardboard box in an alley. As he waited out the storm, JC thought sleeping in a box was better than staying at the hateful place he'd left.

It was dawn when he awoke, and, like every morning, JC took his HIV medication. As he poured the pills into his hand, he realized he was almost out of meds. This was the only thing keeping him alive, but in his haste to leave, he'd forgotten to refill his prescriptions. He'd have to find a doctor soon, but right now he was hungry.

JC climbed out of the box and noticed his shoes were soggy. The noise they made when he walked sounded like a cartoon: *squish, squish, squish*. Across the street, he noticed a man discarding something behind a restaurant. After the guy went inside, JC ran across the street and looked inside the dumpster. There were uneaten eggs and bacon. He scooped up the scraps and shoveled them into his mouth. It was cold and nasty, but he was hungry enough to eat the slop.

As he wandered the streets, JC passed a medical clinic and went inside. He told the receptionist he was HIV positive and running out of his medication. He asked if she could give him more, as if it was that easy.

The receptionist gave him a look of concern and asked, "Where is your mother?"

"She's dead," JC said, not wanting to explain he was a runaway orphan.

That response was not what the receptionist expected. Instead of asking about his father, she handed JC a clipboard and instructed him to complete some forms. When he returned, she noticed he hadn't listed an address or phone number. The receptionist asked JC about it, and he said he didn't have a home or a phone. Then it became obvious the strange little boy was a runaway.

A medical assistant led JC to an examination room. The door opened a few minutes later, and a young black doctor stepped into the room. He offered his hand and greeted JC with a strong African accent: "Good morning, Justin, I am Dr. Amara Abayomi. I understand from your notes you need medication?"

JC was surprised to see a black doctor. The only people of color he had ever seen were himself and Jesús. He told the doctor he was born with HIV and needed more medication. For some reason, JC felt comfortable enough to reveal he grew up in an orphanage and had run away. He handed the doctor three prescription bottles: abacavir, lamivudine, and zidovudine.

The doctor thought this was a curious little boy and smarter than your average ten-year-old. After a brief examination, a nurse came in to draw blood. Dr. Abayomi held JC's hand when he saw the boy wince.

After the nurse finished, the doctor said, "That wasn't too bad, was it? You seem like a tough guy."

JC smiled. "I wish I was tougher so kids wouldn't beat me up all the time."

"You will be one day, Justin," Dr. Abayomi said as he patted the boy's shoulder. "Wait here until I get your test results. Would you like something to drink while you wait?"

"Yeah. Can I have a soda?" JC asked.

"Sure," Dr. Abayomi said. "See you soon."

A few minutes later, a nurse brought JC a soft drink. That helped wash away the nasty taste of the rotten food he'd eaten from the dumpster.

Dr. Abayomi returned with a paper bag. He removed a box of medication and said, "Justin, your blood work looks good. There is no visible sign of HIV in your system. You have done well keeping up with your medication." He handed the box to JC. "This is Trizivir, a combination drug that contains all the medications you are taking. You only need to take one pill a day. I have given you a sixty-day supply. But I want you to come back each time so I can continue to check your health, okay?"

JC studied the package, then looked inside the bag. There were several more boxes of the drug and some cash. JC removed five $20 bills. He said, "Dr. Abayomi, there must be a mistake. There's money in the bag."

The doctor smiled. "It is no mistake, Justin. It is a small gift from me. Use it to get something to eat."

JC returned the money to the bag. "I don't know what to say, Dr. Abayomi."

"You need not say a word, Justin. See you next time."

A moment later, a nurse arrived to take JC to the reception desk. As they got closer, Justin saw two police officers and another man wearing a suit. *They must be here for me*, he thought. There was no way he'd go back to that orphanage.

JC asked the nurse, "May I go to the restroom?"

"Sure, it's down the hall on the right."

"Thanks!" JC said as he sprinted down the hall.

JC hid in the bathroom, then peered out the door and saw the nurse speaking with the receptionist. He sprung from the bathroom and dashed down the hall and out the back door. He needed to find a place to hide and quick. Once the cops realized he had gone, Justin was certain they would look for him.

He saw a dumpster and jumped inside. An hour later, JC emerged when he thought the coast was clear. The police hadn't found him, but he was glad they weren't using tracking dogs because he smelled like garbage. He could not believe he had been in a trash bin twice in one morning. He only hoped this day would get better.

JC needed to change clothes because the smell was overpowering. There was a convenience store nearby, and once inside, he asked the clerk to use the restroom. He locked the door and stripped off the smelly clothes. JC only had one other set of clothing, and he was thankful for that. Otherwise, he would have to spend some of the money the doctor had given him, and he knew it already wouldn't last long.

He used the sink and hand soap to wash his shirt, socks, jeans, and underwear. They had equipped the restroom with a hand dryer but no paper towels. He used the blower to dry the clothing as much as possible and then hung it over a bathroom stall. Then he soaped up his body and splashed handfuls of water over himself to rinse off. The tricky part now was how to dry his body. JC felt like he was doing naked yoga as he contorted into awkward positions beneath the hand dryer.

He dressed in his other clothes and placed the damp ones inside his backpack. Feeling somewhat refreshed, JC unlocked the bathroom door and returned to the store. He picked up a few cheap snacks and walked to the counter.

The clerk said, "You sure took a long time in the bathroom."

JC smiled and said, "I really had to go!"

"You must have," the clerk said with a chuckle.

JC left the store and decided to find a better place to sleep than the night before. At the very least, he needed a bigger box. For the next few hours, he wandered the streets until he passed an elementary school. He spotted a box big enough to hold a refrigerator lying next to a trash bin behind the school. It looked like the perfect spot.

He moved the box away from the trash receptacle and farther down the alley. He didn't want it to be mistaken for rubbish. The way his day had begun, the last thing he needed was being tossed into a garbage truck and hauled to the dump.

The school bell rang, and JC looked over his shoulder to see kids rushing down the street. He sighed and thought of his friend Jesús and how much he'd miss him. But one thing he would not miss were the mean kids at Mission of Hope. He went back to setting up his makeshift home when he heard footsteps behind him. It was four older white kids. JC smiled and said hello.

"What are you doing here? Aren't you on the wrong side of town?" asked the biggest one, clearly the leader of the group.

"Excuse me?" JC asked.

"You know what I mean. We don't allow your kind here!" the boy said while pushing JC in the chest. The bully looked down and noticed JC's bag of medication on the ground. He picked it up and said, "What have you got here?"

"No!" JC exclaimed.

The boy opened the bag and saw the boxes of JC's HIV medication. "What is this? You some kinda drug dealer?"

"It's my medication. Please give it back," JC pleaded.

"Hey, guys! There's money in here too. He must be a drug dealer."

The boys all laughed.

"You won't be needing this," the lead bully said as he held up the bag. "We don't allow your kind or drugs in our neighborhood."

"Please don't!" JC said as the leader knocked him to the ground.

Another boy kicked JC in his ribs.

"Stop!" came a loud voice.

The kids looked up and froze.

"Hey, Big Tony," the lead bully said. "We were having a little fun with this black kid."

"If you want to pick on somebody, then pick on me!" Tony landed a hard right to the biggest boy's head.

JC looked up to see a large hand reaching toward him.

"Let me help you up, little buddy. I believe this belongs to you." Tony handed the bag to JC, then looked at the other boys. "If I ever see you guys picking on this kid again, you know what I'll do to you. Now go!"

The bullies scattered.

"You okay?" the big kid asked.

"Yeah. I'm kind of used to getting beat up," JC said.

"Name's Tony Gallo. What's yours?"

"My name's Justin Carter, but my friends call me JC."

"You can call me Big Tony. That's what the other kids call me," Tony said, smiling. "I guess you can see why."

JC laughed. "Yeah, you are a big guy. Thanks for what you did for me."

"No problem. I can't stand bullies."

"Can I give you some money or something?" JC asked.

"Heck no, but I was about to get something to eat if you want to join me?" Big Tony said.

The boys walked to a hamburger place nearby. When they sat down, Tony said, "I'm sorry those kids did that to you, JC. What were you doing in that alley, anyway? I've never seen you at school."

JC told Tony about his messed-up life and how he had ended up behind the school. Tony could not believe what he was hearing.

When JC finished, Big Tony took a last slurp of his milkshake and said, "Wow, that is unbelievable. But I understand why you ran away." He continued, "Listen, my pops owns a grocery around the corner. It has an apartment over it that's been abandoned for years because it is in such bad shape. Dad never had the money to fix it. You can stay there ... if you want to? They never use it, and it'll be safer than you living in alleys, because you are ..." Tony paused.

JC smiled and said, "What? I'm black?"

"Uh, well, yeah, but I didn't want to say that and hurt your feelings."

"It doesn't hurt my feelings, Big T. I've been called worse. Besides, I can't change the color of my skin, can I?"

Tony laughed. "I guess you're right. And I'll always be fat because I like to eat. That doesn't bother me either."

JC smiled yet again and asked, "Are you sure about your dad's place?"

"Sure, JC! I'll take you over there now."

The boys walked a few blocks, chatting along the way.

When they arrived in front of a small corner grocery, Tony said, "This is my pop's place. It's small but has been in our family for generations. He doesn't make much money at it. I think he just keeps it for sentimental reasons."

They walked around the back of the store and up a metal staircase. Big Tony reached over the door frame and pulled down a hidden key. He jiggled the door before it opened.

He handed the key to JC. "Keep this so you can come and go when you like."

They entered the small apartment, and JC could tell nobody had been there in a long time. The place smelled musty, and dust covered the hardwood floors. The windows were glazed over from ages of neglect.

"Told you it wasn't perfect, but it'll be better than you living on the street," Tony said.

"I don't know what to say, Tony. This is perfect. Are you sure you don't mind?"

"Heck no! It's my pleasure to help you," Tony said. "I'll come by after school to check on you. I hate to admit, but I don't have many friends because I am fat."

"You're just a big guy, Tony. Don't call yourself fat."

"I need to warn you to be quiet up here. My dad is, uh ... he doesn't like black people, or brown people, or Asian people. He's not racist, but he just comes from a different generation."

"No problem, Tony. I'll be as quiet as a mouse. Your dad

will never know I'm here."

"I'll be back tomorrow to bring you a few things. Have a nice night, JC."

"Thanks, Tony. How can I ever repay you?"

Tony smiled. "Your friendship is enough."

CHAPTER TEN

MONROE COUNTY, ALABAMA

Stenson hiked throughout the night and much of the following day. He wanted to get so far away that nobody would ever find him. His back and legs ached from trekking over twenty miles. It was late afternoon when he decided to stop and camp for the night.

News of Stenson's disappearance spread throughout the small town of Polksville, Alabama. The tragic death of Betty Beckett at the hands of her husband was still fresh on people's minds. The Masseys offered a $5,000 reward from their retirement savings to find the child. The Alabama district attorney's office who prosecuted Tug Beckett did the same.

Police and neighbors gathered near the Massey home, where they planned to start searching for the little boy. Luna LeRoux led a group to the tree house that she and Stenson had built. She climbed the tree and found the note he pinned to the wall. It read, *"Dear Luna, I left because I can't face my father in court. What he did to my mama is a nightmare I'll never forget. I'll miss you. Tell everybody I'll be OK. —Stenson"*

Luna climbed down from the tree and handed the note to an officer. Searching for a boy who didn't want to be found would be difficult.

Stenson fashioned a lean-to type of shelter from tree

branches and leaves. He covered the ground with pine needles and unrolled his sleeping bag. It wasn't much, but at least it would keep him dry. He built a campfire and opened a container of cheesy macaroni he had taken from the Masseys' home. He placed the can into the flames and stared at the flickering lights. Stenson thought about his mother and how much he wished she was here right now. He laid another log on the fire and climbed into his sleeping bag. The sounds of the forest and trickling water had a calming effect on his soul. He said his prayers, told his mother good night, and soon fell asleep.

When Stenson awoke, he realized it was the first time in months he'd slept through the night without a bad dream. He stoked the coals in the campfire and heated another tin of food. He walked to the stream and sat beside it, enjoying the morning light on his face. Stenson imagined his mother sitting next to him, admiring this beautiful sight. He thought about Luna and the Masseys and how they were so kind. He hoped his brother James and little sister Mary had found a loving family to care for them.

His father never crossed his thoughts as he stared at the water. The man was more than dead to him, and he felt at peace with his decision to run away. He knew in his heart it was the right thing to do. His father might have taken his mother, but Stenson would never let him steal his soul.

Stenson arose and returned to the campsite. He looked at the pile of wood as he ate his food. He'd need more to make it through the night. He scooped hot coals into the empty can to start another fire later. Then he kicked dirt onto the campfire to extinguish it. Stenson headed into the forest to gather more firewood. Soon nature was calling, and he squatted behind a bush. He realized he hadn't brought any toilet paper, so he grabbed a leaf from a nearby shrub and used it to wipe his bottom.

When he returned to the campsite, he dropped the wood to scratch his butt. He should have used more than one leaf to wipe, he thought. Then he began working on his lean-to shelter. But in a few minutes, his butt was itching more. He started working again, but it wasn't long before his rear end felt like it was on fire!

Stenson grabbed his backpack and ran to the stream. He stripped off all his clothing and jumped into the water. It was freezing cold, but he didn't care. He had to wash his butt! He felt bumps around his anus, then he jumped out of the water and put on a pair of shorts. He grabbed his Cub Scout manual and flipped to the section on poisonous plants. He scanned the pictures and recognized the leaf he'd wiped with. Underneath the photo, it read, *"Poison Oak: Forms a rash on the skin and raised blisters. Can last up to three weeks if left untreated ..."*

If only he'd stayed in Scouts long enough to recognize all the poisonous plants in the region! Stenson dropped the book. There was no way he could tolerate this agony for three weeks. He'd gotten poison ivy on his leg once, and his mother applied calamine lotion, which soothed the pain. He thought, *I don't have any calamine lotion, and this is not on my leg!*

There had to be a town nearby, so Stenson walked uncomfortably until he arrived in Hugitch, population 306. He could not believe the irony of the town's name. Stenson thought, *My butt is on fire. I can hardly walk. And I stumble across a town named Huge-Itch!*

He saw a general store with a pharmacy. Stenson didn't have any money, but he had to get his hands on some calamine lotion before his rear end burst into flames.

A bell rang when he walked through the door and an older gentleman asked, "Hello, young man, can I help you?"

"No sir, just looking around," Stenson replied anxiously.

The clerk was also the store owner, and he noticed something wasn't right with the boy. He seemed fidgety and walked funny. The owner kept an eye on him as the kid scanned the shelves like he was on a mission.

Stenson was happier than a bird with a French fry when he spotted the calamine lotion on the shelf. He looked in both directions and didn't see the clerk. Stenson grabbed the bottle and stuffed it in his pack.

As he headed for the door, he said, "Nice store you have. Gotta go!"

The clerk grabbed Stenson's backpack and stopped him midstep. He said, "You come in here and think you can steal from me? Let's see what you've got in this bag."

Before Stenson could say a word, the clerk opened his backpack and saw the calamine lotion. "What is this? I thought you stole some candy. But you stole calamine lotion? You must be a dumb kid."

Stenson's face turned red, and he stared at the floor. "I really need it, sir. I didn't want to steal from you, but I don't have any money and I'm desperate."

The clerk appeared confused. "You were desperate for calamine lotion?"

Stenson told the owner he'd been camping and wiped his bottom with poison oak by mistake.

The clerk could not contain his laughter. "Boy, I have heard some funny stories, but that is one of the best. Take the lotion; it's on me. But next time you need something and don't have any money, just ask. We are good Christian folks in this town, and we'll help you."

"I'll repay you one day when I have some money," Stenson said.

"You don't have to repay me, son," the clerk said. "That laugh you gave me about why you need it was worth more than the cost of the lotion. I hope you feel better soon." The clerk handed Stenson his backpack.

"Thank you, sir!" Stenson said as he rushed out the door.

The clerk shook his head and laughed again. "No wonder that boy was in a hurry."

Stenson wasted no time once he made it to the woods. He dropped his pants to apply the lotion to his rear. It felt so good, but he couldn't believe he was rubbing lotion on his butt. Stenson pulled up his pants and trekked back to the campsite.

When he arrived at the camp, he set his backpack down and noticed his fishing pole lying there. The weather was nice, and it looked like a good day to go fishing. The coals he'd placed in the can had burned out, so he dumped the ashes to use it to hold whatever creatures he could find for bait.

He wandered through the woods, turning over dead logs to look for grubs or worms. Within an hour of searching, his can was half full. As he walked back to the campsite, he saw another log that looked prime. He rolled the log over and jumped back when he saw a snake!

The creature looked like a poisonous coral snake. Stenson had already had enough poison for one day, and he wasn't taking a chance. Besides, he was certain he'd be dead long before he could reach anyone for help. But as he stared at the snake, it seemed docile and more afraid of him. It was about twenty inches long, with red, black, and yellow rings encircling its body. It was a pretty snake, but he would leave it alone. Stenson returned the log over the snake and said, "Sorry to bother you, little buddy."

When he returned to his campsite, Stenson pulled out his Cub Scout manual. He was curious about the snake. He flipped through the pages until he found a picture. The book identified it as *Lampropeltis elapsoides*, also known as a scarlet kingsnake. It was nonpoisonous and native to the region.

Stenson laughed when he read that it was often mistaken for the venomous coral snake. Now he didn't feel so stupid for not taking a chance with the animal. And he was relieved to know his neighbor would not slither into his sleeping bag and kill him.

Stenson grabbed his fishing pole and headed to the water's edge. He picked out a worm and put it on the hook. Stenson felt bad because he did not enjoy killing anything, and he apologized to the worm. He cast his line into the water, and within a minute, he had a bite. It was a little brim and too small to eat. He unhooked the fish and returned it to the water, then cast his line again. After two hours of catching little fish, he had a strong tug on the line. He reeled in a nice bass that was big enough to eat.

CLICK-CLICK!

A sound behind Stenson startled him.

Then a voice yelled out, "You there! What are you doing on my land?"

Stenson froze and looked over his shoulder. He saw an old man with a shotgun pointed at him.

"Get up slowly or I'll blow a hole in you!" the old man demanded.

Stenson stood up with his heart almost beating out of his chest. He turned toward the man.

"What's your name, boy?"

"Stenson ... Stenson Beckett, sir." He quivered.

"What are you doing here?" the old man asked.

"I'm sorry, sir. I didn't know this was your land."

"Where's your daddy?" the old man questioned.

"In prison, sir."

The old man lowered the shotgun. "Your daddy's in prison? Where's your mama?"

"Dead," Stenson replied.

The old man, who looked like a hermit, dropped his guard as if Stenson had taken the gun away himself. He walked closer to the boy and looked him up and down. The man was wearing dirty blue overalls and his hair was shaggy, with a long gray beard.

"You say your daddy's in prison and your mama is dead?" the old man said, as though he could not believe what he'd heard.

"Yes sir, and I'm camping here because I ran away. They wanted me to testify against my daddy who killed my mama. I couldn't stand to see his face again," Stenson explained.

The old man seemed confused. He walked over to Stenson and sat down next to him at the water's edge. "What happened?"

"I'd rather not say, sir. It's too painful to explain, but ... well, I guess I will, since I'm on your land."

Stenson told the old man the story of how he had watched his father kill his mother. He said how hateful his father was and how he beat him and his mom. Stenson explained that his daddy was a drunk, and that's why he ran away.

The old man stared at the boy. Stenson noticed the man's eyes had changed from anger to kindness.

The man said, "I'm sorry about your mama and what your daddy did to her and you. My name is Haggerty. People call me Ol' Man Haggerty."

"It's nice to meet you, Mr. Haggerty. I'm sorry I set up camp on your land without your permission."

Haggerty knew Stenson was sincere. "No problem, boy. Had a lotta trespassers on my land—hunters and such. I don't care for some folks and don't want 'em around."

"I understand, sir. I'll leave ... if you want me to?"

"Aww, shucks, boy. After what you've been through, you're more than welcome to stay on my land. And stop calling me 'sir.' Call me Haggerty. You make me feel older than my seventy-five years."

Stenson smiled, and the old man did the same, with an almost toothless grin. Haggerty liked the boy, and they talked about everything from fishing to farming. Haggerty told him stories about when he was Stenson's age.

After a while, Haggerty looked at the fish Stenson caught. "You gonna cook that fish or keep it as a pet?"

Stenson laughed. "Well, I was planning to cook it, but I never have skinned a fish before. Not sure how to do it. But I have my Cub Scout manual."

"You don't need no book to cook a fish. All you need is somebody to show you how to do it," Haggerty said. "Stay here. I'll get some stuff and show you how to cook a fish."

Haggerty returned with a skillet, two metal plates, and a funny-looking knife. The old man picked up the fish and walked over to the fire. He looked at Stenson's shelter and said, "Nice place you built. Did that all by yourself?"

"Yep!" Stenson said with pride.

"Build us a fire and we'll get started with your fish-cooking lesson," Haggerty said with a grin.

The old man watched Stenson build the fire. After he was finished, Stenson sat down next to Haggerty.

The old man said, "All, right boy, this is how ya skin a fish. Pay attention."

Stenson watched Haggerty dismember and fillet the fish so fast that he could tell Haggerty had done it many times. The old man put the fish in the skillet and placed it over the fire. A few minutes later, the fish was ready.

Haggerty handed a plate to Stenson. "Ain't nothing better than a fresh fish out of this stream. I used to fish a lot down here but not so much anymore since my wife died."

The two of them ate, and Stenson listened to the old man reminisce. Stenson enjoyed Haggerty's stories.

Awhile later, the old man arose and said, “It’s gettin’ late. I’ve enjoyed having dinner with you, Stenson. Don’t get much company round here.”

“Thank you, Mr. Haggerty. I enjoyed it too.”

“My house is up that way a bit. If you need anything, you come and see me, okay?” Then Haggerty told him, “And stop calling me Mr. Haggerty. It’s Haggerty to you. Ya makin’ me feel old, boy.”

“Good night ... Haggerty. Thank you for teaching me how to cook a fish.”

Stenson watched the old man disappear into the woods. Then he placed another log on the fire and retreated to his shelter. As he lay there staring at the flames, he thought about what a strange day it had been. He was glad he had camped here.

Stenson said his prayers. He prayed for his mother and brother and sister. He said a prayer for Luna and the Masseys. Stenson asked God to forgive him for stealing the calamine lotion. Then he said a prayer for his new friend, Mr. Haggerty—*Oops ... I meant Haggerty!* he thought, smiling. Stenson finished by saying, “Thank you for this wonderful day, amen.”

CHAPTER ELEVEN

DEVEREAUX PARISH, LOUISIANA

Morning light through hazy windows lit the dust in the air like snowflakes. JC felt as stiff as the planks on the hardwood floor in the apartment above the corner grocery. The rumble in his stomach said the tank was empty and he needed to find something to eat.

JC snuck out of the apartment before the rest of the town awoke and strolled to a nearby market. He walked to the register with hands so full that he held the sausage biscuit in his mouth. Out of the corner of his eye, he noticed the local newspaper sitting on a rack beneath the counter. His mouth fell agape, dropping the biscuit to the floor when he read the headline: *"Child Disappears from Mission of Hope."* A large photo of JC, resembling a mug shot, appeared with the story. He told the clerk to keep the change and hustled out the door.

The clerk yelled, "You forgot your biscuit!"

Keep the biscuit, he thought as he hurried down the street with his head hung low. He rushed inside the apartment and slumped in a corner far from any door or window. His heart pounded like he had seen his face on a *Wanted* poster. It was bad enough that he was the only black kid in this all-white neighborhood. Now everyone in town would be on the lookout for a runaway kid who would be easy to spot. He didn't bother to check if there was a bounty on his head.

Can things get any worse? JC wondered. He'd run away from one prison to find himself in another. Hiding from Big Tony's father was one thing. But now he had an entire town on the lookout for him.

Remaining hidden in this apartment would at least keep the townsfolk from finding him. But sitting here all day in total silence would be torture. At least prisoners in solitary confinement didn't have to worry about being quiet. The guards could just ignore you while you bounced off the walls in your madness. But if the "guard" downstairs discovered him, JC knew he might find himself tossed out a second-story window. Then he could scream all he wanted to as he hurtled toward the pavement. Between the silence and the chance to only go out at night, JC wondered if he would turn into some kind of mute vampire.

A rap at the door caused JC to freeze. He didn't stir or even breathe. How had they found him already?

A second knock came, followed by a voice he recognized: "Hey, JC. It's Tony. Open up."

When JC opened the door, Big Tony Gallo saw the terrified expression on the face of his new friend. "You look like you've seen a ghost," Tony said. "Is the apartment haunted?"

"I saw a ghost, but not in here. It was sitting on a newsstand and looked like me." JC told Tony how his disappearance from Mission of Hope was that day's cover story.

"You gotta stay outta sight, dude," Tony said.

"Tell me about it. What am I going to do all day besides stare at these walls? Do you have anything to read?"

"All I have are schoolbooks," Tony said as he looked through his backpack.

"Can I read one?"

Tony looked at JC like he was crazy. "You want to read

schoolbooks?"

"Sure."

"Man, you are weird. I hate school. Take my English books. I don't know why they make me take English, anyway." Then he said, "I need to get to school, but I'll stop by later and bring you some stuff for the apartment."

After Tony left, JC propped his backpack against the wall and opened the English workbook. He noticed Tony had missed several homework assignments. Apparently, his teacher did not approve, based on the red-inked comments. If you missed an assignment at Mission of Hope, they would penalize you by forcing you to skip a meal to complete it. JC laughed, knowing that Big Tony would not like that policy.

Tony returned that afternoon, but this time he knocked in a sequence: *Knock. Knock-Knock-Knock. Knock.*

Big Tony walked in with a bag swung over his shoulder. "From now on, that will be our special knock so you'll know it's me." He set the giant sack on the floor. "I grabbed a few things from our storage shed you can use."

Tony pulled things out of the bag and handed them to JC like he was Santa Claus passing out presents. There was a folding chair, battery-powered lamp, and radio with headphones.

"You like puzzle books?" Tony asked.

"Yeah."

"Good, I hate them. Mom gave these to me," Tony said as he handed JC a stack of puzzle books. "Be right back. I have one more thing."

Tony returned with a portable camping toilet. "I thought you might need this. I didn't want you to hold it all day or go to the bathroom on the floor up here since the toilet doesn't work."

JC laughed. "Good idea. I'll use it as soon as you leave." JC gave Tony his English books. "Thanks for the books. I finished your homework."

"You did?"

"Yeah, I saw an assignment is due, so I finished it for you. I hope you don't mind?"

"Do I mind? I hate homework!" Tony said as if JC had asked him if he liked ice cream or cookies. "Tell you what, since you can't leave, I'll grab some burgers ... if you don't mind eating hamburgers two days in a row."

"I could eat burgers seven days a week!" JC exclaimed.

Tony returned twenty minutes later. The two sat on the floor and talked between bites.

It was getting late, and Tony had to leave. He removed his watch and handed it to JC. "Take this so at least you know what time it is, since you are on a curfew like me."

After Tony left, JC thought about how lucky he was. Despite all the difficulties life had dumped on him, JC considered himself fortunate. Abandoned at birth and feeling unwanted, only to find someone like Dr. Abayomi, who actually cared. He also encountered some of the meanest people, who hated him because of the color of his skin. Then he met the kindest friends in Jesús Alvarez and Tony Gallo, who defended him. He had run away from a hateful place only to find shelter where he felt safe. JC realized how life worked in mysterious ways.

JC spent his days much the same. Big Tony would stop by with breakfast before school, and JC would give him his homework. In the afternoon, the boys hung out at the apartment, enjoying each other's company. At night, JC would sneak out of the apartment and wander the streets to get fresh air. He became an expert at avoiding the local lawman on duty at night, Deputy Pecker. He was the only police officer patrolling the streets at that time. Deputy "Peckerhead," as JC called him behind his back, wasn't difficult to avoid. JC figured he wasn't the brightest in the department, which must have been why he worked the night shift.

The story of the missing boy from Mission of Hope died down. People had other things to think about, like Mrs. Jackson's lost dog. JC laughed that they were more concerned about finding a dog than a missing black kid. The boys went to the park on weekends. The only way JC could go was if Tony accompanied him. The same bullies who had beat JC up the day he'd arrived were always there, and they had gotten bigger. But they still weren't as big as Tony Gallo, and those guys were still afraid of him.

Every sixty days, JC returned to the clinic to renew his medication. His physician, Dr. Abayomi, was interested in the boy's well-being as much as his health. JC would share stories about his friend Big Tony and how he spent his days. Dr. Abayomi would always ask if there was anything JC needed, and each time, he'd say no. But whenever the doctor handed him the bag of medication, it was always the same: a sixty-day supply of meds and $100 in $20 bills.

Dr. Abayomi was more than his physician; he was like a father. JC admired him because he was a professional and a role model for a black kid. On his first Christmas Eve living in town, JC opened the door to go out for his nightly stroll. He found a gift on the stairway. The card under the ribbon read: *"Merry Christmas, JC —The Abayomis."*

He would never forget that Christmas. Dr. Abayomi and his family gave him a warm winter coat and a new pair of sneakers. Dr. Abayomi also gave JC something for his birthday. There would always be a gift waiting for him outside the apartment on special days.

The doctor never let JC thank him for the gifts or the money. Dr. Abayomi told him, "JC, I was not born rich or successful. I grew up in a very poor village in Africa. I worked hard to get where I am today, and I hope you will too. You may not believe it, but God is watching over you. I hope one day you find the same success in your special way. Be an example to others and always remain humble. Share your blessings as I have done with you." It would be a lesson in love, kindness, and generosity that JC would carry for the rest of his life.

JC and Big Tony Gallo's routine was the same for the next seven years. JC hid at the apartment over Mr. Gallo's grocery store while Tony went to school. Justin helped his friend with homework, and Big Tony kept JC fed. They were constant companions and best friends.

Tony's parents gave him a car for his sixteenth birthday. The boys often took road trips together. Once, they went to New Orleans for Mardi Gras. The city was fun, and they agreed that one day they would live there.

Big Tony's high school graduation approached, and it made JC a little sad. He had taken all the classes with Tony, albeit without the classroom. But unlike his friend, JC would not receive a diploma. Tony knew it bothered JC and assured him they would share the diploma together. To cheer him up, Tony told JC he would let him wear his cap and gown. JC said the gown would be too big. Tony laughed and told him the cap would fit and he could use the gown for drapes.

As the date approached, JC thought of a graduation present for his friend. He'd kept a favorite photograph of them from a trip to New Orleans. JC took the photo to a store that made enlargements and had a poster-sized print made and framed. The day before graduation, JC purchased a graduation card and smiled as he wrote a thoughtful note inside.

Graduation morning, Tony stopped by the apartment. *Knock. Knock-Knock-Knock. Knock.* JC laughed when he opened the door. Big Tony was wearing a suit.

JC asked, "Are you going to a funeral or did you join the

mob?"

"Very funny! Mom and Dad are downstairs at the store. Dad forgot to leave a sign saying the store would be closed today."

JC couldn't hide the grin on his face as he picked up the gift for Tony. "This is for you!" As he handed it to Big Tony, the frame slipped from their hands. It made a loud crashing sound as the glass shattered when the frame hit the hardwood floor. The boys heard heavy footsteps coming up the stairs. The door flew open, and before either of them could react, Tony's father entered the room. In the seven years that JC had lived above the corner grocery, he had never been discovered. Mr. Gallo looked around the room and realized someone had been living there, and he didn't recognize JC.

"What is going on in here?" Mr. Gallo yelled.

"Dad, this is my friend JC," Tony mumbled. "I've been letting him stay here. He had nowhere to go."

"You let someone live above my store without my permission?" Mr. Gallo shouted.

"Would you have let him stay here if I asked?" Tony questioned.

"No! You know how I feel about ..." Mr. Gallo said without finishing the sentence.

"About what? Black people?" Tony asked.

"You know what I mean. Get in the car!" Tony's father commanded.

"But, Dad—"

"But nothing!" Mr. Gallo said as he looked toward JC. "Pack your stuff! I never want to see you around here again!"

JC quickly gathered a few things and threw them into his backpack. Tony stood there, embarrassed at the way his father acted. JC walked past them in shame and out the apartment door.

Mr. Gallo was furious and stormed out behind JC. He turned back to Tony and said, "We will discuss this later!"

Tony looked at the gift on the floor, with the wrapping torn. He picked up the card and read: *"To my best friend. Congratulations on your graduation and enjoy your next adventure! —JC."* Tony reached down and removed the torn paper to see the poster of him and his friend under the broken glass. A tear rolled down Big Tony's face.

Tony was silent during the drive to his graduation. He listened to his father rant about a kid living above the store. When Mr. Gallo asked Tony how long the boy had lived there, he didn't reply. Mr. Gallo asked his wife if she knew the kid had been there. Mrs. Gallo had in fact known, ever since Tony told her two years before. When Tony explained JC's situation to his mother, she was understanding and told him not to tell his father.

It bothered Tony that JC had been a quiet prisoner in the apartment for more than seven years. Why today, of all days, had his dad found him? Tony blamed himself for dropping the gift and causing his friend's discovery. Tony was so upset that he didn't want to go to the graduation. It was supposed to be a happy day he could share with his friend. He wouldn't have graduated without JC's help. Instead, the day was ruined and the only thing he thought about was JC.

Tony watched his classmates walk across the stage. They all smiled with the principal as they received their diploma. When Tony walked across the stage, he did not smile at all. Afterward, happy families took photos with their graduates. Tony allowed his father to take a photo of him with his mother. But he refused to pose for a photo with his dad. They returned home to a party Mr. Gallo had arranged for his own friends. Tony's only friend was JC, and he wasn't there. Tony guessed that the party was his dad's way of showing his friends that his overweight kid wasn't stupid. Whatever the reason, Tony didn't care.

Nobody noticed when he left the party. Tony went to his bedroom and removed a suitcase from the closet. He stuffed it full of clothes, then scribbled a note for his mom. He walked out the front door and tossed the suitcase into his car. Tony drove all over town looking for JC. He was about to give up when he passed the clinic where JC got his medication. As he drove by an alley, Tony saw a figure sitting next to a trash bin. Tony remembered the story JC had told him of hiding in a dumpster the day he ran away from Mission of Hope. His heart sank at seeing his friend sitting in that very spot again.

Tony placed the car in reverse and then pulled down the alley. JC didn't notice until Tony rolled down the window and said, "They don't pick up trash until Monday."

Justin looked up to see his big friend smiling.

"Get in!" Tony said.

JC got into the car with Tony, who said, "You know how you wrote in the card to enjoy my next adventure?"

"Yeah?"

"Well, here it is!" Tony said with a clever grin.

"What do you mean?" JC asked.

"We're moving to New Orleans!" Tony exclaimed.

JC did a double take. "We're what?"

"We're moving to New Orleans. I don't want to go to college. You need a place to live. I saved almost $7,000 from my allowance and gifts." Then Tony asked, "Do you have any money?"

"Uh, well, yeah. I've been saving all the money Dr. Abayomi has given me over the years. I have almost $4,000."

"There you go. We've got $11,000 between us, and I'm eighteen. We can rent an apartment. What have we got to lose?"

"I guess nothing." JC shrugged with a smile.

"New Orleans, here we come!" Tony said as he put the car in gear. "On to our next great adventure!"

CHAPTER TWELVE

POLKSVILLE, ALABAMA / MONROE COUNTY, ALABAMA

Richard Massey never gave up searching for Stenson. The boy reminded him of his own son when he had been that age. Richard understood how trauma affects people. He had seen a similar change in his own son during his service in the Vietnam War.

Tim Massey was eighteen years old and a recent high school graduate when he received a draft letter in 1967. He had dreams of going to college, but Richard and his wife couldn't afford to send him to school. His mother was against the war and even suggested ways he could avoid the draft. But Tim felt it was his patriotic duty to serve.

Tim arrived in Vietnam soon after he completed basic training. He joined 1st Battalion, 26th Marines at a base in Khe Sanh near the Laotian border. Richard Massey didn't even know where that was until he bought an atlas.

His son wrote letters every day, though they often came in bursts. He talked about his daily patrols, friends, and the miserable weather. As time went on, Tim's letters grew darker and more graphic in their content. They became too much for his mother to read. Instead, Richard would read them and assure his wife that their son was doing well. But as a father, Richard sensed terrifying changes in his son.

They received no letters for about ten days. Richard wasn't too concerned because Tim was often on patrol and had no way to mail them until he returned to base. Then came the day they heard a knock at the door. It was a day Richard Massey would never forget. Two Marines in dress uniform stood in the open door. Marie Massey wailed the moment she saw them. The master sergeant introduced himself and the other Marine, who was a chaplain. The sergeant confirmed the Masseys' identities before proceeding:

"The commandant of the Marine Corps has entrusted me to express his deep regret that your son, Lance Corporal Timothy R. Massey, was killed in action in the Khe Sanh area of northwestern Quang Tri Province, Republic of Vietnam, on 25 February 1968. Your son was on patrol with 3rd Platoon from Bravo Company when they were ambushed. He and five other Marines were killed in action during the assault. The commandant extends his deepest sympathy to you and your family in your loss."

Mrs. Massey was inconsolable and left the room. The chaplain followed her to offer comfort. Richard did not hear the rest of what the sergeant said as he detailed the return of his son's remains. It was as if some giant vacuum had sucked away Richard's soul, and when it reassembled, pieces were missing.

Those scenes remained as vivid in Richard Massey's mind now as the day they'd happened so many years ago. While he could do nothing to prevent his own son's death, he would do everything to ensure the safety of Stenson Beckett.

Every day, Richard passed out stacks of flyers with information about the missing boy. He delivered them to every store, restaurant, and gas station within a hundred-mile radius of his home. Richard prayed to see Stenson again one day.

Stenson spent a lot of time with Ol' Man Haggerty. He would either stop by his place or Haggerty would visit Stenson's campsite and fish with him. Stenson wondered why the old man liked him so much. He never asked because Haggerty was such a private person. But one day while telling a story, Haggerty mentioned his son and then became quiet. He sat there for a moment and finally asked, "Stenson, did I ever tell you I had a boy?"

"No sir, you never mentioned it," Stenson replied.

"I did. He was a good boy. Died when he was ten years old. 'Bout the same age you were the day I met you. You reminded me of him."

"Did you point a gun at him too?" Stenson asked with a grin.

The old man laughed. "Naw, boy. Sorry 'bout that."

"How did he die, if you don't mind me asking?"

"Consumption," Haggerty replied.

"He died of drinking too much?" Stenson asked.

Haggerty laughed again. "No, tuberculosis. That's what we called it in those days: consumption. At first, me and his ma thought the boy had a cold and it would pass. But it kept gettin' worse. So I took him into town to see Doc Wilkerson. By then, it was too late. He was dead within a week. I've always blamed myself for his death. He'd be here today if I had done something sooner." Haggerty paused, then went on, "Wasn't long after that his mama passed. The grief of losing her only child killed her."

Haggerty and Stenson sat there, staring at the water. Stenson understood why Haggerty had never mentioned it.

He reached over and put his arm around the old man's back and said, "It's not your fault, Haggerty."

"I don't want to talk about it anymore," Haggerty said, then got up and walked away.

One afternoon, Stenson heard voices in the distance while fishing. It sounded like two men talking while walking through the woods. He couldn't imagine what they would be doing on Haggerty's property. The old man had *"No Trespassing"* signs posted all around his land. Locals knew to never step foot there or they might be shot.

The voices grew closer. Stenson laid his fishing pole down and stood up. He was about to turn to get Haggerty when the men emerged from the woods across the stream. They seemed as startled to see Stenson as he was to see them.

One of the men said, "Hey, boy, whatcha doing?"

"I'm fishing," Stenson said. "You know you're on private property?"

Stenson saw that each man had a rifle slung over a shoulder and wore camouflage overalls and caps. They stepped into the shallow stream and waded to where Stenson stood. One man got so close face that Stenson could smell alcohol on his breath—a smell that Stenson was all too familiar with.

The man looked Stenson up and down and said, "Private, huh? Don't look so private with you here, now does it? Out here all by yourself?"

"I ... uh ... no, my friend Mr. Haggerty owns this land, and he doesn't like strangers on his property, especially hunters."

"Where is your friend? Looks like you here all alone. Maybe you're trespassing too?" the foul-breathed man said.

"No, Mr. Haggerty gave me permission to camp here. Y'all need to go," Stenson muttered.

"Roy, I believe this boy is bluffing. What do you think we should do with him?" he asked his companion.

"I don't know, Chet. He's kinda pretty. I think we should have a little fun with him," Roy said.

Stenson froze.

"Pull down your pants, boy," Chet said as he aimed the gun at Stenson's chest.

The other man—Roy—raised his gun.

"No!" Stenson exclaimed.

"You're gonna pull those pants down or I'll shoot you and then pull them down for you," the drunken Chet growled.

Stenson trembled and unbuttoned his shorts, letting them fall to the ground.

"Underwear too," Chet insisted.

Stenson's body shook with uncontrollable fear.

Chet yelled, "Now, boy!"

Suddenly, a shot rang out and the man's chest exploded, spattering blood and bits of flesh in Stenson's face. The drunkard crumpled into a pile of death at Stenson's feet. Another blast roared through the forest, removing the second man's face. Both men lay dead as Stenson turned to see Haggerty step out from the woods.

Haggerty wrapped his arms around the boy as he sobbed. He whispered, "Those men won't ever be able to hurt you, Stenson. I made sure of that. Pull your pants up, son."

Stenson held on to Haggerty as he reached down and pulled his pants up.

Haggerty told him with such regret, "Stenson, you gotta leave. Go far, far away from here. I'll take care of these sons-a-bitches. But folks are bound to come 'round asking questions and I don't want you anywhere near here."

Stenson understood. He looked up at the old man like a son to a father. "Okay, Mr. Haggerty."

He smiled. "It's Haggerty, boy. Call me *mister* again and I will shoot you too," the old man said, winking at Stenson.

Stenson gathered his belongings and stuffed them into his backpack. He walked back to Haggerty, who stood over the dead men's bodies.

Stenson gave the old man a hug and said through tears, "I love you, Haggerty. Thank you for being so kind to me. I'll miss you."

Haggerty said, "I'll miss you too, Stenson. Now go before people start snooping. I've got work to do."

Haggerty watched Stenson disappear into the woods. The old man whispered, "I love you too," as a tear trickled down his weathered cheek.

Stenson was so disoriented when he left Haggerty's that he didn't consider the direction he was heading. It wasn't until he reached the edge of his hometown of Polksville before he realized where he was. It felt spooky to be so close to the place where he'd grown up and then ran away from so many years ago.

The night was pitch-black, and then it started to rain. Stenson had no time to build a shelter, so he looked for a place to take cover. He jogged toward a lone streetlamp and found himself in the middle of Polksville's town square. He grabbed a newspaper from a trash can and held it over his head as he ducked under the canopy of the hardware store. The streets were quiet, except for the *tip-tap* of raindrops. His watch told him it was 2:23 a.m. He shook the water from the newspaper and noticed the headline on the *Polksville Gazette*: *"Retired Business Owner Richard Massey Suffers Heart Attack."* Stenson looked at the date and saw it was yesterday's edition. The article said Mr. Massey was in the intensive care unit at Summer Valley Medical Center. It also stated, *"For the past six years, James Massey has searched for Stenson Beckett, son of Betty Beckett, the murdered mother of three."*

Stenson laid down the paper. He could not believe it. Mr. and Mrs. Massey had been so kind to him after the death of his mother. To think that Mr. Massey had been looking for him all these years. He felt terrible for not contacting the Masseys to let them know he was safe.

Stenson had to see Mr. Massey. He knew the location of the medical center, as it was the same place he had gone for counseling after his mother died. The hospital was about five miles on the other side of town. He looked at his watch again and decided he had to go now. He threw the newspaper down and set off in the rain.

He arrived at the hospital at 4:00 a.m. Drenched to his core, Stenson knew he couldn't just walk in the front door and expect to see a patient in ICU. He had to find another way inside. Stenson crept around to the side of the building and noticed an employee smoking a cigarette. He tiptoed closer and waited for the employee to go inside. When he did, Stenson sprang forward as the door was about to close and stopped it with his foot.

Stenson stepped inside and closed the door. He was in a stairwell. The hospital was only four stories tall, and he guessed the intensive care unit was on top. He snuck up the stairs and reached the fourth floor. It was quiet, with only minimal staff on duty. He figured he had to be out of there before 5:00 a.m. when the day staff would arrive.

He opened the door and went inside. A nurse was sitting at a station in the middle of the hallway. How would he get past her? Then a phone rang, and the nurse left the station. This was his chance. Stenson hurried down the hall, peering into each room. The first two were empty. The next had a patient who wasn't Mr. Massey. Then he spotted him in the last room. Stenson slipped inside. It was the first time he had seen Mr. Massey in six years. A lump formed in his throat at seeing the man who had cared for him, lying there with so many wires attached. The room was silent except for electronic chirps coming from a heart monitor. Stenson walked closer to the bed and noticed Mr. Massey was asleep. He reached over and held his hand.

Mr. Massey opened his eyes and saw the boy's face. He stared at him as if in a dream and then said through labored breath, "Stenson."

"Hi, Mr. Massey," Stenson said with a gentle smile.

"I'm glad to see you. I've been worried about you," Mr. Massey whispered.

"I'm sorry I never contacted you or Mrs. Massey."

"It's okay, Stenson. We understood why you left," he said as he squeezed Stenson's hand.

They stared at each other for several minutes without saying a word. It was as if they were communicating telepathically. Each knew what the other was saying with their eyes.

"I have to go now, but take care of yourself. Don't make me worry about you."

"I'll be okay, Stenson, now that I've seen you."

Stenson leaned over and kissed Mr. Massey on his forehead. "Goodbye, Mr. Massey. Get well soon."

Mr. Massey squeezed Stenson's hand again and smiled. It was hard letting go, but Stenson knew he had to leave. He peeked out the door and didn't see the nurse. He dashed through the hallway and bounded down the stairs. Stenson threw open the door he'd come in through and headed for the woods, vanishing like a ghost in the night.

CHAPTER THIRTEEN

POLKSVILLE, ALABAMA / MOBILE, ALABAMA

After visiting Mr. Massey in the hospital, Stenson spent a damp morning resting in the woods. There were too many bad memories to stay in his hometown for long. However, he had a few things he wanted to do before he left.

It was midmorning when he walked through town. People didn't recognize him since he didn't look like the same ten-year-old boy who had run away so many years ago. Stenson made his way to the street where he'd grown up. The trailer where his mother was murdered had long since been removed. But his stomach grew nauseous as he stood on the empty lot. Witnessing her violent death at the hands of his father would forever stain his mind.

He walked a few yards to the Massey home and knocked.

An older woman opened the door and asked, "May I help you?"

It was Mrs. Massey, but she looked very different from the way Stenson remembered her. Marie appeared to have aged more than twice the number of years he had been away.

"Mrs. Massey, it's Stenson Beckett. Do you remember me?"

Her expression changed to joy when she realized it was him. Stenson wasn't the same little boy she remembered either, but the twinkle in his eyes was unmistakable. Marie gave him a warm hug and invited him inside. Like any mother, Mrs. Massey asked Stenson if he was hungry. He was indeed hungry but didn't have long to stay, so he declined.

She would have none of that, though: "Nonsense, you need to eat. You look thin."

He knew he wouldn't win this battle, so he smiled and said, "Yes ma'am."

Mrs. Massey returned a few minutes later with a ham sandwich, potato chips, and a soda. Stenson had fond memories of eating this same meal for lunch when he lived with the Masseys.

"How have you been?" Marie asked. "Richard and I have been so worried about you."

"I've been good, Mrs. Massey." Stenson shared stories of camping and living off the land. He told her about his friend, Mr. Haggerty. He left out the hardships but assured her he was happy. Stenson told Mrs. Massey he had visited her husband that morning around 4:00 a.m.

She asked, "They let you in to see him at that hour?"

"Well, I kind of snuck in," Stenson replied slyly.

"Did he know you were there?"

"Yes ma'am. He woke up and we talked for a few minutes."

"We never stopped searching. You are like a son to both of us." Mrs. Massey touched the boy's cheek.

Stenson asked about his brother and sister. Marie told him they went to a foster family after the tragedy and they later adopted them. She said the kids seemed happy and well adjusted. Marie paused before asking Stenson how he was doing emotionally.

"It's been a process, Mrs. Massey. I don't think about my father anymore. He's dead to me. I can't change what he did to me or my mom. But I have seen more kindness in people who have helped me heal those wounds. I will not allow those tragic moments in my life to define me."

"I am so proud of you, Stenson."

He gave her a little smile, then said, "I saw my old school building isn't there anymore, so do you know where my brother and sister go to school? I'd like to see them before I leave town."

"You're leaving?" Mrs. Massey asked, as if she expected Stenson to remain in Polksville.

"Yes ma'am. There are too many bad memories for me to stay here. I hope you understand?"

"I do, Stenson," Marie said as she touched his hand.

Mrs. Massey gave Stenson directions to the school and told him that the children's last name was now Wilson. Stenson jotted his email address on a piece of paper in case Mr. and Mrs. Massey ever needed to get in touch with him.

He gave Mrs. Massey a hug and said, "I love you both. I'll never forget all you did for me and promise not to be out of touch for so long."

He kissed her on the cheek before he left. Mrs. Massey was sorry to see him go.

Stenson walked to the school his siblings attended. He sat on a short brick wall across from a line of buses and waited for classes to end. When class let out, he searched through a sea of children. Two kids were walking together, and he instantly recognized them as James and Mary.

Stenson could not believe how much James, now ten, looked like he himself had when he'd run away. And at eight years old, his sister Mary was no longer a baby.

Stenson caught up with the kids and said, "Hi!"

At first, the kids looked at Stenson as if he was a stranger.

Then James recognized him and exclaimed, "Stenson!" He dropped his book bag and hugged his big brother.

Mary joined the hug too.

Stenson said, "Hey, guys! I've missed you! Can I walk you home?"

"Sure!" James said. "We usually take the bus, but we don't live too far away."

It was a happy conversation as the kids told Stenson about school and how nice the Wilson family was. James said they lived in a nice house and Mr. Wilson let them get a dog that they'd named "Stenson."

Stenson laughed. "You named a dog after me?"

The kids giggled.

Mary said, "He doesn't look like you because he has four legs and is furry. But we like the dog as much as you, so that's why we named him Stenson."

The kids wanted to hear all about Stenson's adventures. He told them of camping and fishing and living in the woods.

James said, "Wow, Stenson, you sound like Tom Sawyer."

Stenson thought about it and said, "Yeah, James, I kinda do, don't I?"

When they arrived at the house, Stenson gave them both a hug. He wrote his email address in James's notebook and told him to contact him that way if he ever needed anything. When he said goodbye to them, he saw the same disappointment in his siblings as he had in Mrs. Massey. Stenson knew they wanted their brother to stay.

Stenson kneeled and said, "I will never be far away, and you are always in my prayers." He tried not to cry. "Be good for the Wilsons, okay?"

The kids gave Stenson a big hug, not wanting to let go.

He kissed each of them on top of their heads and said, "Now do your homework. You remember how Mama used to make me before I could play?"

The kids grew quiet.

Stenson realized he shouldn't have mentioned their

mother. He tried to change the mood by saying, "Go feed Stenson the dog before he bites you like I'm going to!" Stenson made a playful biting face and growled.

James and Mary laughed.

Mary smiled at her brother and said, "Okay, Stenson-not-the-dog!"

Stenson waved as the children ran inside. It was nice to see how happy his siblings were and to know how much the Wilsons cared. He thought, *This is the way things should be.*

There was one more stop Stenson wanted to make before he left Polksville. This would be the most difficult. His thoughts shifted to sadness as he took the lonely walk to the cemetery. He found the plot where his mother and her parents were buried. Stenson kneeled and touched his mom's gravestone.

"Hi, Mama. It's been so long since I've seen you. You are in my thoughts every day. I wish I could have protected you better." Stenson looked to the sky. "I feel you watching over me and hope I make you proud. I love you, Mama, and miss your smiling face."

Stenson stared at his mother's name. He wiped away a tear, then leaned down and kissed the stone. "Goodbye, Mama."

Stenson did not know what to do next. He couldn't go back to Haggerty's place and he wouldn't stay in Polksville. He'd always wanted to see the ocean, and the closest one was the Gulf of Mexico. It was as good a plan as any, so he headed south.

Stenson hiked for weeks. He felt like he was in the scene from *Forrest Gump*, where the main character ran until he finally reached the ocean, then turned around again. Stenson only hoped he wouldn't end up in the desert like Forrest when he said, "I'm done running."

Stenson was lucky to have some money from selling fishing bait when he'd lived at Haggerty's. But he was more than tired of eating cheap convenience store hot dogs. What he would give for a big, fat fish or one of Haggerty's home-cooked meals.

He finally arrived at the outskirts of Mobile, Alabama. He'd never seen so many cars and tall buildings. The tallest building in Polksville was the four-story hospital. He knew there were bigger cities than Mobile in the United States. But for a country boy who had never been to a city, this place was big enough.

The ocean must be on the other side of this town, he thought. The only question was how he would get there. Should he attempt to cross an eight-lane, high-speed obstacle course called a highway, or take the long way around? Since he'd walked so far, he decided to take the quickest way possible.

It took several attempts to cross Interstate 65 on foot. He would get a lane or two across, then run back to where he started. There were a lot of impatient people who had no respect for a kid with a backpack. Stenson had visions of being splattered on the grill of one of the big eighteen-wheel trucks. He did not want to be a bug on somebody's windshield. After three attempts and a test of courage, he finally made it to the other side.

The place felt foreign as he walked through suburban neighborhoods. He noticed that all the houses appeared the same, with their neatly trimmed yards. It also seemed like everyone drove an SUV. He didn't see a single trailer home or a broken-down car in the front yard like in Polksville. Everything was nice and tidy. But it reminded him of vanilla ice cream without the sprinkles.

Stenson passed a shopping mall. The building appeared to be the size of ten football fields, and he couldn't imagine what they sold in there. Maybe it was the place someone could buy an elephant or an airplane. *It's certainly big enough*, he thought. He didn't bother to find out. Everything in this town was large. The electronics and hardware stores were bigger than anything he'd ever seen. The grocery store looked like it could feed a small country. Then there were the restaurants lining both sides of the street for as far as he could see. Polksville only had Billy Bob's Catfish Corner and a Dairy Queen. He wondered if anybody in this town even knew how to cook.

He finally reached the center of the city. Stenson stood beneath the tallest building and wondered what they did in there. It was probably something he didn't want to do, considering how the people were dressed. Then he noticed bicycles for rent. People in Polksville owned their bicycles or stole yours. For many, it was their only mode of transportation.

As dusk settled, Stenson wondered where to set up camp. He saw a park nearby and decided it would be as good a place as any. He propped his backpack against a tree and unrolled his sleeping bag. Stenson looked through his Cub Scout manual to see if there were instructions for how to camp in a city. He was about to look for firewood when a flashlight shone in his face.

A voice said, "Young man, you can't sleep here."

Stenson realized it was a police officer. "What do you mean?" he asked.

"It's against the law. You can't sleep in a public park," the officer replied. "Let me see your identification."

"I don't have any," Stenson explained.

"Where do you live?" the officer asked.

"Polksville."

"You're a long way from home. Where are your parents?"

"Dead and in prison," Stenson replied.

That wasn't the answer the cop expected. "I'm sorry, but you can't stay here. It's against the law. There is a rescue mission nearby where you might stay."

Stenson rolled up his sleeping bag and headed to the mission. When he arrived, he noticed several people loitering around the building. The place smelled of urine and alcohol.

A man looking as grungy as he did asked, "Can you spare some change?"

Stenson looked him and said, "Dude, I'm sixteen years old and homeless. Do I look like I have any money?"

He was not in the mood for this but didn't have a choice. He would stay here tonight and find a less funky place to stay tomorrow. A man behind a wire cage explained the rules. When Stenson said he didn't smoke or drink, the guy shrugged as if to say he didn't care. He tossed a key on the counter and directed Stenson to the dormitory.

Stenson shoved his backpack into a locker, then walked down a corridor. The hallway emptied into a room lined with bunk beds on both sides. It was noisy and crowded and smelled worse than outside. There was a colorful cast of characters, consisting of mostly dirty and drunken older men. He did spot one kid who appeared to be around his age, sitting on a bunk at the end.

Stenson walked over and asked, "Mind if I take the bunk above you?"

"I don't care," the boy said without looking up.

"My name's Stenson."

"Charlie Whitehorse."

"Interesting last name. Sounds Indian."

"Very perceptive, Brainiac. Figure that out all by yourself?" the boy asked.

"I thought you were Mexican or something," Stenson

replied.

Charlie looked up at Stenson and smiled. "At least you're honest," he said, offering to shake Stenson's hand.

The boys talked for a while. They were both interested in how each had ended up in this place. Charlie told him he had run away from an Indian reservation. Stenson could not believe Charlie was a real Native American. He thought they had vanished.

Charlie couldn't believe Stenson's wild stories either. "Wow, Stenson. Other than your mom dying, you have had some cool adventures."

The guys were tired and decided to get some sleep. Stenson removed his shoes and placed them under the bottom bunk. He climbed onto the top bed and, despite all the noise, fell asleep.

Two hours later, Stenson awoke to a disturbance below.

"Stenson, wake up! Some guy is stealing your shoes!" Charlie yelled.

Stenson jumped down from the bunk to see Charlie Whitehorse trying to tug one of Stenson's shoes away from a man. The guy was already wearing the other one. Stenson pushed the thief so hard that he released the shoe in his hand. Then Stenson ripped the other one off his foot. The man scampered away like a cockroach when you turn on the light.

Charlie laughed. "Sorry, I should have told you not to put your shoes down there. Happens all the time in places like this. I guess the guy liked your shoes better than mine."

The next morning, Charlie woke Stenson early. "Get up! The church down the street provides free breakfast to homeless people. We need to get there before the rest of these clowns. It's first-come, first-served."

The boys grabbed their belongings and returned the keys to the man in the cage. They walked a few blocks to a Catholic church, where tables were set up to feed the homeless. Volunteers filled their Styrofoam containers with scrambled eggs, bacon, fried potatoes, and fruit. Each boy picked up a cup of juice and found a place to sit. Stenson couldn't remember the last time he'd had a hot breakfast.

After their meal, the boys wandered the streets. Charlie showed Stenson safe places to stay overnight where cops wouldn't bother him. Stenson told Charlie his reason for being in Mobile, Alabama, was to see the ocean for the first time. Charlie took him to Mobile Bay, where several rivers emptied into the bay and then on into the Gulf of Mexico from there. Stenson looked at the water and told Charlie he'd seen bigger lakes. Charlie laughed and said it was just a bay. If Stenson wanted to see the real ocean, they had farther to go.

While they were there, Charlie and Stenson visited Battleship Memorial Park. The World War II battleship *USS Alabama* and submarine *USS Drum* were docked there. Charlie asked Stenson if he would ever join the Navy. Stenson said he liked to swim, but not that much. He would prefer a branch of the military that stayed on dry land.

It was too late to set off for the Gulf of Mexico. So Stenson and Charlie picked up snacks from a small market and walked over to Bienville Square. They sat on a bench in front of a large fountain.

Stenson asked Charlie, "Does it bother you to be an American Indian?"

"Heck no, Stenson. I'm proud of my heritage. We are the original Americans. But it is difficult. Most people think Native Americans walk around wearing war paint with feathers in our hair. They don't consider how much we were hurt when the government stole our way of life. My people were placed on a patchwork of lands that are now filled with poverty, alcoholism, and lack of jobs. It's not fair."

Stenson understood. “I am sorry we did that to you.”

“You didn’t do it to us, Stenson. Your ancestors did.” Charlie patted Stenson on the back. “You’re a good guy, and if you had been in charge, I know we could have worked out a better deal than what we got.”

Neither wanted to go back to the shelter, so they looked for a place to stay for the night. Charlie picked a spot beneath a highway overpass. The noise from the cars made it almost impossible to talk. Charlie assured Stenson it would quiet down later and nobody would bother them there. In the morning, they went back to the church for breakfast.

When they finished, Charlie said, “Let’s go see the ocean!”

A few hours later, they reached Dauphin Island, a barrier island on the Gulf of Mexico. This was what Stenson had envisioned when he thought of the ocean. He looked out toward the horizon and saw nothing but water for as far as he could see. It was almost as if the water was falling off a ledge. No wonder early people thought the earth was flat. The boys explored the island and swam in the ocean. Later, they gathered driftwood and built a large bonfire. They talked for hours until Charlie fell asleep. Stenson walked to the water’s edge and let the waves lap his feet. He stared into the infinite blackness with a blanket of stars and pondered the purpose of his life.

The boys spent the next month living under bridges and eating a single meal a day provided by the church. Their money ran out, and they resorted to panhandling. Not that they didn’t want to work, but neither Stenson nor Charlie had identification. As far as the government was concerned, they didn’t exist.

The holidays soon approached, a time of year that’s always difficult for the homeless. Stenson missed his mom more than usual. Thanksgiving used to be his favorite holiday when his mother was alive. He enjoyed it because it was all about family and food. Not since the year before she passed had Stenson celebrated the day. Even though his family was poor, his mother always prepared an enormous meal. Stenson often wondered where she got the food.

Thanksgiving morning, Charlie and Stenson walked to the church for a special meal. As volunteers plopped the food into each Styrofoam box, Stenson noticed that the items were the same as he used to have as a boy. But the one ingredient they could not provide was joy. While sitting there among the dirty, downtrodden, and hopeless, Stenson wondered what he had to be thankful for. He was grateful for Charlie and this meal, and he also appreciated the people who took time away from their families to serve it. But it was one meal on one day. Tomorrow would be back to the same miserable, struggling *Groundhog Day* cycle he called life.

Maybe living in the city was getting Stenson down. As Christmas approached, he watched everybody pass him without a care in the world. It all seemed so superficial, their arms filled with presents that people didn't need. Money couldn't buy the only gifts Stenson wished for. He'd give anything for another moment with his mom or to see Haggerty's snaggle-toothed grin again.

Charlie tried to cheer him up, but Stenson knew it bothered his friend too. They were a couple of dirty, homeless kids nobody cared about. The one thing Stenson had was faith. It was something his mother had instilled in him as a child. His life might have been a screwed-up mess, but faith always seemed to guide him in the right direction.

Christmas morning, Stenson attended Mass at the church where they received meals. He wasn't raised Catholic, but a church was a church and it was Christmas Day. Stenson asked Charlie if he wanted to go too, but his friend declined. Charlie told Stenson he would catch up with him later. Stenson felt embarrassed when he arrived. Everybody wore nice clothes, and he hadn't bathed in days. He waited outside until the service began, then he stood in the back.

Charlie met Stenson in front of the church after the service. He asked Stenson if he was ready to become a Catholic. Stenson laughed and told him he would have to go to class for that. They did a lot of standing and kneeling and other things they'd never done at the Baptist church Stenson had grown up in. The boys ate a Christmas meal, then returned to their campsite under the bridge. Stenson wondered why Charlie was grinning, until they rounded the corner. There was a funny-looking Christmas tree decorated with empty beer cans and plastic bottles. Beneath the tree sat a brightly colored present.

Charlie picked up the box and handed it to Stenson. "Merry Christmas, my friend!"

Stenson tried to refuse the gift, but Charlie insisted he take it. Stenson removed the wrapping paper and opened the box to find a brand-new pair of sneakers—the same pair that Stenson had told Charlie he would buy if he ever had the money. They cost more than $100.

"I don't know what to say, Charlie. How did you get the money?"

"Don't worry about that. Try 'em on!"

Stenson tried on the shoes and they fit perfectly. "Thank you, Charlie. But I feel bad because I don't have a gift for you."

"Your friendship is all the gift I need, and I get that every day." Charlie smiled at Stenson and said, "Besides, your shoes are falling apart."

By February, the temperature had dropped below freezing for several nights. It was so cold that the boys had no choice but to stay in the shelter. It was another chaotic night among the psychos. The next morning, they agreed they'd rather freeze to death than stay in that nasty place again. They roamed the streets, looking for a warm place to stay. Charlie noticed an unlocked car and climbed inside. Stenson hesitated when Charlie motioned for him to get in.

Charlie got out of the car and said, "Do you want to freeze to death?"

Stenson didn't want to freeze to death, so he got in the car.

They were both shivering when Charlie said through chattering teeth, "I-I'll fix-fix this."

He removed a screwdriver from his bag and popped the lock on the steering column. Charlie fiddled with some wires, and suddenly the car started. He turned on the car's heater and smiled. Stenson looked at Charlie like he'd witnessed a Houdini magic trick.

Stenson asked, "How did you learn to do that?"

"I've been boosting cars for a few years," Charlie said. "A guy taught me how to do it. We have a partnership where I get the cars and he chops them up and sells the parts."

Stenson didn't know what to think about Charlie being a professional car thief. His Indian friend put the car in gear and drove around the corner to an alley.

Charlie noticed the fear in Stenson's eyes and said, "Relax. We're not stealing it. I wanted to move it to a spot where we can leave it running with the heat on."

Stenson didn't argue since he was finally feeling his fingers and toes again. They reclined the seats back and fell asleep. Around 2:00 a.m., there was a rap on the window. Stenson opened his eyes to see a flashlight shining in Charlie's face. Then the light panned over to him.

Charlie rolled down the car window. "Yes, Officer?"

"You boys okay?" the officer asked.

"Yeah. We were tired and pulled over to get some sleep."

"May I see your license and registration?"

"Would you believe I left it at home?" Charlie asked.

The officer shined the light around the vehicle and noticed the broken ignition. "Please step out of the car," the officer commanded.

The officer questioned the boys about the ignition. Charlie lied and said it was broken but failed to mention the part where he had been the one who broke it. The officer ran the license plate, and dispatch reported the vehicle stolen. The officer placed the boys in handcuffs and informed them they were under arrest. Stenson was dumbfounded. He and Charlie didn't say a word on the way to the police station. Stenson wasn't mad at his friend because he knew Charlie had done it with the best of intentions. But the only thing Stenson had ever stolen in his life was a bottle of calamine lotion.

The boys were charged with grand theft auto. After a night in jail, they appeared in court the next morning for their arraignment. Charlie Whitehorse told the judge that he had hot-wired the car and that Stenson had nothing to do with it. Since Stenson had never been in any kind of trouble before, the judge sentenced him to one year of probation. He told Stenson that if he stayed out of trouble, the incident would be removed from his record.

Charlie wasn't as fortunate. He had a previous conviction for grand theft auto when he was fifteen years old. Sadly, Charlie's probation was set to expire one week after the day they were arrested. The judge sentenced Charlie to three years for the violation and being a repeat offender.

As deputies led Charlie away, he looked at Stenson and mouthed the words, "I'm sorry."

Stenson didn't know what to do now. The weather was cold, and he didn't feel safe on the streets alone at night. He had no choice but to return to the dreaded homeless shelter.

One day, he saw a bulletin about a free GED course offered at a nearby community college. He figured that even though he was homeless, at least he wouldn't be stupid and homeless, and so he enrolled in the classes. It would give him something productive to do during the day besides beg. He also volunteered to serve meals to the homeless at the church where he ate every morning.

That was Stenson's life for the next year. He lived at the shelter, fed the homeless, went to class, and studied. He also became friends with the priest at the Catholic church. Father Bala was a Franciscan monk from India. Stenson enjoyed the priest's sense of humor and insight into life. Father Bala enjoyed cooking, and Stenson loved to eat. They had dinner together several times a week.

Instructors were impressed with the pace that Stenson completed his studies. They found it hard to believe the boy only had a third-grade education. Stenson tested out of each grade about every six weeks. At the end of eleven months, Stenson finished studies that took other kids nine years to complete. There were whispers among the staff that the boy was a genius.

Stenson stayed in touch with Charlie Whitehorse through letters. They corresponded about once a week. Stenson laughed when Charlie told him he was learning industrial electricity. After seeing how fast Charlie could hot-wire a car, he wondered if his friend would steal a power plant next.

The testing date for the general education diploma approached. Stenson's instructors spent extra time with him to help him prepare. The exam took four hours one Saturday morning. Stenson listed the Catholic church as the place to mail his test results. He sure didn't want them sent to a homeless shelter.

Father Bala handed Stenson the letter a week later. Stenson

was too nervous to open it and asked the priest to do it instead. Father Bala read the document and smiled. “Not only did you pass, Stenson, but you scored 94 out of 100. Congratulations!”

Stenson was proud to be a high school graduate. He returned to court two weeks later for a status update. The judge was impressed to learn how Stenson had spent the past year. He congratulated him and removed the charge from his record.

At the conclusion, the judge winked at Stenson and said, “Don’t steal any more cars.”

CHAPTER FOURTEEN

MOBILE, ALABAMA / PARWAN PROVINCE, AFGHANISTAN

"Now what do I do?" Stenson asked himself after receiving his GED. He was certain of one thing: he was tired of being homeless. His friend Charlie Whitehorse was in a detention center, and the only other people he knew were a hundred miles away.

Stenson passed a United States Army recruiting station. It must have been a slow day for recruiting because Staff Sergeant Jacobson seemed way too happy when Stenson walked through the door. He offered Stenson a seat and something to drink. The recruiter asked Stenson about his interest in the US Army. Stenson told him he had always considered joining the military. What he didn't mention was that "always" meant as of fifteen minutes ago. Sergeant Jacobson handed Stenson several brochures and inquired about his background and education.

Stenson said he was seventeen years old and had recently received his GED. He admitted he didn't know what to do with his life and believed the military might be a good option. That was music to the staff sergeant's ears. He asked Stenson if he'd taken the ASVAB test—the Armed Services Vocational Aptitude Battery. When Stenson said he hadn't, the sergeant suggested he should take it to help the Army determine the best job for him.

Stenson agreed, and Sergeant Jacobson asked how soon he could take it.

Stenson said, "Uh, how about now? I have nothing better to do today."

The sergeant smiled and wished he had more recruits like this.

Sergeant Jacobson led Stenson to a small room and handed him the exam. The time limit was three hours, but Sergeant Jacobson told Stenson he didn't need to rush if it took him a little longer.

It was 11:00 a.m. when the sergeant said, "You may begin. Good luck."

Stenson opened the packet and scanned a few of the questions. The exam covered math, science, grammar, and mechanics. The questions seemed more practical than the ones he'd answered to get his GED. He finished at 11:45 a.m. Sergeant Jacobson asked Stenson if he had completed the entire test, as he'd never seen someone finish it so fast. Stenson assured him he had, unless it included questions written in invisible ink.

Sergeant Jacobson then handed Stenson several forms to complete. In the section for personal references, Stenson listed Father Bala and Richard Massey. He laughed as he considered listing Ol' Man Haggerty. No telling what that crazy old man would say. He finished the forms and handed them to Sergeant Jacobson. The recruiter told him to return in a couple of days when he should have his test results.

Stenson showed up at the recruiting office two days later. Sergeant Jacobson was all smiles when he saw him. He told Stenson he did great on his ASVAB exam. The only section he did not do well on related to automotive questions. Stenson told the sergeant he knew a car thief who could ace that part of the exam if he wanted to recruit him.

The sergeant said Father Bala and Mr. Massey both held him in high regard. Even the community college where Stenson had received his GED had nice things to say. The sergeant asked Stenson if he'd ever done anything wrong.

Stenson said, "I stole a bottle of calamine lotion from a store once. But that's a long story I'd prefer not to discuss."

Sergeant Jacobson told Stenson his high scores would allow him to choose any job in the Army. The sergeant joked that Stenson might not want to work in the motor pool, though. He suggested something in surveillance or communications. Sergeant Jacobson said there was a $10,000 bonus upon completion of training in those fields. Stenson had never seen $10,000 in his life, and he liked the idea of working in surveillance. Maybe one day, he could even be a spy for the CIA.

He said, "Great! Where do I sign?"

Once again, that was music to the recruiter's ears. Sergeant Jacobson handed Stenson a large stack of documents. After the twentieth signature, Stenson realized he was about to become the property of the United States Army. The recruiter gave Stenson an appointment card to his physical exam. He said if there weren't any problems with his health, his induction would take place in six months.

"Six months?" Stenson asked with surprise.

"That is the normal time we give new recruits to get their affairs in order," the sergeant explained.

"Sergeant, I have no affairs. I'm homeless. My only affairs are finding a place to sleep and something to eat every day. Can I go sooner?"

"Sure, if you want to," the sergeant said, looking at the calendar. "The next induction date is Saturday."

"That's my eighteenth birthday!" Stenson realized.

"That will be a nice birthday present, Stenson: free room and board, three meals a day, and a paycheck."

"Exactly what I need, Sarge!" Stenson shook his hand and said, "I promise I'll be a great soldier."

"I know you will, Stenson. Thank you for joining the United States Army. We are proud to have you."

Stenson took his physical exam the next day, and everything came back normal. The Army arranged for Stenson to stay in a hotel the night before his induction two days later. He guessed it was the Army's way of ensuring recruits didn't back out at the last minute. Stenson didn't mind because it was much better than the homeless shelter.

The induction ceremony took place in a large banquet room. Stenson noticed a lot of family members mingling with their inductees. He wished his mother could be there to share the moment with him. At 8:00 a.m., an Army officer assembled the recruits. He gave a short speech about this being a big step in life. He asked recruits to raise their right hand and repeat the following words, so Stenson did exactly that:

"I, Stenson Beckett, do solemnly swear that I will support and defend the Constitution of the United States against all enemies, foreign and domestic; that I will bear true faith and allegiance to the same; and that I will obey the orders of the President of the United States and the orders of the officers appointed over me, according to regulations and the Uniform Code of Military Justice. So help me God."

The officer congratulated the new recruits and welcomed them to the Army. Families hugged, and Stenson felt his mother's embrace from heaven above. He gathered his backpack and boarded a shuttle, bound for a new adventure. He'd never been inside an airport before. He wondered why he had to remove his shoes when he went through security. *Like somebody would try to put a bomb in their shoes*, he thought.

What was next—people placing bombs in their underwear too? When he said this to the security officer, the man did not seem amused. He only asked, "Don't you watch the news?"

Stenson boarded the plane bound for Fort Benning, Georgia. He buckled the seat belt and waited for the plane to depart. As the plane gained speed, Stenson gripped the armrests so hard that he almost ripped them off the seat. He was glad he had not requested to join the 101st Airborne. Like he'd told Charlie before, he preferred keeping his feet on the ground.

Basic training at Fort Benning was easy for Stenson. He was in great physical condition from all the walking he had done. It also did not bother him when drill sergeants yelled or got in his face. They didn't realize he'd been yelled at far worse by his father. At least the drill sergeants didn't beat him like his old man had.

Stenson stayed in touch with the Masseys during basic training. They attended his graduation and surprised him by bringing his brother and sister. Everyone told him how proud they were. Standing in his dress uniform with the people he loved, Stenson felt joy like he could not remember.

He shipped off to Fort Gordon, Georgia, for advanced training. Over the next twenty weeks, Stenson learned tactical communications and electronic warfare. He excelled in training and graduated near the top of his class.

Next, Stenson arrived at Bagram Air Base in Parwan Province, Afghanistan. The first thing he noticed was the heat. It was the middle of summer, and the temperature was 40 degrees Celsius or 105 degrees Fahrenheit. No matter what temperature it was, Stenson felt like he had woken up in hell.

Stenson's unit supported communications for coalition forces. He would often go on patrols with the US Marines. They joked with Stenson about him joining the Army and said real warriors were Marines. Stenson reminded them that they weren't smart enough to fix their own radios. It was a fun rivalry between the branches.

On his second tour to Afghanistan, Stenson met another US Marine—Sergeant Robert H. "Brick" Brickhouse. He was covered with tattoos and told Stenson he was in a biker gang before joining the Marines. They became friends over beers after realizing they'd both had difficult upbringings. Brick told Stenson he had been to jail several times.

Stenson asked him to elaborate, and Brick said, "Many things: mischief, trespassing, and vandalism."

"Vandalism?" Stenson asked.

"Yeah. I have a bit of a temper, and when a kid pissed me off, I rode by on my bicycle and threw a brick through his window. That's how I got the nickname Brick."

Stenson laughed. He thought it was because his last name was Brickhouse. Stenson said he had been in jail before, charged with grand theft auto. When he explained the story, Brick told him it didn't count since they dropped the charge. Then Stenson told him the story of how he had stolen calamine lotion.

Brick roared with laughter. "Now that's a true crime! By the way, how's your butt?"

The two were kindred spirits. Both had grown up without parents. Brick's parents had been killed in a car accident when he was two years old. His grandparents raised him, and he didn't have any siblings. He told Stenson his life had been adrift after his grandparents died. He bounced between odd jobs and jail until he joined the Marines. Now he felt his life had a purpose.

Brick couldn't believe all Stenson had been through. He admired the fact that Stenson had such an upbeat attitude. Stenson told him it wasn't easy. But he decided a long time ago he would not let bad things change the good person his mother always wanted him to be.

Early one morning while still dark, Stenson was to accompany Brick's unit in a support role on patrol. They were tasked to investigate reports of insurgent activity nearby. Something made everybody uncomfortable. There was a restlessness under the moonlight.

Stenson admitted to Brick, "I have a bad feeling about this, Robert."

"Don't worry, buddy. Believe me, they are more scared of the United States Marines than we are of them," Brick assured his friend. "We are going in to kill. I don't want to, but if I have to, I will."

The Marine and Army personnel loaded into four Humvees, with Brick's group taking the lead vehicle and Stenson in the third one back. They drove around the base perimeter, then extended farther out. Brick had been on many of these patrols before. The thing that always made him nervous was when the roads were especially quiet. Even at 4:00 a.m., there was usually some kind of activity.

BOOM!

An improvised explosive device hit the first Humvee. Small-arms fire rained down from surrounding rooftops and windows. The Marines scrambled from their vehicles and engaged the enemy.

Stenson took cover behind his Humvee and joined the fight. Through the chaos, he heard screams coming from the exploded wreckage ahead. A burning Marine ran out from the flames and hit the ground. Stenson rushed forward to help two other Marines extract bodies from the wreckage. Three Marines were dead, and two more were severely wounded.

Stenson grabbed the legs of the last Marine in the burning vehicle. As he pulled the man out, he recognized it was his friend Sergeant Brickhouse. Brick's flak vest was on fire, so Stenson dove on top of him to extinguish the flames with his own body. Then he felt a sharp stab in his buttocks and knew he'd been shot.

Stenson held up Brick's head and said, "Hold on, buddy!"

Robert Brickhouse looked at Stenson with the most honest eyes and asked, "Am I going to die?"

Time went into slow motion. Despite all the chaos around them, Stenson assured his friend, "Not on my watch!"

While dragging the big Marine to a safe position, Stenson screamed, "Medic!"

The threat was neutralized within minutes, but it seemed like an eternity. Two Black Hawk helicopters soon landed nearby to evacuate the dead and wounded. Stenson limped aboard a helicopter, where a medic tried to check his injuries. Stenson refused the attention so they could work on those more injured as they flew back to base.

Specialist Stenson Beckett's wound ended up being embarrassing but not life-threatening. He considered himself lucky and worried more about the others. Stenson asked the status of Sergeant Brickhouse and was told he was still in surgery. He replayed the events of the morning in his head. It was scary how quickly things had turned so violent. The Marines were used to seeing combat, but it was the first firefight Stenson had been involved in. So much for being there only to fix radios.

Stenson returned to his unit after being released from the hospital. His commander informed him he would receive the Purple Heart. Stenson didn't care about medals. His thoughts were with the Marines who had died, and their families. A few days later, he visited Sergeant Brickhouse in the hospital. Brick was bandaged like a mummy, except for small openings for his nose and mouth. He was awake and sipping a drink from a Styrofoam cup through a straw. As they talked, Stenson sensed that something bothered his friend.

Brick said, "They're sending me home."

His voice conveyed his disappointment. Stenson knew what the Marines meant to him. He tried to cheer Brick up by reminding him of all the hot girls and free beers he would get back home.

Brick didn't acknowledge the joke. He said in a serious tone, "Stenson, you saved my life. I was about to be burned alive if you hadn't pulled me out."

"You would have done the same for me."

Brick had been informed that Stenson was wounded while extracting him from the vehicle. He asked Stenson about his injury.

"I got shot in the ass!" Stenson replied.

Brick almost choked on his sippy straw. "I bet you wish you had that calamine lotion you stole as kid now, huh?"

Stenson laughed. "I was hoping you would scratch it."

Brick chuckled and told Stenson he was on his own with that. Finally, Brick told him, "Get out of here. No sense spending time with me. You have radios to fix and I have hot girls to think of."

Stenson received the Purple Heart at a ceremony a few weeks later. Afterward, soldiers from Stenson's unit mingled over refreshments. Somebody tapped Stenson on the shoulder. He turned to see it was Sergeant Brickhouse, standing on crutches.

"Brick! They didn't tell me you were out."

"How does it feel to be a hero?" Sergeant Brickhouse asked his friend.

"Don't bust me about this. It's embarrassing enough that I'll have to explain to people where I was shot."

They spent the afternoon shooting pool and enjoying

each other's company. Stenson rode with Brick to the airport later. Brick told Stenson to visit him in New Orleans when he got out of the Army. He joked that he would save him a hot woman. As Stenson watched the C-130 taxi away, he already missed his buddy.

The monotony of military life became old for Stenson. He'd had enough of the Army and decided not to reenlist. His nightmares were getting worse and more frequent. He often woke in the middle of the night soaked in cold sweat. Doctors diagnosed Stenson with post-traumatic stress disorder. They offered him different medications and counseling. Neither seemed to work. The medication messed with his head to the point that he was having suicidal thoughts. He considered the counseling worthless. How do you explain to some college graduate about the life he had endured? You had to live it to relate, not read about it in some textbook.

The only "counseling" that helped was the time he spent talking with Brick by phone or video calls. His friend understood PTSD, since he experienced it too. Stenson told Brick he wasn't sure what he would do after the Army. Brick suggested he stay with him in New Orleans for a while. He told Stenson he had a spare bedroom and would enjoy having him as a roommate. Stenson thanked him for the offer.

The departure date finally arrived. Stenson signed the obligatory mountain of paperwork, making him a free man. He boarded the bus to the airport and watched a blur of brown pass by. He had mixed emotions, knowing this chapter of his life was over and a new, unknown blur was about to begin.

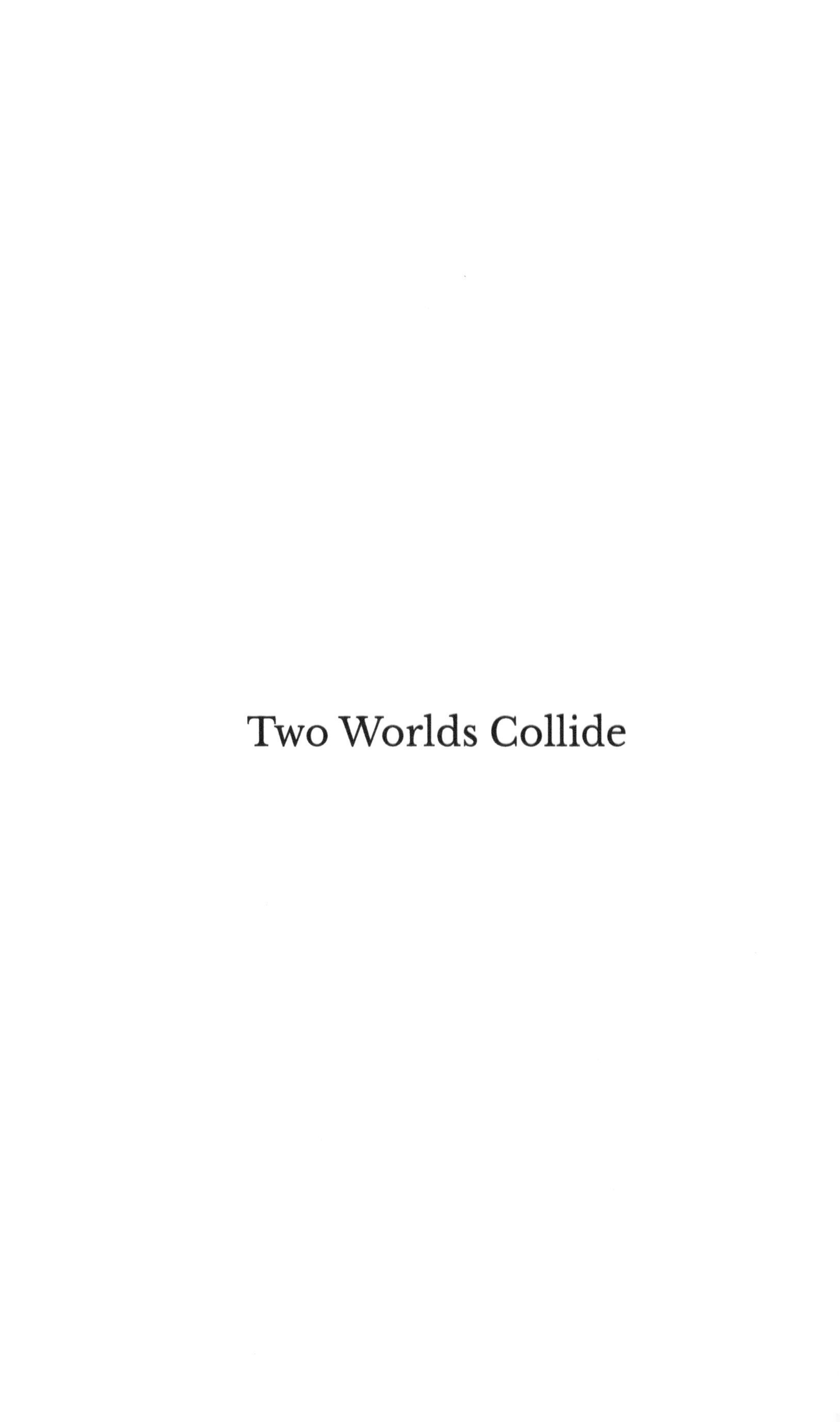

Two Worlds Collide

CHAPTER FIFTEEN

NEW ORLEANS, LOUISIANA

Tony and JC rolled into New Orleans from Deveraux Parish. With $11,000 between them, the boys headed to the French Quarter, where they planned to have fun for a few days. They found a nice hotel with a balcony on Bourbon Street, close to all the action. A well-dressed man at the reception desk said to JC in a feminine voice, "You sure are handsome. Enjoy your stay!"

JC did a double take, then turned to Big Tony and said, "He's a friendly guy."

They hurried to change clothes because these two were ready to hit the town. When they left the hotel, JC noticed two scantily clad men walking toward them. The only clothing one man wore was combat boots and fishnet underwear. JC looked up at the sky, not wanting to see what the man was advertising.

They soon passed a bar near the hotel that seemed interesting.

Big Tony said, "Looks like a gay bar."

JC didn't believe him and walked inside. He was only twenty feet from the door when he saw a bare-chested man in leather pants dancing on the bar. Then he observed two men embraced in a passionate kiss. Without bothering to turn around, JC walked out one of the tall open windows.

When he returned to Big Tony, he said, “Yep, it’s a gay bar. Let’s get out of here!”

The boys wondered what part of Bourbon Street they were on. It wasn’t the same street they remembered from the last time they had been there. Someone told them later there was a section of the street where most of the gay bars were located. Then it all made sense.

Being underage in New Orleans wasn’t as fun since you couldn’t party like the rest of the crazy people. JC and Tony walked up and down the streets, listening to music and watching other people have fun. They were about to give up and go back to the hotel when they passed an alley where a shifty-looking guy offered to sell them fake IDs.

Tony and JC talked it over and decided to buy the forged identification. Mr. Shifty led them to a small doorway in the alley. He took photos of them holding a cardboard cutout of a driver’s license they stuck their head through. Ten minutes later, he produced the IDs. They didn’t look half bad—if someone was drunk and viewing them in the dark. But they were good enough for Walter Smidkiff and Bobby Boladango, the new names for Tony and JC, respectively.

As they walked away, Tony said, “That guy has a good racket. He made two hundred bucks in ten minutes. Can you imagine what he must make in a night?”

The rest of the evening, they went from bar to bar and drank way too much. It wasn’t long before they were intoxicated enough to register on a Richter scale. JC laughed, watching Big Tony dance with a heavyset woman. He decided Tony was having too much fun and joined them in the shuffle. It became apparent JC would not be appearing on any dance shows with his awkward moves. They resembled a combination of a baby giraffe walking for the first time and a person tonguing a light socket—which, with as much alcohol as they had consumed, wouldn't have been out of the question.

It was dawn when the boys returned to the hotel, as plastered as the stucco walls. Tony and JC wobbled onto their balcony to watch the sunrise. JC held on to a steel cable to prevent him from flipping into the street. The wire held a concrete block, which served as a counterweight to the fire escape stairs. When they decided it was time to go to bed, JC let go of the cable. There was a gigantic crash, and the boys turned to discover the balcony railing had disappeared. They looked down to the street below in total disbelief. The concrete had hit the railing and removed it so completely that a welder couldn't have done any better.

JC looked at Tony and said, "I am way too drunk to deal with this right now."

Tony agreed, and the boys went to bed.

They woke at 2:00 p.m. with a banging in their heads like bass drums in a second-line parade. They were so hungover they felt like they would die in five minutes unless they got something to eat. JC and Tony stumbled downstairs in search of food, preferably something greasy. They'd completely forgotten about the balcony incident until they walked past reception. The once friendly manager was not so happy now. He stopped them dead in their tracks before they made it out the door.

"This hotel was built in 1861. We take great pride in this landmark and do not appreciate when our guests destroy it! I have added $1,800 to your bill to repair the balcony. You have also been charged for another night because you did not check out by 11:00 a.m. But I am moving you to another room, and you must check out tomorrow!"

The boys realized there was no point in arguing with the man, even if they could muster the energy.

As they walked out the door, JC turned and said, "Maybe

the balcony fell off because this hotel is old as hell!"

After lunch, Tony and JC wandered New Orleans like a couple of tourists. Their heads were still clanging from the night before, so they went back to the hotel. Mr. Not-So-Happy Manager had moved them to a room at the rear of the hotel that should have been condemned. The smell from the dumpster next to their room did not help JC's stomach. Conveniently, the room also did not have a balcony.

The guys checked out the next morning. Their first priority was to find a cheap place to stay. This adventure had already cost them $2,500 thanks to the balcony incident, fake IDs, and way too much booze.

They found a motel that advertised rooms for $39 per night. The neighborhood seemed sketchy, with liquor stores on every corner. It would have to do for now, since it fit within their budget. The room came with two queen-sized beds, and they soon understood why it was so cheap. The carpet had stains of unknown origin, and there was a musty smell that even the air freshener couldn't disguise. When they turned the light on, a cockroach scampered out the door like, "Get me out of here!" They realized they wouldn't be staying here for long.

It was getting late when JC offered to pick up some food. He walked outside to discover the neighborhood had come alive. Women in revealing outfits walked the streets in front of the motel. JC watched several guys in cars pull over and talk to the ladies. JC was naïve, but not that naïve. He knew what was going on. He passed one of the ladies on his way to the store.

She asked, "Hey, baby, need a date?"

He needed a date, but not that kind of date, so he responded, "No thanks." He took an alternate route through an alley on his return.

Midway down the alley, JC saw a young woman sitting next

to the motel wall, crying. He stopped and asked, "You okay?"

The woman looked up. "Do I look okay, dumbass?"

Her response caught JC by surprise. He noticed she was Asian, and her face appeared swollen. He said, "You are a long way from home, China girl."

"I'm not Chinese. I'm Korean, you idiot!" she snapped.

"Ya'll look the same to me," JC replied.

"All men look the same to me. You are all scumbags."

"Chill out! We all aren't so bad. What's the matter?" JC asked.

"Some guy beat me up and stole my money," she said, "as if it's any of your business."

JC sat beside her and offered her a snack. She sensed something different about this guy, because he didn't run away. For whatever reason, she poured out her heart and shared her story. The lady told JC her name was Pok Kyung-wook, but she went by the name Zabrina. Her family paid to have her smuggled to the US from North Korea two years ago. After she got some work and saved money, she would pay for her parents to join her later. She had never heard from her parents since and worried about them. Upon her arrival in the United States, the Chinese gang who smuggled her forced her into prostitution to repay the debt after they raised the price of her escape. She told JC she was about to pay off the rest of the money she owed them and be free of the gang. That was the money the customer had stolen from her earlier that night. Now she had no money and no place to stay. Her life was hopeless and nowhere near what she had dreamed of.

JC told her he knew what it was like to have no family and be homeless with no money. He said, "Listen, I don't mean to sound forward, but my friend and I have a place at this motel. You can stay with us if you like."

Zabrina looked at JC like he was crazy. "Are you out of

your mind? I don't know you!" she exclaimed. "You could be as psycho as that last guy or maybe you think you'll get some. And I am here to tell you that won't happen. Not now. Not ever!"

JC laughed. "If anyone is psycho, it's you! Look, I know what it's like to be homeless."

Zabrina thought about it. "I don't know why I trust you. But if you try anything, I will slice you up into bite-sized pieces!"

JC laughed at the thought and helped Zabrina up. They walked back to the motel. Big Tony was surprised when JC opened the door and Zabrina was standing next to him. After they talked for a while, Zabrina felt more comfortable around the guys.

When the conversation became lighter, JC told Zabrina, "I bet you know kung fu."

Zabrina looked at Big Tony and asked, "Is he always this stupid?"

Tony laughed and didn't answer the question. The guys agreed to sleep in one bed and offered Zabrina the other. She went to the bathroom to change clothes and walked out wearing a T-shirt and panties. The boys' mouths fell open when she walked by.

Zabrina saw the look on their faces and said, "Haven't you seen a girl before?" She climbed into bed with a warning: "If either of you clowns try anything, I will cut off your favorite appendage and feed it to the rats! I'm sure this motel has plenty!"

The next morning, JC looked at the other bed and noticed Zabrina was gone. He nudged Tony to tell him. Tony pulled the arm wrapped around him closer. At that moment, the boys realized they were cuddling. They leaped out of bed and tried to act macho like nothing ever happened.

They spent the morning searching for a place to live.

They found a one-bedroom apartment in another bad neighborhood, but it was affordable.

When Tony called the place a dump, JC replied, "I've been in dumpsters and this place smells way better."

The manager told them they could move in any day after they paid the deposit. They returned to the motel and found Zabrina sitting outside their room. Her face appeared battered and bloodied. When JC asked what had happened, Zabrina told them that members of the Chinese gang had come to collect the money. When she told them that she'd had the cash but then it was stolen, they beat her and gave her a warning: if she didn't pay in two days, they'd kill her.

JC got a wet towel from the bathroom and wiped Zabrina's face. Tony looked concerned. JC asked Big T to step outside.

JC said, "I know we don't know this girl very well, but this is bad. That gang will kill her. We have the money, so why don't we pay them off so she can be free?"

Tony replied, "You know we'll never see that money again, but you're right: they will kill her."

They returned to the room and told Zabrina they would cover the debt and she could repay them later. Zabrina could not believe two guys she barely knew were willing to help her. She had never known kindness like this, except from her parents.

Zabrina phoned to arrange a meeting with the Chinese gang. She intended to be the one to meet them until JC insisted that he and Tony would go. Zabrina tried to protest, but the boys wouldn't hear it.

Tony drove to an alley and saw a black car parked at the end. As he and JC approached on foot, two men stepped out of the vehicle.

One of them was holding a small machine gun. The other asked, "Who are you?"

"We're friends of Zabrina," JC responded.

"Where is she?"

"Safe. We have your money," JC said as he reached for his back pocket.

The man with the gun raised it at JC.

JC slowly removed an envelope from his pocket and held it in the air. "We don't want any trouble. Here's the money she owes you. Now, leave her alone."

"Or what?" the man asked as he counted out the cash.

"Or our next meeting won't be so friendly," Big Tony replied.

The gangster waved his hand at his partner to lower the gun.

As they returned to their car, JC yelled, "Where are her parents?"

Neither gangster responded before they closed their doors and then drove away. Tony and JC returned to the motel and let Zabrina know she didn't have to worry about them again.

"And my parents?" Zabrina asked.

JC looked at the floor. "I don't know."

The rest of the evening was quiet until Zabrina finally spoke: "I need to go to work."

"Did you get a job?" JC asked.

"You know what my job is, bozo," Zabrina retorted.

"What? You're going to work the streets after what happened to you?" JC questioned. "With your face that messed up, I would never date you."

"You have nothing to worry about, moron. I would never date you!" Zabrina snapped. "Those men don't care about my face; it's the other parts of my body they like. And I don't care about them except for their money. It's all business, and it's the only thing I know how to do."

Tony knew JC could never win an argument with Zabrina,

so he asked, "Do you have a ... you know, a pimp?"

"A pimp? Are you crazy? I'm an independent woman; I can take care of myself!"

"Yeah, like you did this past week?" JC replied.

Zabrina could tell Big Tony had the common sense of the two.

Tony said, "Listen, I have an idea. We can't stop you from doing what you do. But you need someone to look out for you. Why don't you let us watch your back and you give us a small cut of what you bring in? Say, 20 percent? Call it a management fee."

"You want to be my pimp?" she asked incredulously.

"No, we want to be your security," Tony replied.

"So ... 20 percent and you'll protect me?"

"Yes."

"We can try this business arrangement. But if I sense any funny business, I will cut you and your dumb friend up like a kitchen knife commercial."

Tony laughed and JC didn't. Big Tony liked Zabrina's attitude. He told her they were moving into an apartment and asked if she wanted to stay with them until she got back on her feet.

"What? And live with that moron?" she asked, pointing at JC. "I've known rocks with more sense than that idiot!"

Tony roared with laughter, but JC said, "Hey now! I'm not as dumb as you think!"

The next day, they checked out of the motel and drove to the apartment. Zabrina looked at it and called it a dump. Tony agreed but said JC seemed to like it since he was used to hanging out in trash bins. When Zabrina asked about that, Tony said it was a long story he'd tell her later.

They went to the store to buy things for the apartment. Tony found bedding while Zabrina picked out the food. JC walked up holding a basketball.

Zabrina looked at JC. “What is that?”

“It’s a basketball, and it’s only ten bucks,” JC responded.

Zabrina and Tony had the same thought: *This boy is dumb as a brick.*

Tony said, “JC, we’re here to get necessities, and a basketball doesn’t count. Besides, did you see a basketball court anywhere near where we live?”

JC put the ball down. Zabrina and Tony felt like two parents telling a child *no* to every silly thing he wanted. Later, they stopped by a mobile phone store, where Tony purchased three cell phones. JC wanted the latest expensive bling-bling phone, to which Tony and Zabrina again replied, “No.” JC pouted when Tony handed him a simple phone. They returned to the apartment and unloaded the car. Tony laid down some bedding in the living room for him and JC, while Zabrina stocked the kitchen.

Tony told Zabrina, “You can have the bedroom. JC and I will sleep out here.”

“Thank you, Tony. You are so sweet.”

JC whined, “Why does she get the bedroom?”

“Because she’s a girl and needs her privacy,” Tony replied to the silly question.

Zabrina went to the bedroom to get ready for work. She looked like a different person when she walked out. The heavy makeup, false eyelashes, and a revealing outfit hid the beat-up girl underneath.

Tony entered numbers into each of the cell phones and told Zabrina, “Text me whenever you go on a date and give me the info. If you get into any kind of trouble or don’t feel safe, message me and I’ll be there right away.”

Zabrina kissed Tony on the cheek and flipped a middle finger at JC with a wink and a smile. She told the boys to be good as she walked out the door.

JC yelled, "Don't give anybody rabies!"

CHAPTER SIXTEEN

NEW ORLEANS, LOUISIANA

Robert Brickhouse was easy to spot when Stenson arrived at Louis Armstrong International Airport. He wore a black biker vest covered in patches, proudly exposing his muscular, tattooed arms.

Brick had a silly grin on his face when he lifted Stenson off the ground with a giant bear hug, saying, "Welcome home, my friend."

"You mean they let you past security?" Stenson joked.

Brick grabbed Stenson's bag and led him to a waiting car.

Stenson said, "I see you're rich enough to have your own driver."

"No, it's a service. I figured you didn't want to ride on the back of my motorcycle like a bitch."

The car dropped the guys off in front of Brick's home in the Lower Garden District of New Orleans. Brick showed Stenson around the house.

Stenson asked, "How much money does the Army give you in disability? This is nice!"

"Enough that I don't have to work anymore," Brick said with a smile.

He showed Stenson to the bedroom he'd prepared for him and suggested he get comfortable. Stenson removed his Army uniform for the last time and hung it in the closet. He put on a T-shirt and jeans, then returned to the living room, where Brick was sitting on the sofa with his dog. Brick introduced Stenson to the gigantic rottweiler named Mufi.

Stenson hesitated to pet the muscular animal with a head the size of a hippopotamus. He envisioned the dog removing his hand in one bite. Brick assured Stenson the dog was friendly.

"Mufi is a funny name for a rottweiler," Stenson noted as he leaned down to pet the beast.

Brick said, "She had a cold the day I brought her home as a puppy. When she sneezed, it sounded like, 'Muff! Muff!'"

Stenson laughed. "You named your dog after a sneeze?"

Brick handed Stenson a beer and put four steaks on the grill. When Stenson asked if he was that hungry, Brick told him he'd invited some female friends to join them. Stenson was happy to hear that. It had been a long time since he had seen a woman who wasn't wearing combat boots or a hijab.

Stenson's mouth hit the floor when the girls arrived. They were beautiful in their halter tops and shorts.

Brick introduced him: "Ladies, this is General Stenson Beckett, my friend and decorated combat veteran!"

Stenson felt embarrassed. "Don't listen to him. It's Specialist Beckett, and all did was fix radios."

"Nonsense, ladies. Don't let him be modest. He saved my life! He won the Purple Heart for getting shot while he pulled me out of burning wreckage."

The women seemed impressed and asked to see Stenson's wound.

Brick laughed out loud. "I dare you to show them, Stenson!"

Stenson had only been back for a few hours and already Brick was getting him to show his ass. He made up some excuse to keep his pants on while he flipped off Brick for suggesting it.

"Wow! You're a hero. I like heroes!" one of the girls said as she ran her fingers through Stenson's hair.

Stenson's face turned as red as a sunburn. He excused himself to get more beer. They spent the rest of the afternoon drinking and telling funny stories on Brick's patio.

It was getting late and everyone felt a little tipsy when Brick said, "I have a surprise for you, Stenson."

"What's that?" Stenson slurred.

With a sly smile, Brick said, "Ginger and Gina ..."

The girls winked at Stenson. Stenson wanted to run, but each of the ladies grabbed him by the hand, then led him inside.

Stenson looked back at Brick and whispered, "I'm gonna kill you!"

Brick laughed at the spectacle.

The threesome returned awhile later. Brick noticed Stenson had the same dazed look he had seen after they finished a combat mission. Brick could tell Stenson had lost this war. The ladies gave Stenson a kiss on the cheek and hugged Brick as they left.

Brick wrapped his burly arm around his friend. "I told you I'd have something waiting for you when you got home."

Brick gave Stenson a ride to the computer store on the back of his motorcycle. Stenson knew he had to get a car before people got the wrong impression about their relationship. He wanted a classic car with personality. After an exhaustive search, he found a jet-black 1957 Cadillac Eldorado convertible, with a bloodred interior. It had been completely restored to its original glory. The car had a 365-horsepower engine, tons of chrome, whitewall tires, and fins. It reminded Stenson of the Batmobile or something Elvis Presley would've driven.

Stenson contacted the owner and arranged to see the

vehicle. It blew Brick away when he saw it. The ride was so smooth that it seemed to float on air when Stenson took it for a test drive. The owner named a price that was more than Stenson wanted to pay. But he loved the car so much, he agreed to it without haggling. Stenson assured the man he would take good care of it.

They dropped Brick's bike off at the house, then took off to cruise around the Big Easy.

Brick noticed how many women liked Stenson's car and said, "Man, I thought my bike was a chick magnet. It doesn't even come close to this ride!"

They stopped at O'Malley's, an Irish pub near Bourbon Street, to play pool. Stenson noticed a *"Help Wanted"* sign in the window and asked the guy behind the bar about the position. The man introduced himself as Fallon O'Malley, the bar's owner. In a strong Irish accent, Mr. O'Malley said he was looking for a bartender to work evenings. Stenson told him he didn't know much about bartending but had drank his share of beer in the military.

That got Fallon's attention. "Military, eh?"

"Yes sir. Discharged two months ago. Did three tours in Afghanistan."

"Well, my boy, from one soldier to another, this beer is on me," Fallon said as he slid a pint to Stenson. "I served in Her Majesty's Army. Was with you boys in the first Gulf War."

Stenson introduced Brick. The three men spent the rest of the afternoon swapping war stories.

Brick was a little tipsy when he told Fallon, "This man saved my life! Pulled my ass out of a burning Humvee and took one in the butt. If it wasn't for him, I'd be a pile of ash!"

Fallon sensed Stenson's modesty. "*Salud*, young man. Your friend owes you one."

"Oh, he took care of that!" Stenson said and then told the

story of the two girls Brick had arranged the day he arrived.

At the end of the evening, Fallon offered the bartending job to Stenson. He said it didn't pay much, but he could make a few bucks in tips and drink free beer.

Brick and Stenson returned to Brick's place. In a moment of drunken honesty, Stenson said, "I have horrible dreams, Brick. I can't get the visions of my mother's murder or soldiers dying out of my mind. It is like a horror movie replaying over and over in my head. And the medication they prescribed messes me up even worse. I wish there was something I could take to ease the pain without all the side effects."

Brick understood how his friend felt. He had seen some horrible things in combat and knew the symptoms of post-traumatic stress disorder. Brick reached into a wooden cigar box sitting on the coffee table and took out a marijuana cigarette. He lit it and took a long drag, then handed it to Stenson. "Try this."

Stenson had never smoked pot before. He was hesitant at first but took a puff and almost coughed up his lungs. After a while, both men were relaxed and talked about their traumatic experiences. Outside of counseling, it was the first time either discussed the hell they lived with.

The next morning, Stenson met Brick in the kitchen and said, "I slept like a baby last night. It was the first time without a nightmare that I can remember."

"I'm glad you slept well, my friend." Brick handed Stenson a cup of coffee. "Weed has helped with my PTSD. All the drugs they gave me after the chaos in Afghanistan did nothing except mess me up like they did you."

"I find it bizarre the one thing that seems to help either of us is a plant you can grow in your backyard and yet it's illegal."

"Blame it on the big pharmaceutical companies and politicians," Brick observed.

"Where do you get the weed?"

"Some guys I bike with. They're all ex-military," Brick said. "I loan them money from time to time so they can make a big purchase, and they cut me in on the profit. I make a little money, but I do it more to help them out." Brick took a sip of his coffee. "There's a large score they want to do soon, but we don't have enough cash to cover the entire amount. They also need somebody they can trust to make the pickup. None of their guys can do it because they suspect they're being watched."

"How much cash do they need?" Stenson asked.

"About $400k." Brick added, "There's a semi waiting down in Mexico."

"How much do you have?"

"About a third," Brick replied.

Stenson wondered aloud, "What if I can come up with the rest? Will they cut me in?"

"Sure, but where can you get that kind of money?"

"I saved most of my money from the military, and I might know where to get the rest. And I don't mind picking it up if you think they'd trust me."

"Stenson, they would trust you when I tell them you are ex-military and saved my life. But are you sure you want to get into this? You're a good guy and I don't want you to get into trouble."

"I don't think anybody will get into trouble if we plan it right. And I'd pick it up to protect our investment."

Brick said if Stenson could come up with the rest of the money, he'd introduce him to the guys. Stenson got in touch with his friend Charlie Whitehorse, who'd gotten out of prison a year earlier. Charlie messaged Stenson after he received his email and said he was back in business. Stenson knew that it was code for *stealing cars again.* Stenson told him to stop by next time he was in New Orleans to discuss an opportunity.

A few days later, there was a knock at the door.

Brick answered and yelled, "Stenson, Tonto is here!"

Brick invited Charlie Whitehorse in. Charlie thought Brick's comment was funny. But if anyone else called him Tonto, Charlie might scalp them. Stenson gave Charlie a hug. The last time they had seen each other was years ago at their arraignment for grand theft auto.

"I guess you met Brick?" Stenson asked.

"Oh yeah. He looks like a lunatic and much uglier than you described," Charlie joked.

Brick laughed, and the three sat down. Stenson filled Charlie in on the details and asked him if he wanted in. Charlie said he could cover a third of the $400,000 they needed. After they wrapped up the meeting, they went out for Cajun food and beer.

A few days later, they were ready to meet with Brick's biker friends to discuss the deal. Stenson checked his email while Brick took a shower. A lump formed in his throat when he saw *lunajean@...* in his inbox. Stenson had not spoken to Luna LeRoux in years. He thought of her often but was too afraid to talk to her after all he had been through.

He opened the email: *"Hi, Stenson! I hope you don't mind I contacted you. I was back home from college visiting Mom and Dad and ran into Mrs. Massey at the grocery store. She told me she kept in touch with you and shared your email address. Mrs. Massey is so proud of you and bragged about your military service. I finished college with a Bachelor of Science in Information Technology. Kind of spinning my wheels right now trying to figure out what to do with my life. LOL. I want you to know I think of you often. I would love to see you or at least talk on the phone. Here is my contact info ... Love, Luna."*

Stenson opened the email attachment. It was a photograph

of Luna holding her diploma at graduation. She was not the nerdy little girl he remembered. In fact, Luna had blossomed into a beautiful woman. He was staring at the photo when Brick walked into the room. Brick asked Stenson if he wanted something to eat.

Stenson didn't hear the question, so Brick said, "Yo! Earth to Stenson!"

He looked up with a blank face.

"You okay, buddy?" Brick asked. "You look like you've seen a ghost."

"I kind of did," Stenson said as he turned the laptop around and showed Brick the photograph.

"Wow! She's beautiful. Who is that?"

"My friend Luna."

"The Luna you've told me so much about?" Brick asked.

Stenson had spoken of Luna many times when they served together in the military. Brick had noticed that Stenson always smiled whenever he mentioned her name.

"Yeah, that Luna," Stenson said.

"What's the matter? You talk about her all the time."

"She wants to see me or speak on the phone," Stenson muttered.

"So talk to her. Go see her!"

"I can't, Brick. I'm ashamed of who I am. She's a college graduate and I'm a runaway with PTSD who looks like a hippie and is a soon to be a drug dealer. I don't want her to see me like this."

"Dude, she's your best friend and you haven't talked to her in years!" Brick exclaimed. "If she's anything like you say, that girl will accept you for the great person you are today."

"I can't. She deserves a better friend than me," Stenson said, bowing his head.

Brick sat down and put his arm around his buddy. "Stenson,

you are an amazing person and my best friend. If you don't call her today, I'll stab you. And you know I'm crazy enough to do it!"

Stenson laughed. "Fine, I'll call her later because I know you really are crazy enough to stab me."

The guys drove to meet Brick's biker friends to discuss the marijuana deal. Everyone agreed that Stenson would handle the money. Another biker with a commercial driver's license would ride along to Mexico. He would drive the truck back to New Orleans while Stenson followed. One thing Stenson found curious was the amount of money. The seller wanted exactly $401,000. The bikers who arranged the deal said the guy was superstitious and didn't like even numbers. Everyone agreed it was odd, but they would accommodate his price.

On the drive back, Brick said, "You called yourself a 'drug dealer' earlier. That's not true. You are facilitating the acquisition of a product and protecting your investment. You are a businessman, not a drug dealer. Don't be so hard on yourself."

"I've just always wanted to do the right thing," Stenson said. "I always feel like my mom is watching over me. I hope she won't be too disappointed in me doing this."

"You're a good man, Stenson. We should all be more like you."

When they returned home, Brick reminded Stenson he had something to do. Brick handed him the phone and walked into the kitchen.

Brick heard Stenson say, "Uh, hi, Luna? ... This is Stenson Beckett ..."

Brick laughed because Stenson used his last name. Like Luna wouldn't know which Stenson it was ...

The conversation was awkward at first. But it didn't take long before Stenson was laughing and talking a mile a minute.

Brick left to run a few errands so his friend could have some privacy. Stenson and Luna talked for two hours. Luna wanted to see him, and they agreed she would drive to New Orleans to spend the weekend. When Brick returned, he found Stenson sitting on the sofa with a silly grin on his face. Stenson told him that Luna planned to visit this weekend.

Stenson was a nervous wreck Saturday morning. He had gone shopping the day before and bought new clothes and a pair of sneakers. Brick told him he looked like Kid Rock in the red baseball jersey and matching pants.

"Should I change? Is it too much? Do you think I need a haircut?" Stenson asked.

"You look great, but I wouldn't recommend you do any rap videos. Still, Kid Rock would be proud of that outfit and your car," Brick joked.

Brick knew how to make Stenson laugh. He had never seen Stenson so nervous, even when bullets were flying in combat. *Bring a girl to town and the boy is a mess.*

There was a knock at the door. Stenson whispered, "You answer it!" and ran into the kitchen. He began fumbling around like he wasn't waiting for her arrival.

Brick opened the door. "Hi, Luna! I'm Robert Brickhouse. Please come in."

Stenson looked up from the kitchen. "Oh, hi, Luna. Sorry, I was rearranging the silverware drawer."

Luna beamed when she saw Stenson. He looked much different from the last time she had seen him. They embraced in a hug that seemed to last forever. Brick excused himself to the kitchen to resume rearranging the silverware. Apparently, neither he nor Stenson was good at faking being busy. Brick looked up from the kitchen to see them holding hands as they talked.

A few minutes later, Brick walked into the living room.

"Stenson, what do you say we take Luna out and show her a good time in New Orleans? I bet she can dance better than you."

"Anybody can dance better than me!" Stenson agreed.

The three spent the afternoon touring New Orleans. Brick felt like a chaperone to two teenagers. He could tell Stenson and Luna were having fun catching up. The group ended up at Pat O'Brien's on Bourbon Street. Luna and Stenson drank Hurricanes, and Brick knew to stick with beer. Stenson and Luna were feeling good when she asked him to dance.

Brick realized Stenson wasn't lying about his dance moves. He thought, *That boy needs lessons. He looks like the gopher from the movie* Caddyshack.

They dropped Luna off at her hotel at the end of the night, and Stenson walked her to the door. When he returned, Stenson had a goofy grin on his face.

Brick asked, "Did you kiss her?"

With slurred speech, Stenson said, "Heck no! We're just friends!"

"Yeah, right. I wish my friends were that hot. I'm happy when the girls I date have a full set of teeth and fewer tattoos than me."

The next morning, Brick took Stenson and Luna for coffee and beignets. They both had hangovers. Brick asked Luna what she planned to do now that she was done with college.

"Find a job, I guess," Luna said.

"Why don't you get one in New Orleans?" Brick asked.

"I'm not sure Stenson would like that since I made him dance last night."

Stenson laughed. "I'm glad you're still talking to me after seeing that disaster."

Brick said, "You should consider it, Luna. I'd enjoy hanging out with you. You're much better looking than Stenson."

Luna said she would think about it. She didn't want to leave but had a long drive back to her parents' home in Alabama. Brick watched Stenson and Luna hug as they said goodbye.

When Stenson returned to the car, Brick slapped him on the thigh and said, "Now aren't you glad I didn't stab you?"

Stenson gave Brick a shy grin and said, "Yes."

CHAPTER SEVENTEEN

NEW ORLEANS, LOUISIANA

JC woke to the sound of a leaf blower and wondered why landscapers worked so early. Then he noticed the sound was Big Tony snoring. He didn't bother to wake his friend since he looked so peaceful hugging his pillow like it was a teddy bear.

JC plodded into the kitchen and started to make coffee when Zabrina walked in. Her hair was a mess, like she'd been in a tornado, and he could tell she'd had a long night.

Zabrina snatched the coffeepot from JC's hand and said, "Give me that! You need a filter, dummy! Do you want me to choke on the coffee grounds?"

JC laughed. "No, I was thinking it would be more fun choking you with my bare hands, psycho!"

A few minutes later, Zabrina poured a cup of coffee and JC remarked, "Nice hair."

Zabrina flipped her middle finger and stormed out of the room.

Big Tony strolled in and said, "What's all the commotion? It sounded like a bar fight."

"It was me and the wicked witch saying good morning," JC said as he handed his friend a cup of coffee.

Big Tony began cooking breakfast when Zabrina returned after a shower. She gave Tony a kiss on the cheek and sat down.

JC asked, "Why does he get a kiss and you curse me out?"

Zabrina took a sip of coffee. "You figure it out, moron!"

Big Tony chuckled and placed a plate of food in front of Zabrina and then sat down with his own.

JC looked at the empty spot in front of him and asked, "Where's mine?"

Tony pointed to the stove as he filled his mouth with scrambled eggs. JC pouted and got up to make his own plate. Zabrina smiled and winked at Big Tony.

Zabrina told the guys she had mentioned the protection arrangement to her friends. Like Zabrina, many worked alone and didn't feel safe at night. Others had pimps who exploited them. They'd asked Zabrina if Tony and JC could provide the same security for them. Zabrina said she'd told the girls it would them cost 30 percent. She would keep 10 percent and the rest would go to the guys. Tony said he thought 30 percent was high—until Zabrina explained that pimps took 50 percent or more.

Meanwhile, JC was watching a mouse run through the kitchen and then behind the refrigerator, and he missed the conversation.

"What do you think, JC?" Tony asked.

"We need a mousetrap," JC replied.

Zabrina slapped JC on the arm and told him to pay attention. She explained she would run the business, and they would provide security. Everyone agreed it was a good idea, but Tony was hesitant to get involved with prostitution. Zabrina assured him their role would only be as security and management. The cops couldn't touch them if they set it up as a legal company and paid taxes.

It ended up being a rarity when Tony had to deal with situations for the ladies who worked for Zabrina. When he did, his presence alone was enough to settle any disputes with a customer. Tony wasn't the violent type and preferred to resolve things through dialog. But one intoxicated man didn't want to listen to reason. Tony grabbed the naked guy and threw him into a dumpster. They disposed of his clothes and car keys in another trash can a block away. Nobody heard from that guy again until they saw a news story about a naked man who was arrested walking down the highway.

After a few months, Zabrina and the guys were making a considerable amount of money.

Once, JC told Zabrina, "I didn't know prostitution paid so well. Maybe I should be a prostitute."

Zabrina quipped, "I've seen you naked. Believe me, nobody would pay you for that little thing!"

Big Tony laughed and said, "Ouch!"

JC said he was tired of sitting around the apartment playing video games all day. He told Tony and Zabrina he wanted a job. Zabrina asked what he was qualified to do. She mentioned that dumpster companies were not hiring. JC ignored her comment and suggested they open a club. For once, Zabrina thought JC had an intelligent idea—until he said it should be a strip club.

"No, dummy," she said. "Let's open a classy place with good music, expensive drinks, and a great atmosphere. I know my girls would enjoy it ... and where there are beautiful women, there are always men with money."

They began tossing around ideas. The first thing they needed was a suitable location. JC suggested somewhere in the French Quarter, which would cost a fortune. Tony and Zabrina convinced him they should find a place where rent would be affordable. Zabrina reasoned that if they built a nice club, people would find them no matter the location.

They found a warehouse on a big piece of property in an abandoned industrial district, and they figured they could build the club on the opposite end of the property from the warehouse. It would take a lot of work, but everyone believed it had potential. Soon they realized the project would cost more than they expected.

JC asked, "Where are we going to get more money? None of us have any credit. It's not like we can walk into a bank and ask for a loan. What banker will give any money to a prostitute, a runaway, and a guy built like a walrus?"

"Hey, watch it with the walrus comment or I will walrus-smack you upside your head," Tony joked.

"I have an idea how we can get some cash," Zabrina said, then told them how one of her girls dated a biker who had mentioned a drug deal going down in Mexico. Some guys across town had arranged it, and Zabrina thought it would be easy to rip them off.

"So how are we supposed to steal a trailer full of marijuana?" JC asked.

"We hijack the truck at the US-Mexico border," Zabrina said, since she had already formed a plan.

"We *what*? I can't drive a truck and I don't speak Mexican," JC said.

"First, you don't know how to drive a bicycle much less a truck. And second, the language is Spanish, not Mexican, idiot!" Zabrina barked.

Zabrina suggested they bribe a border guard to stop the truck as it crossed into the United States. They would hire their own driver to steal the rig while border patrol was interrogating the real driver. Then their driver would bring the truck back to New Orleans, where they would store it until they could find a buyer.

JC believed it sounded too complicated. "We'll bribe a US border guard like the way you bribed your way into the United States? We all know how well that went."

Big Tony stopped Zabrina from slapping JC's face across the room. Then Tony said, "I see two problems. We don't know any US border patrol officers, nor do we know anyone who can drive a tractor trailer."

Zabrina winked at Tony. "Don't you know the power of female persuasion? A few border officers and truck drivers are friendly with my ladies. I'm sure I can arrange something."

JC and Tony looked at each other. It was a wild idea, but it might work. Zabrina hadn't been wrong so far. In the meantime, they had enough money to continue working on the club. Zabrina put the guys in charge of buying equipment while she went to work on the design. JC and Tony found a restaurant that was going out of business and purchased all their kitchen and bar supplies at a discount. Zabrina decided on a purple motif because it was a royal color and she was also a fan of Prince.

The guys knew nothing about construction. Tony was about to hire someone when a guy walked in the door looking for work. JC could not believe it when he saw it was his friend Jesús Alvarez from Mission of Hope.

It had been ten years since JC and Jesús had seen each other. JC introduced Tony and Zabrina. Jesús told them that Mission of Hope had found a foster home for him with a Hispanic family soon after JC ran away. He had worked in restaurants and construction since high school. Jesús said he moved to New Orleans to rebuild homes destroyed by hurricanes in the Lower Ninth Ward. He recently lost his job and saw the construction materials outside their warehouse. He stopped on a whim to see if they had work. JC realized this was fate, and they offered Jesús the job.

As the place neared completion, they named it Club Empire. When JC told Zabrina he would be king of the empire, she said he should be the court jester instead. Each of the partners assumed different roles. Tony would handle security and host the front door. Zabrina would take charge of hospitality and the back office. JC would manage the bar and music. And they hired Jesús to run the kitchen.

While it wasn't as glamorous as they envisioned because of their budget, they felt the club was ready to open. Besides, after they opened and pulled off the scam on the guys across town, they would have plenty of money to finish the club to its full potential.

Zabrina hired several friends to work as hostesses and bartenders. She chose sexy outfits for the staff that would drive the men crazy. JC convinced the best DJ in New Orleans to play at their club. Tony hired three guys bigger than him to help with security.

Zabrina designed flyers announcing the grand opening. She asked ten of her working girls to hand them out on Bourbon Street. Zabrina told the ladies to only give them to people who looked like they had money. This would be a high-class affair, and she didn't want any losers showing up.

They had done all they could do to get ready for the launch. But everyone was nervous the day of the opening.

"What if nobody shows up?" JC asked.

"Then we spent a lot of money and did a lot of work for nothing," Tony chimed in.

"Relax, guys. The girls told me that many people said they would come," Zabrina reassured.

The opening was scheduled for 8:00 p.m. Tony walked into the office at 7:15 and told Zabrina and JC that people were already gathering outside. Zabrina gave the staff one last pep talk, and everyone assumed their positions. The DJ cranked up the music, and Big Tony unlocked the doors.

Opening night was a huge success. Zabrina estimated that six hundred guests had come through that evening and that they'd grossed more than $90,000. It was not long before Club Empire was the talk of the town and they were rolling in money.

After Empire had been open for a few months, Tony suggested that JC buy a car. He was tired of driving JC everywhere. Tony should have known that it was a terrible idea because the next day JC pulled up in an Audi R8.

Tony shook his head and said, "JC, I drive a ten-year-old Honda and you pull up in this?"

Zabrina walked into the club's office after seeing the car. "See what happens when you get some money, JC? You spend it on stupid things! What are you going to buy next, a tank full of sharks?"

"That's not a bad idea, but it better be a big tank because I need sharks large enough to eat you!"

Big Tony laughed and told JC to watch what he said to Zabrina. He didn't want to come in one day and see little pieces of JC floating in the tank after she threw him in.

Zabrina told the guys everything was set for the Mexican Plan. That was their code name for hijacking the truck full of marijuana. She paid $5,000 to a border patrol officer (who was dating one of her ladies) to stop the truck at the US-Mexico border. Zabrina also found a driver to bring the truck back to their warehouse in New Orleans. She told them the deal would go down the following Saturday.

Then she asked, "What do you guys think about free money?"

"I think I'll use it to buy a tiger cage to put you in!" JC teased.

CHAPTER EIGHTEEN

NEW ORLEANS, LOUISIANA

A few weeks after Luna returned to Alabama, she phoned Stenson to tell him she'd accepted a job in New Orleans. A financial services company had hired her as an IT security analyst. Stenson could not believe she found something so quick. Luna told him it had to be fate, or they just wanted her because she worked cheap.

When Stenson told Brick, he said, "Now you lovebirds can be together."

Stenson tried to convince Brick that he and Luna were only friends. But Brick knew better than Stenson. He had seen the spark, and Stenson was in denial.

Luna moved to New Orleans over the weekend. They met her at her new apartment and helped her unload the car. As she was unpacking items in her kitchen, Luna told the guys she wanted to cook dinner for them sometime. Stenson said she might need a bigger refrigerator because Brick ate like a horse.

Luna started her new job on Monday, and the guys resumed their daily routines. Stenson and Brick went to Luna's for dinner that Saturday night. They saw Luna's apartment was already furnished and decorated when they walked in.

"Where did all this come from?" Stenson asked while

looking at the new furniture. "I didn't know you went to the store this week."

"Haven't you heard of online shopping, Stenson?"

"I can hardly use email and you ask me that? Brick is even worse. He would stab somebody and steal their furniture before he would ever touch a computer."

Brick grinned and agreed.

Luna made veal parmigiana that night and set the table with candles and a bottle of wine. It was a wonderful meal among friends. Brick insisted on doing the dishes so Stenson and Luna could spend time together. Stenson told Luna he would be out of town on business toward the end of the week. He said he was completing a 401(k) plan in Mexico, which puzzled her.

"Why do you have to go to Mexico to set up a 401(k)? Can't you do that online?"

Stenson laughed and said, "Not this kind of 401(k), Luna."

Charlie Whitehorse stopped by the bar the night before Stenson left for Mexico. They went to the office, where Charlie placed a duffle bag with $133,000 on the desk.

Stenson said, "The driver and I will head out in the morning. It may take a few days for them to get it to their buyer. I'll call you to set up a time to give you your cut. We appreciate you helping us put this together."

"No problem, Stenson. I'm happy to do it."

Stenson walked out back with Charlie and put the duffle bag in the trunk of his car. When they returned, Luna had arrived to see Stenson. He introduced her to Charlie Whitehorse. Charlie shook her hand and told Luna she was more beautiful than Stenson described. That made Stenson blush, and he quickly changed the topic. After Charlie left, Luna said he seemed like a nice guy. Stenson told her he might not have many friends, but the ones he had were priceless.

Thursday morning, Stenson met "Chucky" Jones, the biker who would drive the truck. It was 8:00 a.m. when they hit the road. The trip from New Orleans to Juárez, Mexico, would take sixteen hours with a few stops along the way. They planned to return to New Orleans late Saturday.

While they were driving, Stenson asked, "Why do they call you 'Chucky'?"

"My first name is Mickey, and who wants to be a biker with the name of a mouse? A character from a horror movie sounds much better," he said.

Stenson agreed.

They reached the Mexican border around 11:00 p.m. local time. A border guard stopped and questioned them. He seemed suspicious of the long-haired driver and his tattoo-covered passenger. Stenson told the guard they were going to Mexico to do some shopping. He just didn't say what kind.

An hour later, they arrived at the prearranged location. The seller was standing next to the loaded tractor trailer. Stenson and Chucky noticed two men nearby holding machine guns. Stenson wasn't fazed since he had seen a lot of machine guns in Afghanistan. However, Chucky Jones seemed unnerved.

Stenson greeted the seller and asked to inspect the truck. When the guy opened the doors, the odor almost knocked everyone off their feet.

"What is that god-awful smell?" Stenson asked, covering his nose as his eyes began to burn and water.

"We packed the boxes with durian fruit," the seller said.

"Dude, it smells like a fat guy's sweaty jockstrap!"

The drug dealers were smart. Even if they got pulled over, nobody would want to inspect this funky-smelling rig. Stenson handed the money to the man, who counted the cash. Everybody was satisfied, and they concluded their business.

As they walked back to the car, Stenson said to Chucky, "I

hope they wrapped that weed well. Otherwise, your guys will have a hard time selling it."

Chucky climbed into the cab of the truck. When they reached the border, the same guard they'd seen when they entered the country had switched posts and was now in the departure lanes. Stenson watched from three cars back as the guard directed the truck into an inspection lane. He wasn't too concerned and couldn't wait to see the officer's reaction when he opened the trailer doors.

Chucky and the border guard walked to the rear of the trailer. As Chucky and the officer spoke, Stenson saw another person get into the cab. Then, to Stenson's astonishment, the truck pulled away. Chucky tried to run after it, but the officer grabbed his arm.

Stenson pulled up to the checkpoint and Chucky got into the car.

The border officer leaned into Stenson's window and said, "Thank you for visiting Mexico. We appreciate your business, *puta*!"

Stenson looked at Chucky. "What just happened?"

"I don't know! Seems somebody stole our truck from under our nose!" Chucky exclaimed.

Stenson caught up with the tractor trailer. They were determined to not let it out of their sight. They followed it all night and the following day. Neither could believe it was heading back to New Orleans. When they reached the city limits, Stenson hung back a little farther. He didn't want to spook the driver but had to know where they were taking the truck. He watched as the driver backed the trailer into a warehouse in an abandoned industrial area. There was nothing around except some nightclub named Empire.

Stenson would have been prepared to march into the warehouse and get his truck back—if he had a gun. But since he didn't, he would need a different plan. He dropped Chucky off and told him to keep quiet for a few hours before letting anyone know the truck was stolen. It would take some time to figure out who had planned this.

Brick could tell something was wrong when Stenson walked through the door. Stenson was so angry, he threw his car keys hard enough that they almost went through the drywall of the living room. Brick didn't know what to say when he heard the story of the stolen truck. They both found it too bizarre that the truck was now sitting in a warehouse in New Orleans.

Stenson called Luna. "Hey, I need your help. Can you look up an address and tell me who the owner is and any information you can find out about the place?"

Luna called back fifteen minutes later. She said the warehouse was owned by an investment group out of Houston, Texas. But a local company, 21st Entertainment, had leased the building six months ago. The registered agent was a person named Justin Carter from New Orleans. Her research also revealed he was listed as the owner of Club Empire, which was on the same block. Stenson thanked Luna and asked her to stop by after work.

Stenson relayed the information to Brick, who told him the area had been abandoned since Hurricane Katrina. Stenson knew it had to be more than a coincidence the warehouse was next to a new club.

Luna arrived at Brick's house after work. She asked what was going on since Stenson seemed so panicked.

Stenson told her, "Remember that 401(k) plan in Mexico?"

"Yes."

"It's not quite what you think."

Stenson explained the marijuana deal and the theft of the truck. He also admitted he smoked marijuana to relieve his symptoms from PTSD. Stenson asked Luna, "Do you hate me?"

"No, Stenson," Luna said as she reached for Stenson's hand. "That is a crazy story, and I understand why you did it. I'll do whatever I can to help you and your friends get the money back. And as for you smoking pot? I am not as goody-goody as you may think. I smoked it in college with my friends. And if it helps with your post-traumatic stress disorder, I support you all the way."

Brick walked into the living room. Stenson told him Luna would help. She asked what they should do next. Stenson told her to see what more information she could dig up about the guy who owned the club.

Luna was one step ahead of him: "I did more research after we hung up. It appears Justin Carter is connected to an Asian woman named Zabrina Chao. She's been arrested for prostitution several times. After I dug deeper into her past, I found out she's an illegal immigrant from North Korea and her real name is Pok Kyung-wook. Word is she has several girls working for her and is affiliated with Club Empire. It looks like Justin Carter is the front man of the operation. I also ran across another name: Anthony Gallo. I'm not sure what his connection is, but I'll look into it."

Stenson was amazed how much information Luna had uncovered in a short amount of time. He felt certain she'd hacked some databases she shouldn't have seen.

Stenson said, "Let's assume this Justin Carter guy and his people are behind this. How can we get him and my money back without resorting to violence?"

"No violence?" Brick asked.

"No, let's be smarter than him. They were tricky when they stole our truck. Let's be trickier getting it back and maybe have a little fun while we are it."

"What do you have in mind?" Brick asked.

"Have you heard of bullet ants?" Stenson asked. "They say the pain from the sting of one ant is like being shot. Let's break into Justin Carter's place and put some in his underwear drawer!"

"That is wicked hilarious, Stenson! Much better than my idea of shooting the guy," Brick exclaimed.

"The only problem is, where do we find bullet ants and how do we get them inside his place?" Stenson wondered.

"There's a rumor around town about a person they call the Mystery Man," Brick mentioned. "He has a reputation for stealth and will do anything for the right price. But nobody knows what he looks like. I'll ask around to see if anyone knows how to contact him."

"And I'll see what I can do about your ants," Luna offered. "Brick is right: that is a funny way to get the guy back for the trick he pulled on you."

Stenson and Brick drove to the bar. Chucky and Charlie were waiting there when they arrived. They gathered in the office, and Stenson explained the events of the past forty-eight hours. Stenson assured Charlie he would get his money back even if it had to come out of his own pocket. Charlie wasn't worried about the money, and he loved Stenson's plan to get the guy back.

"What I need to figure out is how they knew this was going down," Stenson pondered. "I suspect that prostitute Zabrina has something to do with it. Chucky and Brick, I bet one of your biker friends might have tipped them off—maybe even without knowing it. You guys need to keep quiet until we can figure out where the leak came from."

Chucky and Brick didn't want to believe a biker had betrayed them, but they bet Stenson was right. Luna phoned to say she had found the bullet ants he was looking for. The university she'd attended studied the species. She asked a friend who worked in the department to ship some. Brick made contact with the elusive Mystery Man and set up a meeting.

A few days later, Brick and Stenson waited in the bar after closing time for the Mystery Man to arrive. After an hour, they were about to give up. Stenson shut off the lights, and they headed toward the back door. They jumped when a dark figure appeared in the shadows.

Stenson regained his composure and said, “You must be the ... uh, what’s your name?”

The figure raised his hand like the Grim Reaper, as if to say, “Silence!”

All Stenson could see was a silhouette dressed in a hooded black coat that concealed his face. Stenson asked if the apparition wanted a drink or to sit down. Again, the shadowy figure raised a hand. Stenson realized this person was not much for conversation. Stenson got to the point and explained what they wanted done. When Stenson asked the phantom if he could do it, the shadowy figure nodded yes. Then Stenson asked how much it would cost. The figure raised a hand and spread five fingers. Stenson did not press his luck with a joke about it meaning five dollars or five hundred. So he assumed the spook meant five thousand.

Stenson said he would leave the cash and a jar of ants with an address outside the bar two nights from now. Again, the figure nodded. Stenson looked at Brick. When they turned back around, the ghost was gone. It was like he had vanished into thin air.

Stenson flipped on the light and said, “Man, that was weird. I need a beer!”

Brick felt as spooked as Stenson. “I don’t have enough weed to keep that bogeyman out of my dreams tonight!”

CHAPTER NINETEEN

NEW ORLEANS, LOUISIANA

JC and Tony could not believe how many connections Zabrina had. Members of the New Orleans Saints football team booked the club for a bachelor party. It was the third private event that month.

"Why aren't you dressed?" Zabrina asked JC. "We open in two hours."

"I was at the gym," JC responded.

"Don't lie to me. I saw you playing video games with Big Tony. At least he's wearing his tuxedo. Now go home and get changed!" Zabrina commanded.

JC drove to his apartment and took a shower. He returned to the bedroom wearing a towel around his waist and opened the closet door. He chose a gold lamé jacket, black silk shirt, black pants, and gold tie. The outfit seemed appropriate, considering the Saints team colors were gold and black. Besides, he thought he looked good in gold.

JC opened a drawer and chose a pair of leopard-spotted briefs. As soon as he slipped the shorts on, lightning bolts shot through his groin. It was like somebody had clamped his private parts to an electric fence and shoved a cattle prod up his rear end.

Screaming, JC dropped to his knees. "Oh my God! Oh my

God! Oh Jesus!" He'd never experienced such agonizing pain in his whole life, especially down there!

JC swayed back and forth holding his testicles, causing him to bang his head into the corner of the dresser. Then the pain climbed up his back and down his arms. JC slapped himself all over as the stabbing reached his face. He felt as if he was in front of a firing squad and they were using a million miniature machine guns to shoot him in places you don't want to be shot.

Unable to see since his eyelids were swollen shut, JC stood up and ran around the room, crashing into everything. He knocked over lamps and ripped the blinds from the windows. He grabbed the comforter from his bed and rolled in it like he was on fire. That only made matters worse.

JC crawled to the bathroom, crying like a baby. His testicles, penis, butt, and other body parts were being massacred. He stood up long enough to grab the showerhead and turn on the water. He lay on his back and let the spray wash over him, but the pain would not go away. After more than an hour in the shower, JC turned off the ice-cold water. The hot water had run out long ago, but he didn't have the energy to move. Freezing to death would have been a more peaceful way to die than this.

JC dragged his frozen body back to the bedroom and stood up with help of the dresser he'd banged his head on. He pried one eye open and looked in the mirror. Welts covered his face, chest, and arms. There was also a large knot on his forehead, making him look like a black unicorn. He was too afraid to look down to see the damage to his nether region. Then he noticed the damage to his bedroom. It appeared as if Hurricane Justin Carter had passed through.

JC had to go to the party or Zabrina would kill him. He investigated the open underwear drawer and decided to go commando. He wasn't sure what had happened, but there was no way he would ever trust those underwear again. JC dressed and looked in the mirror. He hoped the club was dark enough that nobody would notice the disaster that used to be his handsome face. As he drove to the club, every little bump shot pain between his legs and caused him to squeak like a rubber toy.

Zabrina was greeting guests when JC walked in. "What happened to your face? Did you get into a fight? And why are you walking funny?"

"Shut up, Zabrina! I am not in the mood for you right now!"

JC made his way to the VIP area with legs spread so wide that he looked like he was auditioning for a part in a Western movie. He attempted to smile when people greeted him. But the smile looked more like the grimace of a madman before he killed you. A waitress asked JC if he wanted his usual drink.

He replied, "Make it a triple and bring me the largest bucket of ice you can find."

Big Tony walked over and said, "You okay, JC? You don't look so well."

"You think?" JC said with an exasperated expression.

Somehow, JC made it through the night.

After the party ended, Zabrina stormed over and yelled at JC, "You didn't do one thing to help me with this event! You sat here like you were king of the world!"

JC would have choked her to death if it didn't involve removing the ice pack from between his legs. He also thought losing one battle a day was enough. JC told Tony and Zabrina what had happened at his apartment.

After the club closed, they went to JC's place to investigate. When they looked inside his underwear drawer, it was still crawling with ants. Tony reached in to pick up a garment, and a single ant stung him on the hand. He jerked his hand out of the drawer, striking Zabrina in the head.

"Sorry, Zabrina, but that hurt!"

"Try putting a hundred of them on your balls!" JC suggested.

Now Zabrina felt sorry for JC and told him she would call an exterminator. She offered to let him stay at her place that night, but JC asked Tony if he could stay with him instead. For all he knew, Zabrina had put the ants in his drawer and might have something more devious planned for him later.

They returned to JC's apartment the next morning to meet the exterminator. The pest control guy told them he had never seen ants like that and he'd had to research what they were. He determined the ants were *Paraponera clavata*, a species also known as "bullet ants." They got the nickname because their potent sting felt like a gunshot. The species inhabited rainforests in Central and South America.

"How did they get here if they're not native to the US?" Zabrina asked.

"That's a good question," the exterminator replied. "You can't import them ... although some universities in the US conduct research with them to study the venom."

"I should donate my balls," JC said. "There's enough venom in them to go on a university tour!"

The exterminator said, "I treated your apartment, Mr. Carter. I recommend replacing your underwear."

"Believe me, the first thing I'll do after you leave is take that drawer outside and set it on fire! Then I'm going shopping for new underwear."

Zabrina wondered how foreign ants had gotten into JC's apartment. Nobody in his building had reported them. And she was sure if there was an infestation of this species in New Orleans, she would have heard about it in the news. JC also had a security alarm, so she was certain nobody could have snuck in and put them there. Something did not seem right. Then

Zabrina wondered if there was a connection to the marijuana shipment they had stolen. It seemed too coincidental that this had happened so soon after that.

When they returned to the club, Zabrina called the girl who had given her the information about the drug deal. The woman told her the guy belonged to a biker gang made up of former US Marines. Zabrina asked her to see what else she could find out. An hour later, the lady called back. She told Zabrina a biker called Brick and some guy named Stenson had arranged the deal, but that was all she knew.

It wasn't much to go on, but the Stenson name was a clue. How many people could there be in New Orleans with that name? She contacted a friend who worked for the police department and asked him to conduct a DMV search on the name. He found one person named Stenson—a Stenson Beckett—in New Orleans and gave her his address and a description of his car.

Zabrina handed Tony the slip of paper with the details and said, "Tony, will you stake out this address? Follow this guy and tell me what he's up to. And look for anyone that appears to be a biker with him."

A few hours later, Big Tony returned to the club. "I saw both guys. One is a long-haired skinny guy, and the other is a mean-looking tattooed guy. I followed them to a bar named O'Malley's on Decatur."

"Watch them for the next few days and find out what their routine is," Zabrina said. "If this is the person who put the ants in JC's apartment, we'll get him back. Two can play this game."

Tony watched Stenson's and Brick's movements for several days. He told Zabrina the Stenson guy worked as a manager at O'Malley's bar. The biker they called Brick was always with him. He also noticed a redheaded woman who visited the bar every evening around 5:30 p.m. and hung out with them.

Tony handed the woman's license plate number to Zabrina.

Later that day, Zabrina asked JC and Tony to come to the office. She told them her friend at the police department had looked up the license plate of the redheaded woman. Her name was Luna Jean LeRoux, and she'd graduated from a university that researched bullet ants. Zabrina confirmed there were only a few institutions in the US that studied them. This had to be more than a coincidence.

During her research, Zabrina also found a news story about Army Specialist Stenson Beckett. The article said he'd saved the life of a US Marine named Robert Brickhouse in a roadside attack in Afghanistan. Zabrina knew the biker gang they'd gotten the information from was made up of ex-Marines. She assumed the Brick guy was Robert Brickhouse.

Since Beckett and Brickhouse were both ex-military and had been in combat, Zabrina wanted to try an experiment. She bet they suffered from PTSD. Zabrina asked Tony to pick up some firecrackers. She told him that when he saw the guys together, he should light the fireworks and throw them on the street nearby. Zabrina wanted to know their reaction.

Tony was laughing when he walked into the office later. He told Zabrina, "That was funny. When the firecrackers exploded, they both dove for cover next to a parked car. Something is definitely wrong with them."

"Perfect!" Zabrina said as she picked up the phone and called JC's security alarm guy. She asked if he could wire a place with sound effects and lighting. It wasn't a normal alarm setup, but he said he could do it and it would take a few days. Zabrina asked him to stop by the club so she could pay him and give him the address.

Stenson and Brick went to Stenson's apartment after the bar closed. When Stenson opened the door, there was an enormous *BOOM!* Brick and Stenson jumped into the bushes.

"What was that?" Stenson yelled.

"I don't know. Did a car backfire?" Brick wondered.

They walked inside and turned on the lights. Suddenly, strobe lights and sounds of automatic gunfire filled the room. Stenson and Brick dove behind the sofa. Brick crouched like he was in combat and flipped off the light. Everything became quiet again.

Stenson yelled, "What the hell is going on?"

Brick looked as confused as Stenson and said, "I don't know, but this is not helping my PTSD."

They sat behind the couch for a minute before Stenson asked if Brick wanted a beer while they figured this out. Stenson walked into the kitchen and opened the refrigerator. There was another loud explosion, and Stenson dove under the kitchen table. This was getting out of hand. He picked up the phone to call Luna, which triggered something close to the apocalypse. Strobe lights and the sounds of sirens, helicopters, machine guns, and bombs flooded the apartment. It was too much for Stenson and Brick, and they ran outside, terrified.

Stenson finally reached Luna from his cell phone. He told her to meet them at a motel and said he'd explain why when she got there. Luna knocked on the motel door awhile later. Brick peeked through the peephole before opening the door. A cloud of pot smoke poured out when he opened it, almost getting Luna high. She found Stenson huddled on the bed, clutching a pillow and rocking back and forth.

Luna was furious after they explained what had happened. She knew this could have only come from one place. Luna didn't know how JC had found out they were responsible for the ants, but it was "Game on!" now.

She said, "Don't worry, guys. We'll get them back. And cheer up, since the bullet ants must have worked."

Luna hired a security company to rewire Stenson's

apartment and change the locks. She told the guys she needed human intelligence about the people they were dealing with. Brick offered to do it, but suggested he kill them instead. Luna told him she had a better plan to get JC back for the stunt he'd pulled at Stenson's place.

She suggested breaking into JC's place and spiking his food with laxatives and ipecac. The guys found the idea hilarious. Brick noted it was messier than stabbing JC and funnier too. Luna asked Brick to get in touch with the Mystery Man and set up another meeting.

Brick said, "I'll get in touch with him, but I hope it goes better than last time. That guy freaked me out!"

Luna asked Stenson to pick up the medications from the pharmacy.

Everyone met at the bar later that afternoon. Brick told Luna he and Stenson would meet the Mystery Man that night. He joked that he would bring a flashlight or night-vision goggles this time.

After the bar closed, Stenson turned off the lights, and again the Mystery Man appeared in the shadows. They were prepared for his entrance but still wondered how he'd gotten inside.

Stenson skipped the formalities and explained the task at hand. When he asked how much it would cost, the Mystery Man held up seven fingers. Stenson figured the Mystery Man knew they'd surely upgraded JC's alarm, so he didn't complain about the elevated price. He placed the bag of medication and money on the floor because he was too afraid to touch the spooky person. Stenson and Brick turned around out of respect, though they were curious to see him leave. They didn't want to spoil the trick since it was like wondering how Santa Claus got up a chimney. Some things were better left to the imagination.

As they walked to the car, Stenson told Brick, "That guy will need to grow more fingers if he keeps raising his fees."

Brick laughed. "Either that or he'll have to show us his toes. By the way, do ghosts have toes?"

The next day, JC returned home from the gym and went to the kitchen to make a smoothie. He grabbed ingredients from the refrigerator and placed them in the blender. He poured the mixture into a large plastic cup and returned to the living room to watch the sports channel.

JC took a long sip of the smoothie and sat on the sofa. A few moments later, his stomach rumbled. At first, he thought it would pass. Then the rumble resembled an earthquake. JC jumped up and tightened his butt, hoping this volcano would not erupt before he made it to the bathroom. He ripped his pants down and almost made it to the toilet when Mount St. Justin Carter exploded. Half-digested smoothie spewed everywhere. It hit the floor, the back of his legs, his pants, and his shoes. He'd had diarrhea before, but never like this.

JC sat on the toilet for several minutes, staring at the disaster until he was sure his stomach had ended its revolt. He was funky, the floor was funky, and his clothes were funky. He stripped and took a shower. JC got on his hands and knees, naked, and scrubbed the floor and toilet. He could not believe the stuff had even splashed onto the vanity. JC gathered the pile of nasty clothes and towels and threw them in the washer. He considered burning them, but the unburned smell was bad enough.

JC put on clean clothes, then walked to the kitchen and opened the fridge. He wasn't sure what spoiled food he'd put in that smoothie, so he threw away the bananas, strawberries, yogurt, and milk. His entire digestive tract was empty, leaving him starving. He removed the leftovers he'd brought from the club the night before. Not long after he finished eating, his stomach gurgled again. This time, it wanted to come out the top of his body. JC did everything in his power to prevent himself from throwing up before he made it to the bathroom. Like before, though, he almost got there in time. His dinner spewed all over the walls, sink, and floor. He held his head over the toilet and vomited so much that he was convinced the next thing to come up would be his guts. JC remained over the toilet for several minutes, praying there wouldn't be more.

He stood up and saw that the bathroom was an even bigger disaster than before. JC shook his head in disgust when he saw a piece of undigested lettuce sticking to the wall. He ripped off the second ruined outfit and took another shower. He got more cleaning supplies and went back to work, doing more naked bathroom scrubbing. The chunky mess and putrid smell made him want to vomit again.

JC wondered if he had a virus. He needed to eat something that would be safe on his stomach. He grabbed a box of crackers from the cabinet and returned to the living room. After a few bites, his stomach churned again. He was not taking a chance this time and ran like Usain Bolt to the restroom.

After he brushed his teeth and cleaned the toilet for the third time, JC returned to the kitchen. He did not trust any food in his apartment and threw everything away. JC emptied the refrigerator, pantry, and cabinets, then looked at the blender. He didn't trust it either and tossed it into the trash bin. He noticed a note stuck to the bottom of the upside-down blender, which read, *"Love, Stenson and Co."*

JC screamed, "That son of a bitch!"

CHAPTER TWENTY

NEW ORLEANS, LOUISIANA

JC stormed into the office at Club Empire and slammed the door behind him. Zabrina and Tony looked at him like he'd lost his mind. JC shoved the note he'd found on the bottom of his blender at Zabrina. He told them in excruciating detail about the tainted food at his apartment. After Zabrina and Tony stopped laughing, Zabrina suggested he buy a gun. JC said he was planning on it, considering how things were escalating. He told them he was ready to go on a shooting spree against Stenson and friends. But before he could go to the gun store, he needed something to eat that didn't come from his apartment.

Tony walked with JC to the kitchen, where he asked Jesús to prepare a plate of spaghetti. Jesús brought it out awhile later and set it on the table.

JC looked at Big Tony and said, "You try it."

"Me?" Big Tony asked. He didn't want to eat anything after hearing what JC had been through with food. But Tony could tell he didn't have a choice from the look on JC's face. He picked up the plate and hesitated before taking a tiny bite.

JC watched, convinced something would happen. Tony took a bigger bite, and again nothing happened.

Tony said, "This is good." Then he spooled up a large

forkful of the spaghetti and shoved it in his mouth.

JC snatched the plate from Tony's hand. "I said try it, not eat the entire plate!"

Tony slurped a strand of spaghetti still hanging from his chin and smiled.

JC drove to a nearby gun shop. He didn't have a clue about guns, since he'd never shot one before. He noticed a guy resembling Kid Rock's twin brother standing at the counter, looking at handguns.

JC walked over and stood next to him. He said, "What's up?"

The long-haired guy ignored him and asked to see a small revolver.

JC stared at the different guns in the case and asked the clerk about a small semiautomatic pistol. Acting like he knew something about guns, JC asked the long-haired guy, "Why are you looking at revolvers?"

"I like the classics," the guy said, clearly annoyed by the question.

"Give me something modern," JC said. "If I'm in a firefight, I can kill people faster than that little thing you're holding."

The man ignored the comment and asked to see a larger revolver. When JC saw the size of the next gun the guy selected, he asked the clerk to see a bigger semiautomatic.

"Why don't you stand over there?" the annoyed man asked as he pointed to the other end of the counter. "You're crowding me."

"Do you know who I am?" JC asked.

"I don't care, bozo. You're getting on my nerves." Then the man asked to look at a .357 Magnum revolver.

Seeing the bigger gun, JC asked the clerk to show him the biggest semiautomatic pistol in the case. It was the last straw for the long-haired man. He told the clerk to let him see a double-barreled shotgun on the wall. JC then asked to see an AR-15 semiautomatic rifle that resembled a military M16.

JC said, "I own a club called Empire and run a gang."

The man paused. "What's your name?"

"JC, and don't forget it."

"Well, my friend, do you know who I am?"

"A redneck hillbilly?" JC replied.

Stenson pointed the shotgun at JC. "No, I'm the guy whose weed you stole! My name is Stenson Beckett!"

JC looked surprised and aimed the AR-15 at Stenson. The clerk didn't know what to do. He had a standoff like the OK Corral in the middle of his gun shop.

"Thanks for the weed. How's your PTSD?"

"Better than your balls after I put those bullet ants in your underwear drawer. How's your digestive system?"

"You son of a bitch!" JC yelled as he pulled the trigger.

Click!

Nothing happened.

The clerk said, "Guys, the weapons aren't loaded."

JC shoved the gun back in the clerk's hands and, as he was leaving, yelled, "I'll get you back! Just wait!"

Stenson smiled and handed the shotgun to the clerk. "I'll take the .357 Magnum and a box of shells."

JC was fuming when he returned to the club. Zabrina asked if he'd bought a gun. JC looked at the floor like a disappointed child who didn't get what he wanted for Christmas and said no. Then he told her he'd run into Stenson Beckett at the gun store. When she asked why he hadn't killed him, JC told her the guns weren't loaded. She reminded him the store also sold bullets. Big Tony felt sorry for JC and gave him his gun.

Zabrina told JC that while he was out not buying a gun, she'd come up with a plan for Stenson. She discovered a new high-powered estrogen being tested to help women grow breasts.

She didn't see any reason the drug wouldn't work on men. Since Stenson and his crew had spiked JC's food, they would do the same to Stenson with the estrogen. She believed she could find the drug but wondered how to get inside Stenson's place.

Tony didn't believe Stenson had ever seen him. He suggested he could pose as a pest control technician needing to spray his apartment. When Stenson wasn't looking, he would contaminate the food with the estrogen. Zabrina liked the idea and said she would locate the drug. Tony left to find a pest control uniform and supplies. JC told him he was going to a gun range to practice shooting in case this plan didn't work out.

A few days later, there was a knock at Stenson's door. A heavyset pest control technician said he needed to spray the apartment. Stenson allowed him to come inside and then returned to the sofa to watch TV. Tony walked around the kitchen until he saw Stenson was distracted. He opened the refrigerator and sprayed the chemical inside several containers of food. A few minutes later, he apologized for the interruption and left the apartment. Stenson was hungry and decided to eat the Chinese takeout leftovers from the night before. He noticed the fried rice had an off taste but ate it anyway. Having been homeless, Stenson never let food go to waste.

One morning, Stenson was standing in front of the mirror, staring at his chest. Something didn't look right. His breasts were swollen, like a pubescent girl's, and they were tender to the touch. Should he go on a diet? he wondered.

The next week, people at the bar began to notice. Drunk people were always too honest. Brick and Luna wondered what was going on with Stenson's body but said nothing. Even his voice sounded a pitch higher than normal. By the third week, Stenson's chest was too big to hide. He stopped going to work to avoid the ridicule.

A week later, Stenson's breasts were size DD and he was forced to wear a bra. His back was killing him, and he had a lot more respect for busty women. He'd only had boobs for a month and couldn't imagine carrying them around for a lifetime.

Luna came over and asked Stenson if he was okay. He admitted he was not feeling like himself. He mentioned he'd been watching romantic movies and crying a lot. Luna asked Stenson to take off his shirt.

When he did, Luna exclaimed, "Oh my God, Stenson. Your boobs are bigger than mine! What have you been eating?"

Stenson told her he ate the same as always and didn't understand what was happening to his body. Luna insisted he see a doctor. Upon examination, the physician suspected Stenson suffered from gynecomastia—an imbalance of the two hormones, estrogen and testosterone. The doctor ordered tests to confirm his suspicions.

Stenson's test results were off the chart. They revealed he had enough estrogen in his body for three adult women. Another test identified a high-powered form of estrogen only available in clinical trials. The real question was: How had Stenson been exposed to the drug?

Follow-up tests showed Stenson's estrogen levels were dropping. The doctor believed his hormone levels would return to normal in time. Luna asked if his breasts would go away. The doctor expected they would gradually lose their firmness. But the excess skin and enlarged areolas would remain.

"He'll be stuck with flabby titties?" Luna asked.

"Unfortunately, yes. But reconstruction is an option."

"You mean to tell me my friend needs a boob job?"

The doctor could not hide his laughter. "Technically, it is a mastectomy. But, yes, he will need a boob job if he wants to get them back to something closer to normal."

"Oh great!" Stenson said, shaking his head.

Luna's mind was spinning as they drove home. She wondered how Stenson had been exposed to estrogen only available through clinical trials. It wasn't like someone could get it at a pharmacy. She asked Stenson to retrace the days leading up to the first time he noticed changes to his body.

It had been more than a month ago, but as far as Stenson could remember, he'd done nothing out of the ordinary. He said it was around the time the pest control technician had sprayed his apartment for the second time. He told her that was the only thing unusual, since they had sprayed his apartment a week before.

"They sprayed your place twice in barely a week? Was it the same person?" Luna asked.

"No, the first guy had been to my place before. But the second guy was a big fellow I've never seen."

A light bulb went off in Luna's head and she called Brick. "Do me a favor. I need you to stake out that Club Empire. Photograph the people who run the place. I'll explain later."

Brick returned to Stenson's apartment that afternoon. He took out his cell phone and scrolled through photos he had taken outside of Club Empire. The first photo was of a black guy wearing a track suit. Stenson told him that was JC, the guy he'd run into at the gun store. The second photo was of an Asian woman who Luna assumed to be Zabrina.

When Brick showed the third photo of a heavyset guy unloading a car, Stenson exclaimed, "That's him! That's the guy who sprayed my apartment!"

It all made sense. Luna knew Zabrina had to be the one who'd come up with the estrogen idea. How Luna would get her back, she did not know. For now, her concern was for Stenson. She helped him find a surgeon and accompanied him to the consultation. They scheduled the surgery for the following week.

Stenson looked scared, lying in the hospital bed before surgery. A nurse entered the room and administered a drug to sedate him. Luna leaned over and kissed Stenson's cheek and assured him everything would be okay. She sighed and said a silent prayer as they wheeled her friend to surgery.

A few hours later, a nurse arrived in the waiting room to tell Luna Stenson was in recovery. She could visit him as he awakened from anesthesia. Luna's heart melted when she saw Stenson in the recovery room. He appeared to be in and out of consciousness.

She leaned down and said, "Hi, how do you feel?"

He mumbled in a drunken slur, "I feel great. Wow, you are so beautiful."

She could tell Stenson did not know where he was because he never talked like that.

Then Stenson said, "I love you."

Now Luna knew he was out of his mind. She caressed his cheek as he fell asleep again. Luna wished Stenson would say those words when he actually knew what he was saying. But she didn't mind hearing it even if it was under the influence of anesthesia.

Luna drove Stenson home after he recovered. He was sore and had bandages wrapped around his chest. Stenson still wore the hospital gown when Luna helped him into bed. She teased him when he bent over, telling him she could see his butt. Stenson tried to laugh, but it hurt too much.

Brick came by to check on Stenson. Luna was so angry that Brick thought he saw steam coming from her ears.

She said, "I'm furious they did this to him!"

"I am too, Luna. What should we do about it?"

"Let's hit them where it hurts the most: their money. But before we do that, I have a little plan for that Zabrina chick. She likes her beauty so much? We'll see about that."

Luna told Brick to get ahold of the Mystery Man. But this time she would meet him. He set up the meeting for later that night. Brick and Luna drove to the bar and waited until it closed. Brick turned off the lights and, sure enough, the Mystery Man appeared in the dark hallway.

Luna said, "Hey Mystery Guy, I'm Luna. You might have heard what some clowns did to my friend Stenson. Here is some hair remover. I need you to pour this entire bottle in that Asian chick's shampoo. There are a few more items in the bag I need you to replace. I don't know where she lives or how you'll get it in there, but with your reputation, I'm sure you can figure it out. Money is no object. How much will it cost?"

The Mystery Man held up a hand with fingers curled into a zero.

"Thank you! We'll catch you next time."

The Mystery Man turned and walked out the back door. Brick was flabbergasted. He and Stenson were terrified of the guy, but Luna commanded the ghost like she owned him. Brick would have to tell Stenson the Mystery Man walked out the door like normal people. It was kind of disappointing that he didn't vaporize through walls as they'd imagined.

Two days later, Zabrina brushed her long black hair after a shower. Suddenly, a thick chunk pulled away from her scalp. She attempted to comb over the spot, but another piece fell. It wasn't long before there were missing patches all over her head and she had a sink full of hair. Zabrina looked like she'd walked out of Chernobyl. The upset Asian knew right away who was responsible for this.

She found a scarf and wrapped it around her head, then

returned to put on makeup. When she applied mascara to her left eye, it immediately glued shut. Zabrina tried to peel it apart or wash it loose, but the eye remained unapologetically sealed. Using her one good eye, she determined that the mascara contained superglue. Zabrina's blood boiled with every passing second. She picked up a tube of lipstick and swiped it across her mouth. There was an unusual tingling sensation. Within a few moments, her lips puffed up like two balloons on a horny baboon's rear end.

Zabrina smashed the lipstick into the mirror and screamed, "I am going to kill Luna LeRoux!"

Stenson told Brick, "Call your tattoo guy."

"You're getting a tattoo?" the muscled ex-Marine asked.

"Kind of," Stenson replied with a suspicious grin.

Robert Brickhouse did not know where this was going, but picked up the phone and called the guy who had done his tattoos. "What do you want me to tell him?"

"Tell him there will be a special tattoo session tonight!"

Stenson left the bar and drove to the French Quarter. He looked for a lady he'd met before—the hottest girl in New Orleans. When he found her, he said, "I need a favor. There is this guy ..." Stenson handed her $500 in cash after he explained what he needed. She loved the idea because she couldn't stand that guy either, after they'd kicked her and her friends out of Club Empire one night.

Stenson drove back to the bar and revealed his plan to Brick. Later, they rolled to Empire and waited across the street in the dark.

JC stumbled out of the club arm in arm with the girl

Stenson had hired. JC was more than drunk, thanks to the flunitrazepam she'd slipped in his drink. Stenson and Brick watched JC wobble to his car and fumble with his keys. He managed to get the door open and sit inside. That was all it took before JC slumped over and passed out, with his head against the steering wheel.

Stenson pulled alongside JC's car with his headlights turned off. Brick got out and grabbed the man, stuffing his ragdoll-limp body into Stenson's back seat.

Two hours later, they returned JC to his apartment. The Mystery Man had given them a key, which was easier than kicking the door down, and they hauled Mr. Unconscious to the sofa.

The next morning, JC woke up with a pounding headache. He wasn't sure what he drank at the club the night before, but he'd never had a hangover like this. He managed to slide from the couch and bumble his way to the bathroom. He flipped on the light and looked in the mirror to see the disaster once called his face. Through blurry eyes, he noticed his forehead. JC looked twice, not believing what he was seeing. Somebody had written *"RESOL"* on his head in magic marker. He wet his finger and attempted to rub it off. It wasn't going away. He rubbed again. Nothing.

Suddenly, he realized it wasn't a magic marker. It was a tattoo! And what was *"RESOL"*? This was too much for JC to handle with his banging headache. He walked outside to check the mail and ran into a neighbor who asked why he had *"LOSER"* written across his forehead.

The light bulb went off in JC's rumbling mind. He yelled so loud that God could hear it: "Stenson!"

Zabrina walked into the club wearing a head scarf and dark sunglasses. When JC saw her, he said, "Hey, gypsy! You telling fortunes now?" Then he noticed her bulbous lips and asked what kind of messed-up cosmetic procedure she'd done.

Miss Bubble Lips was not in the mood for JC's jokes. With her one good eye, she noticed the do-rag JC wore on his head, which came down to slightly above his eyebrows. With the same sarcasm, she asked, "What are you, a wannabe gangster now?"

Before JC could react, she grabbed the rag and ripped it from his head. It revealed that JC had added some writing in magic marker over the tattoo on his forehead: *"Ain't No LOSER."*

Zabrina howled with laughter while Big Tony couldn't contain himself. When they all calmed down, Zabrina removed her scarf and sunglasses to show the guys how Luna had messed her up. They were more determined than ever to get Stenson and his crew back for this disaster.

CHAPTER TWENTY-ONE

NEW ORLEANS, LOUISIANA / MONROE COUNTY, ALABAMA

Attorney Mark Pruitt walked into O'Malley's bar and asked for Stenson Beckett. The attorney introduced himself and asked if there is a place they could speak in private. When they reached the office, Mark Pruitt handed Stenson a binder. Stenson sat down and opened it. He paused when he saw that it contained the last will and testament of Lucius T. Haggerty.

Stenson had not seen Haggerty since the day he'd fled his land so many years ago. That memory would forever be burned in his mind. It was the day the old man had shot and killed the hunters who tried to attack Stenson. His heart felt a piece missing, knowing his dear friend had passed away. Stenson read the handwritten document: *"I, Lucius T. Haggerty, leave my land, home, and worldly possessions to Stenson Beckett, a fine young man. I know he will do good things with it. Lucius T. Haggerty."* Stenson touched the old man's scribbled signature and looked up at the attorney.

Mark said that shortly after Stenson had left Haggerty's land, the old man called and asked him to come over. Haggerty discussed his final wishes with his attorney. Mark told Stenson he had witnessed Lucius sign the document, leaving everything to him.

The attorney said, "He liked you, Stenson. Lucius shared

fond stories of you two fishing and hunting. He said you reminded him of his own son he'd lost years ago. I knew him for a long time and never saw such a sparkle in his eyes as the day he handed me this document. You touched him in a special way." Mark rose from his chair and shook Stenson's hand. "Congratulations, Mr. Beckett."

Stenson thanked the attorney and returned to his desk. He was filled with an overwhelming sense of loss. Stenson missed the old man and his funny stories. It made him sad to think he would never see him again. Haggerty had been like a grandfather to him, and an important person in his life. He often wondered where he'd be if he had not stumbled onto the old man's land. Seeing his handwriting made him feel as if Haggerty was standing next to him.

Stenson closed the binder and said, "Rest in peace, my friend."

That evening, Stenson told Luna and Brick he would be out of town for a few days on business. He loaded his car early the next morning for the long drive to Alabama. Stenson lowered the top of the convertible and popped in an eight-track tape. He never bothered putting a modern stereo in the car because he liked the classics. Stenson fired the engine and cranked up the volume. The first few bars of "Sweet Home Alabama" by Lynyrd Skynyrd played as he headed down the road.

Five hours later, Stenson pulled down a long dirt road leading to Haggerty's home. He smiled as he drove past the many *"No Trespassing"* signs and imagined the old man with his shotgun. He laughed looking up to the sky and yelled, "Don't shoot! I come in peace!"

He parked the car in front of the old man's house. The creaking steps made a sound that was all too familiar. Stenson opened the screen door and placed the key in the lock. Haggerty's place smelled and looked exactly as he remembered. It was as if the old man would walk into the room at any moment saying, "You hungry, boy?" Stenson sat at the kitchen table, remembering all the meals he shared with Haggerty. He smiled, recalling the time Haggerty had made venison stew. He'd told Stenson, "This will put some meat on your skinny bones!"

Stenson walked around the house, wondering what to do with it. It was in good shape, even though it needed a little work. He was gathering a few sentimental items to keep for himself when he noticed Haggerty's photo album. Stenson sat on the sofa, flipping through the pages. Haggerty had shared many stories with Stenson when they looked at those pictures together so long ago. They were memories of a happier time in the old man's life. Stenson picked up Haggerty's family Bible next. It contained the history of the Haggerty family for generations past. Haggerty never went to church, but Stenson always knew he had a faithful heart.

When Stenson looked at the fireplace mantel, he could not believe his eyes. A silver frame held a photograph of Haggerty and Stenson himself when he was a little boy. They were both grinning in the photo as they stood next to the stream, holding fishing poles. Stenson remembered the day they took it. Haggerty discovered a man wandering through the woods and threatened to shoot him. The startled man said he worked for a hunting and fishing magazine. He was photographing wildlife for an upcoming story and did not realize he was on private land. He showed Haggerty pictures he had taken of deer and turkeys on his land. The photographer asked Haggerty if he could take a photo of him and the boy. The man must have given Haggerty the photo later.

Stenson noticed Haggerty's shotgun hanging on the wall over the fireplace. It was the same gun that had saved his life. He pulled the gun from its rack and felt the cold steel of the barrel in his hands. Haggerty had only ever used the gun to scare people, except for that fateful day. Stenson never knew where Haggerty buried the bodies. But he was sure they were out there somewhere.

He gathered the items he'd collected and placed them in the trunk of his car. Stenson drove to the general store where Haggerty used to buy supplies. The owner didn't recognize Stenson when he walked in the door. Stenson reminded him that he was the little boy who'd stolen calamine lotion years ago. The owner smiled, recalling the funny story. He asked Stenson how he had been. Stenson said he was doing well and had returned to handle Mr. Haggerty's estate.

"Can't say many people in this town will miss that cranky bastard," the clerk remarked.

Stenson didn't acknowledge the remark, nor did he feel the need to defend his dead friend's reputation. He asked the owner if he knew anyone in town who did construction. The clerk mentioned a man named Marty Smith and wrote his phone number on a piece of paper. Stenson then asked about the smallest church in town.

"There's an old nigger church down the road," the clerk said.

Stenson couldn't believe what he heard. "Did you just say 'nigger church'? Why didn't you say 'a church down the road'? Do you know what century this is?"

The owner ignored the question since Stenson looked like a liberal. Nonetheless, he gave him directions. Stenson walked out the door, shaking his head and not believing how racist some people were. He called the contractor and asked to him come by Mr. Haggerty's place in the morning to discuss a project.

Stenson found the church a few miles outside of town. It was a tiny white building that appeared to be at least a century old. He walked inside and saw a man standing at the pulpit. Stenson said hello, causing the man to look up from his reading. The older black gentleman seemed confused to see a white guy standing in his church. Stenson introduced himself, and the man said his name was Pastor Samuel L. Jackson as the two shook hands.

Stenson could not resist asking, "Samuel L. Jackson, like the actor?"

The pastor laughed. "He is Samuel Leroy Jackson, the rich one who curses a lot. I am Samuel Lamont Jackson, the poor one who prays for people who curse a lot."

Stenson told the pastor he was in town to attend to the affairs of Mr. Lucius T. Haggerty, who had recently passed away. He also was curious about the history of the church. Pastor Jackson told him it was built in 1810, long before the abolishment of slavery. It served as the only black Baptist church within twenty miles. He had a large congregation, and with the church being so small, he held four services every Sunday. When Stenson asked why they didn't build a bigger church, the pastor said everyone was poor and they couldn't afford to build a bigger one.

"What if I build you a new one?" Stenson asked.

That was not a question Pastor Jackson had expected from the lost-in-the-'70s-looking guy. He said, "No offense, Mr. Beckett, but you don't look like you can afford new clothes, much less a church."

Stenson chuckled and told the pastor he'd be surprised. He wrote directions to Haggerty's place and handed it to the pastor. "Stop by in the morning and we can talk more."

Pastor Jackson walked with Stenson to the parking lot. When he saw Stenson's Cadillac, the pastor said, "Nice car. That is a 1957. I had one just like it when they were new."

Stenson returned to Haggerty's house and grabbed his

backpack from the trunk of the car. He wandered through the woods until he found the spot where he'd camped as a little boy. He laid the backpack down and headed to the stream. Stenson stared at the water, recalling fond memories of this place. He felt as if he was standing here only yesterday.

Like he had done many times before, Stenson gathered materials from the forest to build a shelter. He could have stayed in Haggerty's house, but camping here made him feel closer to God and the old man. He grabbed his fishing pole and cast his line into the water. Before long, there was a tug and he reeled in a large bass. Stenson took it back to the campsite and prepared the fish as Haggerty had taught him.

Stenson woke the next morning feeling more refreshed than he had in a long time. The air was crisp as he wiggled out of the sleeping bag. The dawn light peeking through the trees made the forest look like a beautiful painting. He wished he could save this moment for times when he felt down. Stenson grabbed his backpack and headed back to the house.

The attorney had given Stenson a map of Haggerty's property. He'd known that Haggerty owned a lot of land, but never knew how much because woods covered most of it. He walked around the perimeter using landmarks identified on the map. In two hours, Stenson covered little of the 600 acres.

A car horn sounded in front of the house. Stenson returned to find the contractor, Marty Smith, sitting in his truck. The men exchanged introductions and Stenson invited him inside. Stenson told Marty he wanted to discuss renovating Haggerty's home. Marty inspected the house and noted the construction was solid. He suggested replacing the wiring and plumbing since the house had been built in 1932. It also needed a new roof and paint. Stenson asked Marty to include updating the kitchen and expanding the tiny bathroom.

The men were assessing at the exterior of the house when

Pastor Jackson arrived. Stenson introduced Marty and the pastor to each other, then unrolled the property map on the hood of Marty's truck. Stenson told the men he'd inherited the house and property from the estate of Lucius T. Haggerty. Haggerty's attorney had informed him a manufacturing company made an offer to buy 450 acres of the land. Stenson intended to complete the sale since it would bring new jobs to the community. He had other plans for the remaining 150 acres and house, which was the reason he'd invited both men to this meeting.

Stenson shared his story of the death of his mother and the reason he'd run away. He told the men that he'd grown up on this land and formed a special bond with Lucius Haggerty. Stenson described a life of homelessness and how the charity of a church had kept him alive in both spirit and food. Stenson told Pastor Jackson it would be his honor to build his congregation a new church. It was his way of repaying the charity shown to him.

Pastor Jackson realized Stenson was serious. "I don't know what to say, Stenson."

Stenson smiled and replied, "What you can say is that you will accept my offer and tell Marty and me how big a church you need." Stenson looked at Marty. "That is, if Marty will build it."

Marty exclaimed, "It would be my honor to work with the pastor to build a new church."

Stenson revealed the rest of his plans. He wanted to donate Haggerty's restored house to the community. It was to serve as a temporary shelter for anyone in need. Stenson took out a black marker and drew outlines on the property map. He told Pastor Jackson he was also giving his church fifteen acres for the new church and a cemetery. The remaining 135 acres would be a campground for boys and girls.

"What do you think?" Stenson asked the men.

"I think you are a gift from God," Pastor Jackson replied.

Marty said, "Stenson, it is amazing what you are doing for this town."

"Mr. Haggerty is responsible, and I'm following his wishes. He stated in his will that he knew I would do something good with it. I hope he'll be proud of what I've set in motion." Stenson then made a request: "The only thing I ask is you don't make this about me. I would prefer to remain anonymous. Mr. Haggerty was misunderstood by many in this town. People thought he was a mean old man and never got to know him. Please spread the word it was Lucius T. Haggerty who made this possible."

Stenson pulled out a sheet of paper and drew up a brief contract for the construction and handed it to Marty. All three men signed the document. Stenson reached into a bag and handed Marty $30,000 in cash to get started. He said he would send more once the sale of the land was complete.

Stenson said, "Well, gentlemen, I believe that concludes our business."

As he headed back to New Orleans, Stenson looked to the sky and said, "It's been a great day, Haggerty!"

CHAPTER TWENTY-TWO

NEW ORLEANS, LOUISIANA

Zabrina's stylist greeted her when she arrived at the salon. Soni—a tall, black, transgender woman—realized early in her life that she was a woman trapped inside a man's body. That was when she changed the spelling of her name from Sonny to Soni to sound more feminine. Zabrina adored Soni and considered her one of her closest friends. She often teased Soni about being more attractive than her.

Soni was in shock at Zabrina's appearance. Her once beautiful long black hair was now a patchwork of missing pieces. Soni asked if a three-year-old had cut her hair or if she was part of an art project gone wrong. Then Soni wondered what had happened to her lips, which were three times their normal size. Zabrina removed her sunglasses and showed Soni her glued left eye and explained the whole story about Stenson Beckett and Luna LeRoux. Zabrina told her about the ongoing battle she and JC had with a group across town. When Zabrina told her that she'd spiked the guy's food with estrogen and he grew man-boobs, Soni found it hilarious and said what they did to her was a small price to pay for that incredible stunt. Then Soni asked where she could get some of that estrogen.

There was nothing Soni could do but shave the rest of

Zabrina's hair. The Asian woman wanted to cry when she saw her bald head in the mirror. Now she knew how cancer patients must feel. Soni cheered her up by taking Zabrina to her favorite wig shop. The girls spent the afternoon trying on different wigs. Zabrina chose three in fluorescent pink, purple, and blue. She also bought a short wig in her natural hair color for occasions when she wanted to appear "normal." Soni joked that she looked like a librarian when she wore that one.

Tony and JC were in the office watching the news. A story aired about a group providing Thanksgiving dinners to the homeless. JC could not believe his eyes when he saw the reporter interviewing Stenson Beckett. Stenson's talk about giving back to the community made JC sick. He reached into the desk drawer and pulled out the gun Tony had given him and shot the TV.

Big Tony jumped and looked at JC like he'd lost his mind.

JC screamed, "That son of a bitch Stenson thinks he'll help the homeless? I'll show him! He's giving away a hundred turkeys? Tony, I want you to buy us a thousand turkeys!"

"A thousand turkeys? Don't you think that's too many?" Tony asked, making sure he heard his friend correctly.

"I am ten times better than he is, so I want ten times the birds! And while you're out, pick us up a new TV!"

Zabrina walked through the door wearing a bright blue wig. Tony liked her new style, but JC sarcastically said she looked like an alien—and not the illegal kind. Tony excused himself before the blue-haired alien slapped JC to another planet.

Zabrina noticed the television with a bullet hole in the screen. She asked JC if her assassin had missed killing him. He disregarded the remark and told her about the Thanksgiving story he had seen. He said he would show Stenson by giving away more turkeys than he did. He told her the news coverage would be great for the club. Besides, he looked better on television than that hillbilly. JC asked Zabrina to create a press release and send it to all the media outlets. She knew it was a crazy idea but wasn't in the mood to argue with JC and agreed to do it.

A few hours later, Tony returned to the club dragging a large TV box into the office. He told JC he had to rent a refrigerated tractor trailer. Then he had to drive to fifteen different grocery stores to buy every turkey they had.

JC walked outside with Tony to where the trailer was parked in front of the club. Tony opened the trailer doors to reveal a mountain of frozen poultry.

Seeing that many turkeys made JC wonder if he might have overthought this. Then he asked Tony how much it had cost. Tony guessed he spent about $20,000 for the turkeys and the truck rental. JC shrugged and said the press coverage and appearing more generous than Stenson Beckett would be worth it.

Zabrina walked out with the press release. She looked at the truck full of turkeys and asked JC, "Are you crazy?"

"Relax, Zabrina. I got this. You'll see. We'll get so much great publicity from this and the community will love us!"

Thanksgiving morning, JC woke up in a great mood. He could not wait to get back at Stenson. He expected to see people lined around the block when he met Zabrina and Big Tony at the club. But the parking lot was empty except for their cars and the tractor trailer full of turkeys. JC walked inside and found Zabrina and Tony sitting at the bar. He asked Zabrina what time the media would arrive.

"They won't," Zabrina flatly replied.

"They what?"

"They aren't coming, JC. They said Stenson had a more personal story, so they're at his event."

"Oh hell no! Where are all the people?"

"We only sent press releases and didn't spread the word to the community. And we are in the middle of an abandoned industrial district if you didn't realize. Even the homeless people don't hang out here," Zabrina surmised.

"I have a thousand turkeys sitting in a truck outside. You mean to tell me nobody is coming here to pick them up and we have no media coverage?"

"That sums it up," Zabrina replied.

"I'll fix this. You ever hear of social media? Zabrina, film this on your cell phone while Tony and I give away turkeys. This will go viral!"

JC climbed into the cab of the truck with Big Tony driving. He told Zabrina to follow them to Bourbon Street. They passed O'Malley's bar on the way and saw a line of people receiving free Thanksgiving meals and people doing interviews with the media. Stenson looked up to see JC flipping him a middle finger as their truck drove by. Stenson shook his head and handed out another box of food.

JC told Tony to park in front of Pat O'Brien's. They got out of the truck while Big Tony opened the rear doors of the trailer. A police officer soon pulled up and told JC they couldn't park there.

"We're giving away free turkeys for Thanksgiving. You want one?" JC asked the officer.

"I don't care if you're giving away Fort Knox. You can't park that truck here."

"Where's your holiday spirit?" JC asked.

"It's at home waiting on me to finish this shift. Now move it!"

"Fine, asshole."

"What did you say?" the officer demanded.

"I said, watch out for that hole," JC muttered as he walked back to the truck.

Tony shut the trailer doors. JC suggested they drive through poor neighborhoods and give away the turkeys. He asked Zabrina if she had filmed the cop. He wanted that ungrateful officer on YouTube. She said she got it.

They drove around the Lower Ninth Ward, stopping along the way to give a turkey to anybody they found on the street. When JC handed a turkey to a homeless man, he asked, "How am I supposed to cook this? I don't have an oven."

"I don't care. Build a fire in a barrel," JC said as he shoved the turkey in the man's chest.

The homeless man threw the turkey at JC and walked away while cursing him. JC picked up the turkey and put it back in the truck.

At the next stop, JC handed a person a turkey and said, "Happy Thanksgiving on behalf of Club Empire!"

The person said, "I'm a vegetarian," and handed the turkey back to JC.

JC shoved the turkey back and said, "Not today!"

It was late when they returned to the club. JC asked Big Tony how many turkeys they'd given away. Tony said technically they gave away five. But it was four if they didn't count the one the guy threw in a ditch.

"Dammit! What am I going to do with 995 turkeys?"

"It was your bright idea to get a thousand turkeys, dummy. You figure it out," Zabrina smarted.

"I don't need this right now. Go edit the video you took today and see if we can salvage something positive out of this. Tony and I will figure out what to do with the rest of these turkeys."

"Me?" Tony asked.

"Yeah, you. I can't keep paying $1,500 a day for this truck. We need to move these birds to the kitchen cooler."

After they unloaded the 995 frozen turkeys, JC sat at the bar eating a turkey sandwich. He scribbled notes on several napkins while he ate.

Afterward, he walked into the office and handed the napkins to Zabrina. "I need you to print this."

"What is it?" Zabrina asked.

"It's our new menu," JC replied.

Zabrina looked at the notes. "You must be kidding. Let's see, under appetizers you have Turkey Nachos, Turkey Egg Rolls, Turkey Meatballs, Turkey Chili, and Turkey Lettuce Wraps."

"Right."

"Main courses, you have Turkey Casserole, Turkey Burgers, Turkey Pot Pie, and Barbeque Turkey."

"Continue."

"Under vegetarian, you have a This Can't Be Turkey Burger."

"Clever, isn't it? It's a burger made from ground turkey. I can't wait for our vegetarian customers to say it tastes just like turkey."

"For dessert, you have Turkey Soufflé?"

"Sounds delicious, doesn't it? And it only took me an hour to figure out how to get rid of 995 turkeys and charge people for it," JC said proudly.

"You have got to be the stupidest person I have ever met in my life!" Zabrina snapped.

The next day, JC kept getting questions from the waiters and waitresses. "JC, I have a customer who wants a salad without turkey on it."

"Fine, put it on the side."

"JC, one of my customers does not like turkey and wants a

steak," another waiter said.

JC walked into the kitchen and returned with a plate. "What table is it?" The waiter pointed and JC walked over and sat the plate in front of the man.

"What is this?" he asked.

"It's a turkey steak. Enjoy!"

"But I don't want turkey," the man said.

JC held up his hand to the man's face as if to tell him to be quiet and then walked away. At the end of the night, he asked Jesús how many turkeys they had left. When he said 989, JC screamed. He walked into the office and plopped down in a chair.

"I never want to see another turkey for the rest of my life! How did the video turn out?"

Zabrina played the video she'd uploaded to YouTube. It showed JC confronted by a police officer, homeless people refusing to take his turkeys, and JC assaulting a vegetarian. JC became so frustrated after watching the video that he pulled out his gun and shot several holes in the ceiling.

Big Tony looked at his crazy friend, thinking he never should have given him a gun. The next thing he'd hear would be JC sending him to the hardware store to buy more ceiling tiles.

Zabrina attempted to cheer JC up by telling him she had a plan to get Stenson back. She suggested they set up a fake drug deal to buy a large quantity of marijuana from South America. They would spread a rumor they were doing it to raise money for the club. Zabrina believed Stenson would find it too irresistible not to steal from them like they had done to him. She called the kitchen and asked Jesús to come to the office. When he arrived, Zabrina outlined the plan.

Jesús would go to O'Malley's bar and pose as a disgruntled employee. He would act drunk and talk bad about JC and Club

Empire. After he'd gained Stenson's trust, Jesús would reveal the fake drug deal. They would charter a plane and get Stenson to go with Jesús to South America. Once there, Jesús would return to the plane to retrieve something. While Stenson waited, the plane would take off, leaving Stenson stranded in the jungle.

JC thought the plan was overly complicated but loved the idea of leaving Stenson in a jungle if he would stay out of his hair and away from his wrongly tattooed forehead. And if Stenson died in the jungle, he'd never bother them again.

A few nights later, Jesús stumbled into O'Malley's and took a seat at the bar.

Stenson walked over and asked him, "What can I get you?"

"Tequila! Make it a double!" Jesús slurred.

Stenson poured a double shot of tequila and placed it in front of Jesús. "Rough day?"

"Yeah, homie. I got screwed."

"Sorry to hear that."

"Never trust a black dude. I want to kill that JC guy," Jesús said.

That got Stenson's attention. "Did you say JC?"

"Yeah, that *puta* who runs Club Empire. I gave him the hookup on a big score down in South America and now they cut me out."

Stenson poured Jesús another glass. "Tell me about it."

Jesús laid out the plan just as Zabrina had instructed. He told Stenson he would cut JC out and do the deal himself if he only had the money.

Stenson motioned Brick over. "Why don't you step into the office and tell me and my friend more about this arrangement. Maybe we can help you."

The guys walked to the office, where Jesús told Stenson and Brick that a plane was scheduled to fly to a private airstrip in Peru next Saturday. Stenson asked how much money JC was putting up for the deal. Jesús told him $400,000, with a street value of more than a million. Stenson looked at Brick, who was thinking the same as he was. It would be a perfect opportunity to get his money back and screw JC.

"What if I can come up with the money? Can you get me on the plane instead of JC?" Stenson asked.

"Yeah, homie. I'm the one who arranged the flight and I know where the airstrip is," Jesús confirmed.

"We don't like that guy either. We'll do each other a favor. Consider us your new partner," Stenson said as he shook Jesús's hand. "Leave me your contact information and we'll be in touch to finalize everything."

Jesús left the bar and returned to Club Empire. He told Zabrina and JC that Stenson had taken the bait. Zabrina could not hide her excitement. The thought of leaving Stenson in a jungle and stealing another $400,000 from him was priceless.

Luna stopped by the bar later. Stenson told her about JC's plan. She considered it risky since they knew nothing about Jesús Alvarez. Luna said she would investigate him and see what she could find out about the guy. Stenson told her if it didn't feel right, he wouldn't go through with it. But he relished the idea of getting his money back and messing with JC after everything he'd put them through.

Luna called Stenson the next day. She said she'd found nothing unusual about Jesús Alvarez. He was a naturalized citizen and grew up in an orphanage. Other than that, he had a clean police record. She also confirmed he had once worked for Club Empire as a cook. Stenson thanked her for the information and hung up the phone. He called Jesús and asked him to stop by the bar that evening.

When Jesús arrived, Stenson escorted him to the office, where Luna and Brick were waiting. Jesús filled them in on the details. He said that Zabrina had chartered a plane scheduled to depart from a private airport at 9:00 a.m. Saturday morning. Then Jesús had contacted the pilot and rescheduled the flight to leave at 7:00 a.m. instead. They would be long gone for Peru before JC and Zabrina found out.

Jesús continued: Once they landed at an airstrip in Peru, they'd hand over the money and load the plane. He estimated their total time on the ground would be less than an hour. Then they would return to the same airport in New Orleans. Stenson asked Luna to arrange for a truck to meet them at the airport when they returned. He would contact her from a satellite phone during the flight to provide their exact arrival time.

Wednesday afternoon, Stenson received a call from Marty Smith, the general contractor he'd hired to work on Haggerty's property. Marty told him the remodel of Haggerty's home and the new church were almost complete and asked if he would like to inspect the work. Stenson agreed to meet him the next morning. He told Brick he would be out of town for a couple days and asked him to look after the bar. Then he phoned Luna, who confirmed everything was set for Saturday.

The new church appeared over the horizon as Stenson approached Haggerty's place. Marty Smith and Pastor Jackson were there to greet him when he arrived. The men gave Stenson a tour of the new house of worship. The construction was remarkable.

Stenson asked, "Where did you get the stained-glass windows, Marty?"

"I was lucky to find those, Stenson. They're from an old church that was torn down. They were sitting in a warehouse where I also found the reclaimed wood I used for the flooring and beams. Pastor Jackson wanted the church to have an old character even though the building is new."

"My congregation is excited, Stenson," Pastor Jackson beamed.

"Let me show you what I did with the house," Marty said.

Then he, Pastor Jackson, and Stenson walked to Haggerty's home. It looked brand new. Marty had replaced the roof, windows, and doors. He'd also redone the paint and landscaping. Haggerty's furniture had been replaced, and there was a new kitchen and bath. Marty said local businesses had donated the furniture and appliances. Pastor Jackson told him two families were already living in the home until they could get back on their feet.

Then Marty took Stenson to see the campground he'd created for boys and girls as Stenson had envisioned. Marty had constructed a pavilion and restrooms with showers. He drove around and showed Stenson the new rear entrance they'd cut through the woods. Marty parked his truck beside Stenson's old campsite. There was a pier over the water.

"That wasn't in the plans," Stenson commented with surprise.

"I know, Stenson. But I had a little money left over from your budget and I remember when you told me how much you enjoyed fishing here. I built it so other children can enjoy it too. I hope you don't mind?"

"I love it, Marty. You've exceeded my expectations."

They drove back to the church, where Pastor Jackson was waiting by his car. When Stenson got out of the truck, the pastor said, "Stenson, you have blessed us. We have a special dedication planned for this Sunday. My congregation does not know you are responsible for this. I told them it was a gift from Mr. Haggerty. But it would be our honor for you to attend Sunday and at least allow me to introduce you as his friend. It would mean a lot to all of us."

Stenson could not say no to Pastor Jackson. While he wanted to get back at JC on Saturday, he felt this was more important. Stenson took out an envelope and handed it to Marty. "This is something extra for you and your family. I cannot thank you enough for all the work you have done."

Marty opened the envelope to see a check for $10,000. "Stenson, I don't know what to say but thank you. I wish I could repay you for your generosity."

"You can, Marty. Bring your family Friday afternoon and let's do some fishing together and have a cookout."

"You have a deal, Stenson. My wife and kids will enjoy it."

Stenson phoned Luna after Marty and the pastor left. "Hey, Luna, something came up and I won't be back until Sunday night. We need to cancel the JC plan. I looked forward to getting our money back, but this is more important."

Luna could tell Stenson was disappointed when he hung up the phone. The plan was perfect, and it occurred to her she could go instead. Stenson had already left the money with her. Luna called Jesús and told him something came up and she would be the one traveling to Peru instead. Jesús said he would meet her at the airport Saturday morning as they planned.

Jesús called Zabrina after he hung up with Luna. "There's a problem. Stenson won't be there. They're sending the girl ... Luna."

"That is even better." Zabrina chuckled. "She is the brains behind their operation. I can't wait to get that bitch back."

CHAPTER TWENTY-THREE

NEW ORLEANS, LOUISIANA / MONROE COUNTY, LOUISIANA

Brick lit up like a Christmas tree when Luna walked into O'Malley's on Friday afternoon. "Your boyfriend isn't here," he teased.

Luna laughed as she sat down at the bar. "He's not my boyfriend, goofball."

"I bet you wish he was," Brick deadpanned with a wink.

"No comment," the gorgeous redhead giggled.

Luna and Brick enjoyed each other's company. She understood why Stenson liked Robert Brickhouse. Behind all those tattoos and burly exterior, he was a funny and kind teddy bear. They chatted while Luna ate a cheeseburger.

"Any plans for the weekend?"

"I have a few errands to take care of," Luna said, wiping mustard from her chin.

"Too bad Stenson won't be able to take down JC and Zabrina tomorrow. It was a perfect plan."

"He seemed disappointed," the cheeseburger eater admitted.

"We'll get them next time," Brick said, clinking his glass to hers.

"You mind if I go to the office? I left something the other night," Luna asked her big, tattooed friend.

"Sure," Brick replied, going to attend to other customers.

Luna found the airport address that Jesús had given Stenson, stuck to the bottom of the computer screen. She pulled the note from the monitor and placed it in her pocket, then returned to the bar. She said goodbye to Brick, telling him she had an early start tomorrow.

It was 6:45 a.m. when Luna arrived at the airport Saturday morning. Jesús stood next to the dual-prop King Air 250. She unzipped the duffle bag and showed Jesús the money. They boarded the aircraft and took off fifteen minutes later. Jesús told Luna to get comfortable because it would be a long flight.

"Why Peru, Jesús?" she asked.

"It's a much better deal than Mexico," the Hispanic man replied with a suspicious smile.

Luna didn't ask more. She was tired and settled back into her seat to take a nap.

The plane landed at 11:15 p.m. on what Luna assumed was a grass runway because of all the bumpiness. She looked forward to stretching her legs after the plane came to a stop.

She exited the aircraft with Jesús and asked, "Where are your people?"

"In New Orleans," Jesús replied.

Luna looked at Jesús, confused. "New Orleans?"

Jesús pulled a handgun from his waistband and pointed it at Luna. "Your amigos JC and Zabrina arranged this little trip for you." Jesús took the bag of money from her hand. "They wanted me to give you this," Jesús said as he handed Luna a folded piece of paper. "Enjoy your stay in Peru!"

Jesús boarded the plane and closed the door. Luna stood in disbelief as the plane taxied down the runway. It occurred to her to run after it, but she realized that would be pointless. She stood there in the dark, trying to wrap her head around what had just happened.

She asked herself aloud, "Did I fly sixteen hours with a crazy Mexican to be stranded in a jungle and watch Stenson's money get stolen ... again?"

She used her cell phone as a flashlight to read the note: *"I am smarter than you! Love, Zabrina."* Luna screamed so loud it woke every living creature in the jungle and a few of the dead ones too. She looked at her phone, knowing there was no cellular service. Luna plopped down in the middle of the runway and fumed. She thought about how if she got out of there alive, she would destroy Zabrina.

Stenson enjoyed spending time with Marty Smith's family at the new campground. One of his kids climbed onto Stenson's lap and asked if she could call him "Uncle Stenson." He smiled and hoped one day to have a great family like Marty's.

Stenson phoned Brick to ask how everything was going. He said things were fine and mentioned Luna had stopped by the night before. Stenson told him he'd tried to call her several times but kept getting her voicemail. Brick said Luna had errands today so she was probably busy or out of range. Stenson let him know he would return Sunday after the dedication of the new church.

Since he hadn't planned to go to church this weekend, Stenson had only packed T-shirts and jeans. He drove into town to find something more respectable to wear to the service. Everybody he passed on Main Street waved and said hello. They were either very friendly or somehow knew who he was.

An elderly gentleman greeted him when he walked into the clothing store. Stenson shook his hand and introduced himself.

The man said, "I know who you are. You're Ol' Man Haggerty's friend—Stenson, right?"

"Yes sir, how did you know?"

"Everybody knows who you are. We heard about the new church and campground you built on his land."

So much for remaining anonymous, Stenson thought.

The man continued, "It meant a lot to us, son. You breathed new life into our little town. What can I do for you?"

Stenson said he was looking for a suit. The owner asked if he was going to a funeral or a wedding. He said it was the only reason anyone ever bought a suit in this town. Stenson laughed and told him it was for church. When the owner asked what style he was looking for, Stenson admitted he'd never owned a suit, so he didn't know.

The owner selected a black suit from the rack and helped Stenson try on the coat. Stenson looked in the mirror and told the owner he looked like a mortician.

The man laughed and said, "Nonsense. We'll find a flashy tie to go with it. Morticians don't wear flashy ties."

They chose a shirt, shoes, socks, and a crimson-colored tie. Stenson liked the tie because it was the same color as the interior of his car. The owner told Stenson his wife would make the alterations today. He could pick up the suit in the morning before church. The owner jotted notes on a pad next to the cash register.

Stenson asked how much he owed, and the man replied, "It's free for you, my boy."

"No sir, I can't let you do that. Please let me pay."

"Son, you paid me and this entire community enough with your kindness. It's my pleasure to offer you a nice suit."

Out of sheer exhaustion, Luna slept on the grass next to the airstrip. She had no intention of walking through the jungle at night. In the morning, a rough, sandpaper-like sensation crossed her face. Luna swatted it as if to brush a bug away. Then she heard a growl and opened her eyes to find herself face-to-face with a yellow-and-black spotted cat.

Out of fear or annoyance, she yelled, "Get out of here!" and pushed the creature away.

Her reaction startled the cat, and it headed for the tree line. She rubbed the sleep from her eyes and realized it was a baby jaguar. Then she noticed that it walked with a limp.

Luna rose and caught up to the animal, saying, "I'm sorry. I didn't mean to scare you."

The little jaguar turned and looked at Luna with a childlike expression. Luna approached slowly and sat nearby. Luna stuck out her arm close enough to allow the animal to smell her hand. The little jaguar walked closer and licked her hand with its sandpaper tongue. Luna dared to pet the jaguar's head as if it was a house cat. Remarkably, the wild animal purred.

"Can I look at your foot?" Luna asked.

The animal trusted Luna and allowed her to lift its leg. Luna noticed the padding on the bottom of the foot was torn away. The exposed wound looked so painful that she was surprised the animal could walk at all. Luna removed her shirt and used her teeth to rip a strip of cloth from the bottom. She gently wrapped the fabric twice around the wound, tying it off at the top.

She smiled at the little jaguar and said, "It's not perfect, but I hope it makes you feel better."

Luna put her shirt on and looked around 360 degrees. There was nothing but trees and the airstrip. Unless she grew wings, the only way she would get out of there was through the jungle. She was glad she'd downloaded a map of Peru before she left New Orleans. GPS placed a pin on her current location. She noticed a river somewhere to the northeast. Then she studied the enormous amount of green between the place she stood and the river. No telling how far or how long she would have to walk. As she headed for the tree line, the baby jaguar followed her.

Luna looked at the animal and said, "You should go home. Go find your mama."

She started walking again, and the animal stayed beside her. When she stopped, the cat stopped. Luna asked, "Are you going to follow me all the way to New Orleans?"

The cat growled as if to say it had no better place to go.

Luna smiled and said, "Well, if you walk with me, we should introduce ourselves. I'm Luna. What is your name?"

The jaguar tilted its head to one side as if to ponder the question.

Luna noticed it was a female. "Well, since you're a girl, let's give you a cool female name. How about Spot? Nah, that's too obvious. I've got it! How about Mi Amiga? It means 'My Friend' in Spanish."

The jaguar purred as if to say she approved of the name.

"Okay then. Mi Amiga it is!"

Luna and the cat stepped into the jungle.

Stenson arrived at the clothing store Sunday morning. He tried on the suit and admired the perfect fit. The owner's choice of the crimson tie was the right touch of flashy. Stenson thanked the owner and drove to the church. He said hello to Pastor Jackson and took a seat toward the back. It surprised Stenson to see so many white people at the African American church.

The clothing store owner and his wife walked in along with Marty Smith and his family. Stenson was proud to see the community come together.

The service began with gospel music. It wasn't long before the entire congregation was on its feet, clapping and swaying to the songs. People waved their hands in the air. The white people saw their neighbors of color doing it, and they joined the celebration.

Pastor Jackson welcomed everyone to the service. He told the congregation it was a special day—a day to give thanks to those responsible for their new church. Pastor Jackson preached a raucous sermon about thankfulness and humility. More music followed. Stenson felt a spirit in the air.

The pastor closed the service with an announcement: "This church and the adjoining shelter were gifts from Mr. Lucius T. Haggerty. Through the loving heart of Mr. Stenson Beckett, it has been possible. Mr. Beckett is with us this morning, and I would like to ask him to join me on stage."

Stenson did not expect such acknowledgement. He felt embarrassed standing in front of the congregation.

The pastor looked at Stenson as he spoke: "None of this would have been possible without the generosity of Lucius Haggerty and you. On behalf of the congregation and this entire community, we present you this plaque. It's the same as the one that will hang in our church for as long as it stands."

The congregation rose to their feet and applauded. Stenson's face became so red that it almost matched his tie. Pastor Jackson asked Stenson to say a few words.

Stenson cleared his throat. "I'm honored to receive this plaque on behalf of Lucius T. Haggerty. Many of you may have thought of Mr. Haggerty as a hermit or mean. He was neither. Lucius Haggerty was one of the kindest, warmhearted men I have ever known. He was a shy man and very private.

He did not know how to show you how much he cared when he was alive. But through these gifts, he is showing you now. On behalf of both of us, thank you."

The pastor hugged Stenson as the congregation cheered. The service ended with the gospel song "Stomp!" by Kirk Franklin. Everybody danced, including Stenson. Not one soul left that church until the very last note.

Stenson and Pastor Jackson greeted parishioners as they left. Each shook Stenson's hand or gave him a hug. Then Pastor Jackson invited Stenson to join his family for lunch. After a wonderful meal, Stenson thanked the pastor for the day of celebration.

On his way back to New Orleans, he looked up at the sky and said, "I felt you dancing in heaven, Haggerty. And you dance worse than me."

CHAPTER TWENT-FOUR

NEW ORLEANS, LOUISIANA / AMAZON JUNGLE, PERU

Jesús went to Club Empire as soon as he returned from Peru. He found Zabrina, JC, and Tony sitting in the office. Jesús placed the bag of money on the desk and said, *"Misión cumplida!"*

"Miss Cucumber what?" JC asked.

"It means 'Mission accomplished' in Spanish, homie."

Zabrina unzipped the bag and counted the bundles of cash. She announced with a triumphant smile, "That is $400,000 of Stenson's money!"

She handed $20,000 to Jesús for his efforts and asked how Luna reacted when he left her in Peru. Jesús said the confused look on her face was priceless.

Zabrina replied, "Good. I hope she dies in that jungle."

"Remind me not to mess with you, because I don't want to end up in a jungle," JC remarked.

Zabrina said, "JC, I wouldn't waste my money taking you to you to a jungle. We would go to one of these tall buildings, and I'd tell you there's a basketball court on the roof. When you ask me where the basket is, I'd throw the ball and tell you it's over the ledge. Then I would look down at your dumb, sprawled-out body on the street below and say I slam-dunked you!"

Big Tony laughed as Zabrina put $30,000 in the office safe

for petty cash. She returned the remaining $350,000 to the bag and asked Tony to deposit it in the club's bank account later.

JC told Zabrina he wanted his cut of the proceeds to buy a boat. Besides pointing out that it was a dumb idea, Zabrina reminded JC that he didn't know how to swim. He gave her a pouty look, and she knew it was pointless to talk him out of it. Then she asked JC what kind of boat he would buy with $116,666? When JC realized the odd amount, he told her to give him $116,000. She could keep the remaining $666. He reasoned that it was the sign of the devil and he was superstitious about things like that. As far as the boat, he planned to buy a yacht with the money because he was a businessman. Zabrina shook her head and handed him the money, knowing JC had no clue how much yachts cost.

Stenson walked into O'Malley's on Sunday evening after he returned from Alabama. Brick saw him wearing a suit and asked Stenson if he was auditioning for a new *Blues Brothers* movie. Stenson laughed and said no, but like the Blues Brothers, he was on a mission from God. He handed the plaque he'd received from the church to Brick, who read it aloud: *"Monroe County First Baptist Church and the Haggerty Home for New Beginnings. Dedicated to Lucius T. Haggerty and Stenson Beckett for their generous contributions to our community."*

Then Stenson handed Brick a large wooden plank with hand-carved lettering. It read, *"Camp Beckett, Monroe County, Alabama."* Stenson told him it was the sign that hung at the entrances of the camp for boys and girls he'd had built. Brick remarked that the only thing anybody had named after him was a jail cell.

Stenson was concerned that he hadn't talked to Luna in a few days. He asked Brick if he had spoken to her. Brick said the last time he'd seen her was when she stopped by the bar on Friday. She said she left something in the office, and he hadn't heard from her since. They walked to the office and Stenson looked around. He wondered what Luna had forgotten. Then he noticed the note with the airport address was missing. Brick said he hadn't taken it, and nobody but Luna had been in the office except him.

Stenson said, "You don't think Luna ..."

Brick read Stenson's mind. "She wouldn't, would she?"

"Get that clown Jesús on the phone! I have a feeling this was a setup."

Brick dialed the number and put the phone on speaker.

"Jesús, this is Stenson Beckett. Have you seen my friend, Luna LeRoux?"

"No, homie. Is something wrong?" Jesús asked with a fake sense of concern.

"No, I thought you might have seen her. Did you do that deal in Peru?"

"No, I canceled it because I didn't have the money."

"Okay, thanks." Stenson hung up the phone and looked at Brick. "I need you to go to the airport and snoop around. Something's not right. I have a key to Luna's place. I'll see what I can find out and make sure the money I gave her is still there."

Luna traipsed through the jungle for hours with her jaguar friend at her side. She didn't know the temperature, but felt certain the humidity was 1,000 percent, if that was possible.

Sweat dripped from every pore on her body. Luna removed her shirt and wrapped it around her head like a turban. All the bugs and thorny brush she'd been through had left her covered with scratches and bites.

Mi Amiga, the young jaguar, seemed to know where they were going. It was a good thing too, because Luna's cell phone was about to die. She was exhausted and sat next to a fallen tree. Mi Amiga plopped down across from her.

Luna said, "What have I gotten myself into?"

The animal purred as if to say, "Don't worry, I do this all the time."

Something moist slithered across her shoulder. From the corner of her eye, she saw the head of a boa constrictor sliding down her chest. Before she could react, the jaguar leaped forward and clamped down on the snake's head, ripping it away. With a quick snap from left to right, the cat killed the reptile and tossed it aside.

Stunned, Luna said, "Thank you!" Then she jumped up and began screaming like a madwoman. "I hate jungles! I hate bugs! I hate snakes! And most of all, I hate Zabrina for doing this to me!" She ran around in circles, waving her arms above her head like a crazy person.

Luna regained her composure and looked at Mi Amiga. "I'm thirsty. Let's find something to drink."

The cat stood up and walked away. Luna shrugged and followed.

Stenson arrived at Luna's apartment and used the key she'd given him to open the door. Things seemed normal as he walked through the apartment. But he had an uneasy feeling she'd not been there in a few days. He went to the bedroom and looked in the closet where Luna had placed the bag of money. It was gone. Stenson dialed Luna's number again, and the call went to voicemail. He hung up and called Brick.

"You find anything at the airport?" Stenson asked.

"Yeah, it seems a private plane filed a flight plan for Peru and left yesterday morning at 7:00 a.m. I ran into a maintenance worker who said he saw a redheaded woman and a Hispanic guy get on the plane."

"I'm at Luna's and the money isn't here. I've got a feeling she did the deal herself to help us out. I bet she wanted it to be a surprise. Now I'm concerned something's happened to her. Call Charlie Whitehorse and meet me at the bar."

Stenson's gut wrenched. Somehow, he knew JC and his crew were behind this. When Brick and Charlie arrived, Stenson pointed to the office. He slammed the door behind them.

"I know what's going on here!" Stenson yelled. "Do you think if we call JC or that stupid Zabrina chick, they'll admit to kidnapping Luna? I sensed Jesús was lying to me when I phoned him. I want information about Luna, and I want it now!"

The men discussed how to get the information. Stenson asked Brick about the guy who was always with JC. Brick said they call him Big Tony.

Stenson replied, "They like kidnapping so much? Well, go kidnap that big fella and do whatever it takes to get the information we need out of him!"

Brick and Charlie said they'd be glad to do it. Stenson had other plans to arrange for JC while they were away.

Luna felt the energy seeping from her body with every step

she took. *How can this place be so green with no water to be found anywhere?* She was at the point of complete exhaustion when the jaguar ran ahead of her. Luna caught up to the cat, who was lapping water from a stream. Luna dropped to her knees and stuck her face in the cool water. She took long swallows of the life-giving liquid.

Refreshed, Luna sat next to the cat, who had been watching her. She said, "Mi Amiga, you are so smart. Let me look at your foot."

Luna unwrapped the bandage and gently washed the cat's paw. The jaguar pulled away when she touched the exposed skin.

Luna imagined how much the wound must sting. She reassured the animal, "This will help it get better." Luna rewrapped Mi Amiga's paw and said, "Let's find that river."

They began trekking through the jungle again, with the jaguar leading the way.

JC returned to the club and exclaimed, "I bought a boat! Now you can call me Captain Justin Carter!"

Zabrina said, "What we should call you is Flotation, because that's what you'll be when you drown!"

"Whatever, Zabrina. I want you both to see it!"

"You guys go ahead, I have some work to do around here," Tony said.

Zabrina told Tony, "I'll go so I can see what Captain Bozo Brains spent his money on."

From their car parked across the street, Brick and Charlie watched Zabrina and JC leave the club. The only vehicle remaining was the one they'd seen Tony Gallo drive up in earlier. Charlie pulled around to the rear of the building. Brick tried the back door, but it was locked.

"How are we going to get in here?" Brick asked.

"What are you talking about? I break into cars for a living. This is a piece of cake."

Charlie pulled a pouch from his jacket and removed a device that looked like a staple gun. He inserted it into the lock and opened the door within a few seconds. Charlie smiled at Brick, who was impressed.

The building was quiet as they crept down the hall. They peered into each room, then saw a flight of stairs. Brick and Charlie tiptoed up the steps and quietly opened the door. Brick peered inside and saw Tony Gallo sitting at a desk. He had an idea and whispered it to Charlie. Brick removed a cloth from his jacket and soaked it with fluid from a small bottle he had.

Charlie took a few steps away from the door and yelled, "Hello? Is anybody here?"

Big Tony walked out of the office and said, "Can I help you?"

Brick wrapped his arm around Tony Gallo's neck, placing him in a headlock. He covered his mouth and nose with the cloth and said, "No, but you can help me. Good night, big boy."

Tony Gallo slumped to his feet. Charlie helped Brick lay him on the floor.

Brick put a black hood over his head. He told Charlie, "I've never used chloroform before. That stuff works quick."

"How long will he be out?" Charlie asked.

"I don't know, but I have an entire bottle. Every time he wakes up, I'll knock him out again until we get him where we're going."

The guys lifted Tony and dragged him down the stairs. They shoved him into the back seat of the car, and Brick got in beside him. Charlie drove to the warehouse, where they planned to interrogate him.

Stenson called Chucky Jones, the driver of the stolen truck in Mexico. "Chucky, it's Stenson. I need a favor. Brick mentioned you have a friend who can get his hands on some special merchandise. Any chance I can see what he's got?"

"Let me call him," Chucky said.

A few minutes later, Chucky phoned Stenson and told him to pick him up. They drove to an industrial area near the docks. Stenson pulled up to a building with a sign that read *"Gulf Coast Logistics."* A big, muscled guy with a short haircut met them when they arrived. Stenson could tell right away this guy was ex-military.

"Sarge, this is Brick's friend, Stenson. He's the person I told you about on the phone."

Sergeant John Dean looked Stenson over and shook his hand. "Brick told me you saved his life."

"Does he have to tell everybody that?" Stenson asked.

"Only his friends," Sarge joked. "Chucky tells me you're looking for something special."

"Oh yeah. I need something that will send an unforgettable message."

"Let me show you what I've got."

Sarge led the guys to the back of the building. He lifted a hidden panel and pressed his thumb against a sensor. The wall split apart, revealing a mega-store of illegal weapons.

"Man, you've got everything!" Stenson exclaimed.

Sarge said, "If I don't have it, you don't want it."

The men walked down a long line of tables and shelves. Sarge pointed out several weapons, from .50-caliber machine guns to rocket-propelled grenades. He asked Stenson what he was looking for.

Stenson felt embarrassed when he said, "I was hoping to buy a single grenade."

"No problem, Stenson." Sarge opened a crate. "What type?

I've got fragmentation, illuminating, chemical, and flash-bangs."

"What causes the most casualties in a small area?"

Sarge reached into a crate and handed a baseball-shaped green device to Stenson. "This should do the trick. It's an M67 fragmentation grenade. It will blow in four to five seconds. Injures anyone within fifteen meters and kills within five. How good is your throwing arm?"

"Good enough for what I need. How much do I owe you?"

"You saved the life of crazy Robert Brickhouse. This one is on me." Sarge patted Stenson on the shoulder.

The men left the vault, and Sarge closed the hidden door.

Stenson said, "Thanks, Sarge. Stop by the bar sometime. Drinks are on me."

CHAPTER TWENTY-FIVE

NEW ORLEANS, LOUISIANA / AMAZON JUNGLE, PERU

Zabrina listened to JC brag about his new boat all the way to the marina. By his description, it sounded like he bought the *Queen Mary II*. JC said it was worth over a million dollars. But since he was such a great negotiator, he only paid the $116,000 he got from Stenson's money. He told Zabrina he even named the boat after her.

Million-dollar yachts lined the marina. Zabrina thought for once that JC might have done something right with his money.

When they reached the end of the pier, JC exclaimed, "There she is!"

Zabrina stood next to a large yacht with a sundeck, water slide, and Jet Skis on the back. She said, "Wow! It's beautiful."

"No, not that one," JC said, pointing to the boat next to it. "That one!"

"What? That rust bucket? It's a shrimp boat! What are you, Forrest Gump?"

Zabrina inspected the sad sight and could not believe the thing even floated. The little paint it had was a peeling shade of baby blue. Along with the enormous amount of rust, the boat was a hideous color combination. A two-year-old with an entire box of crayons would've never chosen those two colors.

And the boat smelled of a billion rotting fish.

When she walked to the back of the vessel, JC pointed to the name. "See, I told you it's named after you."

Zabrina read the sign, *"Azun Which,"* then shook her head. She didn't know if she wanted to choke JC or take him to a spelling class.

"You have got to be the dumbest person I have ever known! The word *Asian* is not spelled A-Z-U-N. And the *Witch* that you want is spelled W-I-T-C-H, not W-H-I-C-H. Why am I even explaining this to you? Does that heap of junk even run?"

JC climbed aboard and invited Zabrina to do the same. She refused, insisting she would never step foot on that shipwreck. JC started the engine, and it gurgled like a person whose neck had been slashed and was now fighting for one last breath. The boat belched out a cloud of noxious black smoke that drifted across the marina. Nearby boat owners began yelling, "Turn that damn thing off!" One guy even threatened JC with a speargun. JC killed the engine and stepped back onto the dock.

"Needs a little work, but didn't I get a great deal?"

"You said it was worth a million dollars."

"That's what the seller told me it cost when it was new."

"When? In 1802?" Zabrina asked, not hiding her exasperation. "You couldn't sell enough parts to make up the $116,000 you spent. Your brain needs more work than this boat!" Zabrina stormed back to the car, realizing this was a waste of time she'd never get back.

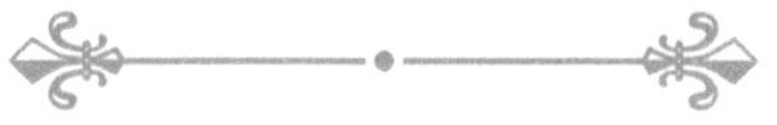

Luna followed the little jaguar through the jungle for hours. She started having severe abdominal cramps. Her stomach rumbled, and she rushed behind a group of ferns and yanked down her jeans. Then she felt her guts explode.

When she returned, Mi Amiga looked at her as if to say, "Are you okay?"

They walked a little farther when it happened again. After the third time, Luna wondered what parasites she must have drank when they stopped for water. She was hot, bug-bitten, dehydrated, and beyond angry at her situation. It was getting dark, and she could go no farther. Luna plopped down at the base of a massive tree. The jaguar sensed they were done for the day and climbed up the tree to find a comfortable spot to lie down.

She said, "You're sleeping up there? Well, I'm staying down here."

Luna fell asleep but awoke a short time later to rustling sounds and itchiness. She lit up her cell phone to see her body covered with thousands of insects and the ground moving beneath her. The jungle had come alive! Luna jumped up, screaming as she attempted to brush away the bugs. Her arms moved so fast she looked like a human helicopter. Somehow, she managed to scamper up the tree to the limb where the jaguar was sleeping.

She told the cat, "No wonder you sleep up here!"

Brick removed the hood from the head of the unconscious Tony Gallo. He slapped him on the cheek and said, "Wake up, big boy."

Tony regained consciousness and saw two blurry shadows standing in front of him. Then realized he was strapped to a chair. A single light shined over his head.

"Where am I?" Tony asked.

"You are in hell and we are the devil," Brick said as he leaned inches from Tony's face.

Tony struggled while Brick suggested, "I wouldn't try that. We weren't taking a chance with you, big fella. Those are industrial-strength zip ties, and for added measure, we used some duct tape and refrigerator towing belts. You won't be going anywhere."

"What do you want?" the big boy asked.

"Information."

"What kind of information?"

"Why don't you start by telling me about a little trip to Peru."

"I don't know what you're talking about."

Charlie Whitehorse lit a blow torch and said, "Maybe this will jog your memory."

That was all the encouragement Tony Gallo needed to realize the seriousness of the situation. He told them Zabrina had arranged the scam to steal money from Stenson and Luna. The plan was to kidnap Stenson and leave him in Peru. But Zabrina was even happier when she found out Luna was going instead. Brick asked where in Peru. As he stared at the torch, Tony mumbled that only Zabrina knew the location.

They'd heard enough. Brick stepped behind Tony Gallo and said, "Thank you for your cooperation. Good night, sweetheart." He covered the big man's face with the chloroform-soaked cloth, knocking him out again.

The next time Tony regained consciousness, he found himself naked in the woods. It was a pitch-black night, and he had no idea where he was. Tony wandered through the forest until he finally came upon a road. He figured he was somewhere in the country because there were no lights for as far as he could see.

Tony followed the road, naked in the dark. Car lights appeared from an approaching vehicle. He placed one hand over his crotch and held his thumb out with the other.

The truck drove by without stopping. The driver looked at his wife and asked, "Did we just pass a fat, naked hitchhiker?"

"He must be on drugs. You know kids these days," she concluded.

Tony kept walking until he came across a lone farmhouse. There were no lights on, but with the pale moonlight, he could make out the silhouette of clothes hanging on a line. As he got closer, he noticed they were all dresses.

"Well, she must be a big woman because this looks like it will fit me."

Tony had no choice but to slip on the flowery dress. Now he had to find a way back to warn JC and Zabrina that Stenson and his crew were out to get them.

It was almost time for the club to open when JC and Zabrina returned from the marina. Zabrina asked if anyone had seen Big Tony. Staff said he wasn't there when they arrived.

Zabrina noticed his car was parked outside. She dialed Tony's cell phone. When it answered, she said, "Hello, Tony?"

The voice on the other end was Stenson Beckett: "Hello, Zabrina. Good luck finding your fat friend. We know you kidnapped Luna. Where is she?"

Stunned, Zabrina hung up the phone and ran to find JC. She yelled, "They got Tony!"

"Who got Tony?"

"Stenson and his crew! They kidnapped him! Stenson knows we set them up and wants to know where Luna is."

"Wait a minute! Don't blame this on us. You set them up and only you know where she is."

"He's after all of us, JC, and only the pilot knows exactly where he left her. And who knows if she's even alive."

"You better figure this out, Zabrina! Tony is my best friend!" JC said as he stormed out of the room.

Brick and Charlie were in the office with Stenson, discussing how to get Luna's location out of Zabrina. Stenson wanted twenty-four-hour surveillance placed on her and Justin Carter. He knew Tony Gallo would find his way back at some point, and they needed to watch him too. Charlie offered to have his guys take care of it.

After Charlie left, Stenson asked Brick to stay behind. He told Brick about the grenade he got from Sarge. He said if they didn't get information about Luna's whereabouts by tomorrow, things were going to a new level. Brick had never seen Stenson so angry.

Brick said, "You love her."

"I do, Robert. And I've been afraid to admit it to myself."

"I know, my friend. We care about both of you, and we'll do anything to help you get her back."

Mi Amiga woke Luna with a rough lick on her face, then jumped down from the tree. Luna felt weak as she lowered herself to the jungle floor. She opened her phone to look at the map. Luna believed they would find the river with one more long day of hiking. She hoped her body would last that long. Just then, the phone battery died. Luna had to trust the instincts of her feline friend to get them there.

The temperature felt cooler and less humid the farther they walked. She listened over the calls of monkeys and birds to hear the faint sound of water in the distance. Her spirits rose, as she believed they were close to the river. She continued to follow the jaguar when suddenly Mi Amiga turned right, away from the sound of the water.

"Where are you going? The water is over there," Luna said as she pointed in a different direction.

The jaguar continued to walk another way. Luna followed the instinctive animal since she had gotten them this far. When she caught up to Mi Amiga, she saw her staring at a corpse. Luna looked closer and realized it was the body of an adult female jaguar.

Luna sat beside Mi Amiga. "Is that your mother?"

The little jaguar looked up at Luna with sadness in her eyes. Luna's heart sank when she realized Mi Amiga was an orphan. She let her friend be alone with her mother. Luna gathered large palm leaves and wildflowers in the jungle. When she returned, Luna noticed Mi Amiga had not moved. She covered the corpse with the leaves and placed flowers on top.

Luna sat beside the infant jaguar. "Mi Amiga, I am sorry you lost your mom. She would be proud of you."

The young jaguar arose and headed back in the direction they'd come from. Luna quietly followed the animal. An hour later, they reached the edge of the jungle. Luna saw the water and wanted to sprint toward it. But Mi Amiga was focused on something in the distance. Luna peered through the trees and saw what the cat was watching. A group of native people was fishing on the other side of the river. They were like nothing she had ever seen before. They had red paint on their faces, with bodies covered in elaborate tattoos.

Luna gathered her courage and emerged from the tree line. The fishermen were startled when they saw her and raised their spears. She thought of running, but then Mi Amiga suddenly walked up and stood beside her. When the fishermen saw the jaguar, they lowered their spears and dropped to their knees.

One of the men paddled a dugout canoe to the bank where

Luna and the cat stood. The native sensed Luna's fear and got out of the canoe slowly, then spoke to her in a language she did not understand. He smiled and pointed at the jaguar. He said a few more words and gestured toward the boat. The man turned and walked back toward the water, and Mi Amiga followed. Luna watched the jaguar jump into the boat. Mi Amiga looked back at Luna as if to assure her it was okay.

When they reached the other side of the river, the fishermen surrounded Luna and Mi Amiga. The men spoke in rapid chatter and pointed to the jaguar. They escorted Luna and the cat to their village, causing a great commotion when they arrived. As Luna tried to make sense of the situation, a Caucasian man emerged from the crowd. He introduced himself as Dr. Eric Fletcher from Michigan State University.

He asked, "American?"

"Yes, I'm Luna LeRoux from New Orleans, Louisiana."

"Wow, you're a long way from home. What are you doing in the Amazon Rainforest? Are you a student?"

"It's a long story," Luna replied.

"Welcome to the village of the Matsés tribe. They are also known as 'the Jaguar People.' I see they like your friend," Dr. Fletcher said, pointing at the cat.

"She's an orphaned jaguar that I named Mi Amiga. She's been my companion, guide, and protector during this wild adventure."

"That's a nice name for her. You look like you've had a rough time. I'll ask the women of the village to attend to you and we can talk more later."

Dr. Fletcher spoke to a group of women in their native language. An elderly woman approached and held out her hand. She guided Luna to a hut while other village women followed. Mi Amiga seemed to enjoy the attention from the tribe and stayed behind.

The eldest woman motioned Luna to remove her clothing, then bathed and washed her hair. Another woman prepared herbal salves and smeared them onto her wounds. The ointments tingled when they touched her skin, then instantly relieved the pain.

The elderly woman handed Luna traditional clothing to wear. It consisted of a skirt made from bright yellow strips of palm leaves and a green wrap to cover her breasts. A woman decorated Luna's forehead and cheeks with a bright red paint like the other women. Then the grandmotherly woman removed her necklace and placed it around Luna's neck.

The women smiled when Luna stood up. Rather than feel silly, Luna felt welcomed as a member of their tribe. The ladies escorted Luna from the hut. The rest of the villagers seemed to approve of her new appearance.

Dr. Fletcher said, "The men have prepared a feast in your honor. I'm sure you're hungry."

"You cannot imagine!" Luna exclaimed.

Luna sat with Dr. Fletcher and the elders of the tribe. Mi Amiga had a special place set aside for her. It seemed she was the real guest of honor. The rest of the tribe, comprising about thirty people, gathered in a circle around a large fire. They ate fish, wild boar, and fruits gathered from the jungle. The men told stories of great hunts and spirits, which Dr. Fletcher translated for Luna. After the meal, they performed traditional songs and dances.

Luna walked with Dr. Fletcher to a small farm near the village. There, she met Eric's Matsés wife and children. Dr. Fletcher told Luna he had been studying the Matsés people for thirty years. He again asked how she had ended up in such a remote part of the Amazon Rainforest. Luna explained the strange story, leaving out the part about it being a drug deal gone wrong. She asked Dr. Fletcher if he had a phone. He said he did not but told her a research site upriver had one. He was planning to visit there in two days and welcomed her to stay with his family until then.

Luna thanked the professor and said she looked forward to learning more about the Matsés people.

CHAPTER TWENTY-SIX

NEW ORLEANS, LOUISIANA / AMAZON JUNGLE, PERU

Brick and Stenson were in the office when the phone rang. Stenson put the call on speaker. It was Charlie's guys giving him an update on the surveillance at Club Empire.

"Stenson, didn't you tell us to keep an eye out for that heavyset guy, Tony Gallo?"

"Yeah."

"Well, a car pulled up and either a fat ugly woman got out or your boy is wearing a dress."

Brick roared with laughter. He told Stenson they'd left Big Tony naked in the woods and figured the big fella must have found a dress to wear. Brick wondered if they should have put makeup on him too.

"That's him!" Stenson shouted. "Please tell me you took photos?"

"Even better. We've got the video."

"Priceless! Are JC and Zabrina there?"

"I believe so. We saw the staff leave earlier, but those two never came out and their cars are in the parking lot."

"Thanks, guys. You can go home."

Stenson and Brick drove to Club Empire and pulled around back. Stenson reached into the glove box and pulled out the grenade he'd gotten from Sarge. They stood beneath the second-floor office window as Stenson pondered the situation.

"How am I going to throw this through double-pane glass?"

Brick understood the dilemma. He looked around and found a concrete block. Brick spun it around like he was throwing a shotput at the Olympics and hurled it at the second-floor window. The glass rained down in a million tiny pieces.

"How about that?" Brick asked with a smile.

Stenson laughed. "Not very subtle, but that'll work."

"They don't call me Brick for nothing," Robert joked.

The commotion caused JC, Zabrina, and Big Tony to gather at the window to see Stenson and Brick standing below.

Stenson yelled, "I told you if I didn't get information about Luna, there would be consequences!" He pulled the pin from the grenade and hurled it through the shattered opening.

Everyone in the office dove to the floor. The grenade landed in front of JC's face. He yelled, "Grenade!" In a split-second reaction, JC grabbed the device and tossed it back out the window, and it fell onto the front seat of Stenson's car. Stenson and Brick saw it just in time to dive to the pavement. Stenson's precious Cadillac exploded in a huge fireball. Pieces of his car flew all over the parking lot. After the dust settled, Brick and Stenson stood up and stared at the flaming debris. JC, Zabrina, and Tony were laughing from above.

Stenson shook his head and looked at Brick, "Well, that didn't go as planned."

Brick pointed at Stenson's head. "Hey, buddy, your hair is smoking."

They took a cab back to O'Malley's. Stenson and Brick were in the office when they heard a loud crash. They walked into the bar, thinking there was a fight.

A customer said, "Stenson, some Mexican dude threw a car bumper through the front window!"

Stenson and Brick looked at each other and said in unison, "Jesús!"

They walked over to see the front bumper of Stenson's Cadillac lying on the floor. There was a note attached to it that read: *"You are out $800,000 and you destroyed your own car. We thought you might want your bumper back. P.S. You will never find Luna!"*

Stenson handed the note to Brick and stormed back to the office. Brick noticed steam coming from Stenson's head as if he was about to burst into flames like some angry cartoon character. Stenson was furious.

He picked up the phone and called Chucky Jones. "Chucky, it's Stenson. Tell your friend Sarge I need to see him right away. ... No, I can't pick you up. I have no car. Come get me. I'll explain everything later."

Stenson slammed down the phone and told Brick, "I've had it with them! I don't care about the weed; I don't care about the money; I don't even care about my car! All I care about is getting Luna back!"

"What are you going to do?" Brick asked.

"You'll see. I've had it with these clowns!"

Chucky Jones rang Stenson to say he was waiting outside. When he asked Stenson what happened to the bar window, Stenson replied, "Don't ask. I'm too angry to talk about it. Just drive!"

Sarge was in the parking lot of Gulf Coast Logistics when they arrived. He saw how mad Stenson was when he got out of the car and asked, "What's going on, Stenson? Chucky said it's urgent."

"I need the biggest, baddest thing you've got, Sarge! I don't care what it costs."

Sarge opened his secret vault and showed Stenson an assortment of heavy weapons. He pointed to a Soviet rocket-propelled grenade. Stenson shook his head and said it wasn't enough. Then Sarge pointed to a TOW missile launcher. Again, Stenson wanted something bigger. Sarge knew this had to be serious. He walked to the back of the warehouse and pulled back a curtain. revealing a British Chieftain MK 10 battle tank.

Stenson took one look at it and said, "Perfect! Sarge, I won't ask you how you got this or how much it will cost me to borrow, but this is exactly what I need."

Sarge opened a large garage door at the rear of the warehouse and drove the tank out. He gave Stenson brief instructions on how to operate and fire the vehicle.

Stenson climbed inside and said, "How hard can it be?"

Stenson looked at the array of levers, knobs, and switches before trying to recall Sarge's directions. He lifted his foot off the brake, making the gigantic machine rumble in reverse.

Suddenly, he heard Chucky Jones scream, "Stenson, stop!"

There was a crunching sound, and the tank came to an abrupt halt. Stenson opened the hatch and looked out to see the sixty-ton weapon sitting atop Chucky Jones's car. Sarge and Chucky stared at the flattened vehicle in utter disbelief.

Stenson said to Chucky, "We'll deal with your car later."

He went back inside the tank and pressed a button, causing the turret to rotate 360 degrees. Sarge ducked as the barrel spun around.

After Stenson returned the turret to its original position, Sarge climbed on top and lifted the hatch. He yelled over the roaring engine, "Stenson, this is worse than teaching a teenager to drive!"

Stenson laughed. "I almost figured this out. Now which one is the fire button?"

Sarge hesitated before showing him. He pointed to the red toggle switch and asked, "Are you sure about this, Stenson?"

"I've never been more sure of anything in my life!" Stenson

replied with a possessed man's determination.

Stenson waited until dark. He knew there wouldn't be much traffic in this part of town on a Monday night. He drove the tank along several side streets all the way to the warehouse by Club Empire. He lined up the tank with the door of the warehouse, where he had seen them park the trailer with his stolen weed. Stenson dialed JC's number and told him to meet him at the warehouse.

JC, Zabrina, and Big Tony couldn't believe their eyes when they saw the tank.

Stenson yelled from the open hatch, "If you don't get Luna back to me, this is only a taste of what I will do to you!"

He closed the hatch and pressed the fire button. The enormous explosion lit up the sky, and the blast threw JC, Zabrina, and Big Tony to the ground.

Stenson rotated the turret and pointed it at JC. He opened the hatch and yelled, "You better get her back now!"

Stenson backed the tank out of the parking lot and returned to Sarge's place before any police or fire personnel arrived. He wished he could have been there when JC explained that someone blew up his warehouse with a tank. Stenson also hoped the fire department would be wearing oxygen masks or else everybody would get high.

Stenson climbed out and said, "Thanks, Sarge! I feel much better."

"I won't ask what you did with it. But I'm sure you had a good reason."

Back at Club Empire, JC yelled at Zabrina, "That guy is a lunatic! Do you see what you got us into? I told you to fix this!"

"I tried, JC. I even chartered the same pilot to fly back to Peru, but nobody can find Luna."

"This won't end well, Zabrina, and it's all your fault! I never wanted to be part of this. You were the one who said it was easy money. Does this even remotely look easy?"

Luna found the Matsés people fascinating. She admired their self-sufficiency. The jungle and river provided everything they need to survive. Their families were close, and they had a spiritual reverence for nature. The Matsés understood medicinal qualities of plants that modern science didn't know. Their rhythmic language sounded melodic, like a song. Luna found the simple way they lived beautiful.

European missionaries had discovered the tribe living along the Javari River in 1969. Things changed soon after outsiders arrived. Now they had motorized canoes and other modern conveniences. But they also struggled with poverty and external dependence they hadn't dealt with before. Companies and the government exploited the rich natural resources of their land. At the current rate of exploitation, Dr. Fletcher feared that the Matsés people were at risk of extinction.

The day arrived for Luna to travel upriver to the research station with Dr. Fletcher. Luna wished she could stay longer with the Matsés. She shared a morning meal with the tribe before she had to leave. The eldest Matsés woman handed Luna her clothes, which they had washed in the river.

Luna felt sad removing the traditional dress and the paint from her face. While she had only been their guest for a few days, Luna felt a kinship with these remarkable people. She emerged from the hut dressed as she had arrived. The villagers gathered in a circle, and the little jaguar, Mi Amiga, stood by the elder woman's side. Luna approached the woman and removed the necklace she had given her. The woman held Luna's hand and smiled. Luna understood the necklace was meant as a gift. She leaned toward the elder woman and kissed her cheek. Then Luna placed her hand on her heart and smiled. The older woman returned the smile and gestured to her heart.

The little jaguar watched the exchange of kindness between the women. Luna leaned down and stroked the animal's head. "I'll miss you, Mi Amiga. Take good care of my friends. I know they'll take good care of you."

A tear rolled down Luna's cheek. She knew Mi Amiga understood this was goodbye.

Luna boarded a canoe with Dr. Fletcher and two of the tribesmen. The villagers gathered on the bank, smiling and waving. Luna returned the wave as they headed upstream. She would miss the Matsés people.

The morning was cool and overcast as they traveled up the river. The boat passed a magnificent waterfall as tall as a ten-story building. It created a rainbow unlike anything Luna had ever seen.

Dr. Fletcher noticed Luna's expression and said, "It's called a fogbow or ghost rainbow. It's rare, and the Matsés believe it's a gift from their spirits. You are very lucky to see it. I've lived here thirty years and have only seen it once before."

They arrived at the research station early that evening. Dr. Fletcher told the researchers of Luna's situation, and they handed her the satellite phone. Luna asked their location and the nearest airport. A researcher pointed to a nearby airstrip on the map and wrote the coordinates.

Luna dialed Stenson's number. It took awhile to connect and then rang several times. She was about to hang up when Stenson answered the phone. She said, "Hello, Stenson?"

"Luna!" Stenson screamed so loud that the researchers could hear him. "Where are you?"

Luna kept the call brief and said she was at a research station in Peru. Stenson told her he would charter a plane to pick her up as soon as possible. She gave him the coordinates.

Before she hung up the phone, she said, "I love you."

Stenson was ecstatic. He began calling charter companies until he found one willing to fly to Peru and land on a grass airstrip. He insisted on leaving that night, no matter the cost. The company said they would be ready to leave in two hours. Stenson shared the news with Brick and asked him to go along in case there was any trouble. He'd spent most of his money on the tank, and the rest had been stolen by Zabrina. Stenson called Charlie Whitehorse and asked to borrow money for the flight.

Charlie drove Stenson and Brick to the airport. Stenson paid the pilot $40,000 in cash and everyone boarded the plane. Sixteen hours later, they were in Peru. The research station heard the plane approaching and gathered along the airstrip. The pilot could not open the door fast enough for Stenson. As soon as it opened, he saw Luna running toward him. She jumped into his arms, and they kissed. Everyone watched their long embrace. Brick smiled at the sight.

Luna asked, "How come you never kissed me like that before?"

"Because I've been too afraid to tell you I love you."

"Tell me now!" Luna insisted.

"I love you with all my heart, Luna Jean LeRoux!"

Luna glowed when she heard Stenson say those words. "I love you with all my heart too, Stenson Beckett!"

Luna hugged Brick. "Hi, ya big lug. Did you miss me?"

"Of course! I'm glad we found you. Your boyfriend was about to kill every person in New Orleans if we didn't."

Luna introduced Stenson and Brick to Dr. Fletcher. "Stenson, Dr. Fletcher is the person responsible for me making it here."

Stenson thanked the professor as he shook his hand. He reached into a bag and handed the professor $10,000. Dr. Fletcher tried to refuse the money, but Stenson insisted. "Please take it and use it for your research. I cannot thank you enough for taking care of my friend."

They said goodbye and returned to the airplane. There was a sense of relief when the plane left the ground. Luna shared stories of her misadventures, the little jaguar, and the Matsés people.

After she finished, Luna said, "Stenson, I hope you're not mad at me. I was doing this for you. It was my mistake. I should have told you."

"I'm not mad, Luna. But next time, if somebody gets stranded in a jungle to play with snakes and wild animals, let it be Brick."

Brick laughed. "Hey now! I wouldn't survive as well as Luna."

CHAPTER TWENTY-SEVEN

NEW ORLEANS, LOUISIANA

Zabrina was an outcast in her own club. Silence and mistrust had replaced friendship and camaraderie. JC no longer teased her with his bad jokes. The always sweet Tony blamed her for the embarrassment he'd suffered at the hands of Stenson's crew. Nobody spoke to Zabrina unless it was necessary. Even then, the conversations were brief. No longer was Zabrina considered a friend or ally; she was a business partner. Nothing more. Nothing less.

With their biggest, most public event approaching, Zabrina didn't need more stress. She wished she'd never concocted the plan that ended up kidnapping Luna LeRoux. Things had gone way too far, and her only hope was fixing it.

Her cell phone rang and displayed the name *Jesús*. She answered it and snapped, "What?"

"You want some good news?" Jesús asked.

"I need all the good news I can get."

"I received a phone call from the pilot we hired to take that girl Luna to Peru."

"And?"

"He told me Stenson hired him two days ago to pick her up. She's back in New Orleans."

"That is great news! Thank you, Jesús!"

Zabrina could not wait to tell the guys. Tony seemed relieved, but JC said, “That solves part of the problem. But how are we going to get the guy’s money back to him? You know he’ll never stop until we do.”

“Relax, JC. I’ll figure out the money. His biggest concern was getting the girl back. Let’s hope he’ll leave us alone until we finish the event next week. Then we’ll have enough money to repay him.”

“We better!” JC exclaimed. “That guy is a nut. He and his crazy biker friend will kill us if we don’t.”

Zabrina had hoped for a better reaction from JC, but he was right. Finding Luna only solved half their problem. The money would be difficult to raise, considering how much of it they’d already spent. She took a deep breath and reassured herself it would not be impossible.

Luna happy-danced her way off the plane when they arrived in New Orleans. The first thing she did was contact her employer to find out if she still had a job. She had requested two days of vacation, then went missing for more than a week. Luna called her boss and told him she got lost while hiking and had no way to contact anyone. It was true, but she didn’t mention the “kidnapped and left in a Peruvian jungle” part. That would have been too much to explain. Remarkably, her employer didn’t ask her to elaborate and told her to take the rest of the week off to recover. She was glad about that, because she had other things to do.

A hot shower never felt so good after the cold baths in the Javari River. As the warm water sprayed down like rain from heaven, Luna thought of the elderly Matsés woman who had bathed her. Never had she known such a tender act of kindness. She smiled, now thinking of the sweet young jaguar, Mi Amiga. What a smart animal, and with the personality of a house cat.

Then her mind shifted to Zabrina. The woman had taken things way too far when she pulled such a dangerous stunt. It was only through divine intervention that Luna hadn't died in that jungle. Things could have been so much worse. Now playtime was over. Luna needed to come up with a plan to take down Zabrina and her friends once and for all.

She phoned Stenson to invite her hero over for dinner later. Butterflies fluttered when she heard his voice. Stenson seemed giggly too. It reminded her of when they were kids and made each other laugh for silly reasons. If this was love, they were both feeling it.

Luna climbed into her cozy bed. She'd never again take a bed for granted as she remembered lying on the jungle floor covered in bugs. A shiver ran down her spine. Luna lifted the covers to make sure there were no insects in her bed, just in case. With all the tricks Zabrina had pulled, nothing would surprise her.

Charlie Whitehorse stopped by the bar to visit the guys after they returned from Peru. He knew Stenson was happy that they'd found Luna. But according to Brick, his friend was so sunny that if you turned off the lights, Stenson would glow.

Charlie asked, "Why is he so cheerful?"

"The boy's in love," Brick said with a smile.

"Get out of here. Stenson in love? Let me guess ... Luna?"

"Head over heels."

Charlie walked into the office and found Stenson on the

computer. "Hey, buddy, what's up?"

"Looking at cars I can't afford. Seems I owe you and some bikers a lot of money. I'll be riding on back of Brick's bike looking like his girlfriend for a while."

Charlie laughed at the thought. "Don't worry about my money. I know you'll get it when you can. You want me to get you a car?"

"Thanks, but I know where you get your cars," Stenson joked.

Stenson stopped by a florist to pick up flowers. He arrived at Luna's apartment at 6:00 p.m.

She answered the door barefoot, wearing an off-the-shoulder black dress. "Hello, handsome!"

Stenson's mouth hit the floor. He had never seen Luna look so sexy. When Stenson handed her the bouquet, she thanked him with a kiss. He thought of bringing flowers every day if this would be how she greeted him.

"I love the sunflowers, Stenson. They're my favorite. Why did you choose them?"

"They reminded me of you—bright and happy."

Luna placed the flowers in a vase and set them on the candlelit table. She poured two glasses of pinot gris, and they sat on the sofa while dinner cooked. Stenson clinked his glass to hers and told Luna how worried he had been when she was missing. She leaned over and gave him another kiss.

"I want to show you something," Luna said as she opened her laptop and handed it to Stenson.

It was a promotional announcement for an upcoming black-tie event at Club Empire. The article listed several celebrities and local politicians who would be in attendance.

Luna said, "Let's take them down."

"What have you got in mind?"

Luna laid out her plan. It was way more complicated than

leaving somebody stranded in a jungle. And it would take all their friends to pull it off. But it wasn't violent, and nobody would get physically hurt. And that bothered her. She could have died in Peru, and she was still angry how they'd affected Stenson's health with the estrogen stunt. He would carry those scars for the rest of his life. When Luna finished explaining the plan, she asked Stenson what he thought.

"I like it. It's brilliant but complicated. If we pull this off, maybe they won't mess with us again. I'm sure Charlie and Brick will help."

Luna pushed the laptop away and climbed on Stenson's lap. She wrapped her arms around his neck and gave him a passionate kiss. Then she jumped up and said, "Let's eat!"

Stenson laughed at the way she teased him. He would rather forget dinner altogether after that kiss. But since Luna arranged this evening to the last detail, he would go with whatever Ms. LeRoux wanted.

Aaron Neville's music serenaded the candlelit dinner. Stenson gazed at Luna's eyes as she rubbed her foot against his leg under the table. They fed each other bites of food, and their conversations were sweet and endless.

They were tipsy from two bottles of wine. When the song "A Change Is Gonna Come" played, Luna held out her hand and asked Stenson if he would honor her with a dance. Stenson wrapped his arms around Luna's waist as she placed her arms on his shoulders. They swayed to the music in the flickering candlelight. Luna laid her head against Stenson's chest and listened to the rhythm of his heart. Neither had felt love like this before.

When the sweet song ended, Luna gazed into Stenson's eyes. She kissed him with such passion that it said they were more than friends tonight. She held his hand and led him to the bedroom. In that moment, two souls became one.

The next morning, Stenson awoke to Aretha Franklin's, "Respect." He walked into the kitchen to find Luna dancing in her pajamas and singing into a spatula microphone. She was having so much fun that Stenson joined her dance party. They laughed as they danced around the kitchen like two crazy kids.

"You're in a good mood this morning," Stenson said.

"I'm in a great mood! How about some pancakes?"

"You don't have to twist my arm. I'm starving!"

After breakfast, Stenson mentioned he needed to run a few errands. Luna offered to drive him home. She still couldn't believe Stenson blew up his own car trying to get information from Zabrina. Luna grabbed her keys and walked out the door.

When Stenson got into the car, he said, "You know you're wearing your pajamas?"

Luna replied, "I'm so happy, I don't care if I'm naked!"

Stenson winked and said, "You mean like last night?"

Brick and Charlie dropped by Stenson's place later to discuss Luna's plan. Brick saw the goofy look on Stenson's face and knew there was only one thing that could make a man smile like that. He was happy for the couple and wondered what took them so long.

Club Empire buzzed with activity in preparation for Saturday's black-tie charity event. Zabrina sent press releases and spoke with media organizations. She invited every high-profile politician, athlete, and celebrity in New Orleans. JC placed orders for extra cases of expensive alcohol. Jesús coordinated the menu with the catering company. Big Tony interviewed extra security and hired a valet service to handle attendees' cars.

In typical JC fashion, he wanted everything over the top. JC told Zabrina to get spotlights like they had at movie premiers and a roped-off red carpet. Any other time, she would have told him it was too much. But considering how mad he had been at her lately, she agreed to his demands.

Luna's plan required more people than Stenson, Brick, and Charlie. Brick recruited his biker buddies, and Charlie enlisted his crew. The Mystery Man was on board with his part, and Sarge provided the hardware. Thursday night, everyone gathered at O'Malley's to go over last-minute details.

Satisfied they were ready, Luna raised her glass and proposed a toast: "Here's to payback!"

The club looked like a chorus of chaos Saturday morning as the crew prepared for the big night. Big Tony supervised the cleaning crew and trained extra security. JC oversaw the installation of new lighting and signed for liquor orders as they arrived. Jesús assisted the catering company in the kitchen. And Zabrina fielded calls from the media and the personal assistants of VIPs.

Zabrina would have pulled her hair out, if only she had any. Instead, she removed the purple wig she was wearing because it was too hot with all the running around. She still had enough time to pick up her dress and make it to the salon. As she was about to leave, Zabrina asked the guys if they wanted her to pick up food on the way back. JC waved her off because he still wasn't talking to her. Tony never turned down food and asked her to grab something for him.

Brick and Charlie met Stenson and Luna to go over final details. Brick said he'd received a message from the Mystery

Man confirming his job was done. Charlie confirmed his team was ready to go. Stenson and Luna had a few more things to do, but they would be ready in time. The four joined hands like a team preparing for a big game and wished each other luck.

Soni, Zabrina's stylist, knew how important the evening was to her. She could tell it bothered Zabrina that she and JC weren't talking. Soni assured her JC would be in a better mood after the successful event tonight. When Soni finished Zabrina's manicure and pedicure, they drove to the dress shop together.

The ladies bought new gowns for the special occasion. When they walked out of the dressing room, each teased the other about who looked hotter. Zabrina said it wasn't a fair competition because Soni was almost seven feet tall in heels and easier to spot. Zabrina dropped Soni off at home, then picked up some food and headed back to the club.

Tony was at the front desk reviewing reservations when Zabrina walked in. She'd forgotten to put Soni's name on the list and asked Tony to add it. Zabrina described Soni as a beautiful, tall, transgender woman. She said Soni wouldn't be hard to spot because she got all the attention whenever she entered a room. Zabrina asked Tony to take special care of her best friend.

When she handed the bag to Big Tony, he said he didn't remember ordering that much food. Zabrina winked at him and said some of it was for Justin. She told him not to tell JC it was from her or he might think she poisoned it. Tony laughed and said he would say it was from him.

Everyone left the club at 6:00 p.m. to get dressed for the event. Meanwhile, Stenson and Luna had their own special outfits planned for the night. They emerged dressed head to toe in black. Stenson said they looked like cat burglars or the

Mystery Man. Luna laughed and said they were kind of the same since the Mystery Man was the world's best cat burglar.

At 7:30 p.m., Tony Gallo held a final briefing with security personnel and the valets. JC had the DJ rehearse the introduction he'd produced to make sure the lights, video, and smoke effects were in sync. He instructed the disc jockey to play it at precisely 10:00 p.m. Zabrina conducted interviews with the media in front of the club. VIPs began to arrive at 8:00 p.m. Light bulbs flashed as expensive cars rolled up to the front doors of Club Empire. Celebrities posed for photographs and briefly spoke to reporters before entering the club.

JC and Big Tony greeted guests at the door, and then attractive hostesses escorted them to their tables. Zabrina's friend Soni arrived around 9:00 p.m. JC's mouth fell wide open when she walked through the door. Soni wore a floor-length, bright red gown with sequins.

JC told Big Tony, "I'll take care of this beautiful woman myself."

"But, JC ..." Tony tried to warn him.

JC ignored him and approached the tall woman. "Hello, gorgeous. Welcome to Club Empire. Are you here alone?"

"Yes, I'm Zabrina's guest," Soni said.

"I won't hold that against you. Why don't you join me in my personal VIP section?" JC offered his arm and escorted Soni to the section reserved for him.

The club was filled with the rich and famous. JC was admiring the sight when a waitress approached and said, "I've received several complaints about the hors d'oeuvres."

"Like what?"

"Like they suck," the waitress honestly admitted.

JC walked into the kitchen and tried an appetizer. He spit it out and screamed, "What is this?"

The caterer said, "Pâté and pear butter."

"No, I'll tell you what it is. It is horse manure on a piece of fruit! Get rid of it!" JC demanded. He poured a box of Ritz crackers on a platter and told the waitress to serve them in the meantime.

A bartender caught JC as he left the kitchen, telling him that customers were complaining about the drinks. When JC asked which drinks, the bartender said all of them. JC went behind the bar and poured a glass of Cristal champagne and spit it out. The only thing Cristal about the champagne was its crystal-clear appearance, because it tasted like flat soda. The champagne had no bubbles. Then he tried one of the top-shelf vodkas, and it was even worse. He didn't understand what could be wrong with the booze because it was brand-new liquor delivered that morning. JC told the bartender to serve the old stuff and tell guests the drinks were on him.

People kept dancing despite the problems with the food and alcohol. JC assumed everyone had arrived drunk, since even a homeless alcoholic wouldn't touch the stuff he was selling. He tried to take his mind off things by asking Soni to dance. When she turned around on the dance floor, JC started grinding on her backside. He believed he might get lucky with this hot woman tonight.

Luna and Stenson were positioned outside the club. She came over the radio: "Is everybody ready?"

One by one, they all said, "Ready."

Luna looked at her watch. At precisely 10:00 p.m., she said, "Let the party begin!"

JC sat with Soni and several VIPs, waiting for the intro to play at 10:00 p.m. He nodded to the DJ, and the lights went down on cue.

A mysterious voice came over the speakers, announcing, "Welcome to Club Empire!"

Fog poured from the ceiling as JC waited for the big moment.

Suddenly, Stenson appeared on every screen in the club and said, "Hello, JC." Then Luna appeared next to him and said, "Hello, Zabrina." Next, Brick appeared with his tattooed arms crossed and said, "Hello, fat boy," referring to Big Tony.

Strobe lights flashed as a video montage played on the screens to the song "Do You Really Want to Hurt Me?" by Culture Club. The video showed clips of a homeless person throwing a turkey at JC, Zabrina with chunks of hair missing, and Big Tony getting out of a car wearing a dress.

JC freaked out! This was not the intro they'd worked on. He ran to the DJ booth and screamed, "What is this?" JC didn't wait for an answer: "Change it quick! Kill the video and do something about these lights! These strobes made one of our guests have an epileptic seizure on the dance floor!"

The DJ tried to stop the video, but the source was coming from somewhere outside the building. He killed the strobe lights, which triggered all the houselights to turn on, blinding the guests. Then the DJ quickly selected a hip-hop song to play. Instead, the theme song from the children's show *Teletubbies* came on. JC looked at the screens to see Stenson, Luna, Brick, and Charlie all dancing in brightly colored purple, green, yellow, and red Teletubby costumes.

Before JC could react, he noticed the crowd covering their faces and gagging. He yelled at the DJ, "What is that god-awful smell? It's like gym socks combined with a portable toilet in a heat wave! Shut off the smoke machine!"

The club was in complete pandemonium as guests stampeded toward the doors. They knocked over tables, chairs, and anyone standing in their way, trying to get out. It was like watching the running of the bulls in Spain. Except in this case, the people running were in tuxedos and gowns.

Zabrina stood outside, trying to apologize to people as they ran out the door. One woman was so angry that she yanked Zabrina's hair, only to rip the bright pink wig off her head. Hundreds of people demanded their cars. Big Tony tried to calm people down while the valets went to retrieve their vehicles. Nobody could believe it when the valets returned and told them their cars were missing. Zabrina and Tony frantically phoned every car for hire in New Orleans. They were so desperate for transportation, they didn't care if donkeys or a space shuttle showed up to take people home.

A woman yelled, "The drinks sucked, the food sucked, the music sucked, and my twenty-five-hundred-dollar dress smells like an outhouse! Now you're telling me my car is stolen too? You'll hear from my attorney!"

Zabrina looked up to see several media outlets filming the chaos. She ran over and began attacking the cameras and screaming to turn them off. A reporter placed a microphone in front of Zabrina to ask her a question. Zabrina punched the woman in the face.

It took two hours to clear everyone from Club Empire. The only people remaining were Zabrina, Tony, JC, and Soni. Even the employees had gone home in disgust. Zabrina saw the fury burning in JC's eyes. Tony was embarrassed by the video of him in a dress. Soni removed her wig in solidarity with her bald friend Zabrina.

Soni's voice became deeper, more like that of a man, as she said, "Everything will be okay, honey."

JC erupted at Soni, "You're a man? You mean to tell me I danced with a faggot? How could tonight be any worse? I'm out of here! And, Zabrina, I never want to see you or that homo again!"

JC screeched his tires as he tore out of the parking lot. As soon as he got home, JC poured a stiff drink. He took the bottle with him as he sat on the couch alone in the dark. How could this have happened? He was born into a ruined life but had worked so hard to make it better. He cried and wondered why God hated him so much. What did he ever do to deserve this?

Awhile later, there was a knock at the door. JC ignored it and slammed down another shot of vodka. The knocking persisted until he finally got up to see who it is. He looked through the peephole and saw it was Soni. "Go away, faggot!"

"I'm not going away, JC. I'm big enough to kick down this door if I have to."

JC was drunk, and that comment made him laugh, knowing Soni was definitely big enough to kick down the door. He opened it and said, "What do you want, homo?"

"I wanted to come by and check on you. I know how upset you are."

"I don't need comforting by a drag queen. Leave!"

Soni wasn't fazed by JC's disparaging remarks. She had heard it all before. "JC, I am transgender. I identify as a woman even though I am stuck in a man's body."

Whether it was because Soni was so honest or JC was so drunk, he let her in and offered her a drink. They returned to the living room and sat on the couch. Neither spoke for a while as they sipped their drinks.

Soni broke the silence: "JC, do you like when people call you 'nigger'?"

"No."

"Do you realize calling someone 'faggot' or 'homo' is just as offensive?"

JC listened but didn't reply.

Soni continued, "JC, I treat others the way I want to be treated, with kindness and respect. I would never intentionally hurt someone's feelings. Why do you think it's okay to hurt mine?"

"Because you have issues. You're a man who dresses like a woman."

"You have issues too."

"No I don't."

"I know you were abandoned as a child and ran away when you were eight. I also know you have HIV."

JC looked surprised. "How do you know that?"

"Zabrina told me. We talk about everything."

"Nobody knows about my HIV status except Big Tony."

Soni said, "Zabrina saw your medication and knew what it was even though you told her it was vitamins. She's not stupid."

JC remained silent.

"Zabrina said nothing because she knows you aren't comfortable telling anyone. Do you think you are homophobic because you have HIV and think people would believe you are gay?"

JC didn't answer.

"Listen, JC, Zabrina loves you and considers you and Big Tony her best friends. And because of what she has been through in life, she doesn't trust many people. What happened tonight hurt her too. She was only trying to help, and it backfired in ways she could never imagine."

JC sighed but didn't say a word.

"Listen, JC, I attend a weekly group meeting for LGBTQ people. You should go with me sometime."

"I'm not gay. I have nothing in common with those people," he replied.

"Nobody thinks you're gay. But I believe you'll find we all have things in common. They're nice people. I'll leave my number on the table. I hope you'll consider it." Soni arose to leave.

JC said, "Thank you for stopping by, Soni. I'm very sorry I called you those names."

Soni hugged JC. "It's okay. Just remember, I might dress like a woman, but I fight like a man!"

CHAPTER TWENTY-EIGHT

NEW ORLEANS, LOUISIANA

The plan to take down JC and his crew went better than expected. Charlie's crew, posing as valet employees, had made off with $3 million worth of exotic automobiles. After guests handed keys to the valets, they drove around the corner and onto waiting car haulers. The automobiles were already aboard ships headed to buyers in Asia and the Middle East. Charlie wished it was always that easy stealing cars.

The video montage that played at Club Empire was Luna's idea. Everyone had fun filming it a few days earlier. The video was an instant sensation on the internet. They kept the Teletubby costumes for their next Halloween party. Stenson was especially proud of the funky fog that sprayed inside the club. He managed to get cases of the nasty smelling Durian fruit that had been used to pack the stolen marijuana. He found it ironic, since the stolen weed had started all the madness.

Brick was happy since he met the girl of his dreams when he offered her a ride home from Empire on the back of his bike. He and Stenson also left the Mystery Man a case of untainted Remy Jackson XO cognac, which JC had special-ordered.

Luna clinked her glass to get everyone's attention. "I saved the best part for last. Tomorrow morning, JC and company will realize they're broke. It seems a hacker transferred their funds to an offshore bank."

Cheers erupted and Brick yelled, "Don't mess with Luna LeRoux!"

The next morning, Zabrina turned on the news. Club Empire was the lead story on every channel; even the national media had picked it up. They were all the same. Irate attendees describing the gruesome events. People saying their valet-parked cars had been stolen, and threatening lawsuits. There was even video of a bald Zabrina shoving cameramen and punching a female reporter in the face.

Zabrina turned off the TV. It only reaffirmed what she already knew: they were ruined. Zabrina phoned Big Tony and asked him to meet her at the club. She didn't dare call JC. She was certain he would never forgive her for what had happened last night. Zabrina instructed the staff who hadn't already quit to not come in today.

Tony arrived at the club to survey the damage with Zabrina. The smell was overwhelming. Tony opened all the doors to ventilate the place. Overturned tables and chairs and broken glass made it look like the scene of a riot. Their once beautiful club was a total disaster.

They walked to the office and sat down. Zabrina asked, "What are we going to do?"

"Rebuild," Tony suggested. "We can rebrand the club. After a few months, people will forget about this. You know how news cycles are."

Tony was right. They didn't have a choice. Besides, she could not let Stenson and his crew defeat them like this.

Zabrina logged in to their bank website to see how much money they had to rebuild. Zabrina's face turned pale with disbelief. "This can't be right!" she exclaimed.

"What?" Tony asked.

"It says our account balance is zero!" She refreshed the

screen, hoping it was an error, only to see it remain the same. "Tony, I checked the account yesterday and there was more than $1.5 million."

Zabrina phoned the bank. A representative confirmed that a transfer had occurred at 10:01 p.m. last night. She mentioned that since it was such a large transaction, they'd phoned to verify. Records showed a person named Anthony Gallo had validated all the security questions. While unusual, the bank approved the transaction. Zabrina asked where they'd transferred the funds. The representative said a bank in the Cayman Islands.

Zabrina slammed down the phone and stared at Big Tony. "Not only did they kill our business, they impersonated you and stole our money!"

"They impersonated me? How?"

"Somehow they knew the answers to your security verification questions. The bank approved the transfer of our funds to some bank in the Cayman Islands."

"Un-freaking-believable! It had to be that hacker Luna. Don't tell JC until we figure this out."

"I know," Zabrina said, bowing her head. "Would you mind cleaning the club for a while? I'm sorry to ask you to do it, but I need time to think. You are the only friend I have, Tony."

Zabrina felt like crying because she was responsible for this mess. If she had never gotten them involved in the Mexico deal with Stenson's people, they wouldn't be in this position. She opened the office safe and removed the only cash they had. The partners had poured everything they made back into the club—except for JC, who poured his money into cars, clothes, and bad ideas.

There was approximately $32,000 sitting on the desk. How could she rebuild a club on that amount of money? They'd invested more than $500,000 to build Empire. And most of that came from the backs of the women who worked for her "side" business. She didn't want to go there again. For the longest time, she had tried to get out of that racket and give the ladies a legitimate way to make money.

But what could she do? She couldn't sell the tainted alcohol inventory. The furniture and fixtures were destroyed. Everything else smelled of portable toilets and vomit from the stink-bomb Stenson's crew had set off in the club.

Tony knocked on the office door. "Zabrina, there's somebody here to see you."

"Tell them to go away. I'm in no mood to talk."

"I believe you should see this person, Zabrina."

"Fine, let them in."

Into the office walked a petite black woman who appeared to be in her early forties. Big Tony shut the door.

"I'm sorry to bother you," the lady said.

"Have a seat. How can I help you?"

"My name is Mattie Carter. I am Justin's mother."

Zabrina dropped the pen she held in her hand. She didn't hear the sound it made when it hit the desk because of all the thoughts rushing through her mind. She knew JC had been abandoned at birth and grew up in an orphanage. He'd told her he never knew his mother, and anytime he mentioned her, JC said how much he hated the woman. Now she sat before Zabrina.

The petite lady said, "Ms. Chao, I saw what happened to you and my son on the news this morning. I feel very sorry for you both. I've lived in New Orleans for many years working as a housekeeper. I've watched my son grow up from the shadows. It's made me proud to see his accomplishments, and I know he could not have done it without you."

Mattie paused, then said, "I would like to see my son. I believe it's time."

Zabrina was shocked but understood. "Ms. Carter, it is the right time." Zabrina wrote JC's address on a piece of paper and handed it to Mattie.

Stenson poured a cup of coffee and joined Luna on the sofa. She smiled and said, "Good morning, sunshine. How do you feel today?"

"Hungover," Stenson barely muttered.

"Me too. That was quite a party last night."

Luna turned on the television. It seemed like the Club Empire story was on every station. Luna laughed at the pandemonium and torrid interviews of patrons. She especially enjoyed seeing Zabrina losing her mind with a bald head. It was the first time she'd seen the success of her trick that had caused Zabrina to lose her hair.

Luna looked at Stenson, who did not seem quite as amused. "What's wrong? Isn't it funny what we did to them?"

"I guess. But I kind of feel bad. We destroyed them."

"What do you mean you feel bad? I was left for dead in a jungle! And you lost so much from everything they've done to you. They got what they deserved!"

"I guess you're right, but I wanted none of this. I'm not a vindictive person. All I ever wanted was to get you back safely and return the money I owe our friends."

"I know you aren't vindictive, sweetheart. But we had to teach them a lesson."

Stenson knew Luna was right. But it didn't make him feel any better about what they had done. In some ways, he knew JC wasn't responsible for any of this. He didn't think JC was bright enough to come up with the scam that started their twisted game anyway. Stenson sighed, wishing none of this had ever happened to either him or JC.

There was a knock at JC's door. He ignored it, just like he ignored Big Tony's call earlier that morning. But whoever it was wouldn't go away. The gentle knock persisted, like some leaky faucet when you're trying to sleep. Finally, he got up and opened the door so he could tell whoever it was to leave him alone.

"Justin?" a petite black woman asked.

"Yes?"

"May I come in?"

"Do I know you?" JC asked as he wondered why she seemed so familiar.

"No, but I know you." The lady paused. "I'm your mother."

JC stood frozen like an iceberg, unable to process what he heard.

She asked again, "May I come in?"

As if on automatic pilot, JC widened the door and allowed the stranger inside. He followed her into the living room, where they sat and stared at each other in silence.

Finally, the woman said, "Justin, my name is Mattie Carter. I'm your biological mother. I've wanted to have this conversation with you for a lifetime."

JC sat stunned, staring at the person who admitted she was the person he hated above all others. He recoiled when she attempted to touch his hand. His head spun like he was in a fighter pilot's training centrifuge. Any moment, he was certain he would black out.

Mattie sensed his hesitation. What was she to expect when

the mother he hadn't seen in twenty-three years—the one who'd left him at a hospital—showed up at his door? This wasn't easy for her either. But she'd come this far, so she would tell him what she had to say. It would be up to him if he wanted to forgive her, and she wouldn't blame him if he didn't.

JC sat in a hypnotic trance as Mattie spoke. She said she'd become pregnant at sixteen years old by a man who did not love her. Her mother insisted she have an abortion so she would not screw up her life as she had. Mattie shared the vivid dream she had while she was pregnant with Justin: that one day her son would grow up to be a great man. Mattie told him about the mysterious voice of a little boy who assured her, "Everything will be okay."

Mattie locked onto her son's eyes and said, "That dream is why you are here today."

A chill ran down Justin's spine as she continued. Mattie told him of her decision to run away. She recounted the horrifying tale of rape by a drug addict in an abandoned railroad car. She told him of the kindness shown to her by the waitress, Annie, who cared for her during pregnancy. Mattie explained the reason she'd left him at the hospital. She believed in her sixteen-year-old heart that it would give him a better life than she could provide as a teenage mother.

Tears welled up in Mattie's eyes. She told Justin how that single decision she'd made as a child had affected both of their lives. She and her son had contracted HIV because of the rape. Her friend Annie died the day she received the news that she could not adopt Justin. Mattie's mother passed away before they could mend their relationship. And Mattie never realized her own dreams of a happy life.

There was a long moment of silence. Finally, Mattie said, "Justin, please know that every day of my life, I have loved you."

The icy walls surrounding JC's heart smashed into a million pieces, and he began to cry like a child. For so long, JC had hated his mother. He grew up believing she threw him away like unwanted trash. He'd cursed her for the stain of a life with HIV. The jaded belief that he wasn't good enough for his own mother made him feel like he'd never be good enough for this world.

His own self-pity never allowed him to consider there might be another explanation. The pain he'd endured paled in comparison to his mother's. How could he have been so selfish and wrong?

JC reached for his mother's hand and looked at her with childlike eyes as he said, "Mom, I didn't understand the sacrifices you made for me."

Mattie had wished every day since she felt Justin in her womb to hear him call her "Mom." But, like most wishes, she never believed it would come true. Especially like this.

"Son, I'm sorry I haven't reached out to you sooner. I've carried this burden of letting you go every day of my life. I cannot forgive myself. How can I expect you, my son, to forgive me?" Mattie paused and wiped a tear. "After I saw what happened to you on the news, I knew this was the time you needed your mother."

JC embraced his mom. His tears flowed like a dam that held back a lifetime of emotions bursting from within his soul. Mattie held his head next to her breast. An overwhelming sense of déjà vu transported Mattie to a time in her past. It was the last time she had rocked her infant son in the hospital the day she said goodbye.

Mattie wiped the tears from Justin's eyes. He looked at his mother's gentle smile. JC studied her face, noticing every tiny detail. He had her eyes, her nose, and her lips. Even their smiles were the same. But it wasn't that they looked alike, or her words about being his mother. It was as if God had left some indelible imprint within JC that told him so.

"Mom, yesterday was one of the most heartbreaking days of my life. I've lost everything. But I gained something more important today that I never dreamed would come true ... you. This is the most precious gift when I needed it most."

Mattie stroked her son's head. "JC, you'll learn as I have that when you think your life is falling apart, sometimes it's falling into place. Life has a plan none of us know."

"Why does it have to hurt so much, Mom?" JC asked.

"I have always wondered that myself, son. Why does it hurt when a mother gives birth to a child? One of the most joyous experiences is also one of the most painful. Maybe these things that happened to you were so painful to guide you down a different path. Would you have changed direction without it?"

JC listened to the wisdom of his mother.

"What I went through to bring you into this world changed my life forever. It wasn't the plan I wanted. I was a good girl and became pregnant with you the first time I had sex. And I never wanted to have sex until I was married, but your father—" Mattie stopped midsentence.

JC sensed that his mother did not want to talk about his father, but he pressed, "Tell me about my dad."

Mattie considered her words carefully. "Justin, Demarcus Jackson is not your dad. He is your biological father—a sperm donor, that's all. As I look back, he lied and said he loved me. At that young age, I believed him. But Demarcus did not love me, nor any of the countless women whose lives he has destroyed. Demarcus Jackson only cares about himself." Mattie smiled at her son. "JC, as I tried to explain to you, my life fell apart the day I discovered I was pregnant. But in some miraculous way, God allowed me to be your mother, to be here with you today.

Our lives have fallen into place in ways we could have never imagined."

Mattie changed the subject: "Enough about me. I want to hear about you. We have a lot of catching up to do."

JC shared stories of his life growing up in Mission of Hope. Kids had picked on him because of the color of his skin, he said. He lived with a disease that made ignorant people afraid to touch him. It hurt that nobody wanted to adopt him. He'd grown up feeling unloved, unwanted, and broken. By the time he was eight years old, he'd had enough. That was when he ran away.

Mattie rubbed her son's hand. JC saw the anguish on his mother's face as she learned of the trials he'd endured.

JC smiled and tried to reassure her, "It wasn't all bad, Mom. I met my friend Jesús at Mission of Hope. And after I ran away, I met Dr. Abayomi, who is a great example of an intelligent black man who taught me to be proud of who I am. Then I met my best friend—Big Tony. If it wasn't for him, I would probably be dead."

Mattie noticed JC had not mentioned Zabrina. "What about your friend Zabrina? She's the person who gave me your address."

"I wish I had never met her. She ruined everything I worked for."

Mattie sensed her son's anger, but asked anyway, "*You* worked for?"

JC looked at his mother as if he couldn't believe the question.

"You're telling me you built Club Empire all by yourself and Zabrina didn't help at all? That Club Empire would have been just as successful without her?"

JC shifted on the sofa as Mattie continued, "Justin, did you stop to think that this has ruined her life too? You can ask me to leave, but as your mother, I will tell you what I think. You are doing what you've done all your life by saying 'poor little me' and not considering anyone but yourself. What happened at Club Empire hurt many people. Reputations have been harmed. Your staff lost jobs. And if you think Zabrina intended for this to happen, you are wrong. I met her, and she is a broken woman right now. But unlike you, she's not hidden away at home not talking to anyone. She is at that club along with your friend Tony, trying to figure out what to do now."

Justin felt the sting of his mother's truth.

"JC, what Zabrina needs is your friendship. You all built Club Empire together, and then you fell together. Don't abandon her when she needs you most." Mattie paused. "You of all people should understand what it feels like to be abandoned and unloved. Now is the time I want you to be the great man I always knew you would be."

Mattie saw tears welling in her son's eyes again. He understood what his mother meant and knew she was right. Mattie squeezed Justin's hand. "Son, forgiving ourselves is often harder than forgiving others."

JC wiped his eyes and asked his mother if he could take her to lunch. He wanted her to meet Big Tony. She would only accept the offer if he also invited Zabrina. When JC resisted the idea, Mattie said, "JC, today is a new day. Don't waste it holding a grudge. I held a grudge against my mother and lost her before we reconciled. Don't repeat the same mistake as me."

He smiled and said, "Well, Mom, as long as today is about forgiveness, let me invite another strange friend." He picked up the phone and called Soni.

It was a beautiful morning at the outdoor café in the French Quarter. Big Tony and Jesús were there. JC's mom especially enjoyed meeting Soni. When Mattie and Soni hugged, the top of Mattie's head came to the height of Soni's breasts.

Mattie laughed and said, "You are a lot of woman!"

Soni was tickled by the remark and said, "You are too, only in a smaller package."

Zabrina was the last to arrive. She hesitated at the entrance to the covered patio. To everyone's surprise, JC rose from the table and hugged Zabrina. He whispered in her ear, "Let's talk later." JC pulled out a chair for Zabrina next to his mom.

Brunch was lighthearted. It seemed like everyone had a funny story about JC: from ants in his underwear drawer to the menu he came up with when he had to get rid of so many turkeys. Mattie enjoyed hearing them all. After lunch, Soni, Big Tony, and Jesús said goodbye. JC and Zabrina walked with Mattie to her car. JC hugged his mother and told her he would call later.

Zabrina and JC strolled through Louis Armstrong Park in the Tremé neighborhood. They sat on a bench near a small lake and watched the ducks.

Zabrina was first to speak: "JC, I am so sorry. I never meant for any of this to happen."

"I know, Zabrina," JC said with a caring expression.

"Please don't hate me. I will do anything to fix this. You are like a brother to me. You'll never know what it meant to me when you and Big Tony took me in at such a low point in my life. Since I lost my family, you two are the only family I've got. And I didn't mean to ruin our business or friendship with my bad ideas."

JC put his arm around Zabrina and said, "Zabrina, I've been a jerk. You have always been the brains of our organization, and we would not have had success without you. Tony and I cherish your friendship. Please forgive me for all the times I've been so self-centered. We will start over and be even better than before."

"There is a problem. They stole all our money. We're broke."

"They what?"

"Our bank accounts are empty."

JC shook his head. "I have to hand it to Stenson and Luna. They didn't just ruin our reputation and destroy our club; they also killed us financially."

"Aren't you angry?"

"Yes, but revenge has gotten us where we are today. Since this has been one of the nicest days of my life, I don't want to ruin it thinking of payback or bad feelings."

"I agree. Let's take the rest of the week off and think about what our next move should be. Thank you for forgiving me, JC."

"Thank you for being my friend, Zabrina."

After Zabrina left, JC decided there was one more thing he wanted to do. He called Soni and asked her if the invitation to attend the LGBTQ support group was still open. She was excited he'd asked and told him there was a meeting that night and she'd pick him up later.

That evening, JC walked into the support group with Soni. At first, he felt awkward being the only heterosexual in the room. Soni introduced JC to a group of friends who welcomed him warmly. He soon realized everyone was as normal or abnormal as him.

Soni offered JC a seat in the circle of twenty chairs. The leader of the group opened the meeting with "A Prayer for Wanderers." JC found the words poignant. People shared stories of discrimination and disownment by families. They spoke of feeling lost and misunderstood. As JC listened, he realized these people had many of the same burdens he had carried throughout his life.

The leader of the group asked JC if he would like to speak.

At first, he didn't want to until Soni encouraged him with a nudge. JC began by thanking Soni for inviting him to the meeting. He told the group that while he was heterosexual, he shared the same emotions as them. He revealed his abandonment issues and hiding his HIV status. He explained he had been homophobic all his life. He thought it was because he feared that people would think he was gay if they knew he had HIV. JC said he didn't realize calling someone "faggot" was as offensive as if someone called him a racist expression for being black. He thanked Soni for helping him understand that. JC said he would never use that word again and asked the group for forgiveness.

When the meeting ended, people told JC how happy they were he attended and appreciated his story. One guy joked that if JC wasn't so homophobic, he would invite him to one of their weekly dinners. JC laughed and said he would love to go if Soni provided security.

As Soni drove him home, JC told her how much he'd enjoyed the meeting. He was ashamed to have been so judgmental of others his whole his life.

Soni smiled and said, "Not your whole life. There is a new one starting right now."

CHAPTER TWENTY-NINE

NEW ORLEANS, LOUISIANA / DEVEREAUX PARISH, LOUISIANA

JC had a new outlook on life. Understanding his mother's hardships allowed him to see things through a different lens. Soni taught him that being dissimilar should be celebrated rather than chastised. Zabrina made it poignantly clear that everyone makes mistakes and desires forgiveness.

But a few things his mother shared left him feeling disappointed, sad, or angry. That his mom and her mother had never reconciled before she passed away bothered him. His grandmother's regret was what sent her to an early grave.

It made him sad to learn the tragic story of the waitress, Annie Barnes. JC wished he could have met the special lady who befriended his mother when she was a pregnant teenage runaway. Her story reminded him how important people could be in a young person's life. It was like how Dr. Amara Abayomi had showed him what it meant to be an intelligent and caring black man. It troubled him knowing that Annie Barnes died the day she found out she could not adopt him. The system chose not to allow a person who loved JC to adopt him because she didn't have enough money. Annie Barnes had a heart whose account overflowed with love. Instead, bureaucrats sentenced him to an unwanted existence in an orphanage. JC pondered the irony of it all.

His thoughts shifted to anger when he learned of the bastard with whom he shared DNA. The way the man had ruined his mother's life and dreams—not to mention JC's own—seemed unconscionable. Everybody talked about forgiveness. But JC knew it would be a cold day in hell before he'd ever forgive that man.

He was ready to start a new chapter in his book of life. But before he moved on, there were things he needed to do to close this one. JC called Zabrina to ask for a favor. A few hours later, she phoned with the information he needed. He rang his mom to inquire about Annie Barnes's burial place. Mattie was touched when JC told her he would travel to Devereaux Parish to visit her grave. She gave him the name of the cemetery and asked him to place flowers for her.

JC phoned Big Tony and told him about the trip, then asked if he wanted to come along. Tony was surprised when he said Devereaux Parish, because JC had sworn he would never step foot in that town again. Tony agreed to go since it would give him a chance to get away from the mess at Club Empire and see his parents.

The road trip was nice. It had been too long since Tony and JC hung out as friends. Their lives since arriving in New Orleans had been all about the money. JC realized that sometimes you forget how much you appreciate someone. They laughed about the day they ran off to New Orleans and what a crazy idea it was. They recalled the fun times over the years and the struggles they'd been through.

When they arrived in Devereaux Parish, JC stopped at a flower shop. He bought three bouquets of flowers: two were for Annie, from his mother and him; the other was for Tony to give his mom.

They drove to the cemetery and found Annie's grave using a map JC had picked up at the office. Tony stood by the car while his friend walked to the grave. JC kneeled and placed the flowers against the tombstone. He touched the marker and said a few words he hoped Annie's spirit could hear.

As they headed to Tony's parents, Big Tony asked, "Are you sure you want to go? You can drop me off. I know you've never forgotten how my dad treated you the last time you saw him."

JC assured him this trip was meant for closure. He told Tony he didn't hold a grudge against Mr. Gallo and hoped Tony's dad did not hold one against him either.

Tony knocked on his parents' door. His father was surprised to see his son, then noticed JC standing behind him. Tony said, "Dad, you remember my friend, Justin Carter?"

"Yes, hello, Justin. Please come in."

Tony could tell JC and his father felt awkward when they sat together in the living room. Tony excused himself to give the flowers to his mother. After Tony left the room, both men tried to speak at once. JC insisted Mr. Gallo go first.

"Justin, I have wanted to apologize to you for years. What I did that day was wrong of me, and I am very sorry. My son has told me so many wonderful things about you. And I know what your friendship means to him."

JC said, "Mr. Gallo, I want to apologize to you too. I should have never lived in the apartment above your store without your permission. I hope you will forgive me."

"Justin, it hurt me most the way I treated you. If I had known your situation, I would have done more to help."

Tony returned to the living room with his mother. They talked for a while longer, and Mrs. Gallo made Tony promise it wouldn't be so long until the next time he visited. She told him video chats were not as good as hugging her son in person. As they left, Mr. Gallo shook JC's hand and asked him to come back anytime. He told JC he was always welcome in his home.

Their next stop was the medical clinic where Dr. Abayomi

practiced. When the doctor saw JC, he exclaimed, "You've grown up!"

"And you've lost your hair," JC joked.

Justin introduced Tony to Dr. Abayomi. The doctor was about to leave for dinner and invited the guys to join him. JC warned the doctor that Big Tony had a big appetite to match his nickname. Dr. Abayomi laughed and assured them they had enough food.

It was getting late when JC told Dr. Abayomi they needed to head back to New Orleans. When they returned to the car, JC told Tony, "I need to make one more stop."

"Where to?" Tony asked.

JC handed him the address. Tony entered it into the GPS and noticed it was a bad neighborhood. As they drove to the location, JC explained what he planned to do. He told Tony he didn't need to get involved. This was a personal matter. Tony wouldn't hear of it. He reminded his friend he always had his back.

When they arrived, JC parked the car and turned off the headlights. He walked through a cluttered yard and then knocked on the door of a rundown row house.

A tall, skinny black man wearing a white tank top and baggy shorts answered. He looked at JC and asked, "What you want, nigga?"

"Sorry to bother you. I was driving by and saw that somebody hit the car parked in front of your house. I thought it might be yours."

The low-rent resident didn't bother thanking JC for the information. Rather, he pushed him aside to inspect his car. When the man walked around to the rear of the vehicle, Big Tony stepped out from the shadows. He punched the guy so hard in the right temple that he crumpled to the ground, unconscious. JC and Tony bound the waste of a human being with duct tape and dragged him to their car. Tony stuffed him in the back seat and climbed inside beside him in case the jerk woke up.

JC drove to a swampy area on the outskirts of Devereaux Parish. Big Tony yanked Mr. Dazed and Confused from the vehicle and dragged him to the front of the car. JC opened the trunk and removed a Louisville Slugger baseball bat.

The man stood up and realized his hands were bound behind his back. Tony ripped the tape covering his mouth, only to hear the man yell, "Who the f— are you?"

JC leaned inches from the bound man's face and growled, "I am your worst nightmare." JC pushed his forehead with the end of the bat, wishing he could shove it through his skull. But there were things to say so that the man would never forget this night. "My name is Justin Carter. Does that last name ring a bell?" JC didn't wait for an answer. "I'm your son. You got my mother, Mattie Carter, pregnant and didn't give a damn about her or me."

JC swung the bat into the man's rib cage like he was hitting a fastball at Wrigley Field. "It seems you have eleven children by eleven different women and never paid a dime in child support for any of them."

JC smashed the bat into the man's left arm. He heard the bone snap and saw the arm dangle in the wrong direction. The man begged him to stop.

"Stop? Now that's funny. *Stop* is what you should have done long ago." JC bashed the man in his kneecap, causing him to collapse to one side. He looked like a lopsided triangle. "You ruined my mother's life. You ruined mine. You ruined so many lives."

JC got within an inch of the man's face with his own. He glared into his eyes with the look of a demon and spit on his face. Ready to take the express elevator to hell, JC roared, "You will never ruin another life again!"

With a stroke like an audition for the PGA Tour, Justin swung the bat between the man's legs. It crushed him so hard that even scrambled eggs cried at the sight. The bastard who'd ruined JC's life fell facedown into the swampy muck.

JC walked to the back of the car as the man screamed in agony and pleaded to die. He threw the bat into the trunk, looked at Tony, and said, "Let's go home."

Stenson flew to the Cayman Islands and withdrew the money they'd stolen from Empire's bank accounts. He returned to New Orleans with two duffle bags stuffed with a total of $1.5 million in cash. Brick watched Stenson place 150 stacks of bound $100 bills on the coffee table. He handed fifteen to Brick and asked him to return it to the bikers. It was repayment for the money they'd lost when the truck was stolen in Mexico by JC's people.

He called Charlie Whitehorse and asked him to meet at the bar later. Then he headed out to visit Sarge. Stenson asked how much he owed for the British battle tank rental he'd used to blow up JC's warehouse. Sarge told him the tank was free, but the round he fired cost $40,000. Stenson handed him $50,000 and told him the rest was gas money.

Charlie was waiting when Stenson arrived at O'Malley's. They went to the office, where Stenson pulled $150,000 from the bag and handed it to Charlie. His friend refused to take it, saying he made more than enough on the vehicles they stole from Club Empire. Then Charlie asked Stenson if he was still driving a rental car. Stenson admitted he was, but the Prius wasn't quite his style. Maybe he'd use the cash to buy a new car.

Charlie handed Stenson a set of keys and said, "Maybe this is more to your liking."

Charlie led Stenson out the back door of the bar. A black-and-white 1956 Ford Sunliner convertible sat in the parking lot. With its whitewall tires, a bloodred interior, and tons of chrome, the car sitting there was exactly what Stenson wanted.

Flabbergasted, he asked, "Where did you steal this?"

"It's not stolen, Stenson. My guys and I chipped in and bought it for you to say thanks. Call it an early birthday present."

Stenson could not believe it. "I don't know what to say."

"Just say you won't drive that Prius anymore. You were embarrassing all of us with that ride," Charlie joked.

The Sunliner drove like a dream when they took it for a spin around the French Quarter. After they returned, Stenson asked Brick if he knew where JC was at. Robert phoned the guy who was keeping an eye on him. The lookout informed him JC was on a boat at a marina and texted the address. When Stenson said he was heading there, Brick asked if he should come along. Stenson declined the offer, saying he would take care of this payback himself.

Stenson wandered around the marina looking for Justin Carter. All he saw were million-dollar yachts, and he knew JC didn't have that kind of money. Then he spotted an old, rusting boat at the end of a pier. JC was sitting on the deck, staring at the horizon.

Stenson approached the old boat and yelled, "Excuse me, Captain, may I board?"

JC looked over to see it was Stenson holding a duffle bag. After the week he'd had, he figured Stenson was there to kill him. JC yelled back, "Can you kill me another day? It's been a long week and I'm not in the mood to die right now."

Stenson laughed as he boarded the boat. "I'm here to give you payback, alright. But I wasn't planning to kill you today ... unless you want me to."

JC laughed and offered his assassin a beer. "What brings you out to my fine sailing vessel if you aren't here to kill me?"

"Believe me, if I was going to kill you, it would be on something nicer than this piece of junk." Stenson popped open his bottle of beer and clinked it against JC's. "I came to offer you a truce."

That was not what JC expected. "A truce?" he asked.

"Yeah. Things have gotten out of hand. I'd like to put an end to it."

"They really have, Stenson, and I'm sorry. It was never my intention."

"Nor mine," Stenson replied. "When your crew stole the weed, which started this whole fiasco, I thought it was clever how you did it. That was a smooth plan. But it was not only my money you stole; it was other people's money I had to get back."

"The whole thing was Zabrina's idea. I couldn't have come up with something so clever."

"I didn't think it was your idea, but I had fun getting you back with those bullet ants in your underwear drawer. By the way, how are your balls?"

"Still sore. But I'll give you credit. That was way more creative than shooting me. How are your man-boobs?"

Stenson chuckled. "Fine ... after I had my mastectomy. I have the scars to prove it. Want to see?"

"I'll pass," JC said, almost choking on his beer.

"But listen, JC, things have gotten to the point where I'm afraid somebody will get hurt. What you did to Luna endangered her life. That's why we hit you back so hard. And while it was appropriate, I didn't enjoy doing it. We don't hate you and your friends. In a lot of ways, we admire you." Stenson took a swallow of his beer, then said, "Like I said, I am here to offer you a truce. We won't mess with your operations and you don't mess with ours. Maybe one day, we can be friends. But I don't want either of us having to always look over our shoulder or worry about the people we care about."

At that moment, JC understood Stenson was not the evil person he thought he was. It seemed to be a theme over the past few days. People weren't who JC thought they were: his mother, his father, Zabrina, or Mr. Gallo.

JC said, "You know, Stenson, I was abandoned at birth and then ran away when I was a kid and grew up in the streets. Life has not been easy for me. Big Tony, Zabrina, and Jesús are my only true friends. I never knew my mother until just the other day. I've grown more in a week than the twenty-three years I've been on this planet." JC stuck out his hand and said, "I gladly accept your truce."

Stenson had known nothing about JC until now. Suddenly, he realized how similar they were. He said, "JC, we are more alike than you know. I witnessed my father kill my mother when I was eight years old. And I also ran away. I grew up living in the woods. If not for kind people who touched my life, I don't know where I would be today. Like your friends, Brick, Luna, and Charlie are the most important people in my life."

They watched boats pass by and sipped their beers and pondered the mystery of their fates. A few minutes later, Stenson pushed the duffle bag toward JC.

JC looked at the bag and asked, "Is that another one of your tricks?"

"Open it," Stenson said with a smile.

JC unzipped the duffle bag to see stacks of hundred-dollar bills. He looked at Stenson in disbelief.

Stenson said, "That's $500,000 to help you rebuild your club. I know we took $1.5 million, but $800,000 was our money and $200,000 went to expenses. This is the rest, and it's all yours."

JC was speechless.

Stenson looked at JC and said, "Money doesn't mean a thing to me. Friendships are priceless, and money can't buy that."

"You must not have my taste in clothing and cars," JC joked in honest humility.

Stenson said, "I have better taste in cars and boats than you. But I could use your help with my choice of clothing."

The guys spent the rest of the afternoon drinking beer and swapping stories. Later, Stenson drove JC around the French Quarter in the old-school convertible. As they watched the world go by, they realized that life works in mysterious ways. Who knew that being double crossed would lead to making new friends?

CHAPTER THIRTY

NEW ORLEANS, LOUISIANA / POLKSVILLE, ALABAMA

For the first time since the infamous night of ruin, JC surveyed the disaster once known as Club Empire. He dared not stop as he walked through the club, for each sticky footstep might leave him glued to the floor. Whatever Stenson sprayed in the building still lingered in the air. He imagined this was what a sumo wrestler locker room smelled like after an exhausting day of practice. The vomit-inducing scent was beyond unpleasant.

A sliver of light shown beneath the office door at the top of the stairs. JC found Zabrina sitting alone in the dimly lit room with her head in her hands. A sole lamp illuminated the worry on her face. Zabrina was so lost in thought that she didn't notice JC enter. He placed a hand on her shoulder and sat the black duffle bag on the desk before her. She looked up to see JC's reassuring smile.

"What is this?" Zabrina asked.

"A present. Open it," JC encouraged.

Zabrina unzipped the bag. She could not believe her eyes when she saw the bag filled with stacks of cash. She looked at JC and asked, "Where did you get this?"

"Stenson."

"Stenson?" Zabrina repeated, as if the answer was more unbelievable than if JC told her he'd robbed a bank.

"Yes. He wanted us to have this to rebuild our club."

Zabrina was at a loss for words. This was the same Stenson who had destroyed their club and blown up their warehouse? She tried to process it all.

JC continued, "Stenson is a nice guy. I'm sorry we ever tried to scam him. We agreed to a truce."

Zabrina asked, "And Luna?"

"Well, Stenson and I buried the hatchet. Your friendship with Luna might take a little longer. She may still hate you for leaving her in a jungle."

Zabrina laughed. "I don't blame her. I'll apologize and hope she forgives me."

Stenson invited Luna to dinner. When he mentioned the restaurant, she asked the occasion for such a special place. He said it was no big deal. He wanted to celebrate their recent good fortune.

Stenson arrived at Luna's apartment at 8:00 p.m. dressed in a suit. He didn't think he'd have a reason to wear it again, but tonight was more special than he'd led Luna to believe. She answered the door wearing a stunning burgundy cocktail dress and invited him in. Stenson handed her a bouquet of long-stem red roses.

Luna said, "Wow, a handsome man shows up at my door with flowers?" She gave him a peck of a kiss, as if to say there would be more of that later.

The nineteenth-century French-Creole building looked as if it belonged on a movie set. A hostess seated them at a corner table toward the rear of the ornate dining room. The soaring columns, mahogany paneling, and antique mirrors perfected the beautiful ambiance.

Stenson told Luna over glasses of wine that he had visited Justin Carter earlier that day. He said JC was a misunderstood guy who had grown up much like he did, running away from a horrible situation. He told her that they'd agreed to a truce and that he returned $500,000 of the money they'd taken—to help JC rebuild his club.

Luna reached over and held Stenson's hand. "This is why I love you, Stenson Beckett. You have a heart unlike any I have ever known."

Neither had eaten at such a fancy restaurant before, and they found the menu puzzling. It was much different from the burgers and fries Stenson usually ate at the bar. He didn't recognize anything on the menu, so he asked the waiter for his recommendation.

They chose the chef's degustation menu of five courses, each paired with a different wine: smoked yellowtail crudo with avocado and summer melons; chilled heirloom cucumber soup with spicy crab and caviar; slow-cooked Spanish octopus with baby lima beans over crispy rice; wagyu hanger steak with artichoke and heirloom tomato; and salted caramel tart for dessert.

Through each course, the couple became more enchanted. Stenson stared at the candlelit sparkle in Luna's eyes. His gaze made her feel as if they were the only people in the room. They were so lost in each other that they did not notice the waiter place the salted caramel tart before them.

Stenson said, "Luna, when you were missing, I realized you mean more to me than a friend." He paused to calm the shakiness of his voice before saying, "That is when I knew I loved you."

Stenson reached into his pocket and removed a small blue-felt box. Luna's heart fluttered and her hands began to shake.

Stenson lifted the lid to reveal a diamond solitaire ring. He reached for her hand and said, "Luna Jean LeRoux, will you marry me?"

Tears flowed from Luna's eyes, and her lips quivered. Guests at surrounding tables watched the romantic scene, awaiting her reply.

She reached out with her left hand and said, "Yes, Stenson Beckett. It would be my honor to be your wife."

Stenson beamed with joy as he slipped the ring on her shaking finger. The restaurant erupted in applause as the two kissed. Guests from a nearby table ordered champagne for the happy couple.

They announced the engagement to their friends at the bar the following night. Brick and his biker friends were there, along with Charlie Whitehorse and his buddies. Stenson also invited JC, Big Tony, and Zabrina.

Brick did not miss the opportunity to tease Stenson with a bear hug saying, "I told you it was more than friendship."

JC and Stenson stood by the bar, watching Zabrina and Luna drink shots together. JC said, "Looks like those two made up."

Stenson replied, "They're drinking tequila. That is the potion of Dr. Jekyll and Mr. Hyde. We better keep an eye on them. They may pull each other's hair out by the end of the night."

JC laughed and said, "Zabrina's hair is a wig thanks to your future wife."

Stenson clinked his bottle to JC's. On the other side of the room, Big Tony and Brick were talking over beers. Stenson remarked they were probably discussing various ways to kill people.

When Stenson took a very tipsy Luna back to her place, he noticed a package in front of her door. He asked Luna if she'd ordered something. In slurred speech, she said, "Only you, baby!"

Once he got his slushy-faced fiancée onto the sofa, Stenson opened the box. It contained a bottle of Armand de Brignac champagne. The note read, *"Congratulations! —MM"*

Luna asked Stenson what was in the box.

He said, "The Mystery Man sent us a bottle of champagne. How does this guy know things before we tell him?"

She grinned and said, "I don't know, but I'm gonna show you some things tonight even the Mystery Man doesn't know!"

Stenson and Luna drove to Alabama to see Luna's parents the following weekend. Stenson wanted to ask her father's permission to marry his daughter in person. Her mom and dad liked Stenson, and her father happily gave him his blessing.

Luna said to her father, "I don't know what I would have done if you said no because I already said yes."

She removed her hand from her pocket and showed her mom and dad the ring. Luna's mother cried and hugged them both. Mr. LeRoux shook Stenson's hand and gave him a hug.

Stenson and Mr. LeRoux stepped outside while the women gushed. Luna's father said, "Stenson, I am proud of you. To endure all you've been through and be the man you are today is impressive. I always knew there was something special about you since you were a little boy. And to tell you the truth, I always hoped you and my daughter would marry. I couldn't imagine her with anyone else."

Stenson replied, "Mr. LeRoux, I am the luckiest man in the world to marry your daughter and my best friend. I truly love her and promise you I will always protect her as you have."

"I know you will, Stenson," Mr. LeRoux said with a warm smile and hug.

The couple visited the Masseys the next day. They had not seen Luna since she was a little girl when she would come over to play with Stenson. They were elated by the news and told the couple they'd better get an invitation to the wedding. Afterward, Stenson took Luna to see his brother and sister. Mary told Luna she was pretty and how happy she would be to have a sister-in-law. She said she was tired of being the only girl in the family.

Luna prepared engagement announcements when they returned to New Orleans. She sent one to their hometown paper, the *Polksville Gazette*. Luna emailed the website link to Stenson. He was at the bar going over paperwork when a chime alerted him to an email. He opened the link Luna sent and smiled when he saw the announcement. The photo she'd chosen was a picture they took the first day Luna arrived in New Orleans. As he stared at the photograph, he laughed to himself and thought how he was glad that Luna was better looking than him. Otherwise, they would have some funny-looking children.

Stenson clicked the homepage of the *Polksville Gazette* to see what was going on in his hometown. A knot formed in his stomach when he read the headline, *"Charges Dropped Against Tug Beckett."*

Seeing the name *Tug Beckett* made Stenson sick. It was a name he had not spoken or thought of in more than ten years. The article revealed his father had been released from prison two years ago. He'd remarried and then stood accused of abusing a child he had with his second wife. According to article, charges were dropped after his wife changed her story. She claimed the child simply had an accident.

Stenson thought, *Accident my ass!* He knew victims of abuse often changed their story. Stenson's mother had never gone to the police when her husband beat her. Stenson never understood why, unless she was afraid her father would kill Tug. Mysteriously, his mom's parents died in an explosion the night his father killed his mother. While police never charged Tug because of a lack of evidence, everyone knew Tug Beckett had done it.

Brick walked into the office and saw Stenson staring at the computer screen. Stenson's furious expression told Brick something was wrong. Before he could ask, Stenson turned the screen and showed Brick the story.

"No way!" Brick exclaimed.

"I've spent a lifetime trying to forget how that jackass destroyed my life. Now he's doing the same thing to another child?"

Brick knew what Stenson was thinking and said, "Let the judicial system handle it."

"Like the system did after he murdered my mom?"

Stenson was right, and Robert Brickhouse knew it. The system had failed his friend miserably. Brick thought that if his own father had done what Stenson's did, he would die a slow and painful death.

It did not take two seconds for Stenson to decide what to do. He picked up the phone and asked Charlie Whitehorse to come to the bar. Charlie arrived a short time later and joined Stenson and Brick in the office. Stenson laid out his plan and asked for their help. Brick and Charlie knew there was no talking their friend out of it. Stenson would do this with or without them, so they agreed to help in any way they could.

Stenson asked Charlie to get a car that could not be traced. He handed Brick a list of supplies he needed. Then he stopped by his apartment and retrieved a bag from the closet. He had dinner plans with Luna that night, but they would have to wait. He drove to Luna's place to tell her in person.

"Hi, sweetie, you're early," Luna said when Stenson walked in the door.

"I wanted to stop by and tell you that something came up

and I need to go out of town for a couple of days."

"What's going on?" she asked.

"Some important business I need to take care of," he said. "Sorry we can't have dinner tonight, but I wanted to see your smiling face before I left."

He kissed Luna goodbye and returned to the bar. Charlie and Brick were waiting when Stenson arrived. They loaded the car and set off for Polksville, Alabama. Five hours later, they checked into a motel outside of town. Stenson told the guys he would spend the next few days surveilling his father until he knew his routine. He asked them to take care of the other details of the plan.

It wasn't long before Stenson located his father. He started with the bar the man had frequented when Stenson was just a kid. Stenson guessed old habits were hard to break. Stenson saw Tug Beckett as soon as he walked through the door. He wasn't worried that his father would recognize him, since the last time he'd seen him, Stenson was a child.

Stenson drank a beer and watched his obnoxious father run his mouth at the bar. It was all he could do to resist the temptation to walk up, smash his beer bottle, and stab the man in the throat with the jagged edges. Instead, he returned to the car and waited several more hours for his father to leave. Stenson followed Tug's pickup truck to a trailer park near where he'd grown up. He watched his father stumble and curse as he kicked a bicycle lying in the yard. Stenson felt like he was watching some twisted replay of his own life.

For two more days, Stenson kept an eye on his father. Each day was the same. Tug went to the bar in the early afternoon and left drunk around 10:00 p.m. Now he had seen enough. Stenson returned to the motel and went over the plan one more time with Charlie and Brick. They decided to go the next night.

The following evening after Tug arrived at the bar, Brick snuck to the man's truck and disconnected some wires. Tug left the bar a few hours later and discovered the truck wouldn't start. He was so drunk that he didn't even bother lifting the hood to inspect the engine. Every person he asked for a ride refused, which confirmed that even drunks didn't like the jerk. Tug cursed the vehicle as he got out and stumbled down the road toward home.

Charlie Whitehorse pulled up alongside the wobbly guy and rolled down the window. He asked, "Hey, you need a ride?"

"Yeah, buddy. Truck broke down and I'm not in too good of shape to walk, if you know what I mean," Tug said, almost falling over.

Charlie opened the car door and Tug Beckett poured inside. Tug looked at Charlie with his head cocked and one eye open like a broken bobblehead toy and asked, "You Mexican?"

"No, I'm American Indian," Charlie replied.

"That's cool, Tonto. Where's the Lone Ranger?" Tug said with a drunkard's laugh at his own dumb joke.

Brick rose from the back seat and pulled a hood over Tug's head. He wrapped his forearm around Tug's neck and placed him in a chokehold. Brick said, "You are about to meet the Lone Ranger, bitch."

Tug Beckett's arms flailed against the passenger seat and door until he passed out.

When Tug Beckett regained consciousness, he was on his knees with his arms and feet zip-tied behind him. A car's headlights blinded his eyes. In his messed-up state, he thought it was daylight. He looked around to see if he recognized his surroundings.

They were in the most remote woods on Lucius T. Haggerty's property. Stenson reached into the trunk of the car and unzipped the long nylon bag he'd brought from his apartment. He slid out Haggerty's double-barreled shotgun. It was the same gun that had saved his life so many years ago. Stenson broke open the shotgun barrel and inserted a single shell. He had no need for two.

A silhouette of a man emerged from the blue haze of the car's exhaust in the headlights. It was like a phantom emerging from the darkness, with vaporous breath from the cold air that made him appear like a demon.

Tug Beckett squinted his eyes to make out the apparition. He yelled, "What is going on? Who are you?"

"I am the Lone Ranger."

"You are who?"

"I'm Stenson Beckett ... your son."

"Why you little bastard! I should have killed you when I killed your mother!"

Stenson smashed the butt of the shotgun into Tug's face and roared, "Remember when I was a little boy and you beat me when I tried to protect my mom?"

"Yeah, and I whipped your little scrawny ass!"

Stenson bashed him again. "You enjoy hurting people weaker than you?"

"Let me up from here and I'll kill you like I killed your mama and your grandparents!"

Stenson cracked Tug Beckett in his nose so hard that it almost pushed the bone up through his brain. The man slumped forward, unconscious. Stenson stood and waited, hoping he hadn't killed the man ... yet.

Tug regained consciousness and sat up. He realized the gravity of the situation and begged. "I'm sorry! I shouldn't have done that. I'm sorry I killed your mama and your grandparents. Please let me go! I'm a changed man now!"

"You're sorry you beat me?"

Stenson smashed the gun into his chest.

"You're sorry you killed my mother and her parents?"

Stenson swung the weapon's butt under his chin.

"Are sorry you orphaned my brother and sister?"

Stenson hit his mouth, ejecting several teeth into the air.

"Are you sorry you scarred us for the rest of our lives?"

The gun crashed into the man's skull.

"Yes yes yes! Please forgive me!" Tug Beckett cried.

"Oh, I forgive you," Stenson said as he raised the shotgun and placed it between Tug's eyes. He cocked the gun and allowed Tug enough time to realize his fate.

Before Tug Beckett could say a word, Stenson pulled the trigger. Instantly, the evil man's face was gone into a mash of brains and bone and blood that flew through the air. Tug slumped backward into the hole that had been dug behind him.

Stenson stared at the body and said, "I hope God does too."

Charlie and Brick walked over without saying a word and picked up shovels. Stenson watched silently as they filled in the hole.

When they walked back to the car, Brick asked, "How do you feel?"

"Guilty," Stenson replied.

"You did what you had to do, Stenson," Brick reassured.

"I guess." Stenson paused. "At least he'll never hurt another person again, and it brings closure to that chapter of my life. But I feel terrible doing such a horrible thing."

Brick placed his arm around his friend's shoulder and said, "Sometimes we do bad things for all the right reasons."

ACKNOWLEDGEMENTS

The author wishes to thank the following individuals for their support and inspiration during the writing of *Double Crossed* ...

Beth Anthamatten
Betty Midkiff
Connor Puckett
Frank Jones
Connie Sandridge
Belinda Dwyer
Rhonda Watts
Stephanie Radford
Jason Good

ABOUT THE AUTHOR

Anthony Anthamatten is a Tennessee native who has enjoyed a career in television, radio, recording, and software development. What he considers his most important accomplishment is being a friend you can call in the middle of the night when your life breaks down.

Double Crossed is his first novel.

www.ingramcontent.com/pod-product-compliance
Lightning Source LLC
Chambersburg PA
CBHW021625030826
48979CB00037B/2334/J
* 9 7 8 1 7 3 5 2 7 2 0 1 6 *